THE ROMANCE TREASURY ASSOCIATION

TORONTO · NEW YORK · LONDON
AMSTERDAM · PARIS · SYDNEY · HAMBURG
STOCKHOLM · ATHENS · TOKYO · MILAN

These stories were originally published as follows:

DESERT HAVEN
Copyright © 1981 by Roumelia Lane
First published by Mills & Boon Limited in 1981

CONNOISSEUR'S CHOICE
Copyright © 1983 by Dixie McKeone
First published by Mills & Boon Limited in 1984

FIRE AND STEEL
Copyright © 1980 by Mary Wibberley
First published by Mills & Boon Limited in 1980

ROMANCE TREASURY is published by
The Romance Treasury Association

Story Illustrations by Muriel Hughes
Book Design by Charles Kadin
Printed and bound by Arcata Graphics
Kingsport, Tennessee U.S.A.

ISBN 0-373-04193-4

Printed in U.S.A.

Romance
Treasury

CONTENTS

Desert Haven
Roumelia Lane

Maybe it was an impossible, sentimental task. But Celia was determined to stay in Bahrain until she located her father's first love, the beautiful Arab girl Nevine.

And simply because he'd rescued her from trouble, that McCord man had no right to lecture Celia on the folly of her mission.

Such an arrogant, infuriatingly practical man! She fervently wished that she didn't also find him so very intriguing....

CHAPTER ONE

THE LOBBY of the Gulf Hotel was a-buzz with the conversation of that breed of humanity who hang around Middle East hotels. Architects, salesmen, women journalists, local executives; no one made a secret of their speciality and all were quenching the thirst of long hours waiting for some contact or other.

Celia was waiting for no one. She sipped diffidently near an archway, thankful for the slight circulation of air which wafted in from the hot, dusty street. Ever since her arrival in Bahrain the previous day she had been striving to come to terms with the dramatic change in climate. To her mind the general crush in the lobby made one barely aware of the air-conditioning.

But she was glad to be here, almost exhilarated to have got this far with her plan. Al Manamah, the capital of Bahrain, was just as her father had described it to her; if anything, more British than even he remembered. Apart from an occasional exotic touch in the decor, there was little to indicate that she was in the Middle East, and certainly the present company were as Westernised and amenable as any she would find at home. This was heartening.

It was only after another wayward glance around that the inclination to add a mild amendment to her summing up of the crowd made itself felt. She had described them as amenable, and so they were. All except one. He was tall, but not outstandingly so, nor was he particularly good-looking, yet she was conscious of a force in him that made her aware of—what was it—his disapproval of her?

She felt a fleeting resentment that there was one man in the room who guessed that she was not like the other worldly, self-assured, never-put-a-foot-wrong types who decorated the lobby.

She decided to ignore him. She would be going out shortly anyway. She had only stopped by for a drink to give her the courage to begin the task she had set herself.

Once her mind reverted to the preliminary steps she must take she forgot the press in the lobby. There were lots of places she could start, of course, but all obvious ones and not for her. No, she must find her first lead alone. Celia more than anyone knew that her reasons for coming to Bahrain were, to say the least, a little bizarre.

She rose and as casually as possible made her way outdoors. The heat was like a blow on her thinly-clothed body. Knowing what she was about, she had put on her flimsiest of sundresses, a daffodil yellow with shoe-lace shoulder-straps for maximum cool.

She soon discovered that she had been hasty in condemning the air-conditioning of the hotel, but still it was good to be wandering through the streets of Al Manamah. She felt elated once again and curiously close to her dead father. How he had loved the East! He had never succeeded in shutting it out of his heart for all his long years later in England.

As she walked she looked around her a little uncertainly. She needed transport, but who in the general hubbub of weaving cyclists, trundling buses, darting urchins in tattered shirts and shorts, the traditional fez in most cases cocked cheekily, and plodding produce carts, could she approach?

She had purposely left the smart neighbourhood of the hotel behind, and though the balconied houses and shuttered buildings were as impersonal as she could have wished they were also unrevealing as to what kind of business went on behind. However, an idea did occur to her when she looked ahead and saw that the maze of streets she had followed was giving way to a stretch of open scrubland.

On a derelict patch was a sight that she would have called incongruous in this most Westernised of all the Arab states had the sand-laden breeze and hot blue sky not reminded her that she was indeed on the shores of the Persian Gulf. But it was the homely feel of the place which guided her footsteps unerringly to where the group of camels lazed, some on foot and others, legs folded under ragged humps, beside their owners.

Of course she didn't intend to adopt this mode of travel in her search, but as these camel-drivers were in the transport business they could no doubt tell her where she could find the four-wheeled kind.

In sentences carefully rehearsed for just such an occasion and with a natural feel for the tongue due to her father's long association with the language she stated her requirements in precise Arabic.

The reaction was both puzzling and disconcerting. She had simply asked where she could hire a car and she was confident her rendering had been impeccable, but by the look on the Bahrainis' faces she might have mouthed the foulest insult.

She quickly tried again, in case there should have been some lapse, and was alarmed to find herself, this time, encircled by the scowling, muttering group and nudged in the most unnerving manner.

Celia's cheeks grew hot. She might have been lightweight in appearance, but running through that slender frame was a thread of steely self-will, and after all, she had only asked a civil question. Unfortunately she was not sufficiently practised in the Arab language to put her point of view across, so all she could do was keep repeating that she wished to hire a car.

If she had tossed a hornets' nest in the midst of the drivers' camels the effect couldn't have been worse. With the blood-chilling feel of hands clutching at her she knew that the situation was getting frighteningly out of control. It was then that a sharp voice cut across the skirmish; an imperious *'Ibiird yadak!'* which had the effect of parting the muttering mob like a whiplash.

Celia's glance flew along with everyone else's to the sleek car that had stopped and the figure emerging. It was the man whose eyes she had met across the lobby in the Gulf Hotel. She hadn't liked him then and she didn't like him now, as he came striding over with an expression on his face which said the scrape she had got herself into was only what he might have expected. This was verified by his opening words to her. 'I knew you were heading for trouble the moment I saw you!'

Celia would have liked to make some withering reply and as he pushed her towards his limousine she managed to retort, 'What makes you think I'd add to it by accepting a lift in a strange car?'

'Get in, and shut up.'

She had to admit that it seemed the wisest thing to do under the circumstances, for although the man's presence had put a brake on the general anger it hadn't cooled the tempers of the surly camel drivers, and feeling herself almost wrenched from their grasp she didn't hesitate to stumble into the plush interior, helped unceremoniously by a pair of firm hands and an adequate width of shoulder which held off the indignant mêlée.

Wasting no time on polite farewells, her tight-lipped rescuer fell in beside her and drove off at speed, leaving the unruly group shaking their fists in the road.

Celia had never pretended to understand their wrath, and tremblingly incredulous she asked herself aloud, 'What did I do wrong?'

'Everything,' came the supercilious reply from the wheel. 'Just like all the others who get bitten with this lure of the East stuff, you choose nice cosy Bahrain because it's typically British. What you fail to realise is that if you scratch beneath the surface of any Arab country that used to be run by us you'll find that old customs and habits remain.'

'Savagery included!' Celia unravelled herself from where she had been pushed, quivering not only from shock but at the man's know-it-all attitude. 'What crime is there in asking to hire a car?' she snapped.

'Being new out here you wouldn't know,' she was told in a pitying, unsmiling way, 'that motor vehicles pose a threat to the camel-driver's trade and livelihood. In the old days the discovery of oil put many with no capital to invest in trucks out of business and those subsisting on the crumbs of the trade displayed their annoyance, sometimes with bullets. Now, with Bahrain's oil supplies running out, the old trouble has turned full circle. The camel owners see it as a return to the ancient ways of travel, so naturally they're not going to go out of their way to push the car-hire business.'

'Naturally,' Celia cooed from a heaving bosom. 'And they don't mind committing murder to emphasise their reluctance!'

Her choice retort made no impression on the granite-faced figure engaged in steering. He was busy with his own thoughts, and voicing them aloud he said, 'I followed you when you left the hotel. I knew you were going to come to grief sooner or later, starting out on your own.'

'So you said,' she purred, loathing his satisfied air.

He unnerved her by turning an arctic blue gaze her way and stating harshly, 'We don't find it funny extricating our own kind from foolish situations involving the locals.'

'Pardon me if I've been an embarrassment to you,' Celia said thinly.

'It happens all the time,' the wintry look returned to the road. 'Cheap air fares and trendy travel tours give the folk at home the idea that hopping over here is little different from sunning themselves on the beaches of Tangier. We're used to the gaffes some of them make, but we don't like it. It's not good for the British image out here.'

'It must be nice to be thoroughly weathered and above making stupid mistakes.' Celia eyed him with anything but admiration.

'It doesn't come from an afternoon sipping tea at a hotel lobby table, I can ensure you.'

Oh, he was insufferable! Of all the types to come to her aid in a sticky situation it had to be a grim, lecturing in-ured-in-the-East expatriate of hers!

Her heart recovering some of its normal rhythm after the disturbing ordeal, she noticed for the first time the views of rambling gardens and palm-screened villas sailing by. 'This is not the road to town,' she said sharply. 'Would you mind returning me to the hotel?'

'Later.' The man beside her drove on. 'I can't take you back like that.'

Celia had been too shaken to give a thought to her appearance, but now, following his glance, she saw that her dress had been torn at the bodice and a dangling shoulder strap showed a portion of creamy lace underslip. Colouring profusely, she clutched at the yellow remnants and to cover her confusion she murmured, 'Of course, I wouldn't want to embarrass you further by asking you to deliver me like this.'

'Nor would you want to advertise the fact,' he said with an exasperating curl to his lips, 'that just like a lot of other empty-headed tourists you drift straight off to the native quarter without taking the trouble to—'

'Now wait a minute! I've stood enough of your categorising, Mr....'

'The name's McCord.'

And fitting too! Celia thought heatedly. His personality was about as flexible as stiffened lanyard. 'Unlike your superior opinion of newcomers to Bahrain,' she went on, 'I'm not here for the willy-nilly purpose of making a fool of myself. I happen to know a lot about this Arab state and my reasons for being here are...well...' Why did she hesitate just then? That was all he needed to treat her to another of his supercilious smiles, even though she finished firmly, 'Not that it's any of your business, but I do have a definite purpose for visiting Bahrain.'

'Don't tell me,' he drawled, 'you've come in search of the Moon God or to investigate the mysteries of Ramadan.'

Oh, he was impossible! She turned away impatiently, partly because she was guiltily aware that his suggestions were not that wide of the mark, and annoyingly too she had a feeling that he sensed it.

He brought the car to a stop at the edge of the desert and viewing the white wedding-cake structure as she alighted Celia carped. 'You didn't tell me we were going to pay a call on the local Sheikh!'

'This is my house,' he said, unamused. 'I have business interests in Bahrain.' He led the way into an interior which was cool and white and richly carpeted, sculptures with an Eastern flavour adding to the elegance and priceless objets d'art blending with the jewel-like colours underfoot.

Where arched windows looked out on to a hot, tawny nothingness Celia was left with the silent movement of pearl-finned fish swimming in a wall-length aquarium. In a moment her tight-lipped host had returned. 'First a drink, I think,' he said in an icy, businesslike way tinged with that familiar sarcastic gleam as he added, noting her trembling frame, 'Something stronger than tea this time, wouldn't you say?'

She had thought he would leave her again, but instead he came up to her and with one deft wrist movement ripped her dress from top to hem.

'What are you doing?' She turned on him with a fury that left him unaffected.

'It will save you having to disrobe in front of the servants,' he said calmly. 'Here, put this on.' He tossed her a silk robe he had brought from another room.

Feeling distinctly at a disadvantage standing there in her underslip, Celia didn't hesitate to do as he ordered, and especially as he wasted no time in pressing a button near his hand.

Before she had barely time to wrap the thing round her a soft-footed figure appeared in the doorway, and though his dark-skinned features were as impassive as one could have wished Celia hated her autocratic benefactor for putting her in the awkward position of having to stand there half buried in a dressing gown obviously belonging to the master of the house, and look as though she hadn't a care in the world.

A rapid spate of Arabic, followed by the daffodil remnants of her dress sailing his way, left the servant in no doubt, it seemed, as to his immediate duties. On his departure she was told, 'Quadi's pretty handy with a needle and thread. He also operates a sewing machine, so the chances are you won't know the difference when you get your dress back.'

Seething Celia took a step forward. 'I don't know what right you think you have—'

'Sit down before you fall down,' came the sardonic interruption.

It was true that since leaving the car the shock of her unfortunate encounter had attacked her limbs afresh, but she remained swaying upright to fume, 'Just because I happen to have started off on the wrong foot on my first outing in Al Manamah it doesn't mean—'

'It's a pity you didn't think to ask some advice first,' he cut in yet again. 'It's fairly obvious to me,' he stood over her, wholly overbearing and objectionable, 'that someone like you wandering into the midst of a bunch of Bahraini camel-drivers and then having the nerve to ask about hiring a car would be like waving a red rag at a bull.'

Someone like her? Was he referring to her looks? Undoubtedly her fair hair and dove-grey eyes seemed to offend him.

In case that was it she countered, 'I don't see why I'm so different. When I arrived yesterday the market-place was full of European ladies shopping and managing on their own.'

'Sure, the frizzy-permed, dyed-in-the-wool ex-Army wives and so forth.'

Celia blinked at this reply. That couldn't be flattery, could it? Not coming from *him?* She didn't know whether to be more annoyed or not at his inference that she was not like the other travel-hardened members of her sex currently languishing with their husbands in Bahrain.

Under the circumstances and considering that, owing to his high-handed action concerning her dress, she could not now leave his house until it was returned to her, there seemed nothing for it but to seek a little support for her legs.

Ignoring his offer of assistance and feeling no match anymore for his sanctimonious remarks, clothed as she was in his ridiculously voluminous dressing gown, she dropped into one of the huge powder-puff armchairs and found the whole of her enveloped in such a fleecy cloud of comfort it was difficult not to give herself wholeheartedly to the experience.

While she was recovering some of her fight, though it wasn't easy with the sensuous luxury of the armchair sapping her will, the man who went by the name of McCord moved to a wall-side drinks cabinet. Gloweringly Celia eyed him at his task. He appeared to be completely at home in this land of robed Orientals. With dark hair and sun-weathered complexion he might have been one himself, except for those piercing blue eyes, of course, and an effortless Anglo-Saxon arrogance that no Arab could emulate.

In the silence of the room other sounds came to her, those of the indistinct tapping of a typewriter perhaps, an occasional footstep across tiled spaces and suggestion of distant activity. As though he read her thoughts her reluctant protector informed her, 'I do some of my office work on the premises. I'm in the refrigerating business.'

'That figures!' Celia said shrewishly. Whether her spirited reference to his icy attitude had gone home she couldn't have said, but as she accepted the glass he offered she thought she saw—what was it—the glimmer of lazy appreciation in his eyes?

'I agree, there's unlimited scope for cooling measures in a country as hot as Bahrain,' he replied deliberately misinterpreting her remark. 'In my years at the job I've had no cause to complain. I've been asked to do everything from freezing the royal palace intake of fresh meat to arranging cold storage for imported medical supplies. At the moment

I'm experimenting with an ice-rink in Manama, as we call it.'

'Shades of Western sophistication,' Celia commented idly.

'It's a sideline I've indulged in mainly through pressure from friends,' he shrugged. 'The Bahrainis are no different from their Arab neighbours when it comes to impressing the world with grand-scale modern amenities. If Saudi Arabia has an ice-rink then Kuwait has to have one. And if Kuwait has an ice-rink then Bahrain...'

'Doesn't intend to be left out in the cold.'

'You've got it,' McCord almost smiled at her innocent pun but not quite. Instead he took a pull on his drink and finished drily, 'But I won't bore you with details of a business far removed from your...er...desert quest.'

It was uncanny, this foresight of his! Knowing that she had been a little crazy to come to Bahrain in pursuit of a dream, Celia said briskly, 'Not that far removed. I once got a silver medal for skating. I could probably show your Arab friends a thing or two...and incidentally, how do they manage in local costume? It must be a bit restricting wobbling around in djellabahs and whatnot?'

'The people in these parts are pretty Westernised in dress—British influence again; though it hasn't reached the stage where girls can trip around in ballerina-length attire, but they cope...'

Celia had a feeling that they were marking time conversation-wise as though there were other more important things waiting to be said. She didn't think it was so much curiosity on McCord's part as to why she was in Bahrain as an imperious right to know. Because she was English he had taken it upon himself, high-handedly again, she thought, to put her straight as to what one did and didn't do in this tiny Arab state.

As she expected, after a moment or two he opened up the subject again with, 'It's not difficult to hire a car in Manama. What was the idea of wandering off the beaten track like that?'

'I had my reasons.' She lifted her chin.

'Reasons that may have cost you dear if I hadn't come along when I did,' he snapped.

She wanted to sound non-committal, but found herself saying instead. 'If you must know, I'm looking for someone.'

'Perhaps I can help.'

At this her lips curved wryly. 'I doubt it. This someone existed more than thirty years ago.'

There was no reply to that, she noticed with guilty satisfaction. He was foxed, and she couldn't blame him. It was a weird mission she had set herself.

He stood with his drink not far away. It was like him, Celia was discovering irritably to wait for further clues. She was prepared to let him wait—indefinitely. She had no wish to confide in him.

She had sipped quite a bit of the amber liquid he had poured into her glass, finding it bitter-sweet but strangely soothing. If it hadn't been for a peculiar lethargy which overtook her then she doubted whether she would have told him anything more. As it was, mellowed against her will by the drink and the cool restfulness of the room, she heard herself drifting into a reluctant explanation.

'My father was a government official out here in those days. He came to Bahrain in his teens and by the time he had risen to a decent level in his job he'd lost his heart to the East. Like most young men, single and content in his new way of life, he fell in love.

'Nevine was a dancing girl in a Manama night spot. But she was also beautiful and intelligent. They saw a lot of one another. It was a courtship made memorable by moonlight strolls through the date palm gardens and days spent on the Zallaq beach—and one that could only end one way. Nevine was terribly in love with my father.

'They planned to get married. Everything was arranged, but the wedding never took place. In those days matches of that kind were frowned upon, and my father was summoned home to England. His family were influential and certain strings were pulled which made it impossible for him to remain in Bahrain. In due course he married my mother, but he never forgot the Arab girl in Bahrain. I know that because my mother has been dead a long time and when two people are as close as my father and I were the old truths come out.'

Celia took a sip of her drink lost in her story by this time. 'I never felt it was breaking faith with my mother's memory discussing Nevine. My father was a kind and considerate husband while she was alive, but he hasn't been able to hide the fact from me that Nevine was the love of his life; especially these last two years when he was bedridden for most of the time. To an invalid memories are all-important, and he loved most of all to reminisce with me about the past. Sometimes it was as though the intervening years had never been and that in thought his life in Bahrain and his happiness with Nevine were as close as if it had been yesterday.

'... I suppose it was when he died two months ago that I first got the idea to come out to Bahrain. Nevine is almost as much a part of me now as she was of my father. I felt I wanted to meet her, to get to know her—the woman he had never ceased to love in all the years they were apart...'

There was a silence, a wholly disapproving one, then McCord set his glass down and bit out, 'Of all the sentimental...!'

'Claptrap?' Celia supplied demurely.

'Thanks for the adjective.' He glared at her. 'Are you trying to tell me that you've come all the way out here—and alone—to try to find this . . . this dancing girl?'

'She was a lot more than that.' Celia's chin went up. 'She was a star performer—and she came from a good family.'

'And what makes you think she'll be around now?'

'She would only be in her early fifties. Why shouldn't she be?'

'I don't suppose it's occurred to you that Bahrain is a pretty small place. She could have drifted off anywhere by this time; into neighbouring Kuwait maybe, or even Saudi Arabia.'

'No, she won't have done that,' Celia said with a distant look in her grey eyes. 'She's here in Bahrain. I feel it instinctively.' She saw his expression and stiffened. 'You can sneer if you like. I wouldn't expect you to understand. And it's precisely because Bahrain is such a small state—apart from its scattering of islands, no bigger than the Isle of Wight, my father used to say—that I don't think my search for Nevine will be too difficult.'

McCord looked at her for a long moment and obviously recalling the skirmish with the camel-drivers he pointed out, 'It still doesn't explain why you didn't order a car at the hotel desk and start your enquiries there.'

Celia fidgeted. 'I suppose I thought they'd . . .'

'Consider it an idiotic errand you'd come to Bahrain on?' he finished for her. 'And so do I. If I were you, Miss . . .'

'The name's Darwell,' she smiled thinly.

He bowed ironically. 'If I were you, Miss Darwell, I'd pack my bags and return to England.'

'You may have business interests, but I don't think you own Bahrain, do you?' Her spirited comment was delivered smoothly.

'I can make it difficult for some fool English girl wandering around on an even zanier lovelorn mission.'

His harsh words made her react involuntarily. 'I don't suppose you can have any inkling of what this means to me?'

'I won't help trying to perpetuate your father's memory by searching out this . . . this Nevine.'

Was that what she was doing? She had to admit it would make her feel very close to her father if she could find and talk to Nevine.

Annoyed at the man's wisdom, she straightened. 'You can make it as difficult as you like, I intend to go through with it. And don't worry, I won't disgrace your Englishman's good name abroad by doing anything else foolish.'

'Do you want to bet?'

Oh, that supercilious look! Never had a man stirred her to such depths of resentment. She had only just met him, but she could cheerfully have hit him.

He took advantage of her being unable to frame a suitable reply to query, 'May I ask if you know any Arabic?'

'I've got a very good phrase book.'

He threw his glance to the ceiling, then nailed her again with it to probe, 'I take it you know the surname of this Nevine?'

'I . . . didn't think to ask my father.'

'Photograph?'

'There . . . was nothing in his effects.'

He let the breath escape through his teeth. 'So you don't know what she looks like and you don't know her name. That's great! It's likely to take you another thirty odd years to solve the mystery.'

'Time isn't an enemy to us all, Mr. McCord.' She countered his scorn with a show of confidence. 'I'm willing to bet Nevine is still beautiful today.'

'So all you have to do is look for a faceless, nameless, fading beauty among three hundred thousand inhabitants.'

'I can take all the discouragement you feel obliged to hand out,' she was then fired to reply. 'I wouldn't expect a hard-headed businessman to know anything about the affairs of the heart. But *I* don't intend to make heavy weather of it. For one thing, I happen to know that English is widely spoken in Bahrain, and as I see it, it's simply a matter of asking around.'

'You might do okay in Manama, but what if you have to go to outlying villages? Chances are you'll have to if nothing turns up in town.'

'I'll cope,' she said hardily. It was strange. Before she had clashed with this hardbitten countryman of hers she had been ready to admit that it was madness coming to Bahrain with the idea of searching out her father's old love. Now she was filled with a drive to prove that it was anything but that. Such were the things that opposition did to one; opposition in the shape of a big, clamped-jawed, disapproving Englishman, at any rate.

CHAPTER TWO

McCORD ADDED nothing to what he had already said, but Celia could almost hear him thinking, 'There's one born every minute!' as he looked at his watch.

It was yet another source of irritation to her to discover that he had timed the repairing of her dress almost to the second, for in the next moment the soft-footed servant reappeared and presented him with the daffodil yellow folds before discreetly departing again.

McCord held up the dress and went over it with his gaze in an aggravatingly leisurely manner. 'I do believe the old boy's pressed it too,' he tossed it her way. 'You're going to look decidedly better leaving the house than you did coming into it.'

Celia changed rapidly, tempted to throw his dressing gown back at him in the same way, but something about the icy spark in his eyes deterred her. She thought it changed to mockery as she opened her handbag, one frayed handle reminding her of her brush with the camel-drivers, to search for comb and powder compact. Perhaps it amused him in a coldly sardonic way to have a woman titivating herself in his wholly masculine domain.

Let him look! She combed her shoulder-length hair to some semblance of smoothness and patted her nose with a perfumed powder-puff. And defiantly too she retouched her lips with a flame-hued lipstick.

Everything replaced and her handbag hung lopsidedly over her wrist, she presumed McCord was waiting for her to leave, but contrary to moving towards the door he pressed another button close at hand and said without stirring, 'There's someone you should meet.'

Celia was hardly in the mood to prolong her stay. The effects of the soothing liquor had long since cleared from her head and, wondering how she could have been so idiotic as to relate her trite story to this man of all people, she said, drily 'I think I've done enough socialising for one day.'

'I wasn't thinking in terms of entertainment' he returned crisply. 'Unless you consider the task you have set yourself falls into this category.'

Everyone seemed to jump to attention when he pushed those buttons, for in no time at all another figure not only appeared in the doorway, but this time walked respectfully into the room.

He was a little younger than his employer, being barely thirty perhaps, and Celia was struck by the contrasting warmth which seemed to fill the room with his arrival. His dark, luminous eyes took in the whole of her at a glance, returning to hover with lazy interest around her mouth. His Western dress didn't quite come up to the tailored perfection of McCord's tropical suit, but he was smartly attired in dark blue and though slight of frame there was a curious magnetism about him, an impish love of life, she felt, held sternly in check by that formal smile.

'Kamel, I want you to meet Miss Darwell.' It was McCord's voice which broke the spell of that look which passed between them, on the young Bahraini's side if not on Celia's; though she had an uncomfortable feeling that McCord had made his own lightning deduction of her reaction to the handsome young Arab. 'She's come to Bahrain to look someone up,' he went on, 'and it will be your job to give her whatever assistance she requires. You will pick her up promptly at nine in the mornings at the Gulf Hotel and deliver her there each day before dark. Is that clear?'

Celia couldn't believe her ears. The audacity of the man, interfering in her affairs this way! Who did he think he was, taking it upon himself to supply her with a guide! And at the precise hours *he* stated too!

She wanted to tell him so to his face, but that would have been insulting the young Arab, who was politely bowing her way, so she held her tongue.

'It's likely to be a prolonged search,' there was no mistaking those sanctimonious tones. 'Miss Darwell will give you all the details herself. Her safety will be your responsibility until she leaves Bahrain. Do you understand?'

'I will do as you wish, sir.' The reply was made in good English while those dark eyes roamed in Celia's direction again.

'Okay, Kamel, you can go now. And don't forget, Gulf Hotel, nine in the morning. You can use a company car.'

Dismissed in the peremptory way he had been summoned, Kamel was nevertheless sent about his business with a smile from McCord. To Celia it was totally unexpected. Hard and reserved, it was every bit in character with the rest of his granite features, yet she was fascinated by it. The shock that he could appear almost human left her with a wry feeling inside.

When they were alone again she wasted no time in letting him know that she was one, at least, who didn't intend to heel to his autocratic ways.

'Why did you do that?' she demanded hotly. 'I'm perfectly capable of making my own plans, thank you.'

'Kamel is one of several assistants I employ. I can spare him for as long as you want to keep up this fool quest.' He spoke as though the matter was closed, and stood aside for her to precede him. 'Shall we go?'

'Nothing would please me more!' It was the only scathing retort she could muster while brushing past him and even this, she felt, was lost on his tough exterior.

They made the drive back to the hotel in quivering silence—on Celia's part anyway. It was so humiliating to have to sit there and subject herself to his forceful handling of the situation. He ran people's lives, it seemed, in the same casual, steely way he was steering the car. She would dearly have loved to argue the point, but he gave her no opening. There was an unspoken air about him that defied the unsure—well, that was what he did to one—to contest his authority.

He came right in with her into the Gulf Hotel. In the lobby Celia said ungraciously, 'Please don't put yourself out for me. I *do* know my way from here.'

'I'm not doing you any favours,' he drawled in his tight-lipped fashion. And looking around, 'I'm here to meet a lady.'

So! He was not too frosted over to appreciate the company of a woman once in a while. For some reason his words struck a further note of discord within her and she was moved to aim at him, 'She has my sympathy, Mr. McCord!'

'Call me McCord,' he smiled as though making sweeping concessions. 'Everybody does.'

She ignored his slight nod as he left her and swung away into the opposite direction, though it was not necessarily the right one for her. Little did he know that she had regarded him as plain *McCord* from the start. As far as she was concerned he was not the type to inspire anything other than the dehumanised approach. She doubted if he had ever *possessed* a Christian name! And cared even less.

CELIA WAS up bright and early the next morning. It was not that she was falling in with McCord's plans... It was just that it did seem to her that the help of someone locally would make her task easier. To be truthful, she had had a go on her own the previous evening, but Manama at night-time was overwhelming and she hadn't known where to start in her search for Nevine. She would need assistance, she saw that now, and while she had no wish to be supplied with a guide out of McCord's camp, the man's integrity she was certain of, whereas if she hired a guide herself, who could say? Besides, she had a feeling that Kamel would be a lot more friendly than his employer.

Just how friendly she was soon to discover! His presence outside the hotel where he waited for her beside a practically dark saloon was eye-catching, to say the least. He was wearing a sand-coloured suit which emphasised his attractive olive-skinned features, and his smile as he greeted her was just about the warmest she had come across since her arrival in Bahrain.

'I am happy to be of service to you, Miss...' he frowned humorously while showing her into the seat beside the driving wheel. 'But it is too beautiful a day to be on formal terms. If we are to be together so much we should start out as friends right away. Don't you agree?'

'Agreed,' she laughed at his easygoing audacity. 'I'm Celia, and I'm glad to know you, Kamel.'

'Celia,' he said it musically. 'I know the name. It has a Greek significance, has it not?'

'They do say!' she replied lightly, settling herself as he joined her behind the wheel.

'Heavenly... that is the transposition in English, I believe,' he savoured the word with sensual lips while his liquid brown eyes amused themselves roaming her face. 'A

charming meaning for a name, and one entirely befitting in
your case, if I may say so.'

'You may.' Celia laughed again. What else could she do?
But as his gaze continued to linger while the rest of the town
traffic went about its business, she said, smiling back her
embarrassment, 'Well, shall we go?'

'Ah yes!'

At this purposeful exclamation Celia was sure Kamel intended to get down to work. He discarded his jacket and
confronted her with a decidedly less formal view of himself
in open-necked sports shirt the whiteness of which did even
more to enhance his attractive physique. Still purposeful, he
started the car and told her, 'First I will take you to Isa
Town, our beautiful garden city. Then I will show you El-
Areen where—'

'But I haven't even explained about my search yet,' she
cut in to remind him.

'Well,' he shrugged philosophically, 'we will find a good
spot where we can talk.'

A little helplessly Celia went along with the plan. She had
had visions of making almost door-to-door enquiries in
Manama concerning Nevine, and to be whizzing along
country roads, albeit surrounded by interesting scenery, was
not her idea of conducting a systematic search. Still, she
supposed she had better let Kamel have his head to begin
with. She had heard that in the East they took things more
leisurely and she supposed it was not in an Arab's nature to
get straight down to business.

She forgot some of her frustration when they came to Isa
Town, a showpiece about eight miles out of Manama; the
gateway to the town consisted of three impressive, futuristic archways, and after that it was gardens all the way. As
she viewed the large concentration of new homes it occurred to Celia that Nevine, in later years, might have

moved out here. She was excited at the thought, but there was little opportunity for making enquiries there and then. Kamel was giving her an offhand account of current development in the area, as though he considered he had certain duties to perform as a guide, and when this was over he promptly left the district for somewhere which was obviously closer to his heart.

The man-made oasis he parked beside some time later she had to admit was a charming spot—and it would serve nicely too, she decided firmly, for describing in detail the plans she had in mind.

'Kamel,' she said, dragging her gaze from the green of slender bamboo saplings and eucalyptus trees against the sapphire sheen of lapping waters, 'don't you think I should tell you now why I'm here in Bahrain?'

'But of course! You must explain everything.' Her heart leapt at his enthusiasm, then sank again as he added, 'But first we will have lunch.'

'Lunch?' she gaped around. 'Out here?'

'Naturally I have come prepared.' He jumped out energetically on to the sand and proceeded to lay out a desert feast which was as incredible as it was inviting. There were cooked meat on little sticks, eggplant filled with aromatic herbs, grape-leaves stuffed with rice and mincemeat, white cheese, flat round bread, and dishes of figs, dates, olives and apricots.

Weakly Celia succumbed to the pleasures of eating. She hadn't allowed for taking time out to indulge themselves in this manner, in her itinerary, but she supposed they couldn't do what they had to do on empty stomachs. There were rugs to recline on and thirst-quenching liquids to go with the meal, and though she was impatient to make some start on tracking down Nevine she felt it would have been petty to throw cold water on Kamel's efforts.

He told her something about the wild-life sanctuary of El-Areen while they ate, and the reserve which was dedicated to the preservation of rare Arabian species, but not with any great desire to impress her with the information. If anything he was inclined to be a little more vague about their surroundings, concentrating more on creating a cosy atmosphere where they were camped beneath the spreading greenery of camphor trees.

Celia was grateful for the shade. She had donned cotton slacks and sleeveless blouse for the day's work, but even these were trying in the soaring temperatures of the Gulf. Her companion, like all Arabs, appeared not to notice the heat. She watched tapering horned oryx at a distance and striped gazelle nervously nibbling beside a fern-like copse. It was a far cry from how she had expected to be spending the first day of her quest; after all, there were no people here, people who might know or have heard of Nevine; just rare and timid animals. But the experience was not unpleasant, and the lapping waters of the oasis were decidedly soothing...

Kamel had a keen mind, obviously, or a man like McCord wouldn't have employed him, but in the few hours she had known him Celia felt it was a condition he was not wont to put himself out about when away from the office. Like now, for instance. Lunch over, he had contrived to position himself next to her and on the intimate note he had fostered throughout their stay at this chosen spot he asked, 'What do you think of our country, Celia?'

'It's hot,' she blew the damp air from her brow, then viewing the pearly brilliance of the sky and exotic scenery she conceded laughingly, 'and exciting, I suppose.'

'You are right. I cannot deny that there is something about the air here in the East that quickens the blood.'

Because he was gazing deep into her eyes Celia said lightly, 'Have you had occasion to make comparisons?'

'But of course! I am a travelled man.' Kamel looked faintly hurt. 'I studied in Beirut with future British Ambassadors to the Middle East, and I have also spent some time in your country. Do you know what they say about Bahrain?' He was comparing the fairness of her hair against the dark cinnamon of his wrist. 'They call it the Welwyn of the Gulf.'

'Is that because of the uncommon amount of Britishers there are over here?' she asked steadily. 'Or because of the garden aspect of the place?'

'A little of both, I think,' he smiled before his eyes took on a luminous urgency. 'But there is no one in Bahrain who so resembles a cool flower in a raging climate. Your presence, like your name, my sweet Celia, is for us Bahrainis— heavenly.'

Celia floundered for a reply. At twenty-three she had learned how to handle persuasive young men. Before her father's illness she had attended the usual social gatherings, and her fair hair and fresh features had made her the inevitable quarry of the bolder members of the opposite sex. But Kamel! He worked faster than the speed of light!

Shaking herself from the hypnotic quality of his gaze, she twinkled sternly, 'You may not know it, but the name Celia also signifies "one who commands," and I think it's time I got down to issuing a few. But first I'll tell you all about my reasons for being in your country.'

'Business! Business! Why does everyone always want to talk business?' he groaned.

'Contrary to common belief,' she teased, 'it's *that* that makes the world go round.'

Much against his will Kamel listened to all she had to say and when she had finished he didn't hesitate to give her his opinion of the matter. 'But that is a stupid idea!' He was petulantly incredulous. 'You cannot waste our time looking for some bag of an Arab woman when we are at the point of something so exciting in our lives.' He waved an arm. 'All this and much more can weave the memories for our future—the bathing delights of El Bakhor; the moonlight paths of Jamrah...'

'You're employed by Mr. McCord, I believe, to do a working day, not to languish in lush tourist spots' Celia pointed out patiently. 'And please don't refer to Nevine in that way. She was quite a bit younger than my father and it's possible she may be still elegant and attractive.'

'But it is not Nevine who beckons across the barren stretches of my heart.'

Kamel could be impishly digressive and Celia had to work hard at pushing home her demands. 'We'll start in town. I think that will be the best place to begin our enquiries.'

'Very well,' Kamel became brisk too. 'We will return to Manama, and I shall be a slave to your wishes. No house or business will escape the purge of our enquiries, but I too have my conditions. After dark is my own time and I shall make a supper reservation for two at the Moon Guest restaurant. We will take up there the quest you force me to abandon now...the linking of hearts.'

It was blackmail in the subtly charming, Eastern tradition, and Celia was mildly apprehensive about the 'linking of hearts' bit, but, worriedly aware that she was now in her third day in Bahrain with only limited resources in her purse, she accepted with a lighthearted 'Done!' and fell to helping him to pack away the picnic things. Any start was better than none.

Kamel was as good as his word. He worked with a conscientiousness that Celia felt any man of McCord's would, approaching owners in shops and town houses and places of entertainment with the courteous affability of his race, and lapsing into fiery Arabic and abuse when dealing with the slow-witted, also a trait in his kind.

Celia possessed no likeness of Nevine, but she did carry a photograph of her father, taken as a young man when he had worked in Bahrain. She showed this around expectantly at first but after much foot slogging and hovering in the background listening to negative responses, her optimism was replaced by acute disappointment, and she began to see that the thing she had set her heart on was going to be no easy task.

No one had heard of any person going by the name of Nevine. Many suggested that it might have been a stage name the dancer had adopted for her profession, but all proffered blank faces and empty-handed gestures. Even the elderly had no recollection of such a woman in their midst.

When the town became lit by the plum-coloured glow of dusk Celia was more than ready to call it a day, and after a refreshing shower in her hotel room and a change of clothes she found she was not averse at all to dining out with Kamel. Work, no matter how exciting in some cases, could pall, she had discovered, if one didn't give it a rest.

She hadn't packed an extensive wardrobe for the simple fact that she didn't possess one, but her dreams of finding Nevine had prompted her to want to look her best for the occasion, so her favourite garments had accompanied her on this trip. One was a summer dress in creamy seersucker which she was wearing now. She pinned on a diamanté brooch to give it an evening touch and with similar winking lights showing when the thick sweep of honey-pale hair revealed her earlobes, she considered the effect wasn't too bad.

Kamel was waiting for her in the lobby of the hotel. It was thickly populated as usual, and as she was crossing the

spaces to meet him she caught sight of McCord in with the
wandering traffic of guests. He had seen her, she noticed—
well, that was possibly an understatement, his eyes were
fixed on her as she moved before him as though he expected her, at any moment, to commit another faux-pas. She
met his gaze somewhat defiantly in passing. He was bound
to see her meet up with Kamel, of course, but so what? This
was Kamel's free time, and he wasn't boss over *that,* was he?

THE MOON Guest Hotel housed a restaurant that was both
intimate and exclusive. The Chinese cuisine and Korean
royal food were an experience for Celia, but neither was as
devastating as Kamel's burning presence. The longing to
participate in something other than knocking on street doors
and confronting blank faces had made her forget the bull-
dozing charms of her Arab assistant.

His attentiveness during the meal would have been embarrassing if she had taken it seriously. But for all her light-
heartedness little whispers of doubt kept coming to plague
her as to the wisdom of agreeing to spend the evening with
him. He could be unnervingly possessive, she was noticing,
and his 'linking of hearts' talk of earlier, and 'weaving the
memories for our future,' caused her some concern behind
her smile.

When they got up to leave after the meal, his arm turned
quite naturally about her waist and he told her close to her
ear, 'Before we go, I have a little surprise for you. Come,'
he indicated through a beaded curtain.

Approaching displays of jewellery and gifts along a carpeted corridor of the hotel, Celia was horrified to discover
that Kamel intended to buy her a trinket. Slant-eyed girls
showed her trays of rings and pendants in imperial jade and
coral brought specially from the Far East, and when her

Arab companion placed a necklace around her throat she gasped, 'Oh, no, Kamel! I hardly know you.'

'What is time, measured in the earthly way?' Those liquid dark eyes met hers. 'You and I have lived a thousand years since meeting. It is certainly the moment to show my appreciation for the gift that Allah has delivered into my arms.'

She wasn't in his arms, nor had she any intention of ending up there, but her polite refusal to accept a trinket from him met with the same charming disregard with which he viewed all her negative responses. In the end she settled for a simple pendant affair of mystic Oriental design which he took great pleasure in fastening about her neck.

Out in the warm, charged air of night-time in the Gulf she knew she was going to have to stand firm, and taking a breezy attitude she said, 'Well, it's back to the hotel now, Kamel. We mustn't forget we have an early start to make in the morning, and I am rather tired.'

'But you know nothing of Manama by night!' He was obviously put out at her rapid rounding off of the evening. 'We have discothèques and—'

'I've seen enough of it by day,' she replied wryly. 'Now are you going to drive me back or shall I take a taxi?'

He gave in peevishly, and later, alighting outside the entrance to the Gulf Hotel, Celia was smitten sufficiently by his glum features to offer, 'Thank you for a perfect evening, Kamel, and I do appreciate the pendant—it's lovely. I hope we'll have another good day work-wise tomorrow.'

'Of course I shall wait for you at the appointed hour,' he said aloofly before driving off.

Despite his polite assurance she half expected to see no Kamel or a very disgruntled one the next morning. But contrary to her expectations he greeted her beside the car with his glowing smile, and radiating his usual warmth and energy; though energy for what? she asked herself with a sinking feeling noting picnic and beach gear as she got into the car. 'First we will go to Yafamas for morning coffee,' he told her gaily, 'then to the beach at Ras-al-Kar. It is a superb day for a swim, there is a cooling *shamal* blowing and—'

'But I don't *want* to swim,' Celia cut across his suggestions firmly. 'I want to find Nevine.'

'So! We have eight whole hours.' He was complacent. 'And if you wish we can ask around along the way.'

'I want to do more than that, Kamel. I want to follow up any line of enquiry which may reveal Nevine's whereabouts,' Celia said patiently.

'That too,' he shrugged flexibly. 'But as it is a tedious occupation conversing with the rabble about some frayed Arab...matron, why should we not enjoy a swim for our labours?'

The way he put it there was little footing for argument and Celia was bound to go along with his bargaining tactics...that day and the ones that followed. Once she got into the hang of falling in with his plans to overwhelm her with his company and the sights of the island in return for his assistance in the matter of Nevine, comparative peace reigned. But it was an uneasy peace where Celia was concerned.

She couldn't complain of any reluctance on Kamel's part to make a thorough search for the woman who had been so much a part of her father's life thirty years before. Besides traversing the corridors of smart seaside apartments and palmshaded communal residences they combed the countryside and outlying villages, stopping at hamlets to knock on decrepit doors and waylaying camel and donkey traffic to enquire of their owners. But balancing with this were the languorous afternoons they spent beside the blue waters of the Gulf and in the garden pools of sophisticated Bahrain hotels, time enough to foster an ever-increasing intimacy between them which she was helpless to counteract.

Though she drew the line at seeing Kamel every evening, pressure in the form of some extra zest on his part in their joint search made her feel obliged to show her gratitude with an occasional supper together; concessions which something told her were far from wise.

She also had McCord at the back of her mind. She had seen him in the hotel again on another occasion, and it would have to be when she was loaded up with beach bag and bathing gear on her way to meet Kamel. She recalled his terse statement that he had not been thinking in terms of entertainment when offering her the services of a guide, and she was reminded rather guiltily that it was McCord who was paying Kamel's wages.

She couldn't help wondering too, at times, about Mc-Cord's mysterious lady friend. He was often to be seen in the lobby of the Gulf hotel, but so far she had spotted no feminine figure at his side. Where did he keep her?

But dominating her consciousness most of the time was the glum fact that she was no nearer to finding Nevine now than she had been at the start. Of course there had been moments when her hopes had soared; when it happened that someone bearing the same name was known to be residing in some out-of-the-way village or backwater section of the town. But each time it had turned out to be a false trail with the woman in question being some stallholder who had worked at nothing else since childhood or a farming type whose whole life had been the land she and her husband tilled.

The days were flying by; a state of affairs that Celia was all too aware of. She was running up a bill at the hotel which threatened to take the last of her reserves. Coupled with

Kamel's ever-increasing possessiveness where she was concerned, things were, to say the least getting out of hand. The moment she knew that she would have to forget her dream of finding Nevine and return to England came when they had just left a hamlet of cubic dwellings with the usual negative results and were driving back to the more populated sections of the island. Palm trees rose in misty splendour beside damply irrigated lush green farm strips and the idea of never knowing the woman whom her father had idolised filled Celia with an intense sadness. But it had been a wild scheme anyway and she should have known that the chances of success were remote.

She chose a relaxed period when they were sipping mango juice at a beachside table to tell Kamel that she was abandoning the search. He made no attempt to hide his pleasure. 'Good!' he beamed. 'Now we can think solely about ourselves.'

'But, Kamel, you don't understand' she explained wearily. 'I came to Bahrain only for a limited stay. Now that time is up I have no choice but to return to England.'

'You have one other choice,' he took her hand. 'Celia, my heavenly Celia, you must know by now that I want to make you my wife.'

'Kamel!' She was staggered, though she fought hard not to show it. 'We've only just met. A fortnight together doing guided tours of Bahrain is not the basis for the kind of partnership you suggest.'

'Nevertheless you shall be my first wife,' he said stubbornly.

First wife! Celia would have reviewed the whole thing with humour if Kamel had not been so petulantly serious. She saw the burning desire in his eyes and wondered if all Arabs worked on making such lightning conquests.

All along she had sensed that her guide was getting a charming fixation about her, but she had not forseen in her farewell speech the possibility of having to make a refusal of marriage. Nor was it as simple as that. As Kamel was a man who obviously didn't like to be crossed she could see she was going to have to oppose the idea with everything she possessed.

The arguments she offered lightly at first and then otherwise had no effect on him. So in the end she told him gently but firmly that she would be catching the plane home the following day, and that in time he would find someone who would make him a much better wife than she would.

It did seem then that her words had got through. 'Very well,' he gave a shrug, his gaze somewhat hooded. 'But before you leave I think there is one more possibility we should try concerning this dancing girl of the past.'

Celia couldn't believe that he was seeing sense at last, but happily this appeared to be the case. A little in wonder, as he had never offered suggestions of this sort before, she said, 'Somewhere where we might find Nevine? But if you think there's a chance why haven't you mentioned it earlier?'

'It has only just come into my head,' he shrugged again, and then with growing enthusiasm, 'But I am sure there is every reason to believe that this time we may be lucky.'

His words triggered off a new excitement in Celia. It had been known before to hunt and hunt for something and then find it under one's nose. And anywhere in the small state of Bahrain that could happen, couldn't it? Her hopes soared unaccountably. It might still be possible to meet and talk with Nevine after all before she had to leave for England. It could be that having got the nonsense of his proposal out of his mind Kamel was thinking clearly for the first time.

Increasingly optimistic, she asked, 'But where is this place?'

'Out in the desert, somewhere we have never thought of looking, and I think we should go there right away.'

Celia was a little taken aback at Kamel's sudden zest for work, but she went along with him happily enough to the car, her mind re-inspired conjuring up pictures of a gentle-featured woman who had once been the young Arab girl of her father's heart.

They drove for some time leaving the beaches of Zallaq behind and making for an area which appeared to be devoid of all living matter, going by the look of the yellow haze beyond the windscreen. But surprisingly, Celia was to discover, there was one habitation in all these barren miles of dusty desert; a cubic dwelling of sorts with onion-shaped archways leading to other buildings, and a minaret and palm trees giving it the look of a traveller's rest.

What was odder still to Celia, for the oasis had a deserted air, was that Kamel drove straight into the sand-strewn courtyard and alighting helped her rapidly from her seat. Hesitatingly she got out and looked about her. 'You can't mean here?' she was frowningly incredulous. 'The place looks derelict...'

'That's the impression one gets,' he took her arm. 'But I do happen to know of a recluse staying here.'

'A recluse?' Celia's heart lifted suddenly. She looked at Kamel expectantly.

'A recluse,' he nodded mysteriously, 'who is known to have been an entertainer in her time.'

Celia was spurred into action. Could it be? Was Nevine, love-lost like her father, living out her life here, lonely and forgotten?—Or so she thought.

Celia almost ran with Kamel to the doorway he indicated. Fleetingly it struck her as strange that he seemed to know his way around. And when he produced a key to the door her whirling senses, thinking only of the prospective meeting with Nevine, were too lit up with excited anticipation to register the fact.

She walked into a low-ceilinged room. Vast and ornately furnished in true Eastern style, it wore an air of outdated luxury. The tasselled hangings, sumptuous sofas, carpets and velvet cushions exuded the musky odour of age, and rich mosaics and lacework drapes had yellowed with time.

Celia had time to notice all this while she waited, keyed up, for someone to appear at their arrival. But all she heard was the slam of the door at her back. At first she thought it was a trick of the breeze which had sculptured the sand-drifts in the courtyard, but when she heard the turn of the key in the lock, puzzlement took the place of her glowing anticipation and she called, 'Kamel! What are you doing? Do you realise you've locked me in?'

His voice came back, soft and caressing close to the door. 'That was my intention, my heavenly Celia. And you will stay locked in until you agree to become my wife.'

Celia listened horror-stricken. 'You mean—there's no Nevine in this place?—It was all a trick just to get me here?'

'I had to think of something.' His tones were peevishly apologetic. 'I decided from the first moment I saw you that I wanted you for my wife. You have upset all my plans by refusing my wish, but I think it will be simply a matter of time before you change your mind.'

'Kamel!' She beat in a frightened way on the door. 'You're not going to leave me here? You can't! I have to return to England tomorrow... and besides, it won't do you any good. You must see the idea of a marriage between us after so little time is rid—'

'I will return in a few days,' the voice came from further away. 'We will see then how strongly you resist my desires to make you my betrothed.'

'A few days?' Celia hammered, panic-stricken. 'Kamel! Let me out at once! Stop this stupid game, do you hear? Kamel!...Kamel?'

The only reply this time was the sound of the car starting up, and soon her cries and beatings upon the door were drowned in its noisy departure. When she listened again the rumble of the engine was fading fast in the distance, leaving her surrounded by an eerie and breeze-whining silence.

Half angry and half laughing at the craziness of the situation, Celia wandered into the room and found a seat. But it had ceased to be funny when the arched windows began to show the blue-black night of the desert and Kamel still hadn't returned.

Exhausted, she curled up as best she could on one of the sofas, reminded for some inexplicable reason in all this faded luxury, of the after-scent of Turkish Delight. But the furtive scufflings around the corners of the room doused any humour she might have felt at the thought and she spent a sleepless night listening to these and other unnerving sounds around the desert outpost.

Dawn came and the morning passed with her pacing the room in between frantic bouts of looking for a means of escape, all of which proved fruitless. Kamel had known what he was doing imprisoning her here. Every entrance she explored outside her immediate surroundings was sealed and the room, despite its elegant trappings of the past, had the barred-in feel of a fortress.

It was just after lunch-time by her watch when she heard the heartening sound of a car approaching. So Kamel had relented and returned! Or maybe he thought she had already changed her mind. Well, she wouldn't be such a fool as to let him believe any different until she was well clear of this place. Conjuring up in her mind the sweet replies she would give him, she rushed to the windows, but they overlooked the rear of the courtyard and she could see nothing. All she could rely on was her hearing, and something told her that the vehicle that was fast approaching was not the one she was used to hearing Kamel drive her around in. The rhythm of the engine was different, for one thing, and suddenly she was filled with a new and blood-chilling fright. What business other than questionable could anyone have in a ghost-town place like this?

Instead of rushing to the door as the car came to an abrupt stop in the courtyard, she backed away. And at the sound of footsteps making straight for the door, *her door,* she paled. *That* certainly wasn't Kamel's soft-shoed tread.

The knob turned right and then left. She watched it hypnotised. Would the caller go away? She stood transfixed, then jumped back a step or two as some great weight was hurled against the door. It was a strongly fabricated structure, but it soon began to give against the powerful force at the other side.

Her blood running cold, Celia knew she ought to *move;* run, hide, anything but just stand there. Yet stand there she did, rooted with horrified fascination as the door began to splinter before her eyes. The sound of laboured breathing came to her ears. An extra, superhuman effort and the door cracked before her and fell away to reveal in its opening an awry and familiar figure.

McCord looked at her in that disapproving way of his, squared himself in the doorway and heaved, 'I thought I'd find you here.'

CHAPTER THREE

STRUGGLING TO appear unaffected by his appearance, Celia replied flippantly, 'Your powers of perception are amazing. Given one unlocked door on these premises and you could have been wrong.'

'Yes, it's a pretty neat stronghold,' McCord acknowledged, brushing himself off. 'And trust you to end up stuck in the middle of it.'

'Well, believe me, I'm not enjoying the experience!' Celia thought she would get that point home. More relieved than she cared to admit at seeing McCord, she asked crossly, 'How did you know I was here?'

'Simple deduction.' He lifted sizeable shoulders clothed in dust-powdered desert garb. 'I noticed that Kamel was back at his desk as usual this morning. But I learned at the hotel that you hadn't checked out.'

'So naturally I was bound to be locked and barred away, in some distant desert retreat,' Celia reasoned satirically.

'That's just about it in Kamel's case.' McCord was unamused. 'It's not the first time he's used this place to try to weaken the opposition where a girl's concerned. Although I employ some of the keenest brains among the local Arab population they do at times tend to revert back to nature, and Kamel has had designs more than once in starting up his own harem here at Al Minbah.'

Feeling more foolish than she cared to show, Celia fumed, 'Well, you might have told me!'

'I thought you would have the good sense to avoid that kind of entanglement,' he snapped back.

'Avoid it?' Celia was stormily incredulous. 'If I'd ridden around in the car trunk all the time I couldn't have escaped Kamel's wooing ways. He has a kind of demolishing approach, as you've probably noticed.'

'As I remember it,' McCord's expression was cynical, 'you were a long way from riding in the car boot. In fact I'd say Kamel was half-way there, with the kind of encouragement you gave him.'

Encouragement! Oh, why was it that whenever she met this man her fingers always itched to come into forceful contact with those self-important, hardbitten features?

Containing her fury, she said with flashing-eyed mockery, 'It would be interesting to know how *you* would have handled the situation had it been a seductive female in the driving seat!'

He looked at her, his blue eyes enigmatically self-indulgent, as he replied, 'I hardly think that has any relevance in the argument, do you?' and she could have kicked herself for giving him the opportunity of demonstrating, once again, his male superiority.

While she was thinking, against her will, about his mysterious lady friend at the Gulf Hotel he added with his usual asperity, 'And as you appear to be unharmed and little the worse for the experience I suggest we get out of here.'

He stood aside for her to step over the remnants of the battered down door, and feeling considerably lightheaded after the eruptive exchanges with her formidable rescuer— his extracting her from sticky situations was becoming a habit, and oh, how he loved to belabour her shortcomings!—Celia made her way unsteadily into the courtyard.

Nothing would have induced her to display the cosy feeling of security which enveloped her in the haven-like interior of McCord's car. She waited until they were speeding away from Al Minbah before putting in smoothly, 'It may sound a silly question, but why didn't you confront Kamel with what you had obviously guessed about me, and ask him for the key to my prison?'

'It wouldn't have done any good,' came the level reply. 'He would have denied the whole thing and probably thrown the key away to detach himself from the matter. The oasis, which was famous in the days before the oil boom, belongs to his family. In his mind you could have become just another part of the past until he felt sufficiently mollified to come and look you up.'

Celia shuddered. She really was glad now that McCord had burst the door in. She had been a lot more frightened than she had let herself believe, and her instincts had proved correct, it seemed. Since she had neither eaten nor slept for more than twenty-four hours it didn't bear thinking about how much longer she would have had to remain in this piteous state had it been left to Kamel. Spent as she was, she couldn't resist a wry smile at the so-called 'affection' of some Arabs.

She hadn't meant to demonstrate further her incompetence where McCord was concerned by collapsing into a deep sleep on the ride back. But the bright outdoors, the steadily drumming rhythm of the car wheels over rough ground, and the barren landscape, all acted like a drug on the mind. And such was her drained state that she never remembered dropping off. Nor had she the remotest intention of letting her head fall to rest on a comfortably-padded shoulder, and horror of horrors, she stirred at one point to discover that she had actually done this. But the deep bliss of this longed-for dreamless state was so all-encompassing she had no real will-power to fight her anti-McCord feelings . . . not for the moment at any rate.

Had she known what was coming when the car stopped she might have made some effort to revive. But there again, perhaps she was too wrapped up in the euphoria of sleep to care much when McCord began to shovel her up in his arms; though she did stir enough to protest dopily, 'Where are we? Oh no, not the Sheikh's palace again!'

'His title now is Emir, he was promoted on independence,' McCord corrected her, making for the indoors. 'And though it may look roomy I can assure you El Zommorro in no way compares with the royal abode.'

Even so, it was a beautiful house, Celia had to admit, if only from what she remembered of it on her last visit. A blur of rose gardens passed her sleepy vision, then she was aware of a whispered commotion in the cool interior as servants were sent on hurriedly ahead.

A staunchly independent type, she couldn't understand this powerful feeling of lethargy; a warm contentment to stay where she was nestled against a hard chest. Distantly in her mind she could hear the solid rhythm of a heartbeat. She was lulled again into oblivion by its comforting thud, surfacing momentarily when her head touched cool pillows, and then only to give a blissful sigh.

When she awoke the sky beyond the windows was aglow with the lilac and amber suffusion of dusk. She raised herself, noticing how the light filled the room with rose-violet tints; a room richly but moderately furnished to give a feeling of airiness.

Over a white carpet, realising that her shoes had been removed, she explored and discovered an adjoining bathroom suite; a sight that had never looked so inviting to her dust-rimmed eyes. It was good too, in the flower-shaped porcelain bath, to soak away all traces of the musty-smelling makebelieve harem where she had been imprisoned for so long. But when she was dressed again, and reasonably groomed, the pale face staring back at her from the mirror was not too heartening a sight for all her efforts.

A reeling sensation reminded her that she had not eaten since lunch-time the previous day. Though she had been too exhausted earlier to think of food, now she realised that she was in urgent need of some kind of sustenance.

The house was silent as though enveloped in the hush of approaching darkness. There was no sound now of the muted office-like atmosphere she had divined on her last visit. Outside her room she followed tiled corridors dimly lit to a curving stairway. Below, doors ajar on all sides showed interiors tastefully lit in a subdued way. Choosing the most open one of these, where slightly more illumination spilled out into the hallway, Celia saw at once that her guess had been correct.

McCord was leisurely pulling on a cigarette in an armchair lit by a pool of lamplight, a sheaf of what appeared to be business papers on hand. He rose when he caught sight of her and, confronted by the length and breadth of him in tailored evening wear as opposed to the desert garb of earlier, she became stiff again and impatient with her lapses of the afternoon.

'I'm grateful for your hospitality,' she offered truculently. 'But I would have preferred you to drop me back at the hotel.'

'Drop might have been the operative word,' he said, observing her drily.

Meaning to say that she would have fallen flat on her face in the lobby from fatigue, no doubt.

'Oh, of course!' She made a show of recollecting a previous conversation. 'We have to remember not to let the side down, don't we?' And recalling how he had transported her in his arms to the room she had woken up in, she added, 'It's amazing the lengths some people will go to, to keep up the image.'

'Isn't it,' he replied noncommittally.

Celia would dearly have liked a chair to support her rubbery legs, but as McCord didn't offer her one she drifted with as much dignity as she could muster to the nearest one and sank down, suppressing an exclamation of relief.

The room, she noticed, was not quite on the grand scale of the others she had seen. Furnished in a more intimate style it was probably a dining room for a table, set in this instance for two, under the golden glow of a low chandelier, was its main feature.

McCord reached to press one of the inevitable buttons and as savoury-smelling dishes appeared in the hands of shadowy assistants he said, 'You'd better get yourself over to the table while you're still upright. You're not exactly a heavy weight to haul around, but I don't fancy having to cart you off to bed a second time—not on an empty stomach.'

Wobbling to a chair which he held for her beside the table, she flashed him a facetious look. 'I'd hate you to miss dinner for me!'

It was impossible to remain wooden with all this delicious food laid out, though she did make a feeble attempt while feverishly helping herself with the remark, 'There was really no need to extend your hospitality to include feeding me. I could have managed quite well at the hotel.'

'What happened at Al Minbah is a company matter,' McCord said, filling her glass and his own with a local wine. 'The unpleasant adventure you got yourself mixed up in involved an employee. As Kamel is my concern it's up to me to make amends for the damage that has been done. Eat.'

Since he put it like that Celia had really no more reservations about digging in. He jolly well owed her some com-

pensation after what she had been through at the hands of
his marriage-crazy guide, and she intended to make the most
of it.

In her undernourished condition the meal was heaven.
Combining European tastes with a dash of Arabic flavour-
ing here and there, every dish sampled was a gastronomic
experience. And there were the usual displays of dates and
fruit and Turkish Delight vying with pastry-thin fibres
baked with nuts and cream or raisin cake steeped in milk, for
sweet.

McCord finished long before Celia did, and while she was
busy peeling her second tangerine he sat back in his chair
and asked, 'How's the search going for Nevine?'

Aglow now and in a much pleasanter frame of mind, she
answered with a sigh, 'Not good, I'm afraid. Kamel and I
have combed the whole of Bahrain—that is, Awal, I think
you call this main island—without so much as turning up a
clue. It's as though she never existed.'

'What about the smaller islands, Muharraq, and the
Hawars?'

'We've had extensive enquiries made in those regions,
with much the same results.'

'Even so, it wouldn't hurt to go there personally and do
some looking around.' McCord was thoughtful. 'Jalal, a
young assistant of mine, is a native of the Hawar Islands...'

Celia looked at him and exclaimed with feeling, 'Oh no!
Not one of your Arab guides again!'

At the stricken note in her voice he reconsidered and said
with a tight grin, 'No, perhaps not.'

He asked for coffee to be served through an adjoining
doorway, and preceding him, Celia found herself in a sheltered balconied affair lush with the tropical growth of pot-
ted palms, climbing vines and sweet-smelling plants.

The furniture was garden-like and the lighting hidden amongst the greenery; not that one needed light with a view like this, Celia mused. There were no gardens at this side of the house, just the yawning emptiness of the desert. But what an emptiness! Stars filled a sky which swept low to distant horizons, spangling the night with a mystic awareness of the heavens and their timelessness.

As though to bring her back to earth McCord said, 'The glow you can see is from the lights and oil flares at the Dahran oilfield. Bahrain,' he went on, 'is fortunate in possessing inland springs which bubble up in the most unlikely places. I chose this site for the house because it has one of the best springs of drinking water on the island.'

'I might have known it wasn't picked for its romantic location,' Celia replied drily.

Nevertheless it was romantic. The peach glow of the oilfields had a remote and faraway glamour and across the barren wastes wafted the warm scents of the Gulf waters and the whispered flurry of night insects.

Unexplainably Celia was filled with a curious desire to flee. Her eagerness to take in the view had brought her to the balustraded edge and though the balcony was by no means cramped the shadowy bulk of McCord close behind her had a stifling effect. She had a feeling that this was one of his favourite retreats at El Zommorro; here where all this thriving greenery—and his own virile presence, she couldn't help adding—cocked a snook at the impotency of the desert.

She also reminded herself that he had rested and dined her solely to compensate for the trouble caused by one of his employees, so it would not be in keeping to go weak-kneed at her surroundings.

With this thought in mind she went briskly to the glass-topped table to pour, and for the next ten minutes or so they sat in silence over coffee.

McCord was the first to rise. Realising that it was time to go, Celia discovered that the restlessness she had experienced earlier had mellowed to an odd reluctance to stir. She was conscious of a great peace here, a magic, one might almost say, which in a way helped her to understand her father's lifelong affinity with the East and Bahrain. And in turn she knew a tremendous melancholy at the thought of Nevine, who had been so close to him, unfound and unknown to her out there.

APART FROM that brief discussion during dinner concerning the search for her, nothing more had been said on the subject of the dancing girl of the past. But when they were in the car on the way back to Manama McCord let it be known that he had had an idea.

'I'm invited to a dinner party over at Rifaa tomorrow night,' he drawled. 'It's where the aristocracy reside. If you fancied coming along you could do some discreet probing among the guests.'

'For Nevine?' Celia sat up straighter.

He shrugged. 'You said she came from a good class family. It was just a thought.'

'Why, yes, I'm sure she was well born, despite the profession she chose,' Celia pondered eagerly. 'Though one can't say whether she's had to suffer any kind of repercussions in later life, because of it.'

'Have your enquiries covered that stratum of society?' McCord asked.

'As far as it was possible to do.' She looked wry. 'The kind of gatherings you mention are not that easy to gain access to in Bahrain.'

'That's why I suggested it.' McCord swung the wheel, his eyes on the road.

Equally detached now, she considered his words and asked, 'Wouldn't I be gatecrashing?'

'Not if you come with me. I'll pick you up at five tomorrow afternoon.'

She crooked an eyebrow. 'Didn't you say *dinner* party?'

'That comes later,' he replied non-committally. 'First we'll have to go through the usual Eastern ritual, which could prove useful for you.'

In what way Celia couldn't be sure, so she thought it best to wait and see. But she was keyed up at the prospect. As her glance strayed towards the outdoors the familiar surge of glowing anticipation rose within her. Another chance! Another possibility of finding Nevine!

They were fast leaving the desert behind and in contrast to its sombre magnificence Manama flaunted like a tawdry woman of the night. There was glamour here of a hardened kind in the strands of twinkling lights, in the flashing neon signs at the tops of high-rise buildings, and the headlights glitter of cars on the dual carriageway beside the sea.

At the Gulf Hotel Celia noticed how McCord accompanied her indoors, and it occurred to her then to remark obtusely before he left her, 'Are you sure I won't be making myself unpopular with…er…your other friends at the hotel if I accompany you tomorrow evening?'

He said with parting irony, 'Don't worry, I'll arrange it.'

In her hotel room around four the following afternoon Celia floundered in a certain amount of indecision. She was quite decided that she wanted to go to the dinner party, but of her escort for the outing she was not so sure. McCord needled her in a way she couldn't explain. He was always finding fault with her behaviour in his precious adopted country, and as an expatriate she fell far short of his ideals;

mainly because since her arrival he had had to fish her out
of one compromising situation after another. It was no good
trying to explain to him that fate seemed to be taking a
wicked delight in landing her in these tight spots. He put it
all down to featherheaded feminine behaviour. And that was
what made her fume. Just because *he* was familiar with the
East she had to put up with his insufferable superiority!

She was reminded that she hadn't thanked him for coming to her aid at the Al Minbah oasis. But then why should
she? He had more or less admitted that the onus of Kamel's
behaviour was on his shoulders. At least, she told herself
consolingly, *he* wasn't likely to spirit her away to some desert love-nest.

The problem was what to wear. If she made the best of
herself McCord would think she had done it to impress him
(heaven forbid!). And if she didn't dress up she might find
herself politely shunned by the aristocracy of Bahrain. She
decided to go the whole hog and laid out her pearl-grey
pleated chiffon. So far McCord had seen her only in simple
sundresses. But it was a matter of extreme importance, she
told herself, working a little unsteadily, to be accepted in a
society where there was a chance she might unearth Nevine.

Shutting out the remembered feel of a hard chest against
her cheek with its accompanying solid heartbeat, she showered away the dust of a visit to the nearby *souk* and was lib-
eral with a rose skin perfume. And rejecting pictures of a
dimly-lit balcony with an all-encompassing masculine presence, she reached for filmy underwear and dressed.

The finished result took her slightly by surprise. The dress
brought out the silvery lightness of her eyes and the tiny
petal-shaped cap of matching material, showing folds of
wheaten hair, revealed the slim contours of her throat.

The outfit was ages old. She had bought it just before her
father had taken to his bed, and since then there had been

so little occasion for dressing up. Still it had retained its freshness she was gratified to note.

Downstairs in the lobby she defied McCord with her look to make any comment on her appearance. Luckily for him he said nothing, though his glance was laconically appraising.

Almost from the start Celia was conscious of a difference in the drive from the routine ones she had made with Kamel. For one thing McCord's personal mode of transport was considerably more luxurious than a company car, and with its cool air-conditioning, motoring, she suspected, could be pleasant.

But it wasn't just the limousine; the driver too was a whole lot different from her over-amorous Arab-guide. If one forgot the expensively tailored suit, and those compellingly attractive-unattractive features, one would still have to contend with a leashed force in the man. In short McCord had a dynamic aura about him, an authoritative air that no lowly Arab employee could hope to emulate.

Rifaa, she had heard, was where the Ruler's palace was situated. It was in the desert some fifteen miles from Manama, and though they didn't actually touch on the Royal abode McCord told her something about the ruined palaces of earlier generations which were dotted on the sandy wastes stretching away into the far distance below the Rifaa escarpment, like a widely scattered desert encampment.

'Most of the owners' families live in modern villas these days,' he said, cruising along the elevated stretch, 'though some of the older members like to preserve the link with their desert ancestry by camping out in the desert in spring, and keeping hawks and saluki dogs. Many of the old robed diehards make for these abandoned courts to pass the time of day among themselves, accompanied by elderly servants and retainers left over from the days when Negro and Abyssinian slaves were fashionable.'

Celia commented with reluctant interest, 'You talk as though you know something about these gatherings.'

'I've been invited on occasions, yes.' His grin was hardly modest, she noticed, perhaps for her benefit. He just couldn't help letting her know how green she was.

'Naturally!' She put enough loaded interference in her reply to shatter his self-assurance, with no effect. One couldn't help sensing, just by looking at the man, that he was something of a force on the island, and irritated further, she mocked in deflating tones, 'I suppose you've had lunch with the Sheikh more than once?'

'I'll admit we're pretty close due to the desalinisation job I did for him in Bahrain.' McCord's light blue eyes were lit with steely whimsy.

Oh, of all the granite smugness! Celia was driven to swinging her own gaze to the front and cursing her luck at being landed in contact with the one man on the island who must be about the worst possible example of complacent male supremacy!

But her annoyance didn't stop her from making the smooth rejoinder, 'What I can't understand is how they get along with you, these *nice,* unassuming Bahraini types?'

'They're not afraid to learn. Scientifically and commercially there's a lot they don't know about their own country, and unlike outsiders, they appreciate advice.' His expression was bland, but the hint was broad enough. Well, if he thought she could do with some lessons on the East, he was the last one she would approach as a teacher. Add fuel to his already inflated ego by looking up to him with girlish questions? No, thank you!

She decided that the views were a lot easier on her emotions, and soon she saw how the roadside thorn thickets gave

way to avenues of oleander bushes and Mediterranean-
styled houses with swimming pools, half hidden in a walled-
in and green-growing privacy. But what was not hidden
from the eye were the kerbside shade trees and tamarisks
and servants and attendants gossiping besides flocks of
goats. Elegant horses too were to be seen idling in their
open-sided barns or airing magnificent manes beneath the
trees, giving the impression of a well-to-do community leisurely engaged in the running of its estates.

It was at one of these secluded villas that McCord eventually pulled in. The interior beyond the high walls was
green and jungly. Generous trees and flowering plants lined
a smooth winding drive. He parked beside other visiting cars
expensively solid in appearance. An Arab attendant in local dress hovered and Celia, a little uncertain, followed
McCord to the open doorway. He stopped and laying a hand
on her arm indicated another path leading through a tunnel
of greenery, 'You go that way. I'll see you later.' As the
smiling attendant took charge he added, with something like
encouragement in his expression, 'It's okay. You're expected.'

Nervous now and trying hard to hide it, Celia followed
her guide through the green archway, past dozens of stables
and into a courtyard where the silence and emptiness did
nothing for her waning morale. They went on down a cloistered walk, and here her glance was drawn to a heap of
slippers outside an open doorway. Inside, from what seemed
a vast area came the hum of voices. She looked around and
finding herself alone on the cloistered walk gathered that
this was where she was 'expected.'

In slippered feet she crossed the threshold. It was like
stepping back into the past, into another world. At first the
darkness was blinding after the brilliant sunshine. Then she
began to make out a long, low-ceilinged area, gaudily dec-

orated and stretching for twenty yards or more. And like flurrying petals over flanking sofas and Persian carpets, the room was filled with women, women, women.

There were the gauzy bundles of local born, bales of saffron yellow, tulip pink and turquoise topped by thick black hair and the shining eyes of the Gulf women. There were also the sleek forms of ambassadresses, cheerful American oil wives, faded English matrons, and the wrinkled-apple faces of the older relatives of the Sheikhdom family.

It took Celia a while to take all this in, of course, for first, as an arriving guest, she had to file with the others down the centre of the room towards the mauve and gold blur which was all they could see of their hostess at the end. A little nearer and she was able to make out a vivacious face, then she was being received graciously by the wife of Sheikh Jussuf Hamed, the owner of the villa and its estates. 'Mr. McCord has told me about you,' Sheikha Jamida said in pleasant tones. 'Your father was very fortunate to love a woman of our race, for when we choose a man who will mould our destiny we seldom allow another to take his place, even after death. I do hope you have some luck in tracing the woman of your father's heart. Feel free to enquire here as you wish.'

The sign was given that the allotted time was up and with a grateful smile Celia moved on. She drifted into the comings and goings in the room, into the shaking of hands and sipping of fruit juice and the non-stop chatter. Everything was being discussed, from the latest jewellery recently flown in from Tiffany's of New York, to the more successful ways of growing dwarf tomatoes and climbing roses. No one paid much attention to introductions, the gossip was general anyway, and Celia found no difficulty in merging with the animated gathering.

What spurred her on mainly was the exciting prospect of stumbling upon some clue as to Nevine's whereabouts. Surely amongst all this bubbling femininity, in a stratum of Bahraini society which could well be Nevine's own, someone would know her, or have heard of her.

Getting into conversation was by no means any problem, especially as she chose to mingle with the dark-eyed local women, the only ones really who could help her. And talking about the past was something these ladies delighted in, for to the more mature types they were always 'the good old days,' not the bad ones, when *al Khalifa,* the ruler, had been in his prime.

But they were not all as forthcoming as Celia would have wished. Unlike the unprejudiced smile of Sheikha Jamida, some of the listeners considered the act of discussing a dancing girl far beneath their level socially and abruptly changed the subject. Others who would have liked to be helpful were bound to admit that they knew of no such person.

After some time spent drifting from one flower-like group to another with no signs of success Celia was overcome by bitter disappointment. She was beginning to wonder if Nevine had ever existed. Was she just a figment of her father's imagination? A ghost who would never materialise? No, she was real enough, Celia knew, and she was here somewhere in the State of Bahrain. Why she was so sure of this Celia couldn't explain, but nothing would move her from the conviction. And failing to locate Nevine was proving the biggest frustration of her life.

A censer of fragrant burning sandalwood was borne round to which the women leaned in turn to fumigate their hair and drapes. Another gauzy bundle brought round bottles of Christian Dior perfume for splashing over limp hands, and Celia took advantage of the break to slip away.

There was no point now in lingering, and she had a curious desire to know what McCord was doing.

As it turned out he was waiting for her at the side of the green archway entrance, looking as though he had been there for a while, if one was to judge by the stub of his cigarette.

'Any luck?' he asked, tossing it away as she appeared.

'None at all,' Celia replied flatly, gratified in a way to know that McCord was also thinking of Nevine.

'You've been gone two hours' he said, looking at his watch. 'I was sure you were going to come out with some nimble-footed Arab matron in tow.'

'Has it been as long as that?' Celia couldn't make out whether he was joking or not. Amazed at how the time had flown, she added, 'I hope you haven't been waiting all that time.'

'Hardly.' His grin was expressive. 'We men have our diversions too, you know.'

'I wonder what *they* are?' she asked darkly, making it known by her look that she was well aware of what the Arabs got up to away from their wives.

On this McCord was his usual noncommittal self. 'It's time we were getting indoors,' he said, taking her arm. 'The dinner party will be well underway by now.'

From the moment of entering the split-level drawing room to which they were directed Celia knew that this was top-drawer Bahrain with a difference. In fact it was hard to believe that the two gatherings were taking place under the same roof; one so steeped in the traditions of the East, the other embracing an extraordinary collection of emancipated types who could have compared favourably with any such turn-out at a London, Paris, or New York dinner-party.

All the women were covered in costly warpaint and wafted the most expensive scents. The men, with the same dark eyes and longish features, which were a Bahraini trait, wore suits with the rich sheen of top tailoring. Celia learned from the introductions that McCord made that they were the sons and friends of the Sheikhdoms' families, important men in government circles and business empires. Some of the wives, she discovered, ran smart boutiques and even did jobs of work at the local hospital or some downtown office.

Many of the sleek European women that she had noticed at the soirée had found their way to the drawing room like herself and now they strolled over the acres of deep pile white carpet on the arms of tall, red-faced husbands.

Celia had grown disillusioned with the business of Nevine. It was McCord who indirectly made references to her search during the casual conversations they indulged in around the room. The results of these exploratory enquiries were always negative. Celia hadn't expected anything else.

The drink flowed freely, another surprise for her in an Islamic society. Glass in hand, she admired the picture window framing a floodlit swimming pool and watched McCord being carried off by a dark-eyed beauty with a lovely smile.

Her admiration of the pool and its garden fairy lights waned in preference to following McCord with her eyes. She knew a sneaking desire to study him from a distance, and doing so her curiosity was aroused. What kind of a man was he? One of integrity, she couldn't deny. But what of his social life here in Bahrain? He wasn't married, obviously— unless one could say he was married to his business—but clearly he enjoyed the company of women. There was his date at the Gulf Hotel for one thing, and the flowery bathroom and bedroom she had used at El Zommorro told her that besides accommodating business associates his house was designed to receive women guests as well. Added to this was the European female contingent in Manama.

During her two weeks exploring with Kamel, Celia had learned a lot concerning the local scene. In most of the Gulf region women were scarce, but not so in Bahrain. There were the several hundred air hostesses who worked for Gulf Air quartered on the island, to say nothing of the secretaries, shop assistants and hotel receptionists who came out from England and elsewhere to work in Bahrain.

In this part of the world wives, sisters and daughters were confined to family life, socially, and an expatriate might have to put up with a male society interested only in business; native Arabs who themselves return each day to the feminine solicitude and affection in their own homes, while he has to be content with the lonely life of hotel rooms, or bored evenings in bars. But Bahrain was different. Here there was one thing a European was not, and that was lonely for feminine company. And that included McCord. And the reaction of the svelte, emancipated types in the room to his proximity made it clear that he would have no difficulty on any level.

In what she considered a detached frame of mind on her own part Celia's eyes were drawn to those vital features as he chatted within a group. Surreptitiously her glance toured the sun-brown planes and angles of his face framed by a neat head of dark hair. It was a strong face with hard clean lines; not handsome but oddly commanding. With his big build yet compact frame, he had a charisma she couldn't deny; a kind of effortless charm which put better looking men unexplainably in the shade.

As dinner was announced he drifted back to her side, little knowing that she had paid scant attention to what was being said in her own group. Filing into the dining area on his arm, she was actually conscious of envy among the female members of the party. What a laugh! They didn't know that she and McCord were poison to each other. He couldn't stand her untravelled naïveté and she had had all she could take of his superior male attitude. And that definitely excluded her from his circle of feminine admirers.

CHAPTER FOUR

THERE WERE three cut-crystal glasses by each place at the table, and the meal was of such sophistication Celia doubted whether she would have survived if it hadn't been for McCord's solid presence next to her. Shyly mirroring his actions, she got through the successive dishes, recalling vaguely the bliss of vichyssoise, a cream soup served chilled, and that the chives were fresh, and the restrained presentation of the canard à l'orange.

The food may have been European but the conversation was Bahrain, and here again Celia's mood was one of detachment. All this now was something of an anticlimax to her expectations. She had come here in the hope of learning something of Nevine, and arriving at the same dead-end she had encountered in other parts of the island, she was feeling considerably dispirited.

Whether McCord was aware of this she didn't know, but fortunately he didn't linger any longer than necessary once the party started breaking up. In the car on the way back to Manama he asked, 'What are you going to do now?'

There was no doubt he was thinking of her quest and she replied, 'What *can* I do? I've explored every avenue without even the hint of success. I'll have to give up the idea; forget it and leave Bahrain to its mysteries.'

'Fly back to England, you mean?'

She nodded. 'I was going to go today, but I held off in the hope that this trip would prove useful. If I'd known I could have saved myself the extra day on the hotel bill.' No sooner had the wry comment left her lips than she wanted to bite it back. She hadn't meant to let that out.

Outside the desert was a black void below the escarpment. Inside McCord was looking like McCord, hard-jawed, supercilious and meditative. 'I thought you were keen to see this thing through,' he said.

'I am! I am!' She swung on him in frustration, then turned to the front again. How could she explain that she was willing to spend a year searching for Nevine but that she just wasn't in a position to do so? How could she say that all the money her father had ever earned had gone during his ill-health? She had spent her own time nursing him, but what did one do in a country cottage where help was not readily available and funds to pay for it even harder to come by? She felt bound to add frustratedly, 'When I first came out here two weeks seemed ample time to do what I had to do.'

How much McCord guessed of her financial predicament she didn't know, but he said no more on the subject. In the silence Celia began to make plans in her mind for a hasty withdrawal from the island. It was late now, but if she packed her things she could leave first thing in the morning and so save herself further expense. Any waiting around could be done at the airport where she could survive on a packet of sandwiches or something until her flight was called.

As she watched the lights of Manama appear that strange melancholy gripped her. It wasn't just knowing that Nevine was here, undiscovered. There was something else that made her regretful at leaving Bahrain. It was odd, this attraction of the East. It wasn't as though there was anything here that was particularly beautiful by scenic standards. She had seen the bleak stretches of the desert, and the island's barren

coastline, and the town with its traditional Arab houses and
big teak doors was secretive—at least in the old residential
quarters—and uncompromising. Yet all of it held some peculiar enchantment for her. It was as though her mind discarded the mundane and heightened the unusual, so that she
thought only of shimmering seas and white sand inducing
colour changes around the coast; palest blues and deep emerald greens, which were dazzling in intensity. Set amid
pearly distances the island was too shimmeringly pale under the desert sun. Topped by a taffeta blue sky its skyline
of buildings, date palms and mosques rising insubstantially
out of the haze had mysterious charm, a mirage-like quality that evoked an odd response in her.

Realising that she had been dreaming, Celia came to, to
discover that they were now in the heart of the town. She
was familiar enough now with the high-rise blocks and
streets of mud houses that was Manama, yet she was sure
this was not the way to the Gulf Hotel. Spotting the name
of a street that she had no recollection of noting before, she
said, sitting up rigidly in her seat, 'You're going the wrong
way.'

'Relax,' McCord threw her a hard smile, 'I'm not going
to carry you off to some Eastern den of iniquity. I'm just
making a slight detour.'

For what? There was no excess of traffic as far as Celia
could see; in fact at this hour of the night the town was
practically deserted. They came to a stop at last in what
looked like a modern building complex. As McCord came
round to open her door for her she asked coyly, 'Is this part
of the detour too?'

'Come and see,' he said drily. 'It's possible you may consider it was worth it.'

She hadn't the faintest idea what he was talking about,
but as she was relying on him to get her back to the Gulf

Hotel, she didn't see that she had much choice but to tag along with him.

In the darkness she could just make out the long black bulk of the building they were making for. At the door McCord chose a key from the key-ring he carried and led the way inside. There was enough subdued lighting to make out a carpeted foyer-like interior and from here he made for another door. Celia didn't know what she expected, but it wasn't the sweet, cool draught of air that hit her on stepping through, nor the fantastic expanse of space that stretched before her. The floor of ice glinted faintly under the sparse lighting and had that eerie quality that all public places of entertainment seemed to possess when deserted.

Because she was puzzled at McCord's choice of surroundings she quipped, 'I've always wanted to see an ice-rink at the midnight hour!'

He moved towards a glassed-in office close by and she followed more out of nervousness at the vast quiet rather than from any particular curiosity. But once inside the spacious interior smelling of new leather and paintwork, which the burst of modern lighting showed as being quite futuristic in design, her attention was drawn to a large photograph over the desk, the only adornment in the office.

The girl in the portrait was enough to claim anyone's glance if the colouring was not overdone, and Celia didn't think it was. She stared at a tumbling mane of chestnut hair with copper lights, laughing russet-gold eyes and a wide white smile that dimpled peach-blushed cheeks attractively. But that wasn't the half of it. It was a full-length photo and below those phenomenally lovely features was a curvaceous form clothed prettily in a short-short skating skirt that displayed to the full a pair of extremely shapely legs. White skating boots and a theatrical stance made the picture a work of art.

'Who is she?' Celia asked, wondering why it irked her to see the photograph so displayed.

'Mandy Bennet, the daughter of an American oil man here, a friend of mine,' McCord said. 'I've known her since she was a tot.'

'She looks like a star performer now.' Celia tried not to sound grudging in her comments.

'Mandy's one of the tops in the ice world.' The grin that accompanied this remark froze any more magnanimous gestures that Celia might have felt obliged to make, and she moved away with a show of studying the rest of the room.

She had no idea that McCord was planning to prolong the social evening until she turned and saw him opening up a cocktail cabinet. 'Like a drink?' he said, setting out glasses and bottle on the desk.

'Are we celebrating something?' Celia asked a little mockingly.

'That depends on you.' That tight smile in evidence, he poured and handed her a glass. She didn't know what to make of being squarely confronted by those somewhat disturbing blue eyes, so she sipped almost obediently and left the way clear for him to go on, which he did with little hesitation. 'I seem to recall you telling me that you'd attained silver medal status in ice-skating. I need someone with instructor's ability to organise the would-be champions who are falling over themselves to learn to skate here.— In other words, I'm offering you a job.'

Celia blinked. 'But I was only sixteen when I passed my silver. I haven't given ice-skating a thought since.' She didn't say that the high cost of training had made further aspirations impossible and that her enthusiasm had soon waned in favour of less expensive pursuits. 'I can't remember the last time I was in an ice-rink,' she finished falteringly.

'Well, you're in one now and I'd like to bet it's like swimming—once you've learned you never forget,' McCord said, sampling his drink. He eyed the huge expanse of ice through the glass partition. 'At the moment it's a bit of a free-for-all here with the blind leading the blind, you might say. An accomplished skater would set the trend, give the young hopefuls an idea of how it's done.'

'Me work here as an ice instructress?' Slowly Celia came round to thinking about it.

'You should cope okay,' the hard blue eyes glinted with something approaching humour. 'At the moment there's only a couple of dozen Arabs who've found the nerve to sample the least known pastime of our degraded Western society.'

'What about the language problem?' she asked.

'You haven't encountered much trouble in that direction so far, have you?'

'No.' Celia had to admit that the Bahrainis, together with the Pakistanis, Iranians and other members of the polyglot race on the island, all seemed to have learned from the same English grammar books.

'It could be the answer to your dilemma,' said McCord with a businesslike smile. 'You can stay on at the hotel, cost of a suite there and meals will be in addition to your salary. And the hours are not long, a couple in the morning and the same in the afternoon and evening. With work you would have a valid reason for staying on in Bahrain, and this would make it possible for you to go on with your search for your father's old flame.'

Celia's grey eyes flared. 'Nevine was not his old flame!' she retorted caustically. 'She was the love of his life, but I wouldn't expect you to understand that.'

McCord propped himself against the desk and relaxing asked, 'What makes you think I don't know anything about this love business you're always toting around like some emblem of a select fraternity?'

Celia thought about it for a moment, then pointed out accusingly, 'You're not married.'

'I'll admit that most men of my age have fallen for some woman's guile,' he shrugged with a cryptic gleam, 'but it doesn't take, necessarily, the marriage vows to make a man a lover. What else?'

She eyed the plush chrome and glass office and the huge expanse of ice outside and replied, 'You're insufferably successful.'

'Meaning that I've never wanted to divide my time between my work and a member of the fairer sex.' His smile was without self-reproach. 'True in a sense, but even a tycoon is not foolproof against the diversions of women as a whole, and surely that's love of a kind?'

'To you men, maybe.' Celia spoke with disdain. 'But that's nowhere enough, nor the basis of true love to a woman's mind.'

'You talk like an authority on the subject!'

At this mocking observation Celia was all at once unsure of herself. True, what did she know of love personally? And was that what McCord was hinting at with his indirect approach? 'My father is my authority,' she said briskly. 'He loved one woman deeply, that I do know, for the greater part of his adult life, and to the end, without the satisfaction of physical contact or reciprocation of any kind. That was some feat in affection, don't you agree?'

'Should be an example to us all,' McCord said piously. Watching her eyes flash their response to his comment, he lowered his glass and straightened. 'But we're digressing; getting away from the subject of this job I'm offering. What do you say? Are you game to give it a try?'

Celia became thoughtful. Something had struck her from the moment that McCord had first made the offer and she voiced her ponderings now. 'You've spent a lot of time and money on this venture, and businessman that you are, I can't imagine that you've done it all without having something lined up beforehand in the way of teaching staff for the place.'

'Well—er—' If it had been anyone else Celia would have said that the lack of firm response stemmed from embarrassment, but with McCord it was simply a matter of finding the right words, of course. 'As a matter of fact, Mandy,' he nodded at the photo, 'was due to fly in a fortnight ago, the day I first spotted you at the Gulf Hotel. I've been waiting for her arrival there every day since, but it looks as though she's not going to make it.'

So *that* was the reason for his frequent visits to the Gulf Hotel! That, or rather she, Mandy Bennet, was his mysterious date, the one that never materialised.

With an odd stab of satisfaction Celia surveyed him quizzically. 'Don't tell me the great McCord has been stood up?'

There was something indestructible in his grin. 'Mandy's been doing exhibitions around the Middle East. The last I heard of her she was in Cairo. We had it all arranged for her to take up a teaching post here at the rink's opening, but I guess she must be knocking 'em cold somewhere.'

Celia digested this in silence. She felt a little aggrieved to discover that McCord was simply depending on her to help him out in an emergency. It would have been nice to think that he had suggested the job as a means of helping her in some way, but he was a businessman, she should know that, and in his way he was offering her a deal: a little of her time for the chance to go on with her search for Nevine. It was

not a bad bargain, she couldn't explain why she should feel
so sour about it.

On the other hand it was tempting to think that she
needn't leave Bahrain just yet. She had felt miserable at the
thought of having to return to England with nothing to show
for her trouble, and one of the things she would miss most,
she had to admit wryly, were these abrasive differences of
opinion with McCord; even though they always left her
emotionally drained.

As she hadn't rushed to give him an answer he probed,
'Got things in England that would make it difficult for you
to stay on?'

'Such as what?' Her gaze was questioning.

He shrugged. 'I thought you were carrying the banner
maybe, for some young fellow over there?'

Celia coloured slightly beneath the smooth grey petals of
her hat. That was the second time in the space of a few
minutes that he had made an indirect reference to the romantic state of her own heart.

Naturally she had had boy-friends in the past, but after
nursing her father for two years she had lost touch with that
side of her life. However, she didn't see why McCord should
know this, so she said, 'There's no one who would miss me
to the extent of coming out here to see what's happened to
me, if that's what you mean.'

His expression was enigmatic. Because Celia knew he was
waiting for an answer she went back to considering his offer. Not that she was in much doubt now regarding her reply. Bahrain had come to mean a great deal to her. And of
course the overwhelming plus point was that she could go on
looking for the Arab dancer who had long ago won her
father's heart.

Because she badly wanted to stay she said, 'If you can
supply me with a pair of skating boots and I find I've for-

gotten nothing of what I've learned on the ice, I'll take the job.'

'Good.' McCord was obviously relieved. He went to a showcase in the office and pointed to a display of top quality skating boots with blades. 'You can take your choice from these in the morning. I'll leave you the key. You should find your size okay.'

They did actually drink on it then and Celia swallowed with a little glow at not having to catch that plane after all. But looking at it another way she did feel that she ought to have her head examined for agreeing to such an arrangement.

All along she had complained to herself about McCord's high-handedness and penchant for running her affairs. Now he *was* her boss!

AT THE stated hour the next morning Celia drove on the route she had memorised to the Alhambra ice rink. Though it was only a few blocks away the company car, which had been left conveniently parked for her outside the Gulf Hotel, proved useful, for even at this time of the morning the heat was colossal and the air-conditioned interior made it possible for her to arrive as fresh as when she had started out.

She parked the car and went indoors nodding to the cashier in the foyer, and to the Arab assistant in charge of skate hire in the rink itself. After depositing her at the hotel last night and handing over the keys to the office McCord had said that he would be here at the first skating session to help her settle in. But he was nowhere around. The result of having too many business projects to attend to, Celia guessed cynically.

She let herself into the office and chose a pair of skating boots from the showcase. None of the staff interfered with her, so she was obviously expected. She found that her size differed only fractionally from the old days and the soft white kid gave support to her ankles without restricting their flexibility. Once the laces were fastened firmly but not too tightly up her shins she was able to balance around over the office carpet to get the feel of her new footwear.

It was funny how just strutting like this brought back to her all the fun of her teenage days. The smooth surface of ice beyond the office doorway looked inviting, and the eagerness mounted in her to test her abilities after so long away from the sport.

She had donned a pair of stretch slacks in leaf-green and a paler cotton-knit top for her job as instructress, knowing that the consistent cool of the ice-rink would allow her to wear the garments with complete comfort. They proved ideal for her work-out too, for once her blades touched the ice it was as though seven years dropped away from her and she glided and spun, rose in the air and landed with the grace and confidence of her youth.

Of course she knew that her butterfly jumps and arabesque spins were less than perfect and that she would never make a star, but she could skate, there was no doubt about that. And what she knew she could pass on to others.

Lost in the task of testing her skills anew on the ice, she had no idea she had caused a minor sensation until struggling tots on rubbery legs and older children wobbling recklessly like miniature Charlie Chaplins came over to gape. Parents too, keen for the prestige of possessing offspring who had mastered the art of staying upright in this weirdest of sports, crowded at the rail, and Celia was inundated with requests to be shown how it was done.

They had obviously seen nothing like it since the rink's opening, though her own performance, Celia knew, fell short of what could be achieved with real talent on the ice.

Still, she was pleased to know that she had retained much of her confidence and finesse, for what it was worth.

Not being in a position to make comparisons the audience considered her some ice goddess, judging by their admiration. Above the clamour and demands to be shown instantly the secret of her winged feet, she had to make it known that anyone requiring lessons would have to book them in the proper way with the tuition clerk. When it was discovered that one had to pay extra for this service the group dwindled considerably, Celia noted with some amusement, but it still left a sizeable band willing to suffer this added indignity, which would give her plenty to do over the coming weeks.

She felt exhilarated and thirsty after her work-out and decided to make for the bar where soft drinks were sold. Walking on blades took a little more concentration than just strolling in shoes, so that it wasn't until she arrived at the colourfully lit alcove that she spotted a familiar figure viewing the rink from the interior.

For a moment her cheeks grew hot when she realised McCord must have witnessed all that had taken place on the ice. The true test of star material, she reminded herself yet again wryly, was to be blissfully indifferent no matter who was watching. She *had* been utterly carefree. It annoyed her to think it was only this man who would have made her feel stiff and inhibited had she known he was nearby. All the more reason to feel relieved, in a way, that she had not been aware of his presence.

'That was quite a performance.' He supported her by the elbow until she had found a comfortable place to prop against the bar and ordered her a drink.

Celia gave a little curtsy and asked preeningly, 'Do I get the job?' She had no idea what prompted her to behave coyly towards McCord. They had already come to an agreement concerning her employment. Perhaps it was her added stature in skate-boots which helped her to confront his own height and breadth. Or the certain feminine knowledge that her face was glowing and her eyes shining after limbering up on the ice, and to offset the shock of discovering that he could make her feel unsure of herself when performing she wanted to flaunt the confidence of knowing she was looking her best, if nothing else.

McCord said with a grin which was not altogether businesslike, 'I guess you qualify.'

'But not in the same way Mandy Bennet would, I bet?' There she was again, saying things she didn't really want to say; giving rein to this inexplicable impulse to confront him archly when she would far rather not blurt her thoughts aloud.

'Mandy's a world name. She collected medals and cups galore before turning pro.' McCord's shrug was eloquent, though whether this made her something more special to him by professional standards or in a more personal way there was no way of knowing.

Celia had sensed his disappointment last night when he had told her that Mandy hadn't turned up for the job. And it was odd how her own small moment of glory on the ice was dampened now by his air of regret. It made her comment a little waspishly, 'It's too bad she left you high and dry with a disorganised rink on your hands.'

McCord's gleam was philosophical. 'There's a saying in the East, *Inshallah*—God willing. Well, in this case Allah appears to be only half willing, but as he's supplied a makeshift answer to the problem I reckon we'll cope.'

And she was the makeshift! While Celia bristled he knocked back his fruit juice and acquiring the look of the tycoon again he added some scant words of praise before preparing to leave. 'From what I've seen of you, you'll make out okay. And by the way, the staff have been informed that they'll be taking their orders from you. They'll be pulling for you whatever policies you decide on for the good of the rink.'

'Hey, wait a minute!' Grey eyes wide, she stopped him as he was about to move off. 'I thought you said that my job was to teach them how to skate?'

'That's right.'

'But now you're talking as though you expect me to run everything around here!'

'Hiring staff for a leisure pursuit that not many people know about in this part of the world was not the easiest of tasks,' McCord explained amenably. 'The ones I managed to recruit are simple souls, they'll need guidance.'

'But I didn't agree to take on the job of supervising your pet venture,' Celia said indignantly.

'Nothing to it. The business runs itself—has been doing for the past three weeks.' Having somehow managed to convey the impression that it would be no comfortable niche despite his optimistic assurances, he eyed her with challenging derision. 'Scared? Afraid that you might make more blunders than you have done already in your two weeks in Bahrain?'

Her dander up, Celia was stung to reply sweetly, 'Have I made all the blunders? You're the one who suggested Kamel as a guide and companion, I seem to recall. And who was it who said I was bound to have language difficulties in my crazy—to you—search for Nevine? But I notice all such obstacles are glossed over when the subject of discussion is the running of your ice rink.' Casting a glance at the olive-skinned clientele who had recently clustered about her in a mildly frightening way, and were now crowding around the booking office for lessons or falling about on the ice, she said, 'I suppose you're aware that I was accosted by all kinds of gibberish out there just now, and wouldn't have known what on earth was going on if I hadn't managed to recognise one or two of the accents as resembling my own.'

'You'll cope,' was McCord's bland reply. Typical, she thought, of a hard-headed businessman interested solely in suiting his own ends.

Nevertheless his challenging speculation annoyed her sufficiently to take on an onus that instinct told her meant trouble by replying, 'Don't blame me if the takings plummet while I'm in charge.'

'I don't think they will.' His blue gaze toured the length of her in leisurely fashion. 'You might prove an asset to the place. In a couple of weeks, who knows, you could be...'

'Knocking 'em cold?' she finished for him innocently.

His expression was one of steely appreciation at her wit. 'Something like that.' He gave her a salute before departing.

But once he was out of sight the honeyed smile left Celia's lips and she clapped her glass on the bar with cynical resentment. What a nerve! She'd like to bet that Mandy Bennet wouldn't have had to take on all these extra chores. *She* wouldn't have been expected to practically manage the place while the boss was otherwise engaged.

Then pushing these thoughts to the back of her mind, Celia braced herself for work. What did it matter to her if McCord was sweet on the girl whose photograph hung in his office?

CHAPTER FIVE

HERDING BEGINNERS round the ice and offering helpful suggestions to the staff was a lot different from the carefree days of her youth when she had simply skated for the joy of it. But miraculously Celia found that she *was* coping and that so far the Alhambra ice rink hadn't caved in because of her inexpert handling. McCord had said the business practically ran itself—and that figured, she considered now with a curled smile, for he would hardly have trusted her with a venture that would die without his own brain on the job.

After a week she was beginning to know what to expect in the way of patrons at the rink. The morning sessions consisted mainly of children, and these were always accompanied by some servant of the household. They were usually offspring of the well-to-do of the town, for the urchins had neither the money nor the inclination to indulge in the pastimes of the rich. The children, dark-eyed and with the glossy blue-black hair of the Arab, were always beautifully dressed; the girls in panty-short skating dresses, their dark-skinned spindly legs making them look like young fawns on the ice. The boys invariably wore white, the favourite mode of dress being tailored monkey-jackets and slim-fitting slacks. They all took their skating seriously and were acquiring a touch of European sophistication, though their *ayahs* were usually shrouded figures seated at the rail and some of those keeping a sharp eye on the whereabouts of their young charges still wore the veil.

The afternoon sessions were quiet, the heat of the afternoon outside prostrating all but the hardy who made the effort to visit the ice palace mainly for a lark, and to keep cool, of course. It was the evening when things at the Alhambra went mostly with a swing. Not only used for skating, it became a meeting place for some of the European element of the town and the coffee lounge, bar and upstairs restaurant were in danger of becoming quite lively.

Then there were those who were keen to master the art of balancing on blades. It was strange to see a young Arab girl in subdued dress clinging to the rail and occasionally managing to glide a few steps, or a thick-set businessman with his rounded wife in tow laughingly going on in the local tongue, each giving advice to the other in the hope of staying upright.

McCord had said that the Bahrainis were proving a little reticent in braving the unknown of an ice rink, and unfortunately, with their tightly-knit family customs and reluctance to shake off old ways, these numbers were not likely to swell much while Celia was in charge. In fact while the Alhambra remained just so pleasantly populated she didn't see that she had much to complain about—except of course the irritating little hang-ups that occurred occasionally. Or perhaps she ought to regard them as the amusing little irritations of an ice rink situated in the East.

Like the music incident.

She was painstakingly organising the glimmerings of a dance session one morning when the wailing over the loudspeakers made her throw a despairing glance to the roof. Drums, cymbals, flutes, zithers, all combined to make a stirring cacophony of sound; great if you were watching some desert festival, but no good at all for gliding around on the ice to.

'One moment, Ahmad.' She left the side of a tallish eleven-year-old who was showing promise as a dancing partner and skated off to the music console on the rink's perimeter. 'Would you mind toning that down!' she shouted above the din in the booth doorway.

The tape attendant gave her an injured look but did as he was asked. 'Look, Yousuf,' Celia explained patiently, when she could hear herself speak. 'You've got to remember that the music you play has to have some bearing on what I'm trying to do out there.'

'But this is the orchestra of the Mahraba desert patrol,' Yousuf's black eyes glowed with nationalistic pride.

'Fine,' Celia smiled lopsidedly. 'But it's not quite the thing for dancing to. What we need is something a little more lilting…something perhaps with a waltz beat. I'm sure your stock of tapes include this kind of thing.'

'Waltzes are insipid.' Yousuf's chin jutted. 'We do not understand the West's preference for this type of noise.'

'But you like our popular music, and this often has a very danceable rhythm,' Celia compromised. 'I'll tell you what. If you can remember to play something of this nature for these partnered sessions, I'm sure it will be all right to put on some local Arab pop music for the rest of the time. How's that?' And hurriedly, remembering his national pride, 'And if you like you can open and close each session with something by the Mahraba orchestra.'

Yousuf's face broke into a smile that showed every one of his numerous white teeth. 'I think that is a splendid idea,' he said happily.

Celia recognised that it was only partial victory, but Arab pop music was better than the wail and boom of drums of the desert patrol!… Then there was her open conflict with old Ibrahim in charge of skate hire. She still recalled the horror of entering the rink one day and finding a great pile of male and female boots in the middle of the skate room floor. Pairing them up and rechecking the sizes was a monumental task, but no greater than trying to explain to Ibrahim that it just wasn't practical to run a skate hire service on these lines. It was fully three days before she could get him to understand that the pigeonholes around the walls were not there for decoration. But she doubted if they would ever agree on the issue of the patrons' shoes, even though she laboriously explained that rooting through a heap for one's property, as though at a jumble sale, was not done in the best of skating circles.

It was during the second week that she began to feel aware of a certain group who appeared regularly for the evening session. Arabs of high breeding unmistakably, they sometimes wore the cotton robes and headdress but doffed these to reveal expensively cut suits when taking experimental steps on the ice. They were young enough to josh one another while precariously balanced, but were stamped with the successful, and sometimes careworn air, of the businessman.

Their number would vary with each session depending, it seemed, on the whim of the individual, but there was one consistent member of the group whose presence Celia was more than a little conscious of; perhaps because his deep brown gaze always seemed to be following her whatever she did.

The evenings were merry with Yousuf's pop music and the club-like air about the place, but there was always someone who, eager to know the rudiments of skating, booked her time. It was usually while she was stressing the importance of good posture to her pupil and demonstrating the correct way to put one's weight on one's blades, that she would look up and find those brown eyes viewing her with a kind of quizzical interest.

She noticed that this slender-built Arab did quite well on the ice and even when he was unsteady he retained a certain dignity. Because he and his companions appeared to frequent the rink mostly for the fun of it, showing little tendency to take the thing seriously, she was surprised one evening to find that, after she had given some last-minute advice to a pupil, the next one waiting to follow her instructions was none other than the owner of the eloquent brown gaze.

They were gentle and kindly eyes, she noticed at close quarters, though as a teacher she gave no hint of her inner reactions. 'Now the first thing you'll want to practise,' she spoke in friendly but impersonal tones, 'is your edges. There are four edges on each foot, forward outside to left and right, and backward outside to left and right. Now if you'll watch me skate this figure eight, Mr....er...'

'Rahma,' he supplied, with humour in his voice.

'Right then, Mr. Rahma, if you'll observe how my feet are now at right angles and how I push off with the whole of the blade, arms outstretched...now see how I lean slightly to the right while keeping my body straight. This gives me a clean outside curve...and here is the figure eight done on the outside and the inside of both blades.'

She had a feeling he was watching her perform while paying little attention to what she was saying. But when she asked him to demonstrate what he had learned he tackled the step-by-step routine carelessly but with the untimid grace of a born skater.

Not that he showed much in his capacity to catch on quickly. Celia had the distinct sensation that if she had asked him to stand on his head he would have done so, so little attention did he appear to be paying to her coaching.

'You're doing well, Mr. Rahma...you're very good.' She felt obliged to give him encouragement, especially as she was only stating the truth. 'If you'll take my hand we'll do an inside edge together—it's important, you see, to put the pressure just about here on the blade...' She went on giving him tips, knowing that the feel of her hand in his was causing him some bemusement. Well, this was more than evident in his eyes, though she remained aloof from what might have been deciphered as the invitation there. Another Kamel she couldn't cope with!

Mr. Rahma reminded her a lot of McCord's office help-cum-guide. He had the same neat build, the same olive-skinned handsome good looks, though these were toned down by a seriousness, despite the smile in his eyes, that Kamel had never possessed. And he was more mature for his twenty-eight or so years too, with an unconscious charm, an air of breeding that singled him out from the others of his kind.

They went on practising for the duration of his half hour lesson, at the end of which Celia released her hand from his and told him, 'You're a very apt pupil, Mr. Rahma. I do hope the points I've made will help you to enjoy your skating.'

He stood aside correctly to allow her to move off to other duties, though his look was slightly teasing as he commented in that voice as dark brown as his eyes, 'I can't wait to learn more.'

He was nice, very nice, but Celia, moving off, didn't intend to let her thoughts show. An instructress had to remain impartial, and after her experience with one other young Bahraini she was determined to carry this rule out to the last letter.

She was friendly yet distant whenever she and Mr. Rahma met on the ice, but unfortunately this control did not extend to other eventualities, namely the snags that hit the rink from time to time, owing to her precarious management.

Like the evening that the ticket machine in the box office seized up.

She had been limbering up on the ice for the first half hour of the session when news came to her that the cluster of people waiting to pay their entrance fee at the door was growing owing to the cashier's mild hysteria at the breakdown of her ticket computer.

Celia had no time to doff her skates, so she clunked out as she was. She hadn't a clue what to do about the gleaming piece of equipment which absolutely refused to produce its numbered receipt or the correct amount of change. And the worst of it was, though the Alhambra was never inundated with customers, they did all tend to converge at the same time, which was what they were doing now, causing an alarming congestion in the street.

Panic taking hold of her, she was unable to think straight. Who among the somewhat unqualified staff could she call on to unravel this muddle? While she was looking about wildly Mr. Rahma came through the door into the foyer, also on blades as though he had noted her rapid departure and followed to investigate. She rather suspected this was the case, but was not in the mood to care when he quickly took charge of the situation.

'Pull yourself together, Safia,' he said in his beautiful English to the plump, distraught female figure at the computer machine. And with stern humour, 'This is not an invasion of the Shashriri tribe who carry off women. It is simply a group of people impatient at your incompetence. Here, give me a coin . . .' He reached into a dish of rejected tender and bent to use a French franc as a screwdriver in the appropriate screw slot. With a few quick turns the press-button fasteners of the removable panel gave way to reveal the jammed machinery.

Celia, stooping with him, watched anxiously. His expressive gaze saying most of what he was thinking, he mentioned only, 'I regret I am not an engineer... but there are ways...' And with this he tugged out the entire reel of tickets and slapped them in front of the cashier with the order, 'Tear off the tickets as they are required. And you—' he roped in the services of the hovering door attendant, putting him in charge of the coinage in the lower tray of the computer cabinet, 'hand out the change as it is needed.'

In no time the congestion dwindled to no more than half a dozen people, but Celia looked rueful. 'The tickets are coded and shouldn't be taken out of the machine,' she said uneasily.

'That is only as protection against dishonesty, but McCord knows that no Arab would steal what is not rightfully his. I would not worry about it.'

At this familiar reference to her boss it came to Celia that McCord had mentioned to her at the beginning that the ice rink was a whim thought up mainly by his Arab friends, and she guessed now that Mr. Rahma and his companions were part of this set.

Annoyed at what she considered McCord's gross neglect of his business, she commented acidly, 'Well, it's his own fault if he doesn't like the arrangement. He's never around the place to see what's going on.'

'But he was here little more than ten minutes ago.' The man who had come to her aid seemed mildly amused. 'I spoke with him myself before he left. And I and my friends have often taken advantage of his presence of an evening to meet with him in the coffee lounge or at the bar.'

Celia digested this with set features. So McCord was dropping in unknown to her when it suited him to see that the place was still on its feet. Well, that was possible. While the rink itself was brilliantly lit the alcove bar and lounges enjoyed only intimate lighting of the cosy ruby-red type, so that out on the ice, which was where she spent most of her time, she was hardly likely to notice who was around.

And then there had been the signs of McCord's brief appearances during the day: a new set of office keys for instance, freshly cut and waiting for her on the blotter of the desk. Her weekly pay packet propped up neatly in the corner of her clothes locker.

While she was prepared to accept now that McCord was too canny a businessman to leave the entire running of the rink in her inexperienced hands it disturbed her, nevertheless, to hear from Mr. Rahma that he was not the phantom boss she had believed him to be.

For no apparent reason her thoughts flew to what kind of a picture she made on the ice. Luckily a weekly income had enabled her to visit some of the better class boutiques in town, and while she couldn't bring herself to display too much of herself in an Arab country with men like Mr. Rahma and his friends around she had nevertheless splashed on several pairs of figure-enhancing stretch slacks in exciting materials and some attractive tops. Though why she should think of this when considering McCord's point of view she wasn't sure.

Naturally she was obliged to look her best in a position where, whether she liked it or not, she was often the focus of attention, but there was no reason to suppose that McCord would care one way or the other as long as she was doing her job correctly. Still it gave her a little glow of satisfaction to know that she had always presented a groomed appearance.

As for her work-outs on the ice, her limbering-ups—was he in the habit of watching them too? With a tingling in her veins Celia recalled her usual carefree way of racing around on blades with the laughter of complete freedom on her lips.

And, cross with herself for reacting in this fashion simply because McCord might have been a bystander on occasion, she said tartly to the Arab at her side, 'You're more fortunate than I am, Mr. Rahma. McCord is one of those bosses who adopts a kind of sink-or-swim attitude when it comes to advising his staff.'

The cashier reorganised herself with some difficulty in the unprecedented practice of actually tearing off by hand the tickets of entry, and though still flustered she managed to cope with anyone who loomed up at her window.

Celia saw no reason to hang about, although some thanks were due to the man who had come up with a lightning solution to the dilemma. 'I can't tell you how much I appreciate your help, Mr. Rahma—'

'Please!' he stopped her, his gaze lit with mischief. 'You cannot go on insisting on formal terms when we have shared the drama of a jammed ticket roll together. I have another name, also handed down to me by my ancestors. To my family and friends I'm known as Tariq. It would give me much pleasure to hear you address me so.'

'All right…Tariq,' she agreed reluctantly, recalling to her chagrin how easy it was to succumb to the Arab charm.

He held the door for her as they re-entered the ice rink area and Celia left him at once with a great show of good duties to perform. Not that this would do her any good, she thought, her smile crooked. Tariq had only to book a lesson to get close to her, and it was patently obvious that he had no burning ambitions where skating was concerned.

But it was McCord who was on her mind for most of the evening. To think that he was often close at hand when she was least aware of it! Of course he didn't drop in for the fun of it, she reminded herself sceptically. As a refrigerator engineer he had to divide his time between the Alhambra and all the other freezing projects he owned in Bahrain. But she would like, just once, to come face to face with him to give him a few home truths about what was lacking in his latest innovation.

The opportunity came much sooner than she expected, and under conditions which were to prove, for her at least, a considerable surprise.

As in all Islamic countries Friday was the weekend in Bahrain, Saturdays being given over to prayer and Koran reading similar to the Christian way on Sundays.

Celia liked the leisurely feeling that always hung over the town on Friday. There was a great holiday exodus to the beach when the oversized cars of the oil-men and their families and the racy Datsuns and Toyotas of the oil-rich Bahrainis crowded the twenty-three-mile stretch of road leading to the lushest seaside spot. There was a gay air too at the ice rink with people dropping in to try their hand (or should she say feet!) at this new-fangled sport before moving on to other weekend pursuits.

She rose after leisurely contemplating the blue sky from her window and let the familiar sounds of city life wash over her as she showered and dressed. Not sounds that one was likely to hear in an English town, she mused; the harsh cry of a driver urging on his team of asses, the shrill rise and fall of bargaining voices in the nearby *souk*. Even the Westernised hum of cars was different, with the gay, uninhibited honking of horns at every turn.

The Bahrainis were very proud of their cars, Celia well knew. Some of the interiors she had seen were like little bed-sitters, with brocade curtains at the windows, brilliant cushions on the divan-like seating areas and ornaments and trinkets everywhere. Once when her own car was being serviced she had had to take a taxi. And that was an experience she wouldn't have missed.

The whole of the inside was done out in shocking pink mohair. From the roof it flowed down over the seat under the feet and even up to the dashboard where the instrument dials were barely visible amid hairy pink wisps. And if this wasn't enough furry puppets with rolling eyes danced at the windows.

There was always something new to discover in Manama, yet she loved the foreign feel of it all and was content at having landed a situation where she could savour it to the full.

Her suite at the Gulf Hotel had the kind of quiet elegance that contributed a lot to this brand of unrivalled contentment. Apple-green walls and white-flowered curtains were cooling and restful, and ivory-tinted furniture on carpeting of a slightly darker leaf green was her idea of harmonious design.

From the balcony of her bedroom she could see the sapphire blue waters of the Gulf and the view of sunlit minarets gave the living room an exotic flavour. The suite was of villa proportions compared to the single room she had originally booked at the Gulf Hotel, to save funds. Even that had been more expensive than she could afford. But coming out to a strange country alone, and especially one situated in the Middle East, she had felt it would be wise to secure board and lodgings in one of the better class hotels.

This was hardly the term for her mode of living at the moment. She dined in the rose-lit restaurant below, winking with expensive crystal-ware, and there were gardens and a swimming pool at her disposal along with the other guests. At first she had been reluctant to partake of anything more than a roof over her head, but when she discovered that McCord had included all such extras at the hotel in part payment for her services at the ice rink, she saw no reason to forgo the pleasures.

This morning she breakfasted where the heat of the Gulf sunshine was dissipated by gay awnings on a garden terrace, then returning to her suite for a last-minute freshen up and to pick up her things, she set out for the rink. Downstairs she had grown accustomed to coming and going with the air of the working girl, and the grand marble lobby with its numerous businessmen and professionals no longer held any awe for her as it had done in her first days.

She noted that McCord was no longer to be seen around the place. Well, he wouldn't be, would he? Not when his star performer had let him down. Celia wondered if he was finding consolation for Mandy Bennet's non-arrival in the company of the sleek women who graced the parties he went to. Then shaking herself for letting her thoughts drift in this fashion she went out to her car.

The Alhambra, when she arrived, was pleasantly populated but not overwhelmingly so. Her lesson book was fairly full and she got straight down to the business of tuition. The younger children, their *ayahs* in attendance, were showing tremendous improvement, and in their pretty outfits like drifting petals on the ice, Yousuf, for once, playing some imaginative music, Celia began to get the feeling that it was all worth it.

She might have known this serene state of affairs wouldn't last.

By mid-morning she had the horrible sensation that something was not quite right about the ice. It was developing a snowy look across its surface and there was the wet sound of blades skimming through slush. When six-year-old Maryam fell for the third time doing simple edge practice Celia picked her up, brushed her down and delivering her to her *ayah* to dry off decided it was time to go and investigate.

After a speedy change of footwear she hurried round the rink's perimeter with mixed feelings. Melting ice was a serious occurrence, but she wasn't quite sure what to do about it. She followed what she gauged to be the freezing pipes under the rubber floor through a door marked STRICTLY NO ADMITTANCE. In the concrete garage-like space out there stood the Zamboni, a kind of tractor, its function being to shave off used ice on the rink and spray new water which froze immediately.

Nothing unusual in that. What did cause Celia some stunned amazement was the complete absence of any freezing equipment. But that was crazy! She had seen enough of the workings of an ice rink in her teenage years, larking about with friends in forbidden areas and chatting up maintenance men. There *had* to be some kind of machinery—compressors, or whatever they were called—to freeze the ice out there.

She looked around for the local technician, but the place was deserted. The only thing she had to go on was the faint but distinct humming noise coming through the open doorways leading into the street. Curiously, her ears tuned, she followed the sound. It seemed to be coming from a huge business concern across the side alley. Bahrainis in working garb were busy trundling cartons of provisions back and forth to waiting lorries. Some in stained white butcher clothing were transferring great sides of beef to parked refrigerator vans.

A big freezing plant. Aha! Now she was getting warmer. Sour humour at her pun changed to a warlike gleam in her eyes as she progressed determinedly, but still very much in the dark, towards an important-looking entrance away from most of the activity.

She climbed a few steps, the hum becoming more pronounced in her ears, and entered a doorway which told her that this was the source of the power she had traced. What she had expected to find she wasn't quite sure, but the scene before her made her grey eyes widen and her jaw drop slightly in awe.

She was in a white moonship-like interior of vast proportions. Gleaming pipes wove intricate patterns around the walls, and complicated dials, switches, winking panels, buttons and knobs made her feel like an apprentice astronaut. But there was nothing out of this world about the set-up, she realised with tightening lips. In fact it was all very down to earth.

Her ice-rink—she didn't stop to wonder at her proprietorial choice of words—was being deprived of vital juice, or whatever it was, so that this...this...meat factory could function at full pressure!

Well, she'd see about that! Her curiosity mingling now with a desire for some kind of positive action, she began to scrutinise the white-painted levers...which one, she wondered, would rejuvenate her melting ice?... This one with the smart blue stripe round its middle?... Or would it be this nice red button on a big raised disc?...

'Don't touch that!'

The voice slicing across what she had thought was a deserted interior startled her to such an extent that her legs almost gave way beneath her. Annoyed at being made to feel caught out, she swung round and lied irritably, 'I wasn't going to,' while her heart reacted peculiarly at the sight of the owner of the voice.

It was McCord, who else! He must have been viewing her from behind glass panels which housed more humming equipment high up in the room.

As he came down the metal stairway his look was not exactly pleasant, being laced with considerable suspicion. 'What are you doing over here?' he asked harshly. 'Your job is to take the customers round the ice, not to wander in places that don't concern you, with a look on your face that says you'd like to put the whole cold storage system out of action.'

These hadn't been quite her intentions, but it was an idea, Celia thought malevolently. This kind of mood coming through in her smile, she said, confronting him, 'It may interest you to know that your precious sides of beef are interfering with my skating arrangements.'

'If you're talking about a slight lowering of pressure,' he studied the sheets of figures on the clipboard in his hand, unimpressed, 'we have an emergency on here. It's been necessary to divert extra energy to cope with it.'

Celia heaved in a breath. She wasn't going to stand there and watch him calmly proceeding with his work. '*Slight* lowering of pressure!' She took him up on the operative word, her grey eyes flaring. 'Maybe you don't know it, but we're on the point of doing our figures over at the rink in ski-snow, not ice!'

'I can't help that.' It was the inflexible McCord talking. 'There are things more important than pretty pirouetting on ice at stake.'

'Well, it's your business,' she shrugged drily. 'If you don't mind running it as a duckpond with toy boats...'

'It won't get as bad as that.' He smiled into her battle-warmed gaze, his own insufferably devoid of emotion. 'Technically it's simple. I've had to slow the brine flow, which means the liquid in the pipes under the ice isn't taking the heat away fast enough.'

'Oh, I must say, that's abundantly clear!' Her look said she was more confused.

'Okay, how's this?' in mildly tolerant vein now. 'What we call the freon gas flow—that's what hardens the ice in your rink—has had to be diverted to the factory's own deep-freezes. For the time being this will make your ice slushy.'

'By that I take it you mean for the next half hour or so?'

'Not exactly.' He hedged at her slightly mollified tones. 'We're dealing with incoming emergency shipments at the moment, which means the relay in normal food supplies has been affected. The arrival of local and overseas stock together has created a bottleneck. I need all the pressure I can get to deal with the overload.'

All these lucid explanations! But Celia got enough of the gist of it to exclaim, 'But freezing extra food stocks... This could go on for days!'

'Or weeks,' McCord acknowledged with the business-man's eye on the main chance.

'But you can't do that to... to the rink!'

'I certainly wouldn't consider doing it any other way,' phlegmatically he chose to differ, 'for a variety of reasons. The main one being that the Alhambra ice rink is nothing more than a sideline of the real cold storage set-up here. Making use of the surplus of freezing energy normally left over from the plant it was devised, as I think I explained at the beginning, at the whim, and for the novelty and enter-tainment of friends. I definitely wouldn't put that before the real issue of vast amounts of frozen food stock.'

How could she expect him to? Deflatedly and with some exasperation Celia commented, 'But you seem to take it for granted that I'll be able to hold all the bits together until the situation eases.'

'I'm working on past performance, Miss Darwell.' There was the old challenge in his mocking grin. 'You've taken to the job like a fish to water...' He ignored her flash of irony, hinting at the fast deterioration of the ice. 'I've seen how you've handled the minor teething troubles of a new busi-ness without losing your head.'

'I haven't had much choice, have I?' she retorted sweetly.

'I like to give my key men ... or in your case—' his gleam took in her militant female form without going into details—'full rein to run things as they see fit. And by the way, coming back to my personal observations and the visits of those who make up the main patronage at the rink,' was some hint of what made him tick betrayed briefly in his eyes then? 'Tariq's a good friend of mine. I don't want you fluttering your lashes at him like you did Kamel.'

'Oh!' A quivering mass of resentment, Celia swung on him. 'Has anyone ever told you, you are the most aggravating man ...'

'Why? Because I keep my staff in line?' He had that kind of smile that made her itch to wipe it off with the full force of her hand.

With supreme control she hit back smoothly, 'You don't own me. I'm just a stop-gap, remember? And regarding some of those you employ, you set your Kamel on me like ... like a friendly puppy. He was all over me within minutes. How do I know that you didn't know full well what you were doing? Perhaps you hoped that one ghastly experience would be enough to put paid to my plans here.'

'Believe it or not,' this sort of theorising seemed to cause him some grim amusement, 'I've got more to do with my time than dream up ways of stopping fool girls who come to Bahrain on harebrained errands. Kamel has had a dressing down for his ... er ... over-enthusiasm and won't be doing guide duties for some time. Incidentally,' McCord referred once more to the clipboard in his hand, 'how's the search going for Nevine?'

Celia took a deep breath to reorientate to this sudden change of topic. 'I've chatted with some of the *ayahs* at the rink,' she said heavily, 'and made enquiries whenever I've visited shops in town. You may not realise it, but programming the routines of your learner-skaters three sessions a day is a highly demanding occupation.'

'You want to try organising your time as I do, Miss Darwell.' The male superiority was coming over again. 'I'm having to deal with the emergency here myself, as good ice engineers are difficult to come by in these parts, and I've a dozen and one other projects simmering in town, but I still find time to relax and take a breather in some form or other.'

Succinctly Celia put in, 'I was wondering if you still frequented those parts where Charrière gowns and chunky diamonds are run-of-the-mill stuff?'

Not slow to divine her meaning, he smiled, 'I do sometimes partner one of these dusky ladies.' And then without warning his quizzical blue eyes met her gaze. 'Does the thought bother you?'

Oh, he really was insufferable! All six self-opinionated feet of him! And this in no way included his nauseating male conceit.

'Only in the sense,' Celia aimed at cutting him down to size before making a serene exit, 'that their ideas on who and what makes pleasant company must be a whole lot different from mine!'

CHAPTER SIX

FROM THAT day Celia's life at the rink underwent a subtle change. Up to then she had had no reason to know of McCord's cold storage factory across the alley at the rear. But she knew of it now all right—and to her mind it was the cause of everything that went wrong at the Alhambra. The soft ice, for instance. McCord couldn't deny that! The trouble was no one else cared tuppence about the less than perfect conditions. The ice was still delectably skateable for the enthusiasts, and for those who were determined to take it seriously there was the added challenge of trying to fall less often and so keeping the snow off one's clothes.

But Celia, the only what one might term expert about the place, knew that there was room for improvement. She gave lessons as usual and did her bit in other quarters, and no one suspected that anything was any different at the rink. But behind the scenes she conducted a one-woman battle with the rock-like McCord across the street, for better conditions.

If he hadn't enough juice to freeze the Sheikh's joints *plus* her ice, why, she wanted to know, did he build the rink in the first place?

This was an emergency which might not crop up again for another ten years, McCord told her blandly, leaving her to stew in the meantime.

Did he *know* that the ice curtain around the rink, that invisible screen of cold air, was in danger of resembling a south sea breeze and soon, if he wasn't careful, he might have a musically lapping tide to go with it?

'You'll cope,' was all she could get out of McCord as he gave his customary prior concern to his gauges and levers in the moonship-like interior of the compressor room.

Miraculously she did cope, but only, she told herself sourly, because there wasn't one customer here who had any idea how a professionally-run ice rink operated—Well, perhaps one.

She sometimes suspected that the expressive-featured, quietly vigilant Tariq knew that all was not as it should be underfoot, though even he booked lessons with her and mechanically sailed through the ritual of enlarging his repertoire on ice while making no secret of the fact that it was not her coaching abilities that intrigued him.

She liked Tariq, for although he demanded a considerable amount of her time at these pseudo-teaching sessions he never tried to intrude across the bounds of professionalism. This was not to say that she was entirely ignorant of the fact that he would very much like to if she gave him so much as a hint that she didn't mind.

Each time she recalled McCord's 'fluttering eyelashes' remark she bristled, but there was no denying that Tariq's presence, although he did no more than hold her hand and talk to her with his eyes, was considerably soothing after her abrasive encounters with McCord. Compared to his flinty-eyed charm the aristocratic Arab's warmth and sensitivity was like a healing balm on her emotions.

She supposed that sooner or later they were going to have to get to know one another better. There was a limit to how much of a barrier one could sustain with a man who was in every essence a gentleman. The moment came one evening when she was sipping a much-needed cup of coffee after making sure that all was as it should be in the rink. Tariq, his own cup and saucer in his hand, drifted over and asked, 'May I join you?'

'Of course.' Celia hedged only slightly. The lounge was almost deserted and there were plenty of free tables, but she knew it would have been petty to refuse the Arab's request.

He lowered himself into the seat facing her and stirring his coffee said with his expressive eyes, 'You have the look of a mother swan whose chicks have been misbehaving all day.'

She looked faintly amused and replied drily, 'Thanks for the compliment, but I don't feel very swan-like skating on a surface that McCord fondly terms as ice.'

'He has his problems.' There was nothing more irritating than one man defending another to a woman, especially the one who is the very source of upset, but in Tariq's case Celia couldn't take umbrage. The genuine concern and affection he showed for his friend in no way detracted from the sympathy he felt for her. 'There is tremendous pressure on at the moment to house all the surplus stock of perishables, but everything will be in order again soon, I am sure.' His very manner was consoling, and while she knew that he couldn't be expected to understand the situation as she did she smiled and changed the subject with, 'What do you know about swans anyway?'

'I have seen your swans of Abbotsbury,' he twinkled proudly, 'and those on the lakes in your parks. But it is wrong to associate them only with cooler countries. We too have a park some miles out of town—admittedly only newly developed—and there are a dozen or so of the species quite happy there. With the right degree of refrigeration in the water—'

'McCord again!' Knowingly Celia couldn't help sounding tart.

She sipped her coffee and found Tariq's warm but searching regard unsettling. She had never before met a man who could break down the barriers of reserve with just a look. 'You do not have the mental make-up for this kind of work,' he said with shrewd humour after some moments had elapsed. 'Tell me, how is it that you are working here for McCord?'

That was a very good question. Celia knew that she had long since grown away from her old affinity with ice. Her enthusiasm for donning skate-boots and speeding over mirrored surfaces had faded with her teenage years, and certainly she could think of more exciting things to do at the moment than instructing mainly frivolous patrons how to remain in a perpendicular position.

True, she wanted to stay on the island in the hope of tracking down Nevine. But work was easy enough to come by in Bahrain, she had discovered some time back. So why was she doing the job? To help McCord out? Did she care whether this lame venture of his survived or not? Another very good question, and one which along with the others she didn't feel disposed to answering at the moment. Though she made a reply in kind to Tariq.

'I came to Bahrain on a sort of mission,' she said, not wanting to bore him with details of her father's past life. 'It...well...ran into difficulties. McCord's choice for the job, a girl he had in mind to act as central figure at the rink, had let him down, and I needed time to make...alternative plans, so I stepped into the breach, you might say.'

'You have exceptional organising talents, but I do not think you are happy playing nursemaid to so many lame dogs,' Tariq joked perceptively.

Happy! That was something else that Celia hadn't given much thought to up to now. She certainly wasn't glowing at the way her life was turning out at the rink, though she couldn't explain why. It had nothing to do with her frustration at present conditions, that much she knew.

She countered Tariq's intuitive probing with a smiling, 'How many of us are completely content in our workaday lives? I bet you come to a dead-end sometimes.'

'International shipping is not the easiest of vocations,' he admitted with a lighthearted sigh. 'But as a member of a family who have been in the line since the days of the old pearling dhows I am committed to do my part.'

Sitting across from him Celia couldn't help noticing his sensitive mouth, the luminous warmth of his dark eyes, and the way the wiry waves of his hair framed attractively his smooth olive-skinned features.

She was bound to make some comment then to fill the somewhat unsettling pause that stretched as his gaze held hers. 'As a shipping magnate,' she said truthfully, 'you don't appear to have an awful lot in common with the down-to-earth pastimes of an ice rink.'

'It has all been one big and rather enjoyable joke,' Tariq laughed, showing teeth reminiscent of those pearls his fore-fathers used to gather. 'We asked McCord to give us something to work off the stale cramp of sitting at an office desk all day. Exercise we have been taught to respect as the alternative to coronaries and arterial complaints.'

'There is all kind of sport here for the businessman, so I'm told,' Celia shrugged.

'But where in Bahrain,' he had a rather engaging grin, 'is it so cool?'

He had a point there. Celia had to admit that she had hardly noticed the heat since her employment at the rink. She supposed she had McCord to thank for that. Drat the man! Irritably she shut off this avenue of thought. She didn't seem to be able to keep him out of her mind for more than five minutes at a stretch.

She said with inquisitive humour to Tariq, 'I get the feeling that you and your friends know something of the adventures of ice skating?'

'My colleagues and I are not new to the bruises that can be collected in the art which you achieve with ease,' he commented with a goodnatured grimace. 'There is quite a grand ice palace in Kuwait. We have been there several times in the past. The interior is as big as a barracks and there are all kinds of cups to be won for keen competitors. But of course it is more convenient to shed one's weight nearer home.'

Eyeing his lean frame, Celia remarked mischievously, 'You hardly qualify for the title of overweight dyspeptic, Tariq! I suspect you and your chums throw yourselves around for the pure hell of it.'

'But I can be serious when it suits me, as you have seen,' he contested with a teasing light. 'And who knows what heights I might attain as your partner on ice. I'm thinking we should practise our talents elsewhere. Fly with me to Kuwait. I would very much like to show you the ice palace there.'

Here it came! Gentleman he was, with courtesy and breeding, but he was still an Arab. And Celia had to keep reminding herself that they conducted their love-life as they ran their high-powered cars—without a minute to lose!

This was the first real conversation they had had since meeting, yet he calmly wanted to whisk her off to Kuwait as though it was a bus ride to the next village!

'I'm afraid I've no time for travelling, Tariq,' she said lightly, thankful to have a valid reason for refusing. 'Three sessions a day keeps me busy here.'

'But in a week's time we have a public holiday in the Arab calendar.' Tariq thought of everything. 'On that day all places of entertainment will close, so you will not have to work, you see.'

'But if the ice rink's closed here, won't it be the same in Kuwait?' Celia asked innocently.

'Ah!' Perhaps Tariq didn't think of everything. With laughter in his eyes he shrugged, 'Well, Kuwait has some very fine scenery.'

They were both laughing at his audacious tactics when a big-built figure moved into the coffee lounge. McCord had seen them before they had seen him, Celia knew, and for this reason she went on making small talk with Tariq. All but the hardy had left the rink and the few beginners were having a last fling before it closed. They needed no help from her, so Celia purposely remained seated. She wasn't going to jump up guiltily just because McCord had appeared. She might work for him, but she wasn't his slave!

He approached their table with a kind of lazy indifference which somehow didn't match the look in his eyes. 'Don't believe anything she says, Tariq. She tries it on all the Arabs.'

He might have been joking, but Celia caught the mocking undertones and her eyes ground sparks as they came up against his.

'In that case I am delighted to be in the line of fire,' Tariq joked back. 'Won't you join us, my friend?'

Unfortunately McCord slid down into one of the other chairs at the table. The air vibrated with his presence, and striving to ignore the fact Celia kept her attention smilingly but grittingly with Tariq.

'I did not go to the Alirezas gathering myself, but I see you were unable to fix up a similar plea of a "previous engagement,"' the Arab deduced with humour.

McCord's casual attitude as he lounged at the table did little to detract from his suave appearance in superbly cut suit and white dress shirt. It was obvious he had been out on the town somewhere, Celia also deduced cynically.

'The party was more than average entertaining, Tariq,' he laid it on, no doubt for her benefit. 'Your people have a lot more tricks up their sleeve than you give them credit for when arranging occasions of this nature.'

'In the shape of lustrous-haired females in expensively simple attire,' Tariq twinkled knowingly. 'I have seen them all, my friend. But for you perhaps it is still an adventure.'

'I don't tire that quickly, Tariq,' McCord's grin was expressive and what was worse, all-encompassing. Celia sat their pretending, with difficulty, complete detachment. 'My staff don't approve—' if he went any further she would locate his shin beneath the table with the nice steel blade of her skate-boot, '—but to my mind there's no better way of relaxing after a hard day's work.'

'You have to understand what he's going through, Tariq.' On the other hand Celia decided perhaps words of a kind were more ladylike. 'He hasn't mentioned it to a soul, I bet, but he's really drowning his sorrows, you know, because his true lady-love failed to turn up as expected.'

'Ah yes, the one who is still floating around in Cairo.' The fact that Tariq knew that much about the absent skating queen caused Celia a dull shock. If she had been discussed between the two men to this extent then Mandy Bennet was a lot more substantial a figure in McCord's life than even Celia had supposed.

'In that case,' Tariq assumed the heavy air of a sympathetic heart physician and slapped his friend's shoulder, 'I recommend a dose of lovely ladies at least once a night.'

This kind of trying conversation, for Celia at least, went on for some time with only Tariq unaware of the subtle innuendoes that gave it bite. McCord's eyes, when they met hers, were lit with lazy malice, but this was nothing, she hoped, to the message of sweet hate that issued privately from her own.

But for all the emotionally draining experience of making apparent light chat with the boss present, closing time came round with her barely noticing it.

The rink had emptied and all the coffee cups had been washed and stacked. It was McCord who rose first, drawing her attention to the fact that the rest of the staff were hovering in the background, anxious to be off. For this reason she idled on at the table finishing a lingering conversation with Tariq about the pearling banks in the Gulf.

At last the Arab rose, after a large hint from McCord with the dipping of the coffee lounge lights. But Tariq was in lingering mood still and as they moved out into the rink area he put an arm round her waist, though she was perfectly steady in her skate-boots, and laughed, 'You see what a fine team we make!'

It was an excuse to revert to a previous conversation, Celia suspected, and sure enough, his smiling dark eyes questioning, he asked, 'What about our date? Will you come with me to Kuwait?'

Celia was breathless. Tariq's nearness was heady enough for any woman. With those dark good looks, his charming personality, and the undeniable attraction of the well-bred Arab, she had difficulty in keeping her boot-clad feet firmly on the ground.

In the shadowy glow of the rink's perimeter she demurred, 'I'll have to think about it, Tariq.'

'If that is what you are going to do, then I am happy.' His quietly elated look told her he had taken her words as an acceptance. He fastened a cotton burnous about him to go out into the street, and flaring as he walked, it gave him the appearance of a dashing desert figure.

Celia watched his departure in the gloom with excitement singing in her veins.

SHE CAME to shortly afterwards, aware of McCord's shadowy shape locking up the music console apparatus, not far away. Cooly ignoring him now that there was no longer any need to put on a polite front for the benefit of others, she made straight for her private locker in the office.

She heard him checking distantly on things around the rink, and feeling wryly that the office was hardly big enough to accommodate the two of them plus the antagonism which seemed a little rife between them at the moment, she hoped to make a hasty departure. But luck would have it that the lace of one boot knotted up, perhaps because of her fumbling fingers, and McCord drifted in while she was still scouting for her shoes.

Fortunately all was in order on the desk. There was not enough going on at the Alhambra to involve a lot of work behind the scenes, and what bills had come in for ordered cartons of drinks or fresh supplies for the upstairs restaurant Celia had laid neatly on the desk.

McCord flicked through them casually. In the bright lights of the office, compared to the dimness on the outside, he was a dominating force which wouldn't be ignored, though Celia worked at it.

He said, tossing the bills down again in a way that boded fresh skirmishing, 'How long have you been selling tickets off the roll instead of through the computer?'

So he was in *that* kind of mood, was he?

'As long,' she said with sublime indifference, 'as your mechanics have failed to find the cause of the jamming metal rod that holds them.'

'The cashier has strict instructions to make no sale of tickets without a computerised check,' he said, moving round the side of the desk.

She had her shoes on now and she skirted him with just the right degree of healthy respect to search for her car keys in her handbag. 'Instructions are all right,' she replied tightly, 'if you're around to back them up. But while you're glued to gauges and thermometers back there,' her glance clearly indicated his meat factory across the alley, 'someone around here has to think fast enough to avoid a police caution for obstructing the pavement outside.'

Surprisingly he grinned, but it wasn't a nice sight. 'You're not telling me it was your nimble-witted idea to deal manually with the customers? As I heard it was Tariq who came to your aid originally when the reel got stuck.'

So he knew all about that. And he knew the ticket office was still causing problems. *His* ticket office. But he was calmly trotting out these malfunctions as though the onus was on *her.*

Oh! Her anger became a quivering nerve in her throat. The worst of it was she couldn't find half of the things she needed to leave, and this involved bypassing him several times to various corners of the room. The sadistic pleasure he was deriving from playing the dissatisfied boss was apparent in every muscle of his suavely groomed frame. And on top of this Mandy Bennet's likeness smiled down on her from the wall over the desk, the silent laughter on those lips, the sparkling friendly eyes lending an almost comical irony to the tense and crackling atmosphere of the office.

When Celia could find her voice she made it sound deliberately smooth. 'Tariq has proved a wonderful help in a lot of ways at the rink. At least the customers don't mind rallying round, even if the owner is for the most part... otherwise engaged.'

The emphasis she put on the last two words was unmistakable, but McCord only sloped his unpleasant smile.

'Perhaps it's the staff who induce the rallying round impulse,' he said hatefully, hinting no doubt at her long session with his Arab friend at the coffee lounge table tonight. 'As I see it Tariq is just a patron and it's not his place to become involved in matters of policy at the rink.'

'Who said anything about matters of policy?' Celia curved her lips into the semblance of a smile, also hinting at her lengthy tête-à-tête with Tariq. The subtle innuendoes in this remark sent her exhilaration soaring. It felt so good to get one back at McCord, even though she was making more of her brief relationship with Tariq to satisfy this burning desire.

But while she put on an air of being in complete control of her feelings Mandy Bennet's merry sparkle following her wherever she went made her want to scream. It was not the first time she had felt the suffocating awareness of the photograph in everything she did around the office, and in the heat of the moment now she was tempted to fly at McCord with the exasperated request to remove the offending image of loveliness.

She didn't, of course. Feminine intuition advised strongly against this kind of hysteria. It was only a photograph, after all, and even if the flesh and blood of it was in McCord's mind most of the time...well...an olive-skinned face floated mentally before her vision, one with fervent dark eyes, quizzical invitation in their depths, and she found the thought of Tariq oddly comforting in that moment.

She unearthed her car keys at last in a drawer of the desk. McCord, who had reacted not at all to her subtle comment that she might have other things besides work to discuss with her friends—well, he was a man of steel anyway, Celia mused in disgust—followed her movements with something of a blue glint. Seeing that she was ready to leave didn't stop him from belabouring the point over outside interference at the rink.

'Just remember to keep your mind on your job, Miss Darwell,' came the drawling order, with just the right degree of implication that McCord was past master at injecting into his tones. 'Who knows, you might find that the only ones disposed to rallying round you then are the ones who get paid for it.'

Celia dropped her car keys into her handbag and picked up her dressing case. She had had about enough of McCord for one evening. 'Going by conditions of late,' she sailed past him, 'we might all find shortly that your sole clientele at the rink are the ones who get paid for it.'

'I doubt it, Miss Darwell,' his voice floated sardonically after her as she barged away along the dimly-lit route towards the street door. 'With you in attendance I doubt it.'

Celia gave him the frigid length of her departing figure as reply. Oh, he could harp on about her friendship with Tariq in his underhand male way, but he needn't think that she was going to hang around to listen. And now when she came to think of it the idea of flying to Kuwait seemed very attractive indeed. She had told Tariq she would consider his invitation and so she had. At the moment she could think of nothing nicer than joining him on the public holiday he had spoken of, for a flip to another Arab country.

But the day in question was a week away; and with the air charged as it was between her and McCord, she was to discover that a lot could happen in that time.

CHAPTER SEVEN

As a means of shutting out of her mind the trials of the ice rink Celia decided to renew her efforts in the search for Nevine. Though her six-hour working day tended to sap her once glowing enthusiasm in this respect she discovered that her free time, between the afternoon and evening sessions, was ideal for venturing abroad. It was cooler then and the town came alive with the real business of the day being done in the shops and bazaars and gleaming blocks of offices.

Taking the car or sometimes going on foot, she wondered how she could have believed in the early days of her arrival that Bahrain was anything but a true portion of Arabia. Her first impressions of a Westernised air about the place now seemed like an illusion as she explored the rectangular warrens and alleys of Manama, with its tunnels and courts, little lock-up shops, and donkey stalls on streets that were little more than arm's-width passages made narrower by the constant flow of humanity.

Often the only European in sight amid varying skin colours and modes of dress ranging from the black veil to camelhair robes and flowing caftans, she pierced the veneer of Manama's outward sophistication to find a centuries-old culture that no amount of foreign influence could eradicate.

Along one narrow alley the scent of teak and pine spoke of carpenters at work. Another was a brilliant stream of Eastern cottons. The goldsmiths too had an alley to themselves, tapping away with their little hammers and a patience as old as time.

One could shop for meat, vegetables, spices and clothing along lanes where conflicting scents and odours knew no boundaries, and the residue of pungent basil, mint and coriander, fresh sawdust, roast coffee, musky perfumes and the barnyard effluence of live chickens lingered like a pall over the neighbourhood.

Frequently it was a shock for Celia to emerge from the world of mud dwellings and cobbled byways to find herself after all in the twentieth century. Even the marble, glass, and concrete of modern Manama failed to dull her growing awareness to the fact that under these blue skies, pearl-sheened by the heat, was a civilisation steeped in the traditions of the East.

But whether she chose to wander in the native quarter or to drive around the more sophisticated residential areas, she made no progress in her search for Nevine.

She knew very little Arabic and though English could be used on occasion it was difficult to start up a conversation which involved going back thirty years in time. Merchants and business people were concerned only with the living impact of the moment, for it was today's takings that counted, not those of three decades ago.

Accompanying Kamel it had been different. With the Arab arrogance of one who has obtained a slightly exalted position in his job he had barged in on the most intimate of business deals or domestic discussions to put his questions across. But Celia was not in a position to behave in this manner, nor quite frankly did she have the nerve. Also in her weeks in Manama she had made an important and not too promising discovery.

Though foreigners and Arabs may live side by side in Bahrain, one was always conscious of the invisible barrier that separated the two societies. Each lived their own lives according to their own customs, and though friendships may blossom and even deep affections there was this unwritten law that kept the Arabs to themselves.

This was one of Celia's main despairs when she thought about her longing to meet Nevine; and the possible obstacles that might prevent this; especially as she was convinced more than ever that somewhere in these multitudes was the woman of her father's heart, and that it was only ignorance of her whereabouts that separated them.

What with her difficulties at the ice rink and her failure to meet with any kind of success regarding her reason for visiting Bahrain, Celia was not in the chirpiest of spirits these days. But there was one aspect of her work which gave her considerable pleasure, and that was the coaching of her star pupils on ice.

Since the early days when they had resembled wobbly-footed elves on blades, the children of the morning sessions had come a long way. Now they skated with the grace and precision of serious professionals, and there was a good half-dozen who showed the makings of budding champions.

Considering the upheavals that Celia had to contend with she was more than a little proud of the headway she had made with her brood, and seeing the *ayahs* nodding and beaming at their charges from the seats around the edge, she suspected she wasn't the only one to feel this way.

Always prettily dressed, the little girls were lightly moving fairies on ice, the boys like miniature gallants in their wake. It would be an idea, Celia mused at one of these sessions, to harness the talents of the children and put on some kind of show.

But where she would find the time to organise a display of this sort was another question. As Jack—or Jill—of all trades at the rink, she found herself doing jobs that were nothing at all to do with her supposedly exclusive position as ice instructress.

The restaurant, for instance. It had a staff of its own, but who would believe it! In exasperation one morning in the office Celia glowered at the catering release slip in her hand which would have to be signed by McCord. How they managed to lumber her with their responsibilities she was never sure. What she did know from past experience was that if she went upstairs now the restaurant would be mysteriously empty, everybody seemingly busy as usual elsewhere with preparations for opening at sundown.

She left the slip until she was no longer needed on the ice, then changing into shoes went across the alley to the cold storage factory. If she didn't act there would be no food for the restaurant tonight, though why *she* should worry about that…? Sourly Celia dismissed the thought and went up the steps into the compressor room.

McCord was in his glass-panelled den high up in the room, and realising after some time that he had no intention of coming down, she was obliged to negotiate the metal stairway into his humming, bleeping domain.

It really was an education to see just what lay behind a little bit of freezing for food storage plus—though why mention it? she thought cynically—her own expanse of ice.

McCord was hardly the scientist in appearance, in well-cut suit, the jacket of which he had tossed over a pipe-junction, his once spruce shirt tugged open at the neck giving disarray to the businesslike knot of his tie.

'You picked a great time for a visit,' he said, rapidly turning a big wheel and watching the reaction closely on a nearby meter face.

Ignoring his sarcasm, Celia asked with an unexplainable desire to get in his way, 'What's that red liquid bobbing up and down?'

'It's the P.S.I. meter,' he explained grimly. 'Pressure per square inch to you. We need another cold room and I'm having to watch the refrigerant fluid.'

With a bored air she waved the chit under his nose and asked, 'Would it survive without your tender care long enough for you to stamp your authority on this?'

He didn't look at the piece of paper in her hand, only at the needle on the gauge to the right of the wheel. When it swung to dead centre at the top of the glass he relaxed his frame slightly and breathed, 'That's better. Now we've got ideal pressure.'

'We?' Her query was delivered mockingly and not a little bitterly. She spared a glance around. 'If I could find the ice rink pressure among all this paraphernalia of levers and switches I'd like to bet it would register anything but "ideal"!'

He ignored that trend of thought, also the catering chit, in favour of another urgent swing of a wheel. Feeling slightly ridiculous left with arm outstretched and the yellow slip fluttering at the end of it like a limp flag, Celia gave up for the time being and drifted round trying to make some sense of all she saw. There was a chattering Telex among a nest of similar machines in one corner. Idly she picked up the jumping tape and read an order being put through for smoked salmon, caviar and a lot more to be delivered to the Sheikh's palace for a forthcoming banquet.

This must have been something McCord was expecting, for he crowded over to absorb the message himself, rapidly typing back a reply, before swinging back to the all-demanding task of keeping the needles and red liquids happy

It occurred to Celia, since she had made the remark, that it might not be a bad idea to do some surreptitious scouting for the ice rink pressure gauge. It would be here somewhere and it *would* be interesting to see what it registered compared to the rest of McCord's pampered equipment.

She must have examined every clock face and meter gauge in the place before she finally spotted it across a space whose distance did nothing to dim the damning evidence before her eyes, of a half-cocked lever.

Well, if that wasn't cheeky! She had no time to take a closer look—not that she needed to, for McCord was suddenly by her side. He flicked the slip of paper from her fingers and signing asked, 'Will that be all, Miss Darwell?'

The challenging whimsy in his blue eyes told her that he had noted the direction of her gaze. His inflexible smile also indicated that he had no intention of acknowledging it.

'That's more than enough, *Mr.* McCord,' she whipped the slip from his hand and made a wooden retreat.

Her connections with the Alhambra restaurant had never been more than shouldering the load of its work-shy administrators, until one evening when Tariq asked her to dine with him there. It had been a particularly exacting day and the thought of lingering in the rose-lit interior whose windows looked over the ice rink at one side and the multi-coloured lights of Manama at the other was attractive indeed. Especially as her companion would be a man she both liked and was strangely attracted to.

She had had no time to dress for the occasion, but sitting in a lamplit glow later, a pretty lace top she had donned for the evening session more in evidence than her slacks under the table, she didn't feel that she was too much of a let-down to Tariq's refined appearance. If she was on view from the office and the shadowy reaches of the rink, now deserted, so what? she mused rigidly. Her work was finished for the day. And in her free time she pleased herself.

The meal was surprisingly good, mellowing her opinions of the restaurant staff. Not that Tariq paid much attention to what was placed before him. He wanted to know all about her. They talked. She talked. Inevitably it came out about Nevine and Celia's frustrated attempts to find her. She wondered why it hadn't occurred to her to mention it to Tariq before. With his shipping business and family connections he knew a considerable cross-section of Bahraini society.

Disappointingly his response was negative. He'd never heard of such a person, nor could he offer any suggestions on how she could be traced. Of course it was obvious by the look in his eyes, which for the most part rested on her, that he more than anyone she had accosted so far had a burning interest in the present, not the past.

Lightly she let the matter drop and for the rest of the evening she allowed her feelings to run riot a little under his intoxicating gaze.

As she had her own car they parted in the restaurant doorway at a lateish hour, but not before Tariq had raised her hand to his lips and brushed them lingeringly around her wrist and with pressure in the palm of her hand, in a form of farewell.

In a way Celia was glad that she had other things to think about beside this dark-eyed Arab with the charming manners.

She put all her efforts into coaching the children in a form of ice-ballet musical interpretation. They were greatly excited at the idea. Each was allowed to choose his or her musical piece, and as enthusiasm grew the costumes visualised were startling at times. Ahmad insisted on interpreting a James Bond theme and saw himself in tight black trousers and shirt, and a gun in one hand. A water pistol, of course. Did little Arab boys have those annoying toys too? Celia wondered in private amusement.

Iffat and Zaki Junaid had decided to do Romeo and Juliet. They were both sensitive little performers and their practising on the ice to the rather touching music brought an ache to the throat of all but the hardiest among the onlookers.

Celia's work had gone rather well at the rink lately. This alone ought to have warned her that it couldn't last. She was used to nursing several grievances at a time over unprofessional conditions at the Alhambra. It was uncanny indeed not to have one grumble worth voicing; rather like an uneasy calm, she felt, that usually preceded trouble.

SURE ENOUGH it came, in the shape of puddles on the ice one morning when she was putting the star performers through their paces. This was to be the complete run-through of the progress they had made so far in the construction of the ice ballet, and the insidious suspicion of water slowly taking the place of the hard polished surface she had always insisted on, together with glistening stretches which were beginning to twinkle weirdly under the roof lighting, made Celia, after all her efforts, see red.

This was the limit! This was more than the last of the last straws!

She told the children to practise limbering-up exercises at the rail until she returned, and after cursing every moment it took her to change into suitable footwear she moved with seething determination towards McCord's cold storage warehouse.

She knew what she was going to do. It ought to have been done a long time ago, and never more than now would she enjoy the counter-blast of exacting what was her due.

There was a white-coated assistant in the compressor room; a bespectacled Bahraini who looked up from the figures and notes in his book at her appearance. Like a whirlwind Celia gusted past him, making straight for the metal stairway. That his jaw had dropped in her lightning passing caused her not an iota of concern. In any case her mind was otherwise engaged reorientating herself to the upstairs laboratory and the whereabouts of the lever that indicated pressure at the ice rink.

She found it with not much stalking around. As usual it was half-cocked. Well, this was something that was going to be changed, and *drastically,* within the next second or two! In half that time she knew the satisfying feel of cold metal in her hand, was poised to push the thing exultantly all the way home, when a hand clamped down on hers and a voice breathless from the dash to reach the lever before she did ground out, 'Get your fool hands off that pressure!'

In the latticework of pipes and fitments she hadn't noticed McCord in the vicinity. But it wouldn't have made any difference if she had. Her determination to see justice done once and for all didn't stop with his appearance; though the steel bands of his preventive embrace were making a good job of squeezing the breath from her lungs.

The pinpoints of fire in her grey eyes emphasised her defiance and all-out intention to upgrade the lever anyway. His own flame-lit look was menacingly and persuasively to the contrary. Celia couldn't think of anything in those seconds that would give her more supreme satisfaction than thwarting his orders.

Clamped against McCord she might have been pitting her strength against the original iron man. Her fingers were growing limp on the lever, and as she fought madly against capitulation the blue eyes blazing into hers were calmly telling her she would capitulate anyway.

Both breathing furiously, neither giving an inch—mentally at least—Celia contended while her body began to cave in. It was a paramount battle of wills, coming to a head as breath mingled with battling breath.

At last Celia threw her head back, her fair hair awry as she gasped for air. Relentlessly the victor, even after her hand had dropped lifelessly from the lever, McCord's steely regard was smoulderingly, and curiously immovable. She felt nailed by the odd light in his eyes, awash in some new emotion that she knew only as a piercing disturbance within her.

So close to the man whom she seemed to have spent her life bickering with, she found she had suddenly run out of steam; though her blazing gaze continued to hit back to cover up her disorganised flow of thought.

Locked together like this, McCord's bone-snapping grip on her, the moments seemed to stretch into eternity, and strangely suspended Celia had nothing to offer to end the scorching impasse. Then as he abruptly let her go, it was several seconds before McCord erupted afresh, verbally this time on her ignorance of freezing methods.

'Have you any idea what chaos you would have caused if you'd pushed that lever home?' he rounded on her. 'All the cold rooms have an automatic safety level, but because of the size and nature of the ice rink the only safety valves it possesses are here in the compressor room. And *because* there's a mile of pipes under the ice there's what's called a "flow-delay," which means that we have to wait up to ten minutes at the pressure wheel to see that the P.S.I. doesn't go too high for the rink—*otherwise* the gas would find a weak point in the tubing and blow a hole through the ice—*And* the refrigerant fluid could start leaking as a gas, and let me tell you those fumes are dangerous—'

Considerably sobered by the technical implications of his explanation, Celia was nevertheless aware that he kept his *own* cold storage monsters well fed, and with another storm brewing in her eyes she said, 'Talking of chaos, have you seen the riverside effect we've got over the road just now? When I took on this job I was of the opinion I'd need skates for the ice, not rubber flippers!'

'Okay, okay, don't lose your hair—it suits you. Come on, let's take a look.'

His unexpected gentleness left Celia without a leg to stand on. Not only had he stopped sounding off to her about his precious gadgets, he was actually offering to accompany her back to the rink to review the position!

Not knowing whether to be mollified or not, she turned and preceded him down the metal stairway. Outside, the refrigerated vans and lorries were cluttering the forecourt as usual. McCord steered her past a metal forklift over-stacked with food cartons and round the damp bulk of a side of beef being transported across her path.

In the rink she was maliciously pleased to see the ice flooding nicely. Now *he* would see that she had just cause for complaint.

McCord's reaction was impossible to fathom. He nodded pleasantly to the staff and even asked old Ibrahim who was sharpening skate blades on the grinding wheel how his wife was.

But the scene on the ice did not indicate a smooth-running concern, Celia noted with renewed satisfaction. The children were seeing who could send up the most spray with their skates, and the *ayahs* looked around and at one another uncertainly, wondering if they should get their young charges dressed and out of the deteriorating conditions.

Black veils were hastily tugged into position as McCord approached. His fluent Arabic and easy manner were devoured by these child-minding and often lonely women. And long before he had finished his lengthy chat, the dark eyes above the veils were smiling at him coyly.

The children had clustered around him at the edge of the ice, and to her disgust Celia discovered that instead of being the ogre of the situation he was fast becoming the star attraction. He had a way with children, she had to admit. He transferred his attention to them as suavely as he had just a moment ago given it all to the ladies, and what he said kept the tots' piquant gazes riveted on him, evoking a titter here, a giggle there, and a squirm of bright-eyed laughter from the older end.

Tiny Maryam, in candy-floss organdy was moved to show off with a charming pirouette, and McCord demonstrated his approval by swinging her up into his arms and allowing small arms to wind lovingly round his neck. Strong, even teeth, just less than white, gave his smile a masculine appeal; something the *ayahs* were not slow to appreciate, judging by the reserved sparkle atop the veils.

Ahmad and young Husain clowned before him as he talked, and left in the dark because of her ignorance of Arabic, Celia asked distrustfully, 'What are you telling them?'

'I'm just apologising for the poor quality of the ice,' he shrugged, 'and explaining that we're doing all we can to put matters right.'

She looked at her watch and seeing that it was only ten minutes to closing time she left him with a dry, 'Well, I'm glad someone appreciates your particular brand of fiction!'

AFTER LUNCH and a lie down at the hotel, Celia went for her usual hour to the pool. Too hot for anything else at this time of day, she had the choice of drifting irresolutely in the air-conditioned comfort of her suite, or splashing in the sparkling water surrounded by shady palms. She had long ago plumped for the latter as a pleasant way of spending the lengthy break between morning and afternoon sessions.

But today she moved languidly through the half-deserted gardens, a fluttering restlessness inside her, the aftermath of her clash with McCord this morning. There was something in that embrace of his in the compressor room that seemed branded on her mind, and though she saw no sense in reliving those heart-thudding moments, she had no real desire to erase them from her thoughts.

Splashing in the pool would help, she decided, and she did three brisk lengths of the pool as a start to her programme. It was when she was emerging dripping from another cooling bout later that the towel she had been about to reach for from her table under the palms was dropped around her shoulders by unseen hands. Startled, she turned and was rocked further to find herself looking up into the same blue eyes which had caused her considerable mental torment this past hour or so.

McCord here! Her surprise must have shown in her face, for, leisurely arranging the soaking, flaxen strands of her hair over the towel, he said easily, 'Relax. I haven't come in a working capacity. At least only to say that I'm closing the rink for the rest of the day.'

Celia was conscious of the world becoming hazy with his appearance; of the sprinkling of guests around the pool suddenly receding beyond the haze so that her own little area beneath the palm was like an island of uncertainty with his fingers arranging the tendrils of her hair.

'Don't tell me,' she tried to sound flippant, 'that you're actually giving me the day off?'

'I've no choice,' he slanted her a begrudging gleam. 'The ice is going to get worse rather than better. But freezing conditions are improving at the plant and after a close down for a couple of days you'll be getting all the pressure you need at the rink.'

Celia sat down in her chair, droplets glistening on her smooth, lightly tanned skin, her brilliant cornflower blue swimsuit still wet. But she needed support for her legs for some inexplicable reason. McCord looked overwhelmingly unbusinesslike in grey slacks and pale checked sports shirt. He had ordered himself a drink, she saw, picking up her own glass, a social touch which left her slightly out of her depth.

'You couldn't be suggesting,' she said over the top of her glass,' a *two-day* break?... But wait a minute...' Something had just slotted into her mind. 'Tomorrow...isn't that the public holiday I've been hearing about?' It was. She remembered now. And if the rink was to be closed for the rest of the day, that meant she wouldn't see Tariq tonight. And they had made no firm arrangements for their date tomorrow, and Kuwait.

'That's right.' McCord was watching her lazily as he replied. 'It seems the ideal time, don't you agree, to leave the ice in suspension until we're back to full pressure again?'

'Oh yes.' Quickly she replied while her mind was rapidly coming round to the realisation that with the Alhambra all locked up for the evening there would be no way of getting in touch with Tariq.

Contrary to her own secret dilemma McCord seemed well pleased with his plan. He lay back in his chair and pulled on his drink, though his gaze on her, intensely blue in the outdoors and faintly hooded, was offputting to say the least when she madly wanted to pursue her own thoughts.

'I ought to point out,' he put in, after idly removing his glance to view the scene of bathers and loungers around the pool, 'that tomorrow will not be entirely a work-free day.'

Celia bristled. 'I might have known! A public holiday, only I don't happen to be a member of the public, is that right—?'

'Let me finish—' His smile was not exactly soothing. 'You're forgetting the one other occupation, aren't you? That of finding your long-lost mother substitute, Nevine.'

Celia blinked. To be truthful she *had* forgotten. At least since McCord had unsettled her with his presence at the pool.

While she was dumbly admitting this he went on, making no effort to keep a slightly sanctimonious note out of his voice, 'As you've given so much of your time to the smooth running of the Alhambra, I consider it only fair to devote a little of my time in assisting you with the job you originally came to Bahrain to do. I think I'm right in assuming that you haven't yet spread your net to the adjoining Banabba islands, so I suggest we take a boat there in the morning and try our luck.'

Celia's eyes, silvered by the sunlight, became round. This was a side of McCord she hadn't come across; not since the early days when he had taken her to the soirée and dinner party at Rifaa for the purposes of asking around. Suppressing an urge to enthuse, she viewed him instead with ironical disbelief. 'The great McCord offering to leave all his pet projects unattended? Actually shelving the pressing call of business for the more frivolous pastime of joining in a missing persons hunt!'

His look was one of mocking regret. 'Maybe I'll do some business in the Banabba Islands. We'll be going on one of the native dhows, by the way,' he added. 'I own a couple, and one of them, the *Sea Roc,* is in harbour at the moment.'

Celia's expression now matched the delighted incredulity in her eyes. 'One of those camel-necked craft with the big rust-red sails and everything. I don't believe it!'

'Be ready at nine in the morning,' he said with an indulgent gleam, 'and we'll pretend we're doing a pirate run.'

She laughed, struck with the idea, but was sufficiently down to earth to make the wicked observation, 'The usual office hours, of course.'

'Sailing's a leisurely business.' Amused, McCord didn't deny that he was a man who normally made every minute count. 'The earlier we start the more ground we get to cover in the time allotted.'

Celia couldn't imagine floating round the Persian Gulf with a man like McCord, engaged in a search, that was, to say the least, far out of his usual realm of operations. But that didn't dilute the tiny thrill of pleasure that was rapidly flowering within her at the thought.

Relaxed now, she sipped at her drink only to find McCord finishing his off with one gulp after a glance at his wrist watch. He rose, towering momentarily, and gave her a brief salute. 'Okay, see you tomorrow. Enjoy the rest of your day, Miss Darwell.'

'Thank you, I intend to, Mr. McCord.' She showed her teeth in a smile that was not meant to broadcast her irritation. Here she was, just coming round to the idea of lingeringly plying him with questions about tomorrow and generally sunning herself, not only in the Bahrainian warmth but in his unaccustomed conciliatory company, when he upped with that all too familiar preoccupied look on his face and smilingly left her flat.

She watched him go with more than a little curiosity. Just what would be the reason for that fleeting look of concern that had passed across his features just now? Something to do with the pressure of business? She didn't think so. He was not dressed for ice-engineering duties, or high-powered technical chat. But what else was there in his work-packed life? Wondering, she gave up after a while and returned to the rosy prospect of staying by the pool the whole afternoon and later taking as long as she liked over dinner in the luxurious ambience of the hotel restaurant.

CHAPTER EIGHT

IT WASN'T until Celia was lying between the sheets after deciding on an early night in preparation for the morrow that it occurred to her to remember Tariq, and then only as a sleepy afterthought. As he was not in the habit of appearing until the latter half of the evening session he would have arrived at the rink only a short while ago to find it all shuttered up. Too late for him to do anything about confirming the plans he'd had in mind.

She was ready long before the stipulated hour next morning. Always an early riser, she loved to witness the day's emergence in a saffron flush which gave the sea the appearance of oiled silk and the island a mystic quality as it rose from the deliciously cooling vapours left over from the night.

Though she supposed she ought to dress for sailing, Celia baulked at the idea of wearing slacks yet again on this, one of her rare days off. So it was in flowered sundress and dainty-heeled sandals that she took up her vantage point in the hotel lobby. Even at this hour the place was crowded, with the usual travelling salesmen, oil personnel and freelance agents dealing in everything from washing machines to private jets. Men in Dacron suits and others more indifferently attired kept their ears tuned for easy pickings that might come their way in the non-stop buzz of gossip.

Celia felt somewhat swamped by the atmosphere, though she had acquired a veneer now against the openly interested glances, and the more blatant ones of out-and-out seduction. McCord, when he arrived, showed some distaste at finding her here, a slender brown and gold figure in fragile cotton. He fished her from the masculine mêlée and was just about to steer her to the outdoors when an arm came to rest heavily around his shoulder and the slurred speech of its owner sounded in their ears. 'Well, if it ishn't my old mate McCord!'

'Mike!' With something like surprised exasperation in his voice McCord gripped the man's arm. 'Do you realise I've been searching the whole damn town for you? For the love of—' he let a curse go under his breath. 'It looks as if you've been here all night, and drinking too!'

While 'Mike,' a thick-set individual in his late fifties, continued to slump, giving Celia a moon-faced smile, McCord said to her, supporting the man's full weight, 'Sorry, but I'm going to have to take him home. He's due at the oilfields at two for a pretty important operation, and there'll be the devil to pay if he's not on the job this time.'

Mike had started to snore happily and showing her concern Celia asked, 'Is there anything I can do?'

McCord thought about it, making clumsily for the outdoors, and nodded. 'We'll take your car. I'll sit in the back to see that the lovable old soak comes to no harm.'

Celia soon saw that he was speaking from experience, for they hadn't been on the road long before Mike leapt up from his slumber like a mad elephant, battling at the doors and windows in a rollicking attempt to find out where he was. When McCord had calmed him and his musical snores were all she had to contend with she was able to make more headway following the directions that would bring them to their passenger's house.

Surprisingly for an oil man, he didn't live on one of the estates provided but in the heart, it seemed, of Manama itself. She turned right, and right again through streets of crumbling mud walls and latticed balconies. Labyrinths, she supposed was what the desert people called these mazes they had constructed for themselves centuries ago.

At the heart of this maze they came to Mike's house. They searched for his key and got him indoors. Celia saw white-washed rooms, also labyrinthine in design it seemed, with hanging lamps and threadbare Persian carpets. The room they were in and most of the others appeared to open on to a half-covered courtyard where the breeze wafted the scents of a eucalyptus tree and other greenery.

McCord eased his lifeless burden into a chair. He had obviously decided against getting him to bed, and Celia could guess why. 'Coffee,' he said. 'We need lots of black coffee.'

'Let me do it.' She looked around for the kitchen.

'Through here.' He led her across the courtyard to a low-ceilinged space pungent with the aroma of hanging herbs. He helped her to locate the things she would need, the two of them brushing close in the small area lined with rough wooden cupboards and shelves. Celia wanted to smile, but refrained from doing so because of the apparent gravity of the situation. The sight of McCord pottering with sauce-pans and supply canisters in the crude domesticity of their surroundings was somehow highly amusing.

He went back across the courtyard and she could hear him working at rousing the recumbent figure with sharp talk. From what she could make out from the snatches of con-versation she caught as she made the coffee, this lapse of Mike's was one of many in the past, and as he was a top man at the oilfield it was debatable how long he was going to be able to hold down his job if they continued.

She could find only a tin mug to hold the coffee. Testing it for coolness, she took it into the whitewashed room and waited for the appropriate moment to get some inside the man.

Some progress had been made, for his eyes were open and registering a vague awareness of what was going on, though his face still wore the rosy hue of too much liquor. It was a good face, mature, with kindly lines; not one that belonged to a confirmed drunk, Celia felt. Viewing it clearly for the first time, she had the oddest sensation that she had seen it somewhere before. Something about the eyes...or was it the smile?... Tantalisingly the memory eluded her...

'Come on, snap out of it, Mike!' McCord slapped the man's face with grim affection. 'You've got what's left of the morning to shake off the booze and make like an oil company exec. And if I see you sinking this low again I'm gonna have your ears, understand!'

'Awsh, McCord...you are the doggonest... shlave-driver...'

'You love your work. Now quit making out you want to commit professional suicide and think about the guys who are depending on you out there.'

At a sign Celia stepped forward with the mug of coffee. She was prepared to have a go at tipping it into the slack mouth, but McCord took it from her with a look that said she was to keep clear and began the operation himself.

She went for more coffee...and more and within an hour they had Mike sitting up straight if a little mystified, and halfway on the road to recovery. McCord began to relax. He even gave Celia a comradely smile. She felt curiously touched, perhaps because they had both worked so hard and fatigue was making her sentimental.

'I've a feeling we're going to do it,' he said, straightening from the constant necessity of cajoling Mike from his stupor. 'But I want to be sure that he gets to the oilfield with no mishaps. Do you think you'll be okay if I slip out and make a phone call?'

'Of course,' Celia nodded. 'Should I keep up with the black coffee?'

'All you can manage.' He looked grateful. 'I'll get one of my men to take over here when we go, and see that Mike gets to work on time.'

He went out quickly, disappearing along the alley, and Celia turned back to keeping an eye on the cheerful hulk in the chair. He had taken to singing snatches of American ballads in between making firm efforts to appear sober. Celia suppressed a smile. It was impossible not to like this friend of McCords, for all his unmanly state at the moment. That he *was* a man of decent morals and firm ideals she felt instinctively, and looking at him while she applied the mug to his lips she wondered about the tinge of sadness that was creeping into his countenance in the wake of the receding euphoria of drink; an habitual melancholy, she would have said, judging by the deep lines scored in the well-moulded features.

It was gratifying to see him showing a lucid interest in his surroundings at last, though he clung to the last vestiges of drunkenness with slurred snatches of song as though reluctant to face the harsher world of sobriety.

Celia reckoned that one more dose of coffee would do the trick. Looming in, she had got quite adept at feeding Mike like an overgrown baby. This time, when a kind of blank recognition showed in his eyes, she supposed it was because he was becoming used to her administrations. Then suddenly he acted completely out of character by gripping her round the waist with both arms and tightening them so that the mug was suspended giddily in space over one big shoulder.

Helpless, she heard the sob that crumpled his face and burying it against her he cried, 'Mandy!—You here? Why didn't you say—why didn't someone tell me?... Aw, Mandy... I didn't want you... to see me... like this...'

Mandy! Celia was transfixed. Not only because she couldn't move a muscle in the bear hug, but also because something had just clicked into place. The round, sunny features of this man and those in the photograph over the desk in McCord's office at the rink! There was no time to do more than glimpse the possibility, for the man whose arms imprisoned her had risen and they were swaying unsteadily like a couple of drunks.

Afraid that they were going to go crashing over, Celia tried a soothing tone. 'You're making a mistake, Mike. *I'm* not Mandy. I'm Celia Darwell... I work for McCord... we've been trying to get you on your feet for—'

'Aw, Mandy, ya should've said...ya should've told me... Look at me... your gin-soaked old man... and you purty as a picture...' Obsessed as he was with a feeling of disgrace, the sobs were those of a man making the traumatic withdrawal from the bounds of intoxication.

But knowing this didn't help Celia. She was locked against his shuddering frame and was beginning to feel about as efficient as a rag doll in helping him over the rough going. The coffee mug crashed to the ground and the sharp corner of some jutting piece of furniture dug into her back as she fought the losing battle to keep them both upright. Overcome with shame and remorse, her captor seemed bent on proffering his apologies with the ever-increasing stranglehold of a love-hug that was plagued with unsteadiness.

About thirteen stone of brawn and brute force levelled against the solar plexus didn't make for easy breathing, and a feeling of faintness warned Celia that struggling would only aggravate her position. She had resigned herself to waltzing in this macabre fashion until one of them caved in when a sharp voice pierced the rushing in her ears. 'Mike! What the hell's got into you?'

McCord! Thank heavens he was back. He strode across the room, an action which only served to tighten the grip of the thick arms around her, if this were possible. 'Mandy!— Mandy!—All I've got . . . all I've got in the world . . . !'

There was something tear-jerking in this semi-comatose baring of the soul. But McCord was anything but dewy-eyed. 'Get back in the chair, old son,' his voice was harsh with rebuke. 'I'm disappointed to find I can't leave you in the company of a lady for five minutes without—'

Mike reacted like a wild bull at the intrusion. 'Nobody comes between me and my li'l girl!'

'I wouldn't dream of it, Mike,' McCord began to extricate Celia from the elephantine grip with a hard smile. 'But this happens to be Miss Darwell, an employee of mine, and if you don't snap out of your daydreams I'm going to have to give you an unfriendly punch on the jaw!'

Something about his steely attitude must have got through to the befogged brain, for with a laugh of bravado which didn't quite mask another rending sob Mike reeled away and landed with unsteady precision back in his chair.

Celia was making good use of McCord's support, for the simple fact that the abrupt release from the tourniquet hold on her had sent the blood rushing to her head in a blinding pain.

'Are you okay?' McCord steadied her against him, feeling the trembling that Celia would have given anything to hold in check.

'I . . . think so,' she gave a shaky laugh. 'I'd hate to know the force of Mike's wholehearted affection!'

'Rest a while.' McCord eased her head against his shoulder, and as he kept an eye on the half-dozing figure in the chair he said, 'Drink does funny things to a man. Such behaviour is totally alien to Mike's nature in normal circumstances.'

'Is he... Mandy's father?' Celia ventured to ask.

McCord nodded. 'Michael Forbes Bennet. He's got a responsible position at the oilfields. It's been his life's work, and with his retirement to think of and a pension that's going to make him very comfortably off, he can't afford to mess things up at this stage.'

'Why should he want to do that?' Celia wondered aloud.

'That's the hell of it, I don't think he does.' McCord sighed heavily. 'His wife died fifteen months ago. He's taken it hard; sold up all he had—a smart villa over at Juffant among other things—and dug himself in here where he lives like a recluse apart from the stints he does at the oilfields. And these are becoming somewhat irregular, due to his penchant lately for turning to the bottle for release.'

Celia said, 'It upset him when he thought his daughter had paid him a visit, but why should it do that? Surely she would be a great help to him at a time like this.'

McCord shook his head. 'Mike's a proud man. Until he's got a grip on himself and learned to cope with reality, he'd rather Mandy stayed away.'

Yes, Celia had seen some of that pride showing even through the disfigurement of drunkenness. Her cheek lay against McCord's chest. She felt calmed in his embrace. And all at once the knowledge that Mike didn't want his daughter in Bahrain was somehow an infinitely comforting thought.

SHE AND McCord ended up having lunch with Mike. As Celia pointed out, he ought to have something inside him before going off to work, to combat the after-effects of alcohol. And once she had convinced McCord that she had suffered no real harm while he had been out of the house, he agreed it was a good idea. The only driver he'd been able to locate on the phone who was not out of town still had a refrigerated load to deliver across the causeway to Muharraq before he could come and pick Mike up for the oilfield, so there was time enough to arrange some sort of meal for him.

They rooted in the small kitchen together, McCord huge in yachting shirt and sailcloth slacks tossing out what he could find from the sparse food store. Celia found a linen kitchen apron for the front of her dress and for the three of them, she concocted a spread of bacon, egg and mushrooms, and segments of mandarins which McCord plucked from a tree in the courtyard.

It was really a very masculine meal, with hunks of American-baked bread which Celia cut purposely for the men, guessing that this was Mike's usual style of eating, with probably every meal coming out of the frying pan.

He had washed and changed before sitting down at the table and though he said little, preferring to coast along on the memory of an all-night binge, Celia felt that they could congratulate themselves that they had once again made an oil official of him. Frequently she met McCord's blue glance across the table or when they were making trips to and from the kitchen across the courtyard, and his bemused light at their joint domestic role, together with something else she couldn't quite fathom, added to her lighthearted feel.

The driver came just when the two of them were doing the dishes. They saw Mike into the car. 'You've got chauffeur service today, you old trouble-shooter,' McCord put an arm around the thick-set shoulders. 'And good luck with the top brass inspection this afternoon.'

'I'll soon put them in their place,' came the confident reply. 'And McCord—' Mike looked towards the doorway
from his open window, '—thanks.'

Celia knew that shyly he had included her in his gratitude, and with McCord she waved affectionately until the
car was lost in the maze of alleys.

It was something of an anticlimax when they turned back
indoors. And not only that but being alone with McCord in
a tiny mud dwelling which had its charm for all its masculine bareness was considerably different from being alone
with him in the clinically businesslike surroundings of the
office at the ice rink. It had to be, didn't it? with them
bumping into each other as they replaced washed pans and
items of crockery.

Celia would have been able to breathe a lot easier if he
had gone to put his feet up like any other man, but though
this was not his natural habitat, obviously, he seemed to
derive a certain amount of lazy contentment in handing her
the things she needed, or removing those which she discarded.

With feminine conscientiousness Celia felt that they
should leave everything as they found it. In fact, the little
living room and kitchen were spotless when she had finished, a state of affairs considerably improved since their
entry.

Eyeing her satisfied expression, McCord handed her her
handbag from where she had dropped it on a chair and
drawled, 'Ready for the boat trip now?'

'Can we still go?' Her heart leapt. Having spent half the
day with Mike she had assumed that the outing was off.

'I told the *nakoda*—or skipper to you—we'd be held up.'
He escorted her to the door. 'The *Sea Roc*'s in the harbour,
waiting for us to show up.'

Celia felt a new zest in his words. She had combed her hair and generally freshened up in the little bathroom, and with the whole afternoon before them it truly felt like a holiday.

McCord locked the door and put the key high up in a nearby window-nook. 'A little secret of Mike's,' he grinned. 'Though he could leave the door open here and nobody would touch a thing.'

'Do they still chop hands off out here for stealing?' Celia asked with grisly curiosity.

'In some places.' McCord handed her into the car with teasing unconcern, relenting only when her grey eyes widened horrifically to amend it with a laughing, 'But locally I don't think you're likely to see anything but a two-handed populace!'

He drove her car himself to the harbour. Aboard the *Sea Roc* Celia told herself she had to be dreaming. The ballooning red sail seemed to tower above her head and the creaking of its timbers as they rode out to sea gave her the feeling that she and McCord had stepped back a couple of centuries in time.

She wanted to laugh at her nonsense, and half did while viewing turban-clad crewmen in flapping trousers and colourful boleros showing sinewy, teak-skinned arms and chests.

Beside her at the rail McCord watched her changing expressions with lazy amusement. 'Believe it or not,' he said, 'the same sailing craft—roughly in design at least—still ply the Persian Gulf today as they did in the seventeenth century.'

'But with different cargoes, I bet,' Celia smiled, turning to join him in facing seawards.

'Not so different,' he shrugged mysteriously. 'Many still have dubious values—contraband gold, for instance.'

She looked at him to see whether he was joking. 'You don't mean these waters are infested with gold-runners!' And not sure what to make of him she added, 'I hope the *Sea Roc*'s not carrying a hold full of the stuff.'

He laughed. 'If it was it would be on the seabed by now! Gold isn't the lightest of metals to cart around.' He shook his head. 'No, we don't go in for precious cargoes…at least, not usually.'

His cryptic gleam as he looked at her made Celia rush on to cover the moment. 'Well, just what are you carrying?'

'If you really want to know I'm afraid it's going to put paid to all those romantic ideas you've been having about our picturesque transport.' He grinned crookedly. 'I have to confess that from the decks downwards the *Sea Roc* is anything but an Arab dhow in the old sense. Her holds are lined and fitted out with the most modern refrigerating equipment, and our cargo, I regret to add, is just mundane packages of frozen footstuffs.'

Celia gave a shout of laughter. Only McCord would be capable of ruining a perfectly good fairy-tale setting with his ubiquitous freezing methods! As her eyes danced at her thoughts they met his blue laughter and she was a little shaken to find herself on such intimate terms with her boss.

It had all started at Mike's house this morning, and if she wasn't careful she was going to have to come to the conclusion that McCord was not all high-geared businessman.

Gazing seawards after that was less disturbing, and viewing their passage over sun-gilded waters she had to remind herself that this was a semi-working trip. Heavens! She had almost forgotten Nevine and the real reason for this outing.

The scenery was magical. If the *Sea Roc* was pure twentieth century below decks nobody would have known, and under a sky like blue silk, its crystal light intensified by the deep peacock blue of the Gulf waters, the dhow sliced the waves as though commanded by Sinbad himself.

They had to sail southwards down the coast of the main state of Bahrain. From the sea the island seemed suspended in a shimmering veil out of which rose the mosques and minarets and mirage-like skyline of buildings, a disembodied cut-out silvered by the refracted rays of the desert sun.

Out at sea everything was blissfully cool. At this distance the low cliffs and escarpments of the passing coastline, the desolated sand flats with their lonely flights of seabirds were softened by the inner oasis of green and lush palm plantations, like an emerald in a rough pewter setting.

McCord pointed out to her the emergence of the Banabba islands, appearing like strips of desert that had inadvertently found themselves afloat in miles of sea. There were no skylines here, just thorn thickets as they approached and the odd Arab dwelling where scant shade offered some respite from the heat. Celia wondered if there was any point at all in coming this far in search of Nevine, but on arrival she was pleasantly surprised to find the scattering of a fishing community and a sturdy jetty along which the produce they had brought in the holds was soon finding its way on to dry land, transported by waiting refrigerated vans.

McCord had to spend some time generally overseeing the unloading of the stuff for outlying villages, and talking with drivers whose routes covered apparently the adjoining islands as well as this main one of Halab. Celia rested awhile in the cabin McCord had put at her disposal for the trip. Afterwards she bathed her face and arms in deliciously cool water coming from refrigerated supplies (naturally) and scorning make-up now that she had acquired a tan which made her eyes look startlingly grey in contrast, she smoothed her hair, noticing how the sun and sea wind had heightened its dusky barley colour, and went out.

McCord was waiting for her on deck. Judging by his expression he had something on his mind, but he didn't disclose what it was until they were walking along the jetty. Perhaps his idea was that the colourful surroundings of fishing dhows and black-shrouded women would offset her disappointment, for taking her arm he said with a dry grin, 'I'm afraid our trip ashore is going to be purely recreational. I've been checking around and no one in these parts appears to have heard of your Nevine.'

Celia stopped to look at him. She *was* disappointed and not a little puzzled. How could he be so sure when they had yet to set foot on land?

Answering the unspoken question in her eyes, he explained, moving on with her, 'I didn't mention it before, but I gave orders on the *Sea Roc*'s last trip here for each driver to make enquiries along his own route regarding the woman in question. As there are important deliveries to be made— special medical supplies mainly—to every populated spot in these islands you'll gather that they've covered the ground pretty thoroughly, and not one of them has anything to report that might help.'

Celia sighed. 'So Nevine *has* to be in Bahrain itself. It's funny, but that's what I've felt all along.'

'If she's not holed up with some ageing Saudi sheikh; still his favourite dancing girl though running to seed.'

Celia flashed him a look 'It might be a joke to you, but *I* happen to want very much to meet the woman who made such an impact on my father's life.'

'So I've noticed' McCord smiled tightly, his hand still gripping her arm as they walked.

The old discordant relationship was showing signs of surfacing and Celia felt a stab of unhappiness at the trend the conversation had taken. McCord had always shown an open impatience at her desire to turn back the clock thirty years in a land where differing customs made such a feat doubly difficult. Conversely it was *because* she was here in the Middle East and because the life style was so vastly different from her own that Celia felt the need to know the woman whose birthright this was.

She wouldn't expect anyone to understand her mixed up reasoning, least of all McCord, who dealt only with contemporary Bahrain and its new crop of businessmen.

'The sun will be down in half an hour.' He handed her into the air-conditioned interior of a small car obviously waiting there for his use. 'Meanwhile we'll tour the sights. What there are,' he added with morose humour.

The scenery seemed to match their mood at the moment; a rapid deterioration, Celia was sad to note, from the one in which they had started out earlier. How was it possible, she wondered, for the atmosphere to cloud over with such speed when only a moment before all had been smooth?

CHAPTER NINE

CELIA GAVE her attention to the views, as bleak as her thoughts. They had left the pocket of activity at the jetty and now there was nothing but a rough shoreline and a dusty mud village in the distance. Feeling that some comment was expected of her, Celia asked, 'How on earth do the inhabitants survive, marooned in a place like this? There doesn't appear to be any industry apart from the boats.'

McCord shrugged. 'Since the palmy days of pearl fishing there's nothing much to keep anyone here. Your guess is as good as mine what they do with their time, or how they make it pay.'

'Pearl fishing!' The very sound of this, the most romantic of occupations, lightened the atmosphere fractionally and Celia, bent on pursuing it, suggested brightly, 'Perhaps it still pays in a small way in these parts, even today.'

'I wouldn't be surprised.' McCord was noncommittal, much to her mild exasperation. He probably knew to the last man what they did locally, but for some reason was not going to expand. However, he did enlarge on the pearling industry generally, and as they crawled, as a way of passing the time, beside the lacy surf of the sea's edge, she listened fascinated.

'It may sound colourful, but it's always been a tough way of making a living,' McCord told her. 'Less than one third of every catch in the old days produced pearls of any value. You could say that the entire Gulf fleet never contributed to more than a couple of the type of necklaces seen on the Edwardian women of the day, in one season.'

'Can one find pearl oysters just anywhere in these waters?' Celia asked.

'Not usually.' McCord avoided a pile of fish traps at the side of the track. 'Oyster beds shift with the tides or after a certain period of time. Sometimes they yield a harvest of good market value. On the other hand, banks have been known to be sterile for years. None of them are charted. The *nakhoda,* the skipper of each craft, has his own theories on where the best pickings are, and what he knows he keeps to himself. There are trade secrets handed down in families.'

Celia mused on this and said with a dreamy smile, 'I wonder if Tariq knows any of these trade secrets? I bet he does.'

'Tariq?' McCord's smile had a faint twist to it. But Celia was too taken up with her own ponderings to notice. It came to her with a mild shock that she hadn't given a thought to the likeable young Arab all day, or felt the slightest compunction at leaving him high and dry when they had had a kind of loose arrangement to spend the day together.

After but a fleeting twinge she said lightly, 'Of course! He's bound to have some idea of where the productive beds are to be found, even to this day, as he's descended from a pearl merchant family. He knows a lot about them. He once told me that his grandfather—or whoever it was—believed that the finest and densest white pearls came from deep water, and those tinted with colour were shallow water yields.' Celia gave a small laugh. 'Although I'll admit Tariq is the least likely of pearl fishers!'

'Why do you say that?' McCord's taut smile lingered.

As far as Celia was concerned the question was superfluous. 'Can you imagine the sophisticated Tariq in ragged turban and swimming dhoti poised on the bow of a pearling dhow?' she said with amusement.

McCord kept his gaze on the rough route. 'Would he appeal to you in that guise?' he asked lazily.

'Appeal to *me*?' Celia was floored by the question. But considering, she laughed. 'I have to admit, no. Despite all my romantic notions about the East I like Tariq as he is. His Westernised business air and mode of dress suits him, although he does have a kind of dashing charm when he puts on one of these burnous things that he sometimes wears, don't you think?'

'I wouldn't know.' McCord brought the car to a stop in the village and clamped on the brakes. 'It takes a woman's eyes to fantasise. A man only sees fact.'

'What a dull time you all must have!' Celia carped, aware by the grip on her arm as he helped her from the car that the conversation had done nothing to ease the antagonistic mood that persisted between them.

However, the scant increase in scenic detail created a diversion. The mud village fronted the beach where goats scavenged among the fish traps. White donkeys idled outside some of the dwellings like privileged members of the family and black-shrouded Arab women busy with outside chores dropped everything like so many black beetles scuttling for cover when they saw McCord's masculine figure approaching.

But there was one dwelling where the reception was different. An elderly Arab almost as tall as McCord emerged from the interior, and though he was roughly clad, he had something of a village-head authority about him. He clasped McCord's hand in his own sun and sea-weathered mahogany one and the two men greeted each other warmly in Arabic.

'Mahmoud is a friend of mine.' McCord drew Celia forward to introduce her to the headman. 'There's nothing he doesn't know about transport in the Gulf. He proved a great help when I was buying the two dhows I own now.'

Though the women of the household had beaten a hasty retreat they were sternly commanded to provide tokens of hospitality for the guests, and rugs and cushions were brought out and arranged with shifty movements beside the doorway where a cool pitcher of goat's milk and rough goblets had been placed on a low stand, itself centred on a ceremonial remnant of tattered carpet.

Traditionally the men sat to one side discussing trade and local commercial trends—at least that was what Celia presumed, as all Arabs appeared to have an avid interest in these topics. For herself she was glad of some small respite from the overpowering effect of McCord's company. It wasn't as though they had said or done a lot since leaving Manama at lunch time, and yet she felt curiously drained as though she had been battling with some unseen force that at times had threatened to carry her along on wings and now fomented the air between them.

But for the moment, with cushions at her back against the cool wall of the mud dwelling, she felt strangely rested. In the silvered light of dusk the sea mirrored the tranquil opaque sky and the sable masts of fishing craft, and distant dhows were stencilled against the fading brightness of day. Her nostrils caught the clean scent of the sea's waft before it was lost in the exuding warmth and distinct odour of the Arab village.

As the shadows lengthened she relaxed, watching where the men sat conversing in rapid Arabic, McCord's less than white smile stirring her in an odd way. She wondered about him, about his younger days, and what it was that had led him to carve a life for himself out here in the Middle East.

But these were questions one didn't ask a man like Mc-Cord. His eyes were wont to reflect his ice-like approach both to life as well as his profession, although of late when he had looked at her... She shrugged mentally. The slight thawing could only mean that he found her a useful component in the workings of his complex business schemes.

In crude lighting the evening meal of the Arab household was served as appeared to be customary out of doors. The women didn't eat in McCord's presence, but as faceless bundles they bustled out with cooking pots and serving dishes, departing with phantom speed when all was prepared. Celia was left to cope as the *infidel* she was in the added masculine presence of sons and nephews who had come home after a day's work at the harbour. Seated at the low table, she had the sinking feeling that she was going to be swamped in the lusty exchanges delivered in the local tongue. But then a pleasant surprise came her way, for Ismael, the oldest son of the household, had heard McCord introducing her in English and below the harsh babble of his relatives he tried a few broken sentences of the half-forgotten language.

'Once I work for oil peoples in Iran,' he told her. 'But it is not my like. The...this how you say with the nose?...*afwan,* the smell. Ugh! I think that to its compare fish is not so bad.'

Ismael had a big black beard and a wicked sense of humour which didn't go at all with the biblical air he evoked in rough robes. His relatives looked on, envious of his ability to bring a smile to Celia's lips and sometimes shy laughter. McCord gave her an enigmatic look during the meal, though she was doing nothing but politely satisfying a healthy hunger with the food which, despite its strangeness, was good. While he was looking at her she had a better view than he had of Mahmoud, the head of the household, whose eyes, twinkling greatly, were musing on McCord's preoccupation with his son Ismael rather than the food.

There were cinnamon squares, poppyseed bonbons and almond cakes to round off the meal; delicacies whipped up at a moment's notice by the servile black bundles, Celia suspected. And as an added honour to the guests Mahmoud brought out a bottle of Pharaoh's wine from his hoard of foreign treasures, reserved for such occasions.

As their religion forbade the drinking of wine, it was Celia and McCord alone who clinked glasses; an oddly intimate gesture amidst the noisy approval of the masculine audience.

The electric blue of the sky and the yellow glow from the crude lamps lit the friendly faces of the Mahmoud Ali Mirza family as Celia and McCord finally took their leave. She shook Ismael's big hand demurely and the rest of his brothers and cousins lined up—some eight or nine of them—to indulge at least in this one Western custom. Her hand somewhat bruised, Celia turned laughingly last of all to Mahmoud, who gave her the old-fashioned salaam instead, but his eyes were gentle and musing and he wished her well, she was sure, in his softly spoken Arabic as she joined up with McCord for the walk back to the car.

She felt that those wise, twinkling eyes followed the two of them for long enough before turning back to the house glow and family matters.

On the ride back to the jetty McCord said with his McCord smile, 'You made a hit with Ismael.'

'His English was hilarious, but he was so nice and unaffected I couldn't let him see that I was amused at anything but his jokes,' said Celia with a comical expression.

It was lost on McCord, whose eyes glinted out into the night.

The *Sea Roc,* its loading and unloading completed, was waiting to set sail when they arrived. On deck later Celia felt choked at the beauty of the evening, the turquoise radiance of the night sky silhouetting the glamorous lines of their transport, the sea like black satin beneath them, reflecting stars that were like dancing fireflies on the heaving calm. It was warmer now than it had been earlier with the sparkling sea-winds, but it was a velvet caress on the skin, made pleasant by nocturnal breezes singing close to the waves.

Celia thought she would die with the exquisite pain of witnessing such beauty—a ridiculous frame of mind, she told herself wryly when McCord was standing beside her at the rail with hardly a look of appreciation on his face. Or at least maybe he was aware of the magic but preferred his usual phlegmatic approach to it all. No, that wasn't right either. Celia gave up trying to analyse the man at her side. She had been doing it most of the afternoon and finding herself deeper in a mesh of irritations and uncertainties at his nearness.

He was the first to speak when they had been sailing for a good twenty minutes, and by the sound of it they might well have been back at the dark beach side, for his opening words were still linked with the brief conversation that had taken place in the car.

'I can see the wisdom of the Arabs in keeping their women segregated,' his steely reflections were delivered more to the ocean than to her. 'Males of any creed tend to be males when exposed to their mating opposites.'

Celia felt the familiar knot of unease burgeoning in her as she replied tensely, 'We don't all regard our opposite numbers as mating potentials. It is possible to have entertaining conversation with the opposite sex without giving the gender a thought.'

'Like you and Ismael, for instance?' McCord's tones were hardened and sardonic. 'You've got to be naïve if you didn't notice the way he looked at you with those "entertaining" black eyes of his.'

'As a matter of fact I did,' Celia felt moved to reply. 'But it does make a change, once in a while, to be treated as something other than a useful fixture in a working combine.' She didn't know why she had come out with that. It was not what she had intended to say. Not at all.

McCord's smile was goadingly masculine. 'The Arabs are never likely to see a woman anyway but for what she's intended.'

Celia felt her cheeks flame. 'Your opinion of them in this field is so low I wonder you've been able to put up with them all these years,' she flung at him. 'Or is it because you're a male yourself you can ride this lamentable fluke in their character?'

'It has its advantages being a man in a place like this.'

'Of course, a man will see that it has!' she was not slow to retort, hinting with distaste at his own party habits where there was no shortage of feminine partners. 'While the womenfolk are expected to remain tucked away in the background, serving useful purposes like back-breaking house labourers, and passive bed-mates. Well, that might be fine for the men here, but if I were one of their ladies I wouldn't stick it for five minutes.'

'The passive bed-mate bit...or the back-breaking chores?' McCord had turned her way and his eyes were lit with a mixture of steely humour and stringent amusement.

'You can laugh if you like.' Celia lifted her chin at him. 'Suffice to say I have no intention of donning the black robe of submission while I'm in Bahrain. As far as I'm concerned the unattached Bahrainis are every bit as entertaining as any Englishman, and as there's no law against it I

shall have as many Arab friends as I like.' She felt breathless after her self-assertive splurge. She had started off defending the downtrodden Arab women and somehow ended
up flaunting the emancipation of her own kind.

It was an attitude that McCord was in no mood to toler-
ate. He grabbed her suddenly in a hold that transmitted
something of the fury of his gaze with its roughness. 'That's
fighting talk,' his smile had a grim curl to it, 'when you
think you came pretty close to being landed with an Arab
for the rest of your life.'

Kamel! Oh yes, it was obvious where his thoughts lay.

'I was a beginner then,' she tried to shake off his hold,
'But you can rest assured I know my way around now.'

His answer to this was to wrench her close to him so that
her feet barely touched the ground. 'While you're under my
protection,' he ground out, 'you'll comport yourself like a
decent British expatriate. And any talk will be the friendly
kind and nothing else.'

'I told you once before, McCord, you don't own me!'
Celia was quivering at these petty bickering exchanges. It
was both laughable and excruciatingly tearful to find one-
self saying the first crazy thing that came into one's head.
How, she wanted to know, had they got into this emotional
upheaval? It was like a giant force that certainly didn't come
from the ultra-calm of the Gulf waters, but its spell was such
that she felt helpless in its momentum.

'No, but I own your time, or most of it.' McCord's darkened gaze blazed down at her. 'And you'll tread carefully
where the Arabs are concerned. That's an order from me.'

All this because Ismael had looked at her in an over-
friendly fashion! What did he think? That every encounter
was going to be another Kamel? It was true she had warily
been of that opinion herself once, but, hardly in the mood
to admit this now, she flashed. 'I'm not one of your ice-

boxes! There's a little more to me than frosted wiring and obedient switches!'

While his face was dark with some inner emotion at her self-willed obstinacy there was a twitch of bemusement around his mouth as he held her panting frame against him. 'Nevertheless,' he bit out, 'you will do as I say and keep clear of the womanising Arabs.'

'I'll do as I please!' Angry breath mingling with angry breath. Celia was reminded of another time, another place—the compressor room at McCord's freezing plant. Was it only yesterday that they had collided head-on, with the same mouth to mouth, body to body clash of wills? Tonight's episode had spiralled out of petty disagreements that were too stupid to recall, but there was a matching choking defiance on her side and the same odd-lit determination on his.

How would it end? Celia had no intention of capitulating this time. There was no lever now that McCord could wrench her from with his brute force. But it was odd too how that same suspended feel froze the moment.

Above her pounding heart she wanted to laugh bitterly at her choice of adjectives. Could anything be more apt where McCord was concerned?... although less ice-like she had never seen him. In fact there was a molten look in his eyes dominating her view now.

Rebellion in every quivering part of her, she matched fire for fire there, then suddenly the moment exploded with his mouth crashing down on hers.

Celia was stunned like a trapped bird. But it was a rosy kind of imprisonment, for a radiance out-glowing angry sparks spread through her, travelling along her veins like quicksilver at McCord's touch. McCord! How often had she wondered what his party partners experienced in his arms? McCord! Who was not just any man when it came to driving his point home, she had long since suspected, and was now patently convinced.

His kiss was fierce, his embrace relentless, and while she inwardly cursed the puniness of her woman's frame, something sang secretly somewhere, the joys of knowing such an affliction. Her thoughts driving out all opposition, she *was* in danger of surrendering; dizzily, drowningly in danger of giving herself to those savagely demanding lips, to his arms which strained her so close she felt almost a part of his being. Perhaps she did. The urge to give as well as receive was powerfully sweet, and for a moment she became two Celias; one snatching the fruits of clandestine fulfilment, the other fighting to be free of all that was potently desirable.

When she saw the stars again it was to vaguely discover that McCord had raised his head. And just as abruptly, while she was still swaying from the effect, he let her go.

It was some time before she could find her voice, and when she did it sounded quaveringly unreal in her ears. 'Why did you do that?' she demanded, while every part of her cried out for him to do it again.

'For a variety of reasons.' His face was peculiarly inscrutable in the star glow, as though it had been an out-and-out demonstration that he was the superior being in more than the employer-employee sense of the word. Then he tacked on, 'The main one being that for a long time I've watched you frenziedly digging up the past, trying to unearth a mouldered love when it's your own life you should be thinking of. I just thought I'd give you a sample of what today's living is all about.'

So that was it! She had known all along, of course, that he detested her preoccupation with Nevine and a life long gone, and tightly she replied, 'Frenzied is hardly the word I would apply to a series of dead-ends revealing absolutely nothing of what I came in search for.'

'And that's not surprising,' was his clipped rejoinder. 'When are you going to realise that your father's dead and gone, and that what took place in his lifetime can have little bearing on your own?'

Celia tasted his kiss on her lips and said shakily, 'You've got very odd ways of putting your views across.'

'Would you rather it had been Tariq who woke you up to your own existence as opposed to mooning over your dreams of the past?' he sneered.

They were back to the Arabs again. A favourite theme of his. And Tariq—where did he fit into this discussion?

A pulse hammering in her throat, Celia fired back, 'He might have been less overbearing at the job.'

'Of course, and under the Kuwait stars too!'

Kuwait! How did he know that they had intended to hop a plane in true reckless Arab fashion? She was perplexed, then suddenly the mist cleared and she knew that he had overheard Tariq making the suggestion that night in the shadows of the deserted rink.

Something else hit her then and it was like a boulder bruising her heart as she asked, 'That couldn't be the reason why you suddenly got the urge to forfeit your time to go to the Banabba islands, could it? Tariq and I had a holiday day lined up. But you suddenly came up with other plans; semi-working ones, I seem to recall was how you termed it.'

McCord shrugged, his face shrouded in shadow. 'I did take advantage of the fact that you were work-beholden to me. I like to keep my employees toeing the line wherever possible.'

'In this case, by closing down the rink, so that Tariq was left high and dry without an explanation.'

'As I say, I like to keep a close-circuit watch on all that concerns the smooth running of my particular terrain.'

Celia bit her lip in the shadows, not with anger now, but with a horrible hurt which was stealing over her. The whole day long some part of her had rejoiced at the knowledge that McCord had offered her his services in the search for Nevine—true, he had carried this faithfully through albeit with no results, and even made it something of a memorable occasion—but all the time it had been nothing more than a ruse to outwit Tariq, nothing more than an excuse for McCord to keep her possessively within the bounds of his business domain.

She saw it all now. Ismael...Kamel...this heated discussion had all been building up to a showdown over Tariq. And McCord's disapproval of her association with the young Arab whom she had grown to like tremendously over these past weeks even outweighed, she was sure, his dislike of her meddling with the past and Nevine.

The tears filled her eyes, the stupid hurt wouldn't go. But she was not that far gone that she couldn't dig deep for something to fling back. 'You fight dirty, Mr. McCord,' she smiled through her tears. 'But then, with your own love life cut up at the moment, your Mandy Bennet, the true star of the show, off the scene as it were, you've got to have your little diversions, I suppose.'

His own mouth twisted, probably at the brightness in her eyes, and harshly he came back with, 'I'll admit life would be a ball if she were around.'

'Well, contrary to your tactics,' she said with brittle exactness, 'you can be sure there'll be no interference from me if that happy day should ever occur.'

'Sore because I messed up your date with Tariq?' His smile was sharp as he looked at her.

'Oh, leave me alone!' She spun away and stumbled below to her cabin, where she stayed for the remainder of the trip. There were more grinding hurts to contend with now, mainly in the shape of Mandy Bennet, and she preferred to come to terms with them on her own.

McCord had made no secret of the fact that he missed the girl whose photograph hung in his office. Why had she, Celia, momentarily let herself assume anything else? It was obvious, wasn't it, that he wouldn't show the concern he did for Mike if he wasn't emotionally involved with the family in some way. And it *was* concern. She knew now that his preoccupation at the hotel pool when he had come to see her yesterday had been for Mike. And when a man goes to the lengths of keeping affectionate tabs on a faltering father, she told herself, as McCord was doing with Michael Bennet, it had to be because he was deeply in love with the daughter.

Celia listened to the creaking timbers and muffled swish of their passage over the waves with a crushing despondency. It had to come some time. McCord, who had never given more than a fraction of himself in the game of love, was now willing to relegate his hard-won professional status and business ambitions to second place for a woman. And that woman was Mandy Bennet.

The *Sea Roc* docked at last and Celia made her own way ashore. Fortunately her car was parked where they had left it on embarking. Wasting no time, she started up and hurtled off alone into the darkness back to the Gulf Hotel.

CHAPTER TEN

MCCORD HAD said that she would have no more trouble with the ice, and he was as good as his word. Every day it shone now with the hard, smooth, glass-like surface that is perfect for skate blades.

It was odd not to have anything to complain about. There was no cause for her to go stalking across the alley to the compressor room. And even when she had to go with the valid excuse of seeking McCord's signature for an office chit, it was always to find the regular compressor technician in charge, who would politely tuck the chit into a pocket until the boss called.

But busy as he was with other projects, McCord made his usual unannounced appearances in the ice rink. Not that Celia, in this case, showed any awareness of his presence. His kiss still burned her lips and would always do in her mind, she knew. As would the knowledge that his fierce embrace had been merely a clinical reminder that one couldn't spend one's time submerged in the past. No, life could be shatteringly overwhelming at first hand, she had discovered.

But she had her work; the children's rehearsals were coming along wonderfully. She also had Tariq's soothing companionship to take her mind off the unsettling Mc-Cord. They had quickly sorted out the confusion over the ruptured date. 'I was surprised to find the ice rink all closed up,' Tariq told her, disappointment in his smile as he referred back to that night. 'I called at your hotel the next morning, but they said you were out.'

'McCord felt that he couldn't go on taking the customers' moncy with the ice as bad as it was,' Celia explained lamely. 'Apparently he regarded the public holiday as strictly a Bahraini affair, so we had a kind of...semi-working day.'

'I shall impose upon you to put matters to rights by having dinner with me tonight.' There had been humour in Tariq's dark eyes as he had held her close on the ice.

'I'd like to very much, Tariq,' she had laughed up at him.

It was a relief to coast along on the undemanding gentleness of the young Bahraini's nature, after knowing the forceful, chaotic nearness of McCord, and Celia fell into the habit of dining with him most evenings, sometimes in the upstairs restaurant, others at some exclusive spot in town. On these occasions she would bring something feminine to slip into after work, and they would leave arm in arm for the outdoors and Tariq's fabulously expensive motor car.

Part of her knew that she was going all out to show McCord that she made up her own mind regarding what company she would keep. But another part of her was aware that Tariq was dangerously attractive, besides having a charming and uncomplicated personality. There was only one hint that unknown currents of passion and feeling flowed beneath the surface of that dark-eyed serenity, and that was one evening when they had met to dine at a famed night-spot.

For some reason, perhaps because it went well with the dress she was wearing, Celia had fastened Kamel's pendant necklace around her throat.

'What is that?' Tariq spotted it straight away, his dark eyes hardening as though he recognised it as local merchandise.

'A little gift that one of McCord's employees bought me... oh, quite a while ago.' Celia fingered it lightly.

'Take it off at once! It is cheap and tawdry. I will not have it tainting your loveliness with its nondescript value.'

'But, Tariq, it's just a trinket... and after all...' With a gesture of impatience he turned her to get at the fastening himself and afterwards flung the offending necklace into the gutter with the words, as he guided her to his car, 'We will see who knows best in the matter of your adornment.'

She was not wearing a low-necked dress, and apart from a slight pang when thinking of Kamel's joy in presenting her with it, Celia didn't miss the necklace during the evening, or for that matter at all. The incident had completely faded from her mind, only to be vividly unearthed one night in the car when Tariq presented her with a velvet jewel-case containing the most exquisite string of pearls she had ever seen.

She sat gazing at them for a full stunned minute before exclaiming, 'Tariq, they're... lovely! But I couldn't possibly wear them. They must be worth a fortune!'

'Were my ancestors not in the pearling business?' he remarked with a smile that deliberately ignored her perplexed state. 'And you see cleverness runs in the family, for only pearls of such quality can do justice to the opalescent smoothness of your skin.' He fastened the clasp under her hair and gazing long at her he said, 'Wear them for me, Celia. Wear them as a token of our precious friendship and,' he brushed his lips against her wrist, 'of our growing affection.'

Celia didn't see how she could refuse after that. To have done so would have hurt Tariq cruelly, she knew. But it was no easy task to secrete valuable pearls in her dressing locker at the rink, so that she could don them for Tariq's benefit later in the evening.

Work and leisure went with a swing. She could even chat coolly to McCord in Tariq's presence, for the two men were good friends and neither allowed Celia to interfere with this; though McCord's eyes when they met hers had a way of saying things that didn't match the pleasant words he mouthed, and in their blue depths she was conscious of a kind of hard light.

She had so little to do with him these days it ought to have been easy enough to put him out of her mind. Yet it was strange how she sensed, one day, that all was not as it should be in the McCord scheme of things. She supposed subconsciously she had begun to take note of his moment of arrival at the rink and the hour of his departure. Whether it was through the day or in the evening, she had to admit she had grown practised in piecing together the pattern of his coming and going, and knew to a moment now when he would show up.

It was certainly no concern of hers when he failed to put in an appearance at all for three whole sessions. And when there was nothing to be seen of him, if only in an ostensibly distant fashion, the next day, she cynically put it down to excess of work. His various freezing concessions around the town were all-demanding, she knew, as well as the mountain of paper-work which had to be presided over from time to time in the office premises integrated in his desert house.

Just the same, the ache of something not right about the days wouldn't be stilled in her, and one afternoon, using a broken piston on the skate grinder as a reason for visiting the compressor room, she looked around for the familiar big frame, the sight of which could somehow jerk at her heart strings.

But there was only Aziz, the trained technician in attendance. 'But I must see McCord,' Celia insisted, after being fobbed off with the usual reply that the boss was not available. 'The skate grinder is a very important piece of equipment. We've got to have some kind of guidance as to ways of getting it fixed.'

The technician considered. 'I should ring up a local engineering shop. It might be quicker than trying to get in touch with the boss.'

'Quicker?' Celia was both puzzled and impatient. 'What do you mean by that? I could ring him myself if I had his number.'

'Not this number,' Aziz smiled. 'Haven't you heard? Mr. McCord has gone to Cairo. I'm sorry, but I have no idea when he'll be back.'

'Cairo!' Celia realised she must have sounded shocked, so quickly she tempered her exclamation with a weakly smiling, 'Ah well, I expect the engineering shop will be best,' and left.

But how she got back across the street she never recalled. Cairo! Cairo! Wasn't that where Mandy Bennet had been working all these weeks? Blind to all but her own thoughts, she found herself back in the rink; a rink that no longer had the reassuring, if annoying, feel of McCord's presence in the background.

Why had he gone to Cairo? As if she didn't know. She blinked back a brightness in her eyes. It was crazy to feel this shattered just because her boss had decided to renew his love life. But she did.

Not even Tariq with his increasing attentiveness could help her to surmount the blackest period of her life, though of course she gave no indication outwardly that all was not as it should be.

She went about her business at the ice rink with a serenity that might have been in danger of cracking if it hadn't been for Tariq's nearness. He was extremely handsome and likeable, she told herself, whereas McCord was craggy, overbearing, arrogant—and she missed him!

But all things pass, or so Celia hoped. Moving close to Tariq in the subdued lighting of some modern discotheque or viewing the moonlit waters of the Gulf with him, she was at last living her own life. And at least McCord would have approved of that, wouldn't he?

She had stopped counting the days of the ice rink's drifting without that certain central force, like a ship without a helmsman; though she, like the rest of McCord's underlings, were well trained by now, Celia conjectured wryly. They all functioned like clockwork with or without his vital presence. And it was like him to reappear after several days' absence, unannounced as usual, as though to bask in the knowledge that he had a well-oiled staff.

He blew in—Celia could think of no better way to sum up his entry—one evening when she was standing with Tariq in the fairly crowded coffee lounge. There was still a good half of the session to go, but as always at this late hour no one had any use for her talents as an instructress, so she was spending the time until they closed, as she often did, in Tariq's company.

He greeted his friend effusively. 'McCord! When did you get back?'

'A short while ago.' A tight grin accompanied the reply. Only minutes by the look of it, Celia thought. He looked travel-weary, or was that a deep-down weariness in his eyes? There was no knowing, for the light in them when he glanced her way was challengingly intense as always.

Her own gaze, she hoped, showed none of the lack-lustre detachment it had acquired during his absence. If it was mildly aglow now it was, of course, because she found Tariq's chat so amusing.

'How was Cairo?' he asked, ordering another coffee at the bar. So Tariq knew about McCord's visit to the Egyptian capital. He probably knew also, as the two men were in each other's confidence, that Mandy Bennet was the reason for the trip.

'Great as always,' she heard McCord replying easily. 'The Midan el Tahir—or should I say Liberation Square—right beside the Nile, was a sight for sore eyes. I had trouble with a hotel booking and had to transfer to the Nile Hilton, but the view more than made up for the misunderstanding...'

Afraid that he was going to get too poetic about his activities, Celia cut in, 'Do you know Cairo, Tariq?'

'But yes,' he smiled, showing his pearly teeth. 'We have shipping offices in the city. Also I have numerous relatives on the east bank. My mother is of Egyptian blood, so our family ties with the country are extensive.' He put an arm round her waist and added, 'You must make the trip with me some time, and meet my Egyptian cousins.'

'I'd like to very much, Tariq,' Celia said for McCord's benefit. He might have spiked her last proposed trip abroad with Tariq, and that was a hint to say that he was not likely to be successful a second time. Her smile said as much. It was scorched momentarily by McCord's flame-throwing, if lazy, blue glance, but there was nothing in his smile to give her the satisfaction she had hoped for in making the remark.

In fact there was nothing at all about him that would give her a clue as to what he had been up to in Cairo. It was galling to have to admit that she was eaten up with curiosity. Why had he made a visit to Cairo at such short notice? To see Mandy? Well, obviously. But was a few days of her company sufficient to console him against her continued absence in Bahrain? How Celia ached to know. And how

difficult it was to have to put on an indifferent front when
McCord was so aggravatingly noncommittal about it all.

She wished now she hadn't stopped him at the beginning, but knowing him he had probably had no intention of
giving them more than a descriptive account of the sea-
sonal splendours of the city, as he was doing now.

HE LEFT before the rink closed, to catch up on some much-
needed sleep, Celia suspected. Or to withdraw to his desert
domain with his recent memories of being alone with Mandy
in an exciting capital like Cairo. The thought ruined the rest
of the evening for Celia, but she was careful not to spoil
things for Tariq, and gave not a hint in her manner that
dinner together at the Holiday Inn night club was not the
best one she had ever had.

She was keyed up all the next day, knowing that the businesslike McCord would have to call in sooner or later to
check on the backlog of order and delivery slips that had
built up in the ice rink office. Though she told herself she
was well prepared for his visit, his arrival when she was just
preparing for the opening of the evening session set her
nerves twanging, and made a knot of the suppressed emotion in her stomach.

His coming made not the slightest difference to her
changing routine, for she only had to replace her shoes with
ice skates. While McCord leafed casually through the chits,
signing one here and there where it was necessary, she busied herself at her locker, making a great show of ignoring
him.

But perhaps her fingers trembled slightly at the charged
atmosphere which always blew up like a sand-storm whenever they were together in the office, for the pearls she was
privately transferring from her handbag to a hidden cavity

in the locker suddenly slithered from her grasp and went clattering across the tiled floor.

Of course McCord would have to get there first, and retrieving them he hung on to them annoyingly with a musing, 'Well, well, well!' as he examined them. Obviously aware of their value, he looked sharply quizzical as he looked at her. 'You're taking a chance, aren't you,' he said, 'leaving your expensive tokens around in a populated place like the ice rink?'

'They're a gift from Tariq,' Celia felt impelled to labour the point carelessly.

'Of course, the pearl fisher himself.'

Did he *have* to refer to their romantic interlude on the blue Gulf waters?

'He absolutely insists that I wear them for our dates after work,' she shrugged, 'so what can I do?'

McCord had moved nearer. She didn't think he looked refreshed after his break from business. If anything he appeared more drawn, or was it his taut smile as he spoke which gave this effect? 'Any more priceless acquisitions I suggest you give to me to put in the office safe. We're likely to have a stampede if you go on hawking them around like everyday trinkets.'

'I'll think about it.' Celia put on a considering look. 'I do think there's a certain taint attached, don't you, to locking away one's personal possess—'

She got no further in her blithe small talk, for McCord had grabbed her to him with a force reminiscent of that night on the deck of the *Sea Roc,* and in menacing tones he bit out, 'You little idiot! When are you going to learn that you're playing with fire, and in the end it's going to be more than those lovely eyelashes of yours that are going to get singed?'

Her heart raced, close to him once again, her whole being rejoiced in his nearness, while her mind supplied her with the cool reply, 'Aren't you over-dramatising things somewhat? I thought Tariq was your friend?'

'He's one of the best I've got, but he's an Arab, a Bedouin, and their ways are not our ways.'

'Our ways!' Celia lifted a disparaging eyebrow. 'You have your ways, McCord, and I have mine. And by the way, how was Mandy when you called on her in Cairo?'

'Very well, as far as I know.'

As far as he *knew!* What kind of a reply was that? Niggled, she felt the need to ascertain, 'You did drop everything and catch a plane, just to go and talk with her, didn't you?'

'That's right, I did.' Everything in her prayed that she had got it wrong somewhere. But McCord's smiling reply, plus the breeziness with which he backed it up, left her with nothing but her superior confidence where Tariq was concerned. As she defiantly put all this into her attitude, locked as she was in McCord's arms, and he arrogantly made it clear that Mandy was uppermost in *his* mind, the sandstorm was in danger of becoming laced with sheet lightning.

But as it happened the only flashes were the flickering of neon lights beyond the office as staff, opening the rink to the public, went round pressing switches. On view from outside now, McCord quickly let Celia go, and trembling more than she cared to show, she turned at once to the task of donning her skate-boots.

If she could have got them on in record time, nothing would have pleased her more than to make a haughty exit leaving McCord to it in the office. But her limbs were weak, and there were more surprises in store.

She had only just got the right boot laced up when she sensed some kind of commotion in the office doorway. Head bent over her task, that was the only way she could describe it, a sort of excited rustling of air, a quivering, laughing force that compelled her to raise her head just as the whirlwind was gusting in.

'Hi, folks, I made it! I skated all the way! No, don't believe that. How could I with these pesky deserts outside every town? Gee, the heat! But oh, the Bahrainis! Can I come in?'

Celia raised herself, riveted at the altogether stage entrance of the girl whose likeness hung on the wall. She would never have believed it possible, but the lovely picture that had tormented her all these weeks was actually insipid compared to the real thing.

Mandy Bennet was five foot something of mercurial womanhood, with laughing hazel eyes and thick, tumbling wavy hair of gleaming copper which on anyone else would have looked slinky, but the fresh almost countrified features toned it down to just plain beauty. She had a figure, clothed at the moment in hip-hugging jeans and frilly top, that no woman should be obliged to contemplate, and a wholly unfeline air that evoked admiration rather than envy.

The shutter of Celia's mind had taken this in, in a fraction of a second, for there was no pausing for breath with this effervescent creature, as she was to find, and in the next one she had hurtled into the room straight into McCord's arms, the attractive American drawl all over him. 'Kent! Garsh, it's good to see you! I got your message and came as soon as I could.'

Kent! Celia viewed McCord with studied irony where he was almost lost in the tumbling tresses. So he did have something as lowly and purely mortal as a Christian name after all! His answering immodest glint held hers momentarily, then Mandy was turning in his arms like a tawny tornado to explain, 'Heck, I'm sorry I wasn't in Cairo when you came. We'd just started off on a local tour... but I expect they told you that at the digs. I was in El Faiyum, as a matter of fact. You know the sheikhs are crazy to see us flip around on the ice. But if you have to do a solo stint in some official gathering they expect you to make like a tent on skates in the regulation caftan. Can you imagine!'

Her laughter was light as candyfloss which could quickly melt to self-reproach, and with her curving red lips smooching against McCord's cheek, she was, in the next breath, all apology. 'What hellish luck, you coming all the way to Cairo to see me. Was it too awful, honey?'

'As a matter of fact, no,' McCord grinned after he had held her close enough for long enough, heaven knew, Celia thought. 'I managed to fill in the time in a professional capacity. There's no shortage of work as an ice-engineer in a city like Cairo.'

Of course not, and how typically McCord-like to fit business in somewhere. His love life had suffered a temporary setback with Mandy missing from the scene, but he had made good use of the time, and she was here now, obviously as keen to be with him as he was to be with her.

Celia bolstered her plummeting spirits with bright thoughts of her own Arab boy-friend. Well, they would make a striking foursome—Mandy and McCord, and herself and Tariq.

'Oh, what a tactless screwy I am!' Celia realised that this bubbling contrition was for her ears. 'Please forgive me for hogging McCord like this. I'm always forgetting my manners.'

'This is Celia Darwell, who took over the job you were going to do,' McCord made the introductions. 'Miss Darwell, meet Amanda Bennet of world-wide skating fame.'

'Ignore the showbiz plug,' the coppery radiance said with a merry gleam. 'And McCord knows I'm Mandy to all my friends.'

Celia had expected a formal handshake, but discovered instead her cheek brushing the other girl's as she was given a friendly hug. Her warmth was catching and Celia found herself saying, and meaning it, 'Welcome to the Alhambra, Mandy. I hope you'll have many happy skating days here.'

'That all depends on what the big boss has got lined up for me.'

A conspiratorial twinkle accompanying this remark was not lost on McCord, and unhesitatingly he replied, 'There's enough work here to keep two ice instructresses going. You'll be able to take some of the pressure off Miss Darwell, Mandy. She's been feeling the pace lately...what with one thing and another.'

There was no mistaking the hidden meaning in the tail end of his comment. Not to Celia, at least. She knew he was referring to Tariq, and her spirited glance momentarily tying with his told him what she was always at pains to point out. That he might own her working time, but he didn't own her!

However, deep down inside her there was another kind of commotion going on. Mandy's finally turning up for her role at the rink could have had other repercussions. Celia could have found herself out of a job. Was there really enough work for both her and Mandy? she wondered. What doubts she had were dispelled by the easing of some inner tension. McCord seemed to think so, and after all, he was running things.

He was saying now, 'I'll leave it to the two of you to work out your duty programme. No doubt you'll have your own ideas of how you want to run things between yourselves.'

Mandy shrugged. 'Celia knows the ropes. I'll fall in with her way easy enough, I guess. I don't have any plans for messing up what's probably a settled routine.'

'But, Mandy!' Celia was amazed. 'You've had masses more experience than I have. Of course you must take charge now.'

The other girl laughed and linked her arm in McCord's. 'We're all in this together, honey. And I reckon we'll make out as a team. What do you say, boss?'

McCord's reply was to untwine his linked arm and put it squeezingly round the ice star's shoulders. 'Sounds fine to me,' he smiled. 'In any case, it's good to have you here at last, Mandy.'

Celia had to stand by and watch this demonstration of affection. And if she was left in any doubt as to his satisfaction in having Mandy with him, here in Bahrain, McCord's blue glint directed across the top of the tawny tresses her way clinched it.

CHAPTER ELEVEN

TWO PAIRS of feet instead of one certainly made things smoother at the Alhambra ice rink. Mandy Bennet was beautiful, talented and utterly likeable; a combination practically unknown among the female species, and especially in the show business field. Celia felt decidedly drab by the side of her mercurial charm. Not that she was given any reason to, for Mandy played down all her advantages.

She was quite content to dress in conservative slacks and top for her job as skating coach, as Celia did. And though she obviously possessed tremendous skill on the ice, she did her work-outs privately before the public were allowed in, and without any fuss.

But Celia was not entirely in agreement with this dousing down of one's natural talents. She had practically got a show organised with the help of her star pupils, and it struck her that Mandy would be magnificent in the leading role.

She put it to her one afternoon when trade was slack and they were enjoying a soft drink at the bar. Mandy pondered, having heard Celia's description of the show so far. 'You mean you want me to flip around a bit in some spangled, feathery get-up?'

'Oh, have you got something like that?' Celia pounced on the idea enthusiastically. 'It would be just the thing to give our small effort some professional glamour.'

'Well, I brought a few show dresses with me. I reckon I can deck out in ostrich feathers and sequins and do one of my solo routines, if you're sure you don't mind?'

'Mind?' Celia echoed smilingly. 'They're going to be tumbling over themselves at the door to get a look at the world-famous Mandy Bennet! And that will be wonderful for the children's morale.'

'Okay, consider me roped in,' Mandy said with good-humoured resignation. 'When is it to be, this world pre-miere of ours?'

'In two weeks' time on a Saturday night. The children are having their costumes made for the performance and as I'm learning,' Celia said with a wry grin, 'nothing moves with any great speed out here.'

With the work shared nowadays there was often time for a chat, and on another occasion Mandy started off, a little out of character for her, in a subdued way, 'You've met my father, I believe?'

Celia nodded, not knowing quite how to frame an an-swer. 'I like him a lot,' she smiled. 'You remind me of him in many ways, Mandy... although I can't say our meeting gave me much opportunity to—'

'Yes, I know,' the other girl cut her off. 'He... he wasn't himself. McCord told me all about that day when the two of you had to take Dad home, and how you helped to get him... on his feet again for an important oilfield pow-wow... I've been wanting to thank you for some time...'

'I was just glad to be of some use. It was nothing re-ally...' Celia's throat grew pink. What she had done for Mike had long since slipped from her mind, but apparently it hadn't McCord's.

Mandy's subdued gaze had grown distant. 'It's been bad for Dad. Since Mom died he seems to have lost the spark for making a life for himself. I've had my work, friends, the discipline of performing before an audience. It hasn't been easy, but I've gotten over the worst. With Dad it's different. He married Mom when she was just eighteen, and from the start she went with him on every oil assignment. Their travels to every part of the world were just one long honeymoon.' Mandy gave a lopsided smile. 'They didn't even decide to have me until their marriage was fifteen years old.' And then heavily again, 'Mom fell sick almost overnight. She'd lived and thrived in some of the lousiest spots on this earth. She was as strong as a donkey—or so we all thought—but pneumonia's a strange malady. She died within a few hours of being laid low.'

There was a silence when Mandy had finished. Celia could think of no words of consolation. Nor did she feel that Mandy needed them now. It was Mike, Mandy's father, who had to be shown that a partnership could continue, even if one could only go along beside the other in spirit.

McCord seldom came to the ice rink office these days. That he was busy with his deep-freeze plants and refrigerating schemes and deliveries of iced foodstuffs for the Sheikh's banquets Celia didn't doubt. But his evenings were reserved for Mandy, that much she knew.

Dining with Tariq in the upstairs Alhambra restaurant, she was discovering, was not only being in a position to be seen from the shadowy areas of the closed rink, but also to see. And many were the nights when her digestion was upset at the sight of McCord and Mandy talking earnestly in the dimly-lit office below, or leaving together with McCord's protective arm around the other girl as they disappeared towards the outdoors.

Celia didn't know why she should let herself feel so miserable on these occasions. After all, she knew the score where the two of them were concerned. McCord had flown to Cairo to tell Mandy that he wanted her close to him in

Bahrain. And would Mandy have turned her back on fame and fortune as a world star for a lowly job as ice-instructress, if she wasn't in full agreement with this?

Celia made every effort to dull her awareness of Mandy's and McCord's togetherness by losing herself doggedly in Tariq's company. She was really extremely fond of her Arab escort and he gave every indication of being devoted to her. Of course, by now she had been in his arms often, under the Gulf moon on midnight strolls, and in the shadows of the rink's car park, if they were going their different ways after the evening session. But never once had she been able to stop herself comparing Tariq's kiss with that of McCord's that night on the deck of the *Sea Roc.*

One was like the pleasant caress of the sea's ripple on an acquiescent shore; the other a crashing, earth-moving force that pounded the rocks of her defences demanding not only acquiescence but all-out and uncompromising surrender. And it wasn't just the anger of the moment, or the impatience in that embrace on the starlit deck. It was something else; something that would always be there waiting to be sparked off in the same way. And she despaired of knowing it in any other man.

THE DAYS at the ice rink were growing busier, with more people, mainly the European contingent, trying out their skills on the ice. But the evenings were inclined to be social affairs when the Alhambra was used mostly as a meeting place. This allowed for lots of free time for drifting around the coffee lounge.

Tariq had many friends among the Bahraini patrons and Celia often chatted alongside him. Some nights Mandy and McCord joined them. For Celia these were the more trying occasions. She was impressed by Tariq's loyalty to her, when there were delectable, effervescent redheads around like the

American ice-star. In fact it helped her to ride McCord's, as always, unappreciative smile when her glance ran up against his.

Mandy joked with Tariq and he with her, but it was in a frothy way with no depth and they both knew it was simply a device for passing the time. In any case, Celia reminded herself, as they were good friends each man would obviously respect the other's property.

Celia made a wry face to herself at the thought of being owned by any man, yet she was not without a certain awareness that she was sailing dangerously close to becoming Tariq's exclusive possession.

Just how close was brought home to her one sunny afternoon when she had left her suite at the hotel, after the lunch break, to start out for work. Not only was it a surprise to find Tariq waiting for her in the lobby, it was also a puzzlement, for he invariably spent long hours in his office and had little time for social calls through the day.

'Tariq!' She voiced her thoughts with the laughing exclamation. 'What on earth are you doing here at this hour of the day?'

'I wanted to see you for something very special.' He kissed her fondly and for Celia a little embarrassingly among the coming and going of the hotel guests. Then taking her hand he said blithely, 'Come. You will see that I have left my desk for an excellent reason.'

The mystery deepening, Celia went with him to the outdoors. They bypassed her car outside the hotel, and his own parked next to it, and she tilted an eyebrow wonderingly. Tariq never went anywhere on foot...

She was conscious of the minutes ticking by. She had already left herself scant time to get to the rink before opening time. And though she would not have wanted to spoil

Tariq's obvious pleasure in what he was about she did have
to stifle a mounting irritation at these wasted moments.

They stopped on the corner of the hotel block at last.
There was little traffic here. What now? She resisted the desire to take a look at her watch, and saw Tariq snap his fingers in the autocratic way of the well-bred Arab. The next
moment a gleaming silver shape was put into motion under
a hotel parking archway and with the whispering of its expensive inner parts slid to a stop right beside them.

Celia forced a smile. 'I'm sorry, Tariq, I really can't go
anywhere with you now... I'm already late for—'

'*I'm* not going anywhere, my dear,' Tariq smiled. 'You
are. This will be your mode of transport from now on in
Bahrain.'

Celia was dumbstruck. She stared at the Lamborghini, a
silver dream of a car, priceless in its field, with every known
luxury attachment incorporated in its low, wide, stream-
lined magnificence, and dreamlike herself, she exclaimed,
'Tariq! I couldn't drive round town in this!'

'Why not? I do in mine,' Tariq laughed. 'And how do you
propose to get to your work, my love?' With this his glance
had moved playfully along the street to where his chauffeur, who had unknown to her left the Lamborghini, as
though obeying orders, was now climbing into her car. The
next moment she saw it move away and disappear along the
street into the busy stream of traffic.

'Oh no!' She looked at her watch. 'Now what am I going
to do?'

'You have but one choice, darling,' Tariq twinkled. He
opened the door of the Lamborghini with a flourish and a
trace of that insistence that had accompanied his presenting her with the expensive pearl necklace. 'I wish you to accept this little gift, not only because for you to do so would
mean a great deal to me, but also as an Al Rahma I cannot

have someone who is close to my heart driving around in a nondescript vehicle of a type used by the lower classes in the town.'

Celia wanted to ask why not? But she had no time to waste in arguing. Mandy would not cope on her own now with the somewhat rougher types who were frequenting the ice rink in the afternoons. As though reading her thoughts Tariq said, 'Your car has gone to join its workmates in McCord's garages. This now is for your comfort and my family's prestige. Accept it with my love and I will be the happiest man in the world.'

Celia felt that prestige and love had a way of becoming confused here, but it was not something she could put into words. Nor could she think of a thing to say in response to the stunning realisation that Tariq calmly expected her to take over some thirty thousand pounds' worth of glittering car, and regard it as her own. She could only smile and say, 'We'll talk about it later, Tariq.'

She might have known that whatever she said he would regard as an acceptance, for smiling too as he helped her into the car, he said obliquely, 'We will meet tonight as usual...and you may thank me any way you wish.'

He closed the door and gave her a wave before hurrying back to his own jade and chrome palace on wheels. Celia had gathered earlier on in their relationship that Tariq belonged to a wealthy family, but this, she told herself, eyeing the leopard-skin covered seats of her own interior, the walnut and gold panelled dashboard, was ridiculous!

She was treated to another gay wave as Tariq slid away from the kerb, and then flicking the keys of her own machine, not without a certain amusement at the sly way Tariq had left her without a leg—or a wheel in this case—to stand on, she gave a sigh of resignation and set off for work.

Actually the Lamborghini she was driving attracted no special attention on her way to the ice rink. Practically every well-to-do family owned some such status symbol of wealth in oil-rich Bahrain, and the streets were more inclined to be cluttered with these high-powered jewels of the road than the lowly runabouts, similar to her usual form of transport.

As for speed, her present steed certainly got her to work in record time, but parking on this and successive occasions proved difficult.

Of course Celia had known from the start that she couldn't accept the Lamborghini as a permanent gift. But she was aware also that she would have to use caution when returning it to Tariq. He could, as she had seen, be somewhat rigorous in his desires, and it might soften the blow if she waited until she found a way to reclaim her company car.

In the meantime finding a place for the Lamborghini in the small space allocated for staff parking behind the rink, was proving a headache. It was not only that it took up more than twice the space of her other car. It also had the embarrassing effect of standing out with a kind of obscene opulence when ranged alongside the modest and sometimes decrepit runabouts of the rink employees. She had often gone indoors feeling uneasy about its ostentatiousness. But as it was too long to park in the street there was nothing to be done but edge the Lamborghini in somewhere each time she came to work, even if it did appear to take up all the space and more available.

Of course it would have to be at its most awkward angle one night when McCord drove up just as she was leaving.

TARIQ HAD had to miss the evening session because of a dinner with business associates and Celia was looking forward to a pleasant soak in the bath in her suite at the hotel and an early night. Mandy was still indoors and Celia would have preferred to make a quick getaway before McCord's arrival to pick her up. She and McCord seldom had a word for each other these days, and to have to witness his devotion to the other girl, fond as she was herself of Mandy, was something that Celia had no stomach for.

But luck would have it that she was just making for the Lamborghini when McCord swung in and found his way barred. But of course that didn't stop McCord. He manoeuvred a passage for himself despite the scant lighting at the rear of the building and, paintwork almost mingling with paintwork, brought his own car to a stop in its usual haunt.

Celia heard the door slam and across the gleaming width of the Lamborghini bonnet, the bulk of McCord appeared almost with a leisurely air. But there was a hard light in his eyes and a twist about his smile in the shadows as he spoke. 'It would be a great help,' he said, 'if you would keep your expensive trinkets from under other people's feet. This, as you may have noticed, is a parking lot, not a display area for your romantic acquisitions.'

The harsh sarcasm in his tones brought the colour to Celia's cheeks. 'It happens to be the form of transport I prefer,' she lied. 'And as I'm only a simple employee here, I've no choice but to put my "trinket" in the space provided.'

'It would be more at home, I'm sure, in the patrons' parking area. There's bound to be at least one other trendy example of Arab over-indulgence with which it would make a cosy twosome.'

Celia knew that in his satirical way he was referring to Tariq's car, and as subtly as she could manage she replied, 'Obviously it's more suited to the roominess there. If you have no objections...'

'None at all,' said McCord before moving indoors. 'It will
be nice not to have to clamber over the oversized token of a
tender relationship every time one wants to get in the rink.'

Left alone in the darkness, Celia closed her eyes over her
choking resentment. That did it! She hadn't wanted the
Lamborghini. She hated its ostentatious opulence, but she
would drive it now. Oh yes! For as long as she stayed in
Bahrain at least she would consider it her personal property. And she would continue to leave it in the employees'
parking space. There was room for both hers *and* Mc-
Cord's, as he had demonstrated, and gritting her teeth as she
extricated herself from the predicament he had left her in,
she sailed away without a scratch on either vehicle to prove
it.

And she went on proving it in the days ahead. Tariq was
delighted to see her using his gift to her with such gay abandon, so at least someone was pleased, Celia mused sourly.

How far her defiance of McCord's advice was taking her,
she had no time to worry over, for all was now constant activity at the ice rink in preparation for the ice carnival.

Mandy had done most of the organising. For a start she
knew all about show business, but more important than this
was the fact that she had only to make some request to
McCord either for extra seating round the ice, or colourful
spotlights to be mounted, and the thing was done.

Celia had decided to take no part in the show herself. She
wanted to be on hand to give encouragement to the children behind the scenes, and though Mandy was reluctant to
occupy the limelight, she had to agree that Celia would be
needed backstage.

On the night of the performance there was an atmosphere of pleasurable anticipation in the interior of the rink.
Coloured lights lit the expanse of ice that would be 'the
stage,' and friends and relatives of the Arab children, those

who were not tied by family traditions which would prevent them from attending such a function, filled the extra rows of seats around the edge.

When the music started for the opening of the display Celia found she was more jittery than any of the children. Eleven-year-old Ahmad was the first out into the spotlights, and she saw at once through a gap in the back curtains that her choice had been right. Ahmad was always supremely confident on the ice, and tonight with members of his family present he demonstrated his abilities to whizz around on blades with verve and polish. Perhaps he put a little bit too much drama in his actions when interpreting his choice of music, but this only delighted the audience and brought him a terrific burst of applause when he was completing his final spin.

The other children were inspired by the sound. Eager as they were to show off too, and with none of the inhibitions and shyness known by children of a more sophisticated society, it became a contest to see who would induce the most enchanted reaction from the people in the seats.

Of course there were disasters. Seven-year-old Husain, a little too keen, got his skates entangled at the start, and slid out into the centre of the ice on his bottom. But with childlike unconcern he picked himself up and went on to do his spot as though all entrances were made this way. Pretty Latifa had a fall during her interpretation of The Swan. She came back behind the curtain to recover, then went out to execute a charming performance for one so small.

Yes, sometimes with a little dampness in her eyes when she peeped out through the curtains, Celia felt she had just cause to be proud. All her pupils were showing that her coaching had proved worth it, and that for any teacher was the finest reward.

In the glow beyond the ice she could make out the faces of the audience. Many of the Bahrainis she knew quite well by now, especially the *ayahs* of the children who were out in force to beam on the marvels of their own individual charges.

McCord was there, standing offside, a little aloof, as befitting the boss of the place. He had entered into the spirit of the thing by wearing evening dress. Celia felt an odd catch at her heart at the sight of him, making everyone else in the place appear so insignificant, or so it seemed to her, with his vital presence.

She had just cause to thank him for providing unstintingly everything that had been needed to give a show atmosphere at the rink; although, she reminded herself, Mandy had done all the asking, not her. And it was for Mandy, she was certain, that everything had been done to ensure the show's success.

The other girl was kept busy doing pantomime bits which allowed for the children to be on the ice all at the same time. The two of them had worked this out as a way of breaking the monotony of continuous solo performances, and the idea was proving a success. Mandy was wonderful as the Pied Piper with all the little tailed marvels on the ice following her make-believe flute. And in a mock desert encampment with stuffed toy camels in reclining pose and sleeping mats and cooking pots over red glows, to give the effect of night time, the ice-star was magical as a midnight marauder.

But the highlight of the show was to be Mandy in her solo spot for the finale. When the time came the atmosphere in the rink was tense with expectation. The children, having enjoyed the tumultuous applause for their efforts, went to sit with their families on the rink's perimeter. And with no duties for the moment to keep her behind the scenes, Celia, in a dress of dove-grey watered silk, tiny diamanté stars in her ears giving her a poised look, joined Tariq who had just recently arrived.

Unfortunately he had chosen to pass the time between the scenes by chatting to his friend the rink boss. Celia would have preferred to be anywhere but right next to McCord at this moment, considering what was about to take place. But when the music started and the lights dropped low she concentrated on the expanse of ice.

Mandy appeared like a golden vision in the spotlight and had the audience transfixed from the moment she struck off at speed. In saffron ostrich feathers and sequinned primrose tunic, shapely legs unadorned for freedom of movement, she was truly a queen on blades. Though she made no great effort to overshadow the previous performances of keen young amateurs her very presence on the ice was bewitching, riveting all who watched her.

She had chosen music lilting, but with fire, and the more difficult her programme appeared the more she seemed to float smilingly through the tremendous leaps and splits and whirling contortions that made her a world name. Moved at the girl's tremendous skill, Celia obeyed an impulse to slant her gaze sideways. The stark appreciation displayed on McCord's face as he watched the beautiful nymph-like figure speeding like the wind over the glossy surface was not entirely unexpected, though for Celia it was like a knife-thrust in her heart. At the last goddess-like leap and fountain-flow of a spin, she clapped as loud as the rest, but that look she had seen on McCord's face would, she felt, remain forever engraved on her heart.

Tariq, his arm about her waist in the commotion of the lights going up and people preparing to leave, was keen too to make for somewhere where he could have her to himself, now that all the fuss was over. But Celia's work was far from finished. 'I can't go yet, Tariq,' she explained smilingly. 'The children will need help with their dressing, and I'll have to see that there's no mix-up with the costumes that they'll want to take with them. You can wait if you like, but I don't expect I'll be through until late.'

Tariq shrugged and kissed her there and then under the bright lights. 'I am very jealous of these young performers who take up so much of your time,' he flashed her a half-laughing look. 'But as tomorrow is Sunday and we can spend the whole day together, I will allow myself to be up-staged this time.'

Celia hurried off towards the area behind the curtains, more as a means of escaping McCord's all-pervading presence than with any great enthusiasm for work. She found the American girl trying to establish order in what sufficed as a dressing room. 'Mandy, you were terrific!' Celia went to embrace her.

'Thanks.' Always modest, Mandy put on a dry look. 'I guess I dazzled the audience a bit, but I think the kids stole my thunder.'

She helped for a while in righting things behind the scenes, but then Celia sent her on her way. It had been a strenuous evening for Mandy with her numerous appearances on the ice, whereas she, Celia, had been just a general factotum behind the glamour, and it was up to her now to clear away where it was necessary.

It was after midnight before she had satisfied herself that all was in order apart from the dismantling of the back curtains which the workmen would attend to another day. The rink was totally deserted by this time and sunk in the gloom of disuse. She made her way out into the night with mixed feelings. Part of her was happy at what the children had achieved this evening, but out-weighing this was an acute feeling of dispiritedness.

She was rooting for her car keys in her handbag beside the Lamborghini when a voice from the interior said, 'The door's open.'

Celia peered in, startled. McCord! When she had recovered herself she said with annoyance and distrust, 'You've been rifling my locker at the office.'

'That's right. I took the liberty of filching your keys. As you've been working with such devotion for the good of the rink, I thought the least I could do was chauffeur you home.'

She didn't know what to make of his tones. She thought she sensed menace there, certainly sarcasm and a kind of steely self-restraint. But she was tired and in no mood to pit herself emotionally against his granite charm.

She dropped into her seat, and as he closed the door across her there was a look on his face which she found vaguely disturbing. But was there ever a time, she asked herself wearily, when McCord wasn't disturbing?

She left it to him to see her back to the hotel. The first inclination she had that he had never had any intention of driving her straight there came almost in the first moments, for he thundered away with unnecessary speed from the parking lot. Then before she knew it they were hurtling towards the highway out of town.

So THEIR few moments together were destined, as always, to be explosive, and she draped back with resignation. She had no fear with McCord at the controls, but when they were approaching more than a hundred miles an hour on the deserted highway she was sufficiently angered to remark, 'It's a little late, don't you think, for games? Some of us have had a long day.'

'And a long night too... some of us,' came the drawling reply. Celia couldn't make out what he meant by that, unless he was hinting, as usual, at the time she had spent with Tariq, during working hours. 'And what better way to round off such a great evening,' he went on with a grim smile, pushing up the speedometer, 'than to see just what this oversized token of friendship we're travelling in is capable of on the road. Don't you agree?'

'I know that I'm tired,' she said flatly, ignoring his mood and the alarming speed they were doing. 'And I would like to turn in before the dawn hours if that's possible.'

'Oh, you'll be doing that.' There was something distinctly ominous about his grin. 'In fact you should be all tucked up, I'd say, within the next half hour.'

Whatever it was that had driven him to race the Lamborghini almost to its limits through the night seemed to peter out, for with no less dark-faced intensity he slackened down to a more breatheable speed after a while.

It was then that Celia saw where they were heading and, stiffening, she said, 'Unless you're planning to make the return trip in the same crazy fashion you're going to be hard put to it to get me back to the Gulf Hotel in the time stated.'

McCord said nothing for a moment. His face seemed carved out of teak in the shadows. Only his narrowed eyes and his smile gave any indication of thought or feeling—and what they were was anybody's guess.

Just when Celia thought no answer would be forthcoming he put in, 'I forgot to mention, you won't be staying at the Gulf Hotel any more.'

The apprehension that had been building up in her all evening she had put down to the strain of having to nurse the show through to its final stages without any major disasters. Now she knew that that had been child's play compared to what she was going through at this moment.

Forcing herself to speak evenly, she said, 'If this is another way of telling me I've got the sack, aren't you being rather elaborate about your choice of setting?'

'Who said anything about the sack?' He steered with a casual air. 'We don't work that way in Bahrain. If you remember, I agreed to employ you so that you could remain on the island. The papers I signed gave me full control of your services for a period of six months. You've worked for me how long? . . . four months? . . . That means as your employer you still owe me two months of your time.'

The rush of relief in Celia was almost like a pain, though she spoke ironically enough. 'I think I can just about finish my stint at the rink, as I've come this far.'

There was another silence which, to her seemed to build up to nerve-racking proportions, then McCord said, 'That's something else I forgot to mention. I'm closing the rink as from tonight. It's proved a success in a way, but it's not quite my line.'

Celia was shattered by this news. 'The children are going to miss their practice,' was the only comment she could salvage from her devastated thoughts.

'They'll find other outlets for their energies,' McCord shrugged. 'I don't think Bahrain is going to fold up exactly at finding itself without an ice rink.'

Celia felt numbed. But through the shock of what she had just heard something like an explanation came to her.

Why did it have to be tonight that McCord had decided to close down the rink? For it was a snap decision, she was sure. She gulped quietly. Did she have to ask herself this question when she had seen that look on McCord's face during the show? He had decided that he didn't want to share Mandy, who had been dazzling on the ice, with anyone; least of all, all the other males whose gazes must have been every bit as appreciative as his, if Celia had thought to look around.

It was drastic action, to close down the rink because of a personal possessiveness, but only what one would expect from a man like McCord.

A new kind of resentment flared in her at finding herself without a job or a roof over her head in a matter of minutes and she spoke up quiveringly. 'I suppose it suits you to play the iron-handed boss, once in a while?'

'Annoyed because of all the fun you'll miss?' His smile held a certain sadistic satisfaction.

Celia let him have his little joke, which went a lot deeper, she felt, than she had the clarity of mind to fathom. Besides, they had arrived at El Zommorro and she was curious as to why he had brought her here at this hour of the night—or should she say morning?

There was a hush over the grounds as they alighted from the car. The house resplendent and white under the glow of a crescent moon, stood amid green stretches, and the perfume of night blossom and roses hung on the air. Celia was reluctant to stir from where she could see the gardens stretching to the edge of the desert. Even McCord's presence had little effect on the spell of witnessing the beauty and the savagery of nature in one setting; perhaps because for all his city dealings he belonged here, was part of these conflicting surroundings. One felt that.

He did finally break the spell by mentioning, 'Much of the greenness was here before the house was built, due to the underground springs. Even the name El Zommorro comes from the old days when it was an oasis. It's a corruption of the word meaning emerald, and somebody must have thought it fitting, surrounded as it is by wilderness.'

Celia was conscious of a strange and abiding peace here. It wasn't the first time she had experienced this sensation and abruptly she cut off any more mind-meandering by asking. 'It may seem a silly question, but where do I fit into your scheme of things, if, as you say, the ice rink is no longer in existence?'

'I thought you'd gathered.' He took her arm and steered her towards the house. 'As you know, the office side of the business is done mainly here on the premises. It's a thing that's grown with time. In the old days I used to do a lot of the paper work myself, but like all successful businesses it's grown into something of a monster, and soon the whole thing will be transferred to a suitable office block in town. But for now an extra hand on the staff would be useful. No special qualifications are needed.'

They were indoors now, and in the muted glow of the house lights he went on, 'You'll occupy the quarters you used before where you'll find your bags from the hotel have been unpacked. On Monday morning you'll be directed to the office wing and shown your duties.'

Celia digested all this without a word. If she had been about to comment McCord put in, 'Oh, and I should point out that leave from your place of employment is pretty restricted.'

Celia flared then. 'You mean I'm forbidden to leave the house? But that's—'

'I don't think you quite understand how binding a work agreement is in an Arab country,' he cut in smoothly. 'As your employer I have full control of your time.'

'In other words, you've bought me!'

His crooked smile more than a match for her icy satire he left her at the door of her suite with the words, 'You could say that.'

CHAPTER TWELVE

IN THE days that followed Celia found herself yet another component in the McCord business set-up, though she couldn't complain of overwork. The office staff, with the exception of Kamel, who kept her at a cool distance as though what had happened between them was entirely her fault, were friendly and helpful. Her rooms were part of the household and she dined downstairs of an evening waited on by Quadi, the softfooted Pakistani servant. But of McCord she saw nothing at all.

With the house and grounds, it seemed, at her disposal she wandered at will. The loveliness and peace of the gardens made her realise how much she had missed the secluded out-of-town life she had been accustomed to in England. Indoors, idling through the cool and beautiful rooms with the masculine touches, the thought that McCord's possessions looked as uncompromising as the man himself brought a wan smile to her lips.

Of course she knew why he wasn't around. He had closed the rink so that he could have Mandy to himself. And by the look of it they were spending every possible moment together. Celia considered she had the whole thing summed up, but then all her surmising was sent awry when Mandy came one afternoon to say goodbye.

'I hope I'm not interrupting work output,' she said mischievously when Celia came to see her after receiving a message in the office.

'Hardly,' Celia smiled leading the way to garden seats on the shady terrace. 'If there is any output I've a feeling I'm not much part of it.'

'I can't stop, honey,' Mandy put out a hand as Celia would have ordered drinks. 'Dad and I are due at the airport in about an hour.'

Celia looked a little stupid. 'Are you leaving Bahrain?'

'Yep, we're going back to the States,' Mandy said happily. 'Dad's been offered a desk job back home—McCord's wangled it, you might know, with the oil chiefs—and we're going to set up house in Beaumont, Texas, not far from his work. It's something I've dreamed of for a long time—the house, I mean, and Dad and I. That's why I hung on in Cairo as long as I could. You need hard cash to buy property, and as I told you, the sheikhs pay well for their entertainment. But then McCord came and told me that Dad was getting deeper into the doldrums...'

'You mean,' Celia did her best *not* to look stupid, 'McCord came to see you in Cairo to tell you that your father needed you in Bahrain?'

'That was the message I received,' Mandy nodded. 'He told me later that it was you who suggested that I would be more help to Dad here, and you were right. So you see I've got a lot to thank you for. That's why I wanted to do it personally before we left.'

As the other girl gripped her hand warmly Celia said with a sudden pang, 'Then this is goodbye?'

'I'm afraid so,' Mandy grimaced smilingly. 'But we'll keep in touch, and who knows...one day...'

Celia knew a glimmer of pleasure at the unspoken pact, though hardly listening, she couldn't stop herself from asking, 'But...what about McCord?'

'McCord?' Mandy looked blank. 'Well, what about him? He's worked like crazy to get Dad this transfer and he knows

I'm grateful, but—Hey, wait a minute!' With a dawning look Mandy chuckled, 'You didn't think that McCord and I...?' At Celia's expression she looked doubly amused. 'What, McCord with the computerised emotions? No, he's just a very dear friend of the family.' She became pensive. 'Pop's the only man in my life. We're gonna have a ball setting up house together. I'm gonna train him to put his feet up nights, when he comes home, and try my hand with some of his favourite recipes in the kitchen...'

No mention was made of the word sacrifice, but Celia knew. The ice-star was turning her back on fame and success for a worthier cause, and the two girls hugged each other with a choking feeling of affection.

'Goodbye, Mandy!' Some moments later Celia waved her to the car. 'I hope you get everything you've worked for.'

'You too, honey. I'll write.' Mandy threw her a last smile before driving off.

It was some time before Celia could get her mind to function normally again. So it was true what she had thought at the start. The woman who counted first in McCord's life would have to have a powerful attraction to come between him and his work. Mandy, with her freshness and youth and unselfishness, had proved that.

Still she felt a meagre lifting of her spirits as she went indoors. His work was finished now in town. He had done what he could for Mandy's father, which meant that at any moment he would be coming home.

She spent the time listening for his car, and when it arrived, it was silly, she knew, but she went hurrying out on to the drive to greet him. But she had been hasty in assuming that it was McCord's car, for it was Tariq, not he, who stepped out of a chauffeur-driven limousine to meet her.

Perhaps it was her disappointment that gave her the impression that Tariq looked a little sinister in cotton headdress and flowing robe. The kindliness in his eyes had been replaced by a certain annoyance, and when he spoke there was no warm smile to accompany his words. 'It has taken me a week to discover your whereabouts,' he said. 'McCord is never available when you want him and since the rink's closure I haven't had a thing to go on. It was only by insisting on information at the Gulf Hotel that I have managed to trace you here.'

'It's simply a transfer of employment.' Celia tried to make the comment sound light.

'So I have heard. But that of course is out of the question. As my fiancée you must come with me at once.' He took her arm and began to steer her towards the car.

Gripped by a peculiar apprehension, Celia shook herself free as pleasantly as she could. 'I can't leave, just like that!' she gave a strangled laugh. 'There are certain rules—'

'All of which mean nothing when considering the fact that you belong to me. Now must I be more persuasive, or will you accompany me in a sensible manner to the car?'

Sensible! Celia resisted leaving El Zommorro with everything she possessed. She had a feeling that if she went now it was the end of something imperative in her life. But Tariq called for his chauffeur's assistance and against her will she was bundled into the car and driven away at speed.

When she had recovered her breath she sat up to confront her abductor. 'I don't think this is very funny, Tariq!'

'I am not out to amuse, nor am I myself amused. As you are my future wife your duties towards me should be quite obvious.'

His words annoyed her. 'It's customary to ask a girl first, not just assume that she's ready for marriage,' she said crossly.

'I have been patient,' he shrugged. 'I know the reputation my countrymen have for pushing matters of this nature. I have given you time to familiarise yourself with the idea of being betrothed to an Arab. Now I shall waste no more time. The wedding will take place tonight.'

'Tonight?' In panic Celia argued, 'But, Tariq, you don't understand! I like you . . . I like you a lot . . . but not enough to marry you . . .'

'This has all been decided long ago, my dear. The gifts I made to you . . . the pearls, the powerful car . . . Your acceptance of these things was, in a way, your acceptance of me as the man who will share your marriage bed.'

'But I never intended to keep the gifts, don't you see?' Celia was desperate. 'I just did it to get back at McCord. He was always making out that he owned me, or at least my time—' She swallowed on this. As it had turned out, he did! 'I just wanted to let him see that what I did in my free time was my own business.'

'You should have thought of the consequences earlier, my dear. Not that it would have made any difference. My mind was made up from the moment I first saw you, and the culmination of that dream will be in the nuptial ceremony in a few hours from now. You will be dressed as a woman of my country, and later subject yourself to my will as befitting an Arab wife.'

Celia couldn't believe her ears. It was all so matter-of-fact. No tenderness now, just clear-cut orders and instructions. As she eyed Tariq's shrouded profile from where she was huddled in a corner of the car, it seemed to her a little hawk-like in the failing light, and she was reminded of a desert falcon who, having wheeled and idled long enough, swoops without emotion on his prey.

THEY HAD reached Manama and were speeding over the causeway which led to the adjoining island of Muharraq. Apart from being aware that this was where many of the merchant families lived, Celia knew little of this section of Bahrain, and the onion-shaped mosques against the darkening sky and faded family mansions were as strange to her as another land.

When they stopped she had scant time to take stock of her whereabouts, seeing only a magnificent house built alongside a rambling mud warren which in the old days must have been the dwelling place for the members of the Rahma family; then she was hustled indoors to another warren-like interior, along passages, up winding staircases and eventually into a room that smelled strongly of incense.

'Here you will be bathed and dressed for the ceremony.' Tariq was all Arab as he bowed his way backward to the door. His dark eyes lit with passion as he left her with the words, 'I shall await your company with eagerness.'

The first thing Celia did was rush round to try all the doors, but each one was secure and she was a prisoner in a balconied harem-like interior whose glazed, latticed doors showed glimpses of a calm, indifferent sea, and innocently winking stars.

Oh, what a fool she had been, she wailed to herself, to tamper with the affections of an Arab. But then Tariq had said he had desired her from the start, so what could she have done to avoid it?

She paced, determined not to go through with this crazy wedding, but frighteningly certain that she had no choice in the matter. It wasn't as though Tariq had endeared himself to her in this last hour. He was cold and proud and totally unlike the kindly, gentle person she had assumed him to be.

She fingered the tinselled robes laid out for her on a divan and dropped them in panic and distaste. Oh, she had been warned! Once an Arab, always an Arab, and a Bedouin at that. Hadn't they once been a nomadic race? As McCord would have said, Tariq had simply reverted to nature.

There was the sound of someone at the door and knowing that at any moment a team of handmaidens would file in to bathe and anoint her for the nuptial ceremony, she tensed. But only one person entered the room—a mature woman with a neat figure in a Paris afternoon dress and white winged strands at the temples threaded through the rich dark gloss of a coiffured hair-do.

As she came forward Celia saw at once the likeness of Tariq in a face that had a kind of ageless beauty, despite its faint aura of sadness. 'I am Tariq's mother.' Her smile illuminated all but the shadowed depths of her eyes. 'I have come as a mother should, to welcome her daughter into the family.'

'Mrs.... I mean, Madame Rahma...' Celia floundered. How did one address an Arab lady? 'I don't want to sound discourteous, but no one has bothered to ask my opinion regarding this marriage.'

Tariq's mother looked concerned, but not surprised. 'My son has always been headstrong,' she said, taking a seat on the divan. 'He tells us nothing of the affairs of his heart, but we are a close family, you understand, and when we are summoned to meet his bride, we assume that she is a willing party to the arrangement.'

Celia said nothing to stress the fact that she had not been consulted, and with a searching sympathy the Arab woman smiled. 'Have you known Tariq long?'

'Oh yes, for several weeks.' Celia's eyes clouded. 'But tonight he's different. I can't believe he's the same charming, kindly man whose company I have often enjoyed.'

'These are the ways of the East, my child.' The sadness in the dark eyes was evident in the smile. 'In our country the wooing ceases at the moment of union and from then on the wife is just the chattel of her husband.'

Celia suppressed a quiet horror at the thought, but she was struck by the way Tariq's mother seemed aware of Western comparison, probably because, as a merchant's wife, she met many Westerners in her daily life.

As they sat together on the divan, the dark eyes had a twinkling scrutiny as they roamed over Celia's smooth features and fair hair. The Arab matron said after a moment, 'I hope you will not be offended if I tell you that I admire my son's taste.'

There was none of the animosity that a mother might feel for a foreign intrusion in her family, but there was no doubt that she was aware of Celia's comparative newness to Bahrain, and with a warmth that was reminiscent of Tariq in the early days the woman asked, 'What brings you to a country so far from home, child?'

Celia smiled forlornly. 'It's a long story. One that I've grown tired of repeating.' She sighed, realising that some explanation was expected. 'You see, it was a crazy idea in the first place. My father was a government official years ago out here. He was going to marry a dancing girl called Nevine, but the wedding was stopped at the last moment and my father was packed off back to England. He married eventually a woman of his own kind, but he was widowed early in life, and from being very young I suppose I've always known that Nevine was the one and only love of my father's life.' Celia let out a breath. 'He died about four months ago and I had this wild urge to know the dancing girl who had meant so much to him, but I've never had any luck in my search for her.'

Without noticing that the woman's features had turned a little waxen she produced the photograph she always carried on her, and shrugged disconsolately. 'No one seems to recall anything surrounding the young government official who was posted here thirty years ago.'

Tariq's mother took the photograph of the smiling fair-haired young man. Her face had gone a strange putty colour under its olive-skinned beauty, and it seemed that the deep well of inner sadness came brimming to the surface in her eyes as a whispered exclamation escaped her lips. 'Peter!'

Celia went rigid where she sat. Never had she heard her father's name spoken in this way before.

As the glistening dark eyes of Tariq's mother turned slowly her way Celia's own eyes were shining suddenly with tears of joy, and without needing to ask she leaned in to touch the faded cheek with her own. 'Nevine!'

'And you...are Peter's daughter?' The embrace was emotional. Some time later, when eyes had been laughingly dried, Tariq's mother said, 'No one knows me as Nevine now. From the days when I ceased to appear as a dancing girl my name has been Nadia. After your father left, my family were in despair for my reputation. But we are of Egyptian stock, a highly prized status in Bahraini society, and Tariq's father was persuaded to overlook my questionable past for the privilege of rearing fine, intelligent sons. We have a large family and he at least is content.'

There was no bitterness in Nevine's explanation, just smiling resignation, but Celia knew, just as she had known with her father, that the years had done nothing to extinguish the love that had been born between them so long ago, here in Bahrain.

'Of course Tariq knows nothing of my past,' Nevine added. 'That is something between my husband and me, and he has not spoken of it since the day of our marriage.'

Celia nodded absently. That would explain why nothing had come of her enquiries in these parts. But something else was on her mind. She repeated dreamily, 'No, Tariq knows nothing of your love for my father, but you and I know.' At the older woman's questioning look she rushed on, 'Don't you see? This alters everything! Tariq is your son. And I'm . . . Peter's daughter. A match that couldn't take place thirty years ago can, in a way, do so now.'

She stopped herself then, wondering at her impulsive proposition. Could she be happy here with Tariq, in the clamour and clutter of town life? Ironically these people had left the spaces and the desert behind, but she felt that something called to her out there, and it was all tied up with McCord in some way. But McCord was a businessman and he only had work plans, hadn't he? Trying to turn despair into practicality, she laughed harshly, 'What better way to link two people who never made it than to go ahead with this wedding now?'

Nevine didn't answer for a long moment. Celia felt that those searching dark eyes held a wisdom that saw deep beyond one's smile. When she spoke her own smile was gentle. 'I knew the moment I entered the room that you were not in tune here, child, and you yourself admitted it. Do you think a second unhappiness will wipe out that of the past?' She rose. 'You must do as you wish. If you marry Tariq I shall love you as the daughter I consider you to be. But if you decide against it all will be solved. It has been the wish of my husband for some time to put Tariq in charge of the shipping offices in Cairo and he has cousins and friends there who will soon have him joining in their parties. I too have a home there, so you see, after tonight, if this is your choice, our paths will not cross again. The decision is yours to make.'

She drew Celia into her arms, and after a long and tense embrace when eyes of East and West were damp again she turned and walked out of the room.

Celia stood around for a long while in a semi-trance, and when the handmaidens came in to prepare her for the wedding ceremony she did nothing to prevent it. Later, in filmy gold-braided robes and headdress, alone for a few moments before the attendants would come to lead her to Tariq, she raised her eyes to the stars, searching, hoping, but there was no mystic reply.

What there was was a distinct hammering on one of the balcony doors.

Hardly had this registered on her mind than the glazed parchment and latticework was splintering and shattering, giving way under the force of a great weight levelled behind it. Standing there transfixed, Celia had the curious feeling that she had watched it all before.

When the door was matchwood and the debris scattered McCord said, stepping through the dust, 'Don't think I'm going to spend the rest of our lives fishing you out of these kind of crazy situations!'

Our lives! Celia felt a joyous pulsing rushing to her head. She had forgotten all about the filmy raiment she was wearing, and with his blue eyes whimsically appraising McCord snapped, 'Put something on over that ridiculous get-up and let's get out of here.'

As overbearing as always! Unable to bring herself to obey meekly, Celia lifted her chin. 'There's something you don't understand. I've made an important discovery. Nevine is Tariq's mother. She's been here under our noses all the time...and now that I've found her I've decided to join Tariq in a marriage that will make some amends for the past.'

'Over my dead body!'

Her carefully worded speech shot to pieces by his clipped comment, she said witheringly over a sneaking, soaring happiness, 'Do you have to be so melodramatic?'

'You pick these corny scenes, not me.' He swept her up in his arms and made for the outdoors.

The route down from the balcony round turrets and over ledges was painstakingly precarious, and gripped tight against McCord, Celia said with sarcasm, though she didn't raise her voice, 'Wouldn't it have been easier to knock at the front door and ask for Tariq?'

'I think I explained once before,' came the heavily breathing reply, 'that there's no talking to an Arab once he's made his mind up.'

They reached the ground and made for a path leading to the street. McCord looked back momentarily at the brightly lit household and growled, 'It took me one hell of a time to work out which room you were locked in.'

As there appeared to be no visible means of escape Celia asked testily, 'What are we going to do now?'

'I came in the Lamborghini,' McCord replied, unbuttoning his jacket, 'but that stays here now. Tariq will get the message when he knows I've delivered it back from my place.' With his off-white smile he draped the jacket round Celia. 'There's nothing for it but to take a taxi.'

'A taxi?' She was indignant. 'Like this?' But McCord carted her off in his arms again, and later, when she was being bundled into the furry inside of a hired cab, she had to suffer the knowing looks of the winking Bahraini driver, and McCord's grin didn't do one thing to dispel the suggestion that she was being abducted against her will for some dark desert rendezvous.

She fumed all the way to El Zommorro, though below the paper-thin surface of her annoyance was a delicious, singing contentment.

It swelled within her as the undulating gardens and the desert house came into view, and he didn't let go of her until he had paid the man off and they were inside the rose-lit interior.

He had put her down in her favourite room where the chandelier winked over the dinner table set for two and the view through the open doorway of the palm-laden terrace was of a sky starlit and mystic in quality and desert stretches softened in the aura of night.

But there was nothing soft at the moment about McCord's attitude. Putting up with his grim surveillance where his jacket had slipped from her shoulders to the floor, Celia said pettishly, 'Well, don't just look at me as though I'm something the servants have forgotten to remove!'

'I happen to be looking at the world's prize idiot,' he barked, pacing. And levelling a finger at her in his old menacing way, 'Do you realise I've had to question the entire office staff to find out what happened to you? No one saw you leave. No one could tell me anything beyond when you were last seen. After fruitless enquiries in town I was left with the obvious conclusion that Tariq was behind your disappearance.'

Celia blinked, with a rosy glow in her heart. He had gone to all that trouble for her?

Still menacing, he went on, 'You've been a pain in the neck ever since I met you. I only gave you the job at the ice rink to keep you out of trouble, and what did it get me? A whole load of trouble!'

'You could have sent me back to England,' she said guilelessly.

'That's beside the point,' he waved a hand brusquely. And sticking with his own line of thought, 'You've found a way to get under my skin at every turn.'

'Don't tell me your work hasn't been the same since I arrived?' Celia asked with gleeful innocence.

'That's putting it mildly,' he eased out a breath. 'That damnable defiance of yours has given me more headaches than any business deal.'

'And the party nights? Haven't they been the same either since I messed up your life?' Feeling deliciously malicious, she wanted him to keep making music in her ears.

'With you causing me endless sleepless nights, what good am I at a party?' He was moving in threateningly.

Celia sought to check him in mild panic with, 'If you hadn't been so overbearing maybe I wouldn't have rushed into Tariq's arms.'

'You would have gone anyway because you had to satisfy yourself that you'd got me in a spin.'

She mused over his words with pleasurable wonder. Could that have been why she did it? But on her guard again, she tossed at him, 'How could I suspect any such thing with you throwing Mandy at my head at every opportunity?'

'I had to do something to cut you down to size.' The ghost of a grin tugged at his mouth. 'You were so full of Tariq I reckoned a bit of outside competition would take some of the wind out of your sails.'

'Oh yes?' Celia ached to be convinced. 'Well, I saw the way you looked at Mandy that night of her solo spot on the ice.'

'Oh, you did?' Something twitched at his lips and his gaze had become slightly quizzical. 'And is it the same way I'm looking at you now?'

Celia was moved by an overwhelming tenderness in his eyes and every part of her being answering that deep emotion she replied with a dash of mischief, 'You're looking at me with the possessive eye of some desert sheikh.'

'Quite right,' he nodded. 'I played one for a while in abducting you here away from the distractions of the ice rink.'

She eyed him with mock severity. 'And you made out it was for the purposes of work.'

'So it is in a way.' He pulled her into his arms. 'You're going to have your work cut out crossing me in my own house.'

'Are you going to be here?' She looked at him archly. 'Don't tell me you're thinking of relegating most of your work to other capable hands?'

'What do you think I've been doing all these weeks?' His arms were crushing her. 'I've got to have peace of mind somewhere.'

The song inside Celia trilled to a final, piercingly lovely note. Was *she* going to be his peace of mind!

Recapping, she said dreamily, 'What gave you the idea that I should want to cross you?'

Finding her soft and pliable in his arms, McCord murmured, 'At the moment I can't think of a thing.' He sought her lips with a hunger that was devastating, but sweetly so, for with the same urgent need Celia clung to him, letting the tide of his love wash over her now, all-conquering, as she had always known it would be.

His mouth pausing briefly away from hers, he smiled hoarsely, 'You and I should get married right away, Miss Darwell.'

Celia raised her lips for more and said demurely, 'I'm in accord, Mr. McCord.'

THE AUTHOR

Roumelia Lane has earned a firm place in the world of romance fiction with more than twenty Harlequin Romance novels to her credit. Originally from England's Brontë country, Yorkshire, the author now lives with her husband on the Mediterranean island of Majorca, in a house backed by mountains and overlooking a picturesque village. She has two children and three grandchildren.

Connoisseur's Choice

Dixie McKeone

Marlie had been working for her uncle in Virginia Beach every summer for years, and she knew everything there was to know about his business. If she had only known as much about Greg Alston, her uncle's most important customer, things might have turned out differently.

She might not have insulted the man within minutes of their first meeting. And he might not have retaliated with such impossible demands.

Marlie was prepared to play the game. But once again, she seriously underestimated the resourcefulness of her opponent.

CHAPTER ONE

'THAT'S JUST what I needed,' Marlie Richmond growled. 'That was really necessary to the fulfilment of life!' She frowned at the green paint that dripped from her fingers. It trailed down the side of the wooden duck decoy and spattered on the butcher paper that covered her worktable.

While the paint dripped from her left hand she held the nearly full can in her right. She hefted it, judging the weight, the amount of damage it would do if she threw it against the wall, and the release of frustration the act would afford.

Not that a little decorating would do the place much harm, she thought. The chaos of wood, sawdust and machinery that made up the production area of her uncle's wood speciality shop was too overwhelming in its confusion to be affected by a little paint on the wall. The rough lumber which comprised the bins, holding the various sizes and lengths of wood, resembled unfinished packing crates. The odd assortment of bandsaws, band and flap sanders, and the huge automatic carving machine took up most of the floor space. Over everything lay a thin blanket of sawdust. Cleaning only seemed to move most of it from one spot to another. No, a little paint would hardly matter.

The temptation remained, but Marlie Ann Richmond had not been taught to throw tantrums. With a sigh she released her grip on the container and thoughtfully pushed it aside. There was too much paint left. The damage would be worse than the surrounding chaos deserved. She would just have to relieve her frustrations by cleaning up what was already spilled.

'Of course, you understand, that's not the way to do it,' she explained to the half-painted and mottled wooden duck on the workbench. 'The idea is to throw first and worry about the consequences later. My problem is, in twenty-six years, I've never caught the knack of tantrums.'

Marlie picked up the carved bird, wiped away the excess stain and put it on the high shelf over her worktable. It would dry over the weekend, and Monday one of the workers would give it a good sanding, clearing away her mistake. But for the present it sat with splotched green spots on its back and one wing, staring at her balefully with its half-finished eye.

'Is it camouflaged for the army, or are you doing ducks in decorator colours?'

Marlie jumped at the voice and nearly knocked over the can of paint again. She whirled to face directly into a beautifully tailored linen jacket. As she tilted her head her gaze travelled up the lapels, continuing past the strong brown neck, the firm jaw and straight mouth. It met a pair of dark grey eyes that showed none of the humour his remark implied. In the pale blue casual suit, he stood out in surrealistic cleanliness against the background of the dirty, dusty factory. He appeared to be about thirty-five.

Marlie was tired after a day of working in the ineffectual air-conditioning and already irritated by spilling the paint. Angered by the fear that had come with being badly startled, she answered back with a sharpness that was so unaccustomed, she surprised herself.

'We're carving attack ducks for the army—they'll be trained to go for the buttons.' Her answer was as ridiculous as his question. 'What do you mean by sneaking back here?'

Obviously he did not care for being accused of furtive movements. His dark grey eyes which had held a carefully controlled irritation, glinted with anger. His jaw tightened, and he crossed his arms, looking down a well-shaped nose. Marlie felt the power of the man and thought she might have stepped back if the worktable had not been directly behind her.

'Nobody sneaks through an unlocked door,' he snapped. 'Your security system is hardly better than your—' He didn't finish his remark, but the direction of his glance, travelling to the decoy on the shelf, said it for him.

Marlie bristled. Who was he to criticise what she was doing? Even if it had been wrong, it was none of his business. She glowered up at him, feeling at a disadvantage.

He had to be all of six foot three inches tall, but yet it wasn't his height, nor the magnificent shoulders that were intimidating. There was an air of unassailable confidence, as if in speaking he created fact with his words. The power and strength that emanated from his presence lent the additional weight, but Marlie was not one to be put in the wrong with impunity.

She felt his gaze as he assessed her. His eyes seemed to see through her clothing, at the same time as taking in her surroundings and her job. There was something so intrinsically male in that look that she quivered under it without realising why. His was the eye of the casual but experienced hunter, automatically sizing up any possible quarry.

She ruefully considered her clothing and the dishevelment after a day at work and knew she must have been rejected in the same automatic way she had been judged. Her mood darkened, but she was not going to let him know he had affected her.

'Forgive me,' she said sweetly. 'I wasn't aware we were expecting an art critic—but you still don't belong back here.

This machinery can be dangerous. Our insurance doesn't allow for visitors.'

He turned his head as he looked over the surrounding equipment with a deliberate hauteur. Despite his attitude, Marlie thought she had never seen a more arresting masculine profile.

'You may be right,' he answered. 'I can see it's ready to jump its mountings and reinforce the attack ducks.'

'I wouldn't be surprised—everything's set on automatic,' Marlie retorted. She forgave herself for blatant untruth, justifying it by thinking nothing compelled him to be insulting. Still, she could hardly believe she was behaving with no more maturity than the third graders she taught during the winter months.

She recognized his elegant cleanliness as the spearhead of her resentment. No advocate of dirt or sloppiness, she was acutely aware of her own appearance. In threadbare jeans, torn sneakers, and one of her uncle's discarded shirts, she looked as if someone had dragged her from the rag pile. In addition, she was paint spattered and grimy with the inevitable sawdust of the factory in her hair.

That morning, in a spirit of fun and a desire to beat the heat, she had put her shoulder-length blonde hair up in two pony-tails that bounced on the sides of her head like the ears of a cocker spaniel.

For him to stand there looking as if he had just stepped from the door of his tailor's, observing her in all her dirt was enough to be upsetting, she reasoned.

She reached up to sweep a wayward strand of hair back from her forehead, at the same time taking a swipe at the small beads of perspiration on her nose. She saw green. Jerking her hand away, she realised there had still been paint on the back of her hand, and she had transferred it to her face. A green line bordered the lower periphery of her vision. She crossed her eyes, agonisingly aware of the paint on her nose.

Marlie whirled back to face the worktable, but the rag she had been using for cleaning up the spilled paint was saturated. The others were just as bad because of a clumsy day. Her last resort was the ladies' room, but she could hardly leave the stranger alone in the shop.

Turning back to him, she eyed him with speculation. He was certainly no thief. If he was, she amended the thought, the cut of his clothing showed he didn't bother with small places like her uncle's company.

Her wondering about him came to a halt as indignation took over again. The corners of his mouth were twitching as he enjoyed her discomfort. Mustering her shredded dignity, she looked him square in the eye.

'Do you have a reason for being here, other than to practise your insults?'

'I'm looking for some merchandise,' he replied. 'I think the shipment may have been lost.'

So he was a customer, Marlie thought, and felt better. Considerably better. Perhaps he would be dropping in from time to time. She resolved right then to start paying more attention to her appearance when she came to the factory. She forced back her shame and embarrassment at being caught in such a mess, and tried to be more co-operative.

'If you go into the office, my uncle will be back shortly. He just went—' Marlie wasn't allowed to finish what she intended to say.

'Oh, no,' he said with authority, reaching over to catch her by the arm. 'I had trouble enough finding you. I'm not sneaking around any more. I didn't undertake a career in locating your personnel. I've got you, and you can find what I want.'

'But I don't know anything about the shipping,' Marlie insisted as he propelled her towards the front of the building. As he kept her close at his side, she was once again impressed by his height. She felt his strength, and her senses were affected by his arrogant masculinity. His aftershave was a light, elusive scent that hinted of sunlit meadows.

Both his tone and his grip on her arm said he would brook no alteration of his decision. The humorous look in his eyes as she tried ineffectually to rid herself of the stain on her nose showed he was enjoying her embarrassment. That was enough to bring out her innate stubbornness.

Let's just see how much satisfaction you get out of it, Marlie thought, and stopped struggling. Instead she walked at his side, determined not to let him intimidate her again. After all, she had been working, and what was wrong with looking as if she had been involved in honest labour?

Her dignity lasted until she entered the office. It was torn to shreds again as she saw the man had not arrived alone.

Sitting in her uncle's desk chair, looking like a princess out of a modern fairy-tale, was one of the most beautiful women Marlie had ever seen. The elegance of the white linen sundress was reinforced by the delicacy of the high-heeled sandals. Her haircut just had to be a creation of one of the leading stylists. Everything shouted she was most definitely from the same world as the irritating male who still gripped Marlie's arm. Marlie did not care for the heavy, musky perfume the woman wore—it filled the office, hanging in the air like an oppressive atmosphere before a storm.

But she of the white linen and platinum-blonde hair looked as out of place in the office as the man. In the litter of a dozen model ducks, sample pieces of wood, and the clutter that a man like her uncle considered necessary for a comfortable existence, she was obviously both disdainful and uncomfortable. Marlie watched with a small satisfaction, because when Miss White-and-bright started to lean forward, she almost put her hand on the desk that was lightly powdered with fine sawdust. She hesitated, wriggling her fingers in fastidious distaste, and put her hand back on her knee. Her expression showed the poise of a select girls-school training. By a slightly raised eyebrow she gave her opinion of Marlie's general appearance before she turned her attention to the man.

'I wondered what had happened to you, darling,' she drawled. Marlie could hear the possessiveness in her voice.

Don't worry, dearie, Marlie thought. You can have him for all I care. Still, thinking of the handsome man at her side with a woman Marlie knew must be unpleasant, made her slightly resentful on his behalf. As if it were his fault she had been drawn to his defence, she made a point of tugging her arm from his grasp. She walked over to the filing cabinets, eyeing them critically. She wondered how much she could remember of her uncle's erratic system. The sooner she answered his question and sent him on his way, the easier her life would be, she reasoned.

'We file by single order and regular customers. Which are you?' she threw the question over her shoulder.

When his answer was not immediately forthcoming she turned, intending to look him straight in the eye. The afternoon sun was slanting in through the half-drawn blinds, and a ray struck her in the face. The green stain that covered the tip of her nose seemed to glow, drawing her focus inward. When she was able to concentrate on him again, the twitch of his lips had become a grin.

'Well, which is it?' Marlie demanded, feeling every inch the fool.

'You might say I'm a regular customer,' he replied with a curious nonchalance. The female, sitting at the desk, gave a low laugh.

'Name of the firm?'

'Alston.'

Marlie swallowed hard. That was the name of her uncle's largest customer, which accounted for almost a third of their business. While she was reaching for the top drawer, the street door opened. Marlie's uncle, the owner of the small factory, strolled in. Howard Richmond opened his mouth as if to speak and then closed it. He viewed the scene with steady blue eyes much like Marlie's, but his were set in a wizened, wrinkled face.

'Uncle Howard, this—' suddenly Marlie realised the stranger had not given her his name, '—gentleman is from Alston's, checking on a lost shipment.' Marlie had no intention of casting a slur on the tall man when she hesitated before saying 'gentleman', but his mouth tightened. Only after she spoke did she guess he would take her pause to be some socially-affected insult.

I bet I know where you learned to watch for that type of slur, Marlie was directing her mental comments towards the tall stranger, but she was thinking of Miss White-and-bright who was clearly bored, disgusted at her surroundings, and distastefully wiping a speck of dust off her white patent-leather bag.

Marlie had known her uncle too long to think he had been fooled by the atmosphere. With an unerring ability to reconstruct what had happened before he arrived, he knew the attitudes of the three in the office. He nodded to Marlie's opponent and turned his attention to the woman in his chair.

'It's too nice an afternoon to be cooped up in this dirty office,' Howard Richmond smiled at her, showing his appreciation of his visitor without being offensive. 'We're civilized enough to have a Coke machine if you'd like a soda—I'm afraid that's the best I can do.'

Well, so much for manners, Marlie thought, blushing. Where had hers been? she wondered. She had condemned Miss White-and-bright for her disapproving look, but it had been Marlie's place, as an employee of the company, if nothing else, to extend some greeting, something more than the brief curt nod she made when entering the room. If her third graders had behaved as rudely, they would have heard from her. She was thoroughly ashamed of herself. Her only excuse was her irritation at the tall man who stood by her side, looking as chastened as she felt. They had been so busy with their battle nothing else seemed to matter.

'No thank you, we'll have to be going.' Miss White-and-bright's attitude to Marlie's uncle was tightly friendly, but the sharp look she threw her escort showed she wasn't mollified.

Then he turned to Marlie's companion, his hand outstretched. 'I'm Howard Richmond. I take it you're Tom Jordon. We've spoken on the phone many times.'

'No, Alston. Jordon, my buyer, is still in New York. This is Miss Joan Owens-Lane.'

Marlie felt herself blanche. She had been dealing with Gregory Alston, the millionaire-owner of a chain of exclusive haberdasheries. Her sharp tongue could bring about disaster for her uncle's business and his employees as well. All her wisecracks came echoing back. She had been hot and tired, true, but that was no excuse. It wasn't like her to behave so badly. Was he to blame? No, she decided. She would keep the responsibility for her actions on her own shoulders.

And Mr Fred Owens-Lane was a well-known hotelier, and Marlie was sure Joan was his daughter. She was impressed.

Even Howard, a man not usually caught at a loss, was unsettled that Alston in the flesh was checking on a shipment.

'Well, uh, glad to meet you, Mr Alston. Your shipment is late?' Howard frowned, looking thoughtful. His eyes seemed to turn inwards as if he kept all the company records in his head. 'I can't understand it. We've shipped your last orders.'

Now that her uncle had arrived and taken charge, Marlie sidled towards the door that led back into the factory. She stopped abruptly when Greg Alston, a flick of his glance showing he had interpreted her plan, stepped between her and the door. All Marlie's shame at insulting him, as well as her intention to behave like an adult, were lost under her seething anger. The flicker of amusement in his eye and his hand, negligently braced against the doorframe, added up to a deliberate refusal to let her pass. His eyes looked past her to Howard, but the resolution with which he ignored her showed he was as much aware of her as she was of him. He was having trouble keeping control of the right corner of his mouth. Every time it quirked to smile, Marlie sizzled.

Howard went to the files, pulled out a drawer and extracted a folder with the ease of complete familiarity. He spent a minute examining the top sheets and looked up, chewing his lips thoughtfully.

'I don't have an explanation. I gave Jordon a shipping date of the thirtieth of last month. We had a chance to get a little ahead so we shipped on the twenty-fourth. Everything certainly should have arrived by this time.'

Greg's brows drew together. 'No chance it was overlooked—that it's still here?'

Marlie watched the wide smile transform her uncle's face. He had overcome his surprise at finding the famous haberdashery chain-store owner in his factory.

'Look around you, Mr Alston. We're a small operation. When we pack an order for you, it clogs the entire building. We're climbing over it for days. Sorry it was sidetracked, though. I guess you've got enough to do without chasing down lost shipments.' Howard sounded genuinely sorry, but there was no fawning in his voice. He was one businessman talking to another on equal terms. He did look a little puzzled, however. Marlie thought he was probably wondering, as she was, why a man of Greg Alston's position was chasing his own orders.

'I'll get a tracer on it first thing Monday,' Howard said, looking up. The other three in the room glanced up also. Their gaze followed his to the clock on the wall. It was well after five.

The time brought out an objection from Miss Owens-Lane. 'Really, darling, we are due at the Smithsons' right now. Can you finish this discussion so that we can go?'

'Sorry, Joan,' Greg Alston's reply was perfunctory. 'Why don't you go on without me? I want to talk to Mr Richmond. You'd be bored. I'll join you at the party later.'

But Joan had objections. She stood, and Marlie gave a mental sigh of envy at the socialite's tall, willowy figure. She thought, though, the blonde was far less attractive as her face sharpened in lines of anger. Her mouth took on an obstinate line that indicated to Marlie a high degree of selfishness.

Don't let her boss you around, Marlie silently rooted for the tall stranger, and then she brought herself up short. After all, it was none of her business, and she should be glad to see that autocratic nature given a setback. Still, she did not feel the socialite was the one to do it, but she was giving it a try.

'I do think, if I could spend my afternoon sitting here, you could return with me for the party,' complained Joan. She seemed to think nothing of the insult she was giving Marlie and Howard. Their type of business did not cater to walk-in customers, so no provision was made for the comfort of clients, but to suggest that the bare twenty minutes she had been waiting seemed like an entire afternoon was a little exaggerated.

Marlie and Howard exchanged glances. Whether or not her statement was true did not seem to bother Joan. She had given an order, and she expected it to be obeyed.

'I'll join you later,' Greg answered, apparently undisturbed. He took a thin leather key-case from his jacket pocket. 'You take my car back and I'll call a taxi or something.'

With his hand on her arm he ushered his companion to the door. Marlie, seeing the thunder cloud had not receded from Joan's face, took the opportunity to escape the room. If a storm broke, she wanted to find safe shelter. She headed for the ladies' room. Finally she could remove the paint from her nose, and she could thank Miss Joan Owens-Lane for the diversion.

The rumble of voices reached her through the door as she washed her face. The cool water raised her spirits and calmed her irritation. In its place came wonder. Greg Alston! The photographs in the newspapers had never done him justice.

Marlie had begun reading the society columns three years before when her parents, because of her father's study of foreign affairs, had started travelling for the State Department. She often read about people they mentioned in their letters, making her feel closer to her parents. In the circles of the rich, the powerful and the beautiful, Greg Alston figured prominently.

No wonder she had felt the power of his personality, the magnetic pull of his masculinity. Few women could remain unaffected by the gaze of those deep grey eyes. Hey, watch it! she warned herself. She knew that getting interested in him was asking for trouble.

Deliberately she forced her mind to the evening and the things she needed to accomplish. She had used a deplorable lack of foresight in not wearing more presentable clothing, covered with a smock. That morning she had been late in getting her clothes together for their two days out of town, and in the process she had forgotten she would not be driving straight to her apartment for a refreshing shower and a change of clothing. Normally she and Howard went out to the cabin at the weekends. On the way they usually stopped at the bank, a store or two, depending on what they needed, and always at the grocery store to pick up fresh fruits, vegetables and meats. For the nth time that afternoon, she looked down at her shoddy outfit and shook her head ruefully.

Just as she stepped out of the ladies' room, she heard her uncle call her name. Reluctantly she went back into the office where she saw Greg and Howard inspecting a carved decoy. It had been painted in surrealistic colours, someone's attempt at creating an ultra-modern style. For years it had been sitting on the shelf above the painter's bench. To Marlie it was jarring to her concentration. She had carried it to her uncle's office, hoping he would either have it sanded clean of the silver-and-black paint, or get rid of it.

'Who did this?' Howard asked as she walked up. 'I don't remember seeing it.'

Marlie had spent many of her adolescent summers running in and out of the factory. While only an emergency could get her into the office, she was as familiar with the workings and history of the firm as her uncle. In the matter of the signatures on the bottom of the decoys, a pattern of dots placed there by the painter, she often outdid her uncle in memory. She took the wooden carving with the offending paint and turned it over.

'What was his name?' she mused over the pattern of black dots that formed a flourishing number two. 'I can't remember his name, but it was that lanky college student who was here one summer.'

Greg Alston quirked his eyebrow in surprise.

'I thought you were the duck painter,' he said. 'Are you sure you didn't make some experiments? I thought it looked like your work.'

As her anger rose, Marlie wondered why this man had the power to throw her so off balance.

'I would never do that to a perfectly respectable duck!' she retorted and turned to Howard. 'The thing has been glaring at me, and I brought it in here. For heaven's sake—and mine—do something about it.'

'Relatives,' Howard sighed. 'Don't know why I hire them. She's been here two weeks and she's driving me crazy.'

'They'll get you every time,' Greg said solemnly. 'I try to stay away from mine, and never accept the responsibility for the ones I can't control.'

Marlie gave her uncle a dark look. His complaint was their private joke. This wasn't the first summer that he had been pressed for help. She had taken the job to assist him, but she couldn't complain that duty alone drove her to it. The factory was hot and dusty, and she had a choice of dressing like a raggedy-Ann or ruining good clothes. But after months of teaching, the work at the factory was a vacation in itself. Still, Howard didn't have to make Greg think she was there on her uncle's sufferance, as if she could do nothing on her own.

But Howard Richmond's mind had travelled elsewhere. He looked up at Greg with a shrewd expression.

'We're wasting your time, I guess. You didn't come here to look at duck models, and a man who probably doesn't know how many stores he owns, seldom traces his own shipments. You said you had something else in mind?'

Greg nodded. 'I did—I do.'

Both Howard and Marlie watched him as he frowned, thoughtfully rubbing his chin with his left hand. Marlie, the more impatient of the two, broke the silence.

'What was it?'

A smile, half sheepish, crossed his face, taking Marlie's breath away. In it she saw the little boy that hid inside the man with the rich and powerful reputation. She saw why his name was constantly in the society columns, most often linked with this or that socialite. His was a smile to melt a stone heart, and Marlie's lacked even a shell.

Careful, she told herself. Don't allow yourself to be drawn. There are too many females trying to snare him now. He's never going to look at a teacher who covers herself with paint in the summer.

The smile that grabbed at Marlie's heart was soon gone. In its place the businessman had returned. Though his voice held a thoughtful hesitancy, he was back to his original purpose.

'I don't know how to explain what I'm looking for. I was in Europe a few weeks ago, and there's a half-formed idea in my head—maybe I should say the glimmering of an idea. What I should like to do is see your machinery in action.' The smile came back for a moment and Marlie felt her heart grabbed again. 'If I'm wrong on my theories, I don't want to look like a fool, so I'd rather not say what I have in mind—until I know it's practical.'

Howard nodded. There was a full understanding in his smile.

'You deliberately came late, hoping you could run the machines yourself.'

The barely perceptible nod from Greg Alston showed he wasn't surprised at being caught with his intentions down. Without a word he peeled off the tailored linen jacket and started rolling up his sleeves. To Marlie, it seemed that an unspoken conversation was travelling between the two men. Greg had not asked for permission to run the machines nor had her uncle granted it, yet they started together for the back of the factory. Both curiosity and a desire to see Greg Alston out of his role as a corporate businessman drew Marlie along in their wake.

CHAPTER TWO

WHILE HOWARD Richmond gave Greg Alston a grand tour of the factory, Marlie sat on a stool and watched. The men walked from bin to bin, looking at the rough, sawed lengths of wood that filled the large topless packing crates. They were as absorbed as if they were viewing some marvel of science or nature. A running conversation continued as Marlie's uncle answered Greg Alston's questions and listened to his comments.

In keeping with her earlier irritation with Greg Alston, Marlie tried to hold it against him that he was keeping her uncle after hours in the hot factory. They had planned on going to the cabin for the weekend. Since she and her uncle were both riding in the same car, Greg Alston was tying up her evening, too. She held the thought as long as she could, but not being by nature a person who dwells on the unpleasant, her mind kept swerving over to curiosity. Why would a man as rich and powerful as Greg Alston risk dirtying his expensive, tailored suit and his perfectly white canvas shoes—canvas shoes? Who wore canvas shoes with a suit? Marlie let the questions about his footwear go. That was less of an enigma than his poking around in a dirty factory. After all, he had employees by the bushel to run his errands.

Like Howard, she, too, was wondering why he had made the trip to the factory. Maybe he really did want to run the equipment. He certainly didn't come to check on the shipment. Howard had been dealing with the Alston chain for years, but had never met the big man personally.

The men made an absorbing tour of bandsaws, belts and flapper sanders and had what seemed to be an inspired conversation over several electric hand-tools. Then they threaded their way between the equipment and wood bins towards the true heart of the factory. Backed against the rear wall, as if to defend itself from the world, stood the old automatic carving machine. In its day it had been the 'state of the art'. Modern advances had made smaller, more efficient models. They were computerized and outrageously expensive but, to Howard and Marlie, not one could compare with the old Howler, as they called it.

Marlie hooked her heels over the top rungs of the stool and smiled as she considered what Joan Owens-Lane would have thought about it. The belle of society would have seen it as an awkward conglomerate of frames, cables, motor and control box, all painted an eye-jarring bright orange. For years Marlie had considered it almost one of the family. When she returned at the first showing of summer, it was the first thing she visited after saying hello to Howard.

'Marlie!' Howard Richmond's voice was a combination of mild frustration and helpless plea. He stood at the control panel, looking over his shoulder at her.

'What is it?' she asked, wondering if the machine had broken down. She hopped off the stool, concerned as if something had happened to a dear friend.

Howard looked sheepish. 'You know, I haven't run this thing in five years. I'm not sure I remember how. You show Greg how it operates.'

Why you old liar, Marlie thought. You could take that machine apart and put it together wearing a blindfold.

She could see his intention and was irritated by his efforts. He was deliberately pushing her and Greg together.

Did he think he was playing Cupid, or did he just enjoy a fight? He was perfectly capable of either, she knew. She longed to tell him what she thought of his ploy, but it would be too embarrassing in front of Greg. She would have to settle for raking him over on another subject.

'If I were you, I wouldn't admit that in front of Mr Alston,' she said. 'That tells him we're vulnerable. After all, I'm only here during the summer. If Fred got sick during the winter, there'd be no one to get out the Alston orders, would there?'

'Well, I did know,' Howard spoke up in his own defence. 'I could figure it out or read the instructions again if you weren't handy.' Howard gave Marlie a sharp glance, letting her know she had hit the target.

Marlie's reasons for not wanting to operate the machine were purely vain. Some years before, she had helped Howard during the summer by operating the Howler when Howard needed assistance. Then, three years ago, Fred had been hired. He had proved so steady and dependable that Marlie had not been needed again. She hoped she remembered. If she made a mistake, Greg would be watching. The splattered duck, sitting on the shelf over her workbench, had given him cause to look down his nose at her. There would be no repetition of that if she could help it.

As she reached for the switch, Greg intercepted her. His long muscular arm stretched over her shoulder, turning on the power. Slightly startled, she glanced up at him. His mouth was still set in a straight line, but there were asterisks of laughter at the corners of his eyes.

'I can do that much already,' he said, as if he thought he deserved a medal for it.

'Then perhaps you can handle the rest,' Marlie retorted, a smile taking the sting from her answer. 'Next you insert the pattern. If you'd like to do that, I don't mind. They have a tendency to become weighty problems.'

Marlie pointed to the nearest pattern in the rack of un-likely shapes. She watched as Greg tried to keep his fea-tures from twisting into a frown.

Regardless of the size of the item carved, the patterns all measured close to a meter in length. The one she pointed out to Greg in no way resembled the shape of a duck. From the square fittings on each end, it tapered to what appeared to be a long fat steel rod with a curious, off-centred lump in the middle.

The wood, after being carved by the machine to resemble the pattern, had to have the supporting ends cut away be-fore giving evidence of a mallard duck. Even then it was just the body. The head was carved separately and attached with wooden dowels.

Greg eyed the pattern, gave Marlie a doubting look and carried it over to the machine that hummed its readiness.

She watched him as he held the heavy mould, turning it to consider the shape of the ends and the corresponding fit-tings on the machine.

Marlie felt a thrill of interest as she watched him. The weight of the steel pattern was considerable, making the muscles of his arms bulge with the strain of lifting it. The swelling of the muscles in his forearms and wrists she could see, so it wasn't difficult to imagine what was taking place beneath the silk shirt as it was pulled tight against his shoulders and back. When he knelt, his well-formed thighs strained against his linen trousers.

He's quite a man, she admitted, and stopped that train of thought immediately. Just admire the view, but don't get too interested, she warned herself.

Marlie saw his recognition of where to place the mould in the slight movement of his shoulders and a small indrawn breath. He was silently congratulating himself on his ability to figure it out without recourse to her advice.

His face had been turned away from her as he puzzled over the mechanics, but as he turned his head, his expression surprised Marlie. He was boyishly happy, learning something new, and she could see a hint of pride that, far from being autocratic, was a childish pleasure in showing her he could figure it out for himself.

He's trying to impress me, Marlie was slightly stunned, but there was no denying that look. She saw it every year as her students competed with each other. But to see it on the face of the great Greg Alston was incomprehensible. She denied what her eyes saw.

So you think you're so smart, she thought, but inside she knew she had been rooting for him. Nor did he turn cocky after his first success. Realising the pattern had to be fastened in place, he considered, and chose the correct handle to activate the clamp. He looked to her for direction before moving it.

Well, you're certainly nobody's dummy, Marlie thought. The Howler was designed to be simple to run. Still, as a corporate owner, the management of unwieldy carving machines hardly fell within the field of his everyday experience.

Fair, was fair, she decided, and went to the bin to get him a wooden blank, originally a length of eight by eight-inch timber. It had been trimmed on the bandsaw to make the shaping on the Howler a quicker operation. Silently she handed it to him and watched as he worked out the problem of how to insert it. He checked with her to make sure he was correctly securing the wood in place. Only when he was ready to put the machine in operation did she stop him.

'Here,' she handed him a pair of goggles. 'Put these on if you intend to see anything tonight.'

Marlie enjoyed the consternation. He was blaming himself for not thinking about the sawdust the machine would put out.

One up for the duck, she thought, and by his sharp look, her small win had shown on her face.

He pushed the button and the Howler roared into action. It clanked and growled, throwing sawdust into the air as if announcing. 'Hey, look at me! You talk about a worker, now see one in action!'

'You ham!' Marlie remarked to the machine as it shaped the body of a wooden duck. She was rewarded for her criticism with a mouth full of sawdust.

Greg, who had obviously been watching her, laughed at her for her error in judgment and found himself in the position of trying to get the flying particles of wood out of his own mouth.

So no one won that round, Marlie thought, heading for the water fountain. There was nothing left to do but to wash the sawdust out of her mouth in the restroom, though she had heard there was nothing harmful in swallowing it.

Howard had backed away from the Howler, but he was watching the operation as well as the continuing battle between Marlie and Greg. As she passed him, she noticed the curious, pleased expression he wore.

'What do you think you're doing, leaving me to show him how to handle that machine?' she asked as she went by. 'I warn you, that fellow and I just may come to blows,' she muttered, first making sure Greg was out of her hearing.

'Haven't had a good fight around here in years,' was Howard's comment. 'Besides, I bet nobody ever argues with him. He probably enjoys it.'

Marlie went into the ladies' room, taking time to rid her hair of sawdust while she was there. It occurred to her that her sudden flurry of hair combing made little sense, especially if she were going back out to the machine, but she let it pass without careful examination of her motives.

During the next hour and a half, Marlie sat on her stool, watching as the famous Greg Alston, corporate executive and society playboy, laboured over the making of ducks. Since the heads were carved separately and attached with dowels, he was not satisfied with just running the machine, but with Howard's and Marlie's help, he trimmed, sanded, drilled and doweled those he had carved out on the Howler. Some purpose of his own driving him, he went back to the big machine again and carved out several more bodies.

Marlie had drawn back, letting her uncle aid him with the smaller machines, but after one attempt at each piece of equipment, he continued without assistance.

Howard had located a second stool and joined Marlie as they sat watching Greg work. When he returned to the Howler and put another blank in the machine, Howard shook his head.

'I'd sure like to hire someone with his energy,' he said.

'I wonder what he's up to?' Marlie wriggled on her stool as a sudden, unpleasant thought occurred. 'He couldn't be planning on opening his own factory—'

Howard Richmond gave her a hard look.

'That wouldn't make sense. Too time-consuming for what he'd get out of it. No, I think it's like he said—he's got an idea and he wants to pull it off.'

'Working that hard on something he doesn't have to do?' Marlie countered.

'Mmm, maybe you're right. People don't do what they don't have to,' Howard replied in a lazy drawl. His exaggerated seriousness warned her he was aiming a thrust of wit in her direction. 'I would know better than to—say—try to get a schoolteacher to work during her vacation.'

'You should, unless that schoolteacher planned on inheriting the family conglomerate,' Marlie retorted.

Greg Alston turned off the Howler and strode over to where Marlie and Howard were sitting. He appeared to be a different man from the vision of expensive cleanliness that strode into the factory less than three house before. His pale blue slacks and shirt were nearly the colour of the sawdust that covered the rest of the building's interior, as was his dark hair. The once sparkling white canvas shoes were as filthy with grease and grime as Marlie had expected.

He pulled off the goggles and laid them aside. His tanned skin, his dark eyebrows and deep grey eyes contrasted sharply against the beige dust on the rest of his face. He looked as if he were wearing a Technicolor mask. He grinned at the two who had been watching.

'That's some machine! That fellow should be able to do anything!'

'Well, it won't,' Howard said with an unexpected moroseness. 'Just try to get it to type.'

Greg nodded. 'Probably won't spell, either,' he suggested.

'No, it's not too good with English,' Marlie added her bit. 'It emigrated from Austria, you know.'

'That accounts for it,' Greg wiped a grimy hand across his chin and looked down at his soiled clothing. 'Do you have a place where I can wash up? I'll call a cab, but the driver would take one look at me like this and run like crazy.'

'Sure,' Howard said, rising slowly from his stool. 'Where do you have to go? Marlie and I are leaving now. Could we drop you?'

'Might be out of your way.'

'Try us and see.'

Ten minutes later, the three were crowded together in the front seat of the battered station-wagon. Both Marlie and

Howard owned newer vehicles, but with the back seat folded down, the old wagon held the laundry, supplies, fishing gear, coolers and any last-minute items they decided to cart back and forth. The old car might sputter and heat up on hills, but it took the roads through the flat back areas of Virginia Beach with the slow roll of a battleship.

Marlie, sitting in the middle, kept her feet up on the hump in the floorboard, drew her knees in and tried to make herself as small as possible. She was conscious of Greg at her right, the proximity of his wide chest to her shoulder as his left arm lay across the back of the seat. She tried to concentrate on the road ahead, wishing she were not so aware of him, of his shaving lotion, of his relaxed breathing, of his aura of total masculinity.

He was naturally a large-boned person, and unused to being tightly squeezed into a small area. He lounged back, taking more than his third of the seat, as unconsciously as he took a big and successful man's share of life.

Marlie tried to keep her eyes on the road, but the rear-view mirror was in her line of vision. As she stared into it, she got a classic view of the cargo carried in the back. She doubted if Greg, with all his money, had ever ridden in anything as battered or as jumbled. He appeared unconcerned, but she wondered what he thought about it.

She kept tilting her head, curious about the route her uncle was taking. She had assumed Greg was staying in one of the luxury hotels near the beach, but they weren't heading in that direction.

Their speed was slow because the evening traffic was heavy. Summer brought vacationers to Virginia Beach from all over the country, and many parts of the world. The gulfstream, travelling reasonably close to the coast, warmed the water, and the natural gentle slope of the shore bottom was sandy with no rock or coral to cut the feet of visitors.

The city gave its attention to maintaining the golden sands, keeping them clean and litter free, and going to great expense to rebuild the beaches when the occasional hurricane created havoc along the coast.

The result was an influx of holiday-makers as soon as the weather would permit, and a holiday atmosphere that continued through the summer and up until the autumn storms drove the sun-worshippers from the beach.

For many blocks in from the shore, private residences and large apartment buildings catered to the tourists, and while they might be half empty and desolate during the winter months, during the warm part of the year they carried an air of one huge block party.

As Howard eased his way through traffic, Marlie savoured the atmosphere. Singly, in couples, in groups and family parties, people strolled across and along sand-dusted streets. They wore bathing suits or shorts, sunhats and dark glasses. On street corners they called farewell or suggestions for meeting later to bosom friends they had met only that day.

The air, blowing in the open windows of the slowly moving car seemed full of the prevailing spirit. It smelled of ocean, sand, suntan oil, hotdogs and charcoal smoke. Marlie watched one couple as they strolled down the street. They alone of all the people she had seen, took no notice of the holiday spirit. They were too caught up in each other. Without noticing, without gazing at each other, there was an absorption about them that excluded everything around them and left their world undisturbed. Marlie felt a longing suddenly, and realised it was centring on the large, relaxed man at her side. Then she felt, rather than saw him turn his head, as if he were reading her feelings.

'I'm taking you out of your way,' he said, making casual conversation.

Afraid he had noticed her self-consciousness, Marlie tried to be flippant.

'Oh, are you driving from that side of the car?' Marlie was brought up short by her own remark. She intended to be witty, but had she sounded as shrewish to him as she had to herself? If so, he apparently took no notice of it.

'In a manner of speaking,' he said casually. She saw his head turn to look over her shoulder, into the back of the car. He shifted slightly as he reached back, but she couldn't see what he was picking up.

'Humm, a Flueger,' he mused. 'You must have good fishing out your way.'

'Some of the best in the country,' Howard replied as he made a left turn, causing Marlie to wonder where he was going. 'We're just off Back Bay, you know.'

'Bluegills,' Greg said with decision. 'I've heard they are fighting little devils.'

'We call them bream,' Howard said as he slowed for two small boys to carry a large rubber raft across the street. 'Handled right, they're good sport and good eating.'

'I thought you went for the big fish,' Marlie said, biting her tongue after her admission. She hadn't meant to say anything about seeing his picture in the paper with a record-sized marlin, caught off the shore of Florida.

'Oh, there are fish and there are fish,' Greg said lazily, his grin telling her he knew exactly what was behind her remark. She bit her lip and looked ahead into the glare of the lowering sun as Greg leaned forward to speak around her.

'What test line is a fair handicap?'

Howard was silent for a moment. 'Remember what we bought last time?' he asked Marlie.

'No, but we special ordered a very light line, that I do recall.'

'Wish I could remember,' Howard sounded irritated. 'Good for bream though. They're small, but for its weight, you won't find a better fighter in the world.'

'I'd like to try them,' Greg mumbled and reached back again to turn over the box that held the Flueger reel.

Marlie hadn't heard the conversation that included their destination, so she was surprised when they pulled into the yacht basin. Most of the boats were small cabin cruisers. At one long pier several large yachts were drawn up.

It was natural, she thought, that Greg should have a yacht, and she thought it would probably be one of the larger ones. Had he been on an ocean cruise? Then she remembered he could have been travelling the inland waterway. Not too many people knew of the continuing path through bays, canals and rivers. It allowed ships of ocean-going size to travel from New Jersey to Florida and then on to Texas protected from the elements on the ocean and the gulf.

At Greg Alston's direction, Howard drove the battered station-wagon up to the parking area at the end of the pier, and parked. Marlie had expected Greg to get out of the car as soon as he opened the door, but as it swung wide, letting in the breeze off the water, he hesitated.

'How about coming aboard for a bite to eat? I'm interested in hearing more about your freshwater fish, and I'm hungry. How about you?'

'Not dressed like this!' Marlie was firm in the face of Howard's wavering hesitancy. She, too, was hungry, but the sound of a party could be heard from one of the other large boats, and she had visions of being compared to the beautiful Joan Owens-Lane again.

'And if I remember right, you were supposed to attend a party, right?' She put forward another reason why she felt it unwise to go aboard.

Greg shrugged, but there was a hint of obstinacy around the corners of his mouth.

'I've got other things on my mind. If you're upset about your clothes, that's a suitcase back there, isn't it? I'd feel better if I could shower and change before I ate. You could, too.'

'That suits me,' Howard said, overriding the objections Marlie planned on making. 'Are there three showers aboard? I'm for that, and I could eat a horse.'

'You'll have to settle for a seahorse, if I know my cook,' Greg said, getting out of the car. Once straight, he gave Marlie a bow. 'Just show me what you want carried on board, and I will be your own personal stevedore.'

'Oh, how the mighty have come down in the world,' Marlie said as she took the proffered hand, stepping out on to the sand-covered surface of the parking area.

During the winter, Marlie had chided herself after succumbing to the lure of a sale and buying a new set of luggage. Then it had seemed the height of the ridiculous to use an expensive set of pale blue suitcases, complete with matching dressbag just to go back and forth to the cabin on the river. Now she was glad she had spent the money. As she followed Greg Alston who carried the dressbag and weekend case on to the boat, she felt they somehow made up for her shabby appearance.

The yacht was everything she could have imagined if she had decided to dream up a luxury craft. It was probably not in the style of those owned by the legendary Greek shipowners, she reasoned, but in her opinion it was perfection. She guessed its length to be close to a hundred feet overall. In comparison with the other boats close by, it was outsized, and stood tall in the water when put against the smaller launches and the low profile of the sailing yacht moored next to it.

The gleaming white of the hull and superstructure contrasted with the dark water and the rich brown-gold wood teak of its trim. The wide fantail was designed to be glass enclosed, but when they arrived the panels had been folded back to take advantage of the evening breeze.

To Marlie, who sailed when time and opportunity permitted and was therefore used to boats being built close to the water-line, the superstructure seemed enormous. The enclosed area on the main deck was larger than many small residences. Above that was another large deck only partially filled by the wheel-house, and the captain's quarters, Marlie supposed.

The portholes in the hull were standard, but the wide square windows that looked out on to the main and upper deck were large, square, and in her opinion, far from nautical.

That same lack of shipboard flavour continued and was strengthened as they entered the salon. Formality prevailed in the guise of velvet-upholstered, high-backed easy chairs, a comfortable-looking cushion-backed sofa in a muted floral pattern and a dark green carpet that was thick and soft. The end tables and lamps could have been in any house where the owner had the taste for antiques and the wherewithal to buy the best.

The odours of diesel fuel, oil and gas that always seemed to prevail around the docks was lost once they boarded. As they passed through the salon Marlie caught a whiff of something delicious being prepared in the galley.

She followed Greg down a ladder—she reminded herself of the nautical term—though in reality it was a stair, only slightly steeper than usual. As they walked along a companionway she could see, through open doors, into the mahogany panelled staterooms. Where was that efficiently designed, but cramped style usually found aboard boats? she wondered, as she gazed into the spacious areas.

Greg led the way into the third area and laid the suitcase and dressbag on the bed.

'We're very civilised. The shower works just like any other. No strange handles to manipulate,' he said. 'See you on the deck in half an hour.'

'I'll be there,' Marlie answered and walked over to peer through the porthole. To approach her luggage would put her too close to Greg for her comfort, so she waited until he left the stateroom. Once the door was closed, she made a dash for the zippered bag, jerking the handle in her haste to get it open. Then she sighed in relief. The peach-coloured, spaghetti-strapped sundress was there. She had tried to remember, as she had been walking up the gangway, whether she had brought it or not. Her packing that morning could only be described as helter-skelter, since she had slept through her alarm clock's buzz. Dinner on a yacht had not been a part of her plans.

The shower was warm, washing away the grime and the petty problems of the day. Marlie stepped out of the stainless steel cubicle refreshed and prepared for a glorious evening.

As she wrapped a large soft towel around her body, using another to absorb the water in her hair, she smiled down at the large monogram on the towel. She wondered if her expectations for the evening were because of, or in spite of, Greg. The earlier arguments in the factory seemed a world away.

Had she really jumped on the man with both feet, as the saying went? There was no denying she had, and the memory surprised and shocked her. Had he really done anything to deserve it, or had the entire episode been her fault?

Perhaps it was the result of fatigue, the heat, and her frustration when she spilled the paint.

Working in the factory might be harmful, she thought. A winter spent in a classroom with energetic eight- and nine-year-olds was a strain. The vacation she could be enjoying was being taken up by the labour in the factory as she tried to help Howard catch up on back orders. They were almost up to date, so before long she could take some time off.

She dried her hair and decided she was being dishonest in her reasoning. Nothing could make her ill-tempered and snappish unless she allowed it. If she was shrewish, she alone was at fault. The decision was hers, and there would be no more of it.

She heard the roar of a speedboat, and shortly afterwards she felt the slight movement of the deck under her feet as the ship reacted to the smaller boat's wake. It brought her out of her reverie and reminded her she was keeping two hungry men waiting.

From the zippered carry-on bag that held her few cosmetic concessions to vanity, Marlie pulled out the blow-drier and went to work on her hair. As the warm air blew across the strands, she pushed it into a page-boy that waved slightly as it fell just below her shoulders. She surveyed the effect as it gleamed back at her from the small mirror over the built-in vanity. Because of the dying light, she flipped the wall switch. In the brightness her hair glistened and looked far different from the sawdust-filled mop she sported when she first boarded the ship. Not as striking as if it were platinum blonde, she thought, but then what was? Dismissing that little envious thought, she 'did' her face with a dusting of powder, added a light touch of eyeshadow and decided to leave off both blusher and mascara. Her eyelashes were thick and surprisingly dark for one of her colouring, and with the golden tan she had been building since the summer began, the blusher was unnecessary.

From the weekend bag she took the low sandals that were no more than leather soles in which long strings were threaded through loops, criss-crossing her feet, and wrapping around her slender ankles. They showed off her well-formed feet and legs and, by careful planning, she had been able to get narrow grosgrain ribbon to match many of her outfits, including the peach-coloured dress.

A glance at her thin gold watch as she fastened it to her arm, told her she was at the end of the half an hour her host had given her. She stepped into the dress, put her things back into her bags and closed them, making them ready to be carried to the car when they left.

A last look in the mirror assured her the dress was all she had expected it to be. The close-fitting bodice over the flaring skirt showed off her feminine but not over-full figure. She was unable, in the small mirror, to check the hemline, but looking down, she was pleased with the effect of the shoes and skirt together.

All hands on deck, she told herself as she left the stateroom.

CHAPTER THREE

WHEN SHE arrived in the salon, she found Greg alone. All the evidence of his labour in the factory had disappeared with his shower and change of clothing. His hair was still damp, and she noticed he had combed it while it was wet, with no thought of drying or styling it. Around the edges where it had begun to dry and was free of the restrictions of comb and moisture, the waves had begun to form. She felt an unaccountable pleasure in knowing he was careless about his natural good looks.

In wine trousers with a wine-and-white patterned shirt, he was casually dressed, but again that tailored elegance she had noticed in the factory was apparent. Still, he seemed more human. Was that because she knew him better now, because she was not shown up at a disadvantage? Possibly her more gentle feelings came about because she had decided not to allow the less attractive side of her nature to hold sway.

He had opened a glass door on a built-in bookcase, and had removed a wooden duck decoy. Marlie had noticed it as they passed through the salon earlier. It appeared to be one made, painted and antiquated in her uncle's factory but it was hard to be certain.

'One of ours?'

Greg looked up as she spoke. 'One made by your uncle. I don't know who painted it.'

Marlie stepped closer, her knowledgeable eye travelling over the markings on the wings. It was a decoy that had been made years before when the little curves that indicated the feathers had been put on with a thin brush and black stain. Now they used black, felt-tipped pens. The number of feathers indicated told her who had painted it. In the days of the brushwork, the markings had been kept to a minimum because of the time and risk involved. Only one painter had ever taken that much time with each decoy.

'Sally Marshall,' Marlie announced, remembering how Howard complained about the time Sally had put into each decoy, often making the shipments late.

'She knew how to paint ducks,' Greg replied, and the slight emphasis on the word 'she' brought Marlie to instant attention.

'Just what do you mean by that?' Marlie demanded. Her voice was sharp, made more so by the memory of chiding herself in the stateroom, accepting all the blame for the argument earlier in the day. Obviously she was wrong. He was deliberately provoking her.

A sharpness in Greg's glance indicated his surprise that she should take offence, but a mulish expression formed around his mouth, as if caught in a stance he was committed to defend. An odd humour glinted in his dark eyes.

'I didn't mean anything by that, but since the subject came up, you could take a few lessons from her technique—and her colouring. She's really very good.'

'I'm glad you like her work,' Marlie said stiffly. 'Perhaps if you speak to my uncle, he will get her back to do your work—if you're willing to absorb the cost of the time she takes.'

Marlie had been standing, her chin out, shoulders back, and eyes blazing. Greg Alston gazed down at her from the pinnacle of his superiority. She had struck an artery with her

jab, that much was apparent. His voice was cold, belying
what she had at first thought was a twinkle in his eyes.

'Alston's carries only the best. Our customers expect it,
even if they have to pay more. I've dealt with your uncle
because his work has always been superior, and on time—
until now.'

Until now. Superior and on time until now? The words
rang in Marlie like a fire gong. He was not only telling her
she didn't know how to paint ducks, he was laying the blame
for the lost shipment at her door. She took a backward step,
feeling herself revert to the seven-year-old tomboy who
wanted to punch her enemy in the nose.

'Sorry it took me so long,' Howard's voice from the
companionway interrupted the argument. Greg Alston
turned to greet Marlie's uncle with all the urbanity of a man
who had been marking time by discussing the weather.

'I thought it was a woman's privilege to be late.' Marlie
had tried to make her comment light, but the tremor in her
voice told her astute uncle the entire story. She saw his eyes
narrow for a moment before he turned his attention to their
host.

'I'm glad to meet your lovely lady,' Howard said. 'She's
like vintage champagne—getting better with age.'

'Is she better for the ageing, or does she just seem that
way when compared to the younger generation?' Greg
asked.

Marlie wondered if that, too, was some slur on her until
she realized they were talking about the boat. In her state of
agitation, even that bothered her. What was it with this man
that he and her uncle could talk in a language all their own?
It seemed they instinctively knew what the other meant, and
she felt left out of the conversation.

What is the matter with you? she demanded of herself.
Why are you suddenly a war looking for a place to happen?

Where was the Marlie who had a sense of humour, who was a happy young woman enjoying the labours of the factory after the brainwork of the winter? Why did she allow this man to get under her skin? He obviously didn't object to her duck painting. He had been getting her work for years as she had often helped out in the factory, so what were his complaints?

While she was wondering, Greg and Howard had been busy at a small bar. Howard handed her a glass filled with tomato juice and garnished by a stick of celery. She arched her brows, but his grin was reassuring.

'Made yours straight,' he said.

That, in their particular jargon, meant straight tomato juice, since Marlie had never developed a taste for alcohol. She took a sip and looked at the glass again. Something had definitely been added in the way of spices. The drink had a bite of its own and was delicious. Wrapping a napkin around the outside to prevent the condensation from dripping on her dress, she followed the men out on to the deck.

The sun was just dipping down behind the trees, and across the wide expanse of fresh water, the reflection rippled in wavelets of gold. The breeze, crossing the narrow strip of land that separated them from the ocean, had made the heat of the day a memory. As the glowing orb in the west slowly disappeared into a rim of brightness and then was gone, the lights of the other boats came on, glittering across the water in a multiplicity of dancing reflections.

The sounds that were somehow muffled by the day were more noticeable in the darkness. The tinkle of ice in glasses, the well-modulated voices of people enjoying a quiet but convivial gathering drifted from the nearest boat. Farther along the pier a child was relating some experience of the day—a young voice, pitched high with excitement.

While the men discussed draft and displacement, Marlie walked to the rail and stood looking out at the reflections of the light on the water. As usual, being around water brought out a peace in her. She had often wondered if there was any truth in the theory that man, like all life, came out of the sea. Like so many other people, she had an affinity with the water that refused to be denied.

'Hey,' Howard called to Marlie. 'You can admire the view later. We're hungry.'

She turned, feeling guilty that she was keeping them from their dinner, and returned Greg's smile as he motioned her to precede him into the dining room.

Again a semi-formality prevailed. The dark wood of the furniture and walls was a contrast to the snow-white table linen, the patina of old silver, and the sparkle of the glasses. A centrepiece of daisies and yellow candles added colour.

By a buffet laden with covered dishes, stood a short, chubby man in a white steward's coat. The aroma of the food drew Marlie towards the table along with Howard and Greg. She had forgotten how hungry she was.

Even if her work hadn't given her an appetite, she would have done justice to the dinner placed before her by Henry the cook, steward, and jack of all trades, as she was soon to learn. The tossed salad was garnished with a dressing made of vinegar and oil with spices that gave it a distinctive and unusual flavour. Crabflake *au gratin* and a baked potato were followed by a strawberry torte that could have made her jealous of the cook. But she was too grateful for excellence of a meal she had not laboured to prepare. Still, she gave Henry the satisfaction of knowing her feelings.

'I'm so jealous of your skill,' she said as he removed the dishes from the table. 'Is there any chance of kidnapping you? With your permission I'll torture you for the secret of that salad dressing.'

Henry grinned and started to reply, but Greg broke in smoothly.

'Henry's knowledge he keeps to himself, but I warn you, any attempt to steal him away would be useless. I keep a guard on him night and day.'

'But what guard can stand against both determination and ingenuity? You never know how far someone will go to get what they want.'

Marlie smiled over the candles set in tall glass cylinders. She sounded brash, she knew, but she wasn't going to let him have the last word.

'That's true enough,' Greg replied, a small smile softening his face. 'But trespassers should know about paying penalties. It would depend on relative values. Is what you're after worth the risk if you're caught?'

Marlie started to retort when she realised they had left the subject of Henry and were moving towards more dangerous ground. Greg was leaning back, watching her from under half-lowered lids, the smile that played across his face was that of a predator, stalking, watching, ready to pounce. She lowered her eyes for a moment, knowing his words held a trap. She was not going to fall into it, she decided. As if it were a physical action, she was aware of his emotional balance—mentally poised, waiting to parry and return a thrust. It occurred to her that the best way to catch him totally off guard was to remove his target, leaving him nothing to fight.

'Oh, well,' she sighed, shrugging her shoulders as if in defeat. 'Henry, your dressing is good—but there's a limit to everything.'

Her victory was Greg's impatience as he crumpled his napkin, laying it by his plate.

Henry served coffee by the loungers on the rear deck. Marlie sipped the strong black brew and turned her gaze back to the lights reflected on the water. The breeze from the ocean had cooled the air. The tiny wavelets of the inland bay were breaking against the side of the boat, creating their own music. The night was clear, full of stars, and the moon was rising.

Moonlight and romance. Marlie felt the words going through her like a song. Without conscious intention, she looked over at Greg. He was deep in conversation with Howard, telling a story about a fishing trip. She watched him as he talked, noticing the absence of gestures.

The deck was lit by torches. They served the dual purpose of keeping away insects and adding atmosphere. Greg Alston, she thought, should always stay in torchlight.

The flickering illumination brought out a primitive, an almost savage quality to his naturally good looks. The planes of his face created highlights and shadows. His eyes caught and reflected the flames that seemed to come from within.

When women write love songs, he's the object of their compositions, Marlie thought. Then unbidden came a less welcome idea. Miss White-and-bright would be the counterpart they had in mind.

'Ahoy—the *Veronica!*' came a call from the dock. Marlie looked over the rail to see several people start up the gangway. Leading the group was a tall blond man who waved a bottle of champagne like a flag. Behind him came Joan Owens-Lane and two other couples.

Was it her imagination, or did Greg show some reluctance as he rose and went to greet his guests? He introduced Lyle Kearns as the man with the bottle. Mr and Mrs Caulder were a pair of physical mismatches in Marlie's opinion. He was tall and grotesquely fat while she was short and must have weighed all of ninety pounds. His eyes measured everything in terms of possible cost, because his wife's arms and fingers dripped with jewels, making them a psychological match. Marlie had not caught their first names.

Kara and Bill Holmes were two of the beautiful people, tall and slim. They were open and friendly with Greg, Joan and Lyle, but their condescending air towards the Caulders said as much about them as it did the older couple.

The six people had come from another party, it was obvious by their dress. The men were wearing dinner jackets, and the women, floor-length attire. Mrs Caulder had unfortunately chosen to wear a long-sleeved mauve caftan which not only looked out of place and uncomfortable, but her hair, which had a slight reddish tint, made it an unflattering colour.

Kara, with her dark hair in braids that looped below her ears, was exotic in a silver, backless jumpsuit. Joan too wore a jumpsuit of sorts, a white close-fitting garment that was both backless and strapless. The loose, gold gauze jacket did nothing to hide her considerable charms.

Marlie thought the baggy jacket with its long sleeves and improbable length, it came almost to Joan's knees, would look ridiculous on anyone else. But grudgingly she had to admit Joan seemed to show up the others, Marlie included. Amazing what some women could do with style, she thought.

Joan had attached herself to Greg the moment she stepped on board, and after a sharp look of recognition at Marlie, she tightened her hold on his arm.

Marlie chided herself for that feline pleasure she felt, but it was clear in the factory that Joan had looked her over, summed her up in the light of possible competition and dismissed her. But since then, with a shower and a change of clothing, Marlie had taken a step up in the socialite's estimation. Joan clung to Greg, her voice so honey-sweet and false, Marlie wondered how he could stand it.

'Darling, I was worried about you,' she murmured just loud enough for everyone to hear. 'I was afraid you had been devoured by all those wooden ducks.'

'I was rescued just in time.' Greg's answer, Marlie noticed, showed more patient boredom than genuine interest.

Don't think like that, she warned herself. You're not in their league. She had to be practical or she was in for trouble, she knew. Still, the thought left her feeling a bit chilled and empty.

Henry appeared with more champagne and glasses. For a few minutes the guest mingled as glasses and drinks were passed about. Marlie, not at all interested in champagne, opted for another cup of coffee before the pot was removed.

Marlie had expected Joan to keep her stranglehold on Greg's arm for the entire evening, but the tall, silky Kara had other plans. She drew Joan away to the aft end of the deck with some gossip. Mrs Caulder followed. They gathered around a small table near where Marlie sat on a chaise-longue. By Joan's careful placement of her chair, so her back was between Marlie and the others, she effectively cut Marlie out of the conversation.

Between Kara and Joan, the talk was blatantly full of names often read in the papers, and Marlie noticed Mrs Caulder was also being excluded from the intimacy. She was not one to allow much of that, so she kept interrupting with titbits of information obviously gleaned from the gossip and social columns of various papers. Marlie felt sorry for the little woman, who looked winded by trying to keep pace with the others. She seemed determined to worm her way into the higher social structure.

Marlie let their verbal struggle go over her head as she looked out over the bay. The scene was still the same, the lights still danced, but the mood was lost under the hubbub of the boat. She tried to keep her mind on what she was seeing, but she was aware of the tensions surrounding the three women. Joan was tense, as if, in turning her back on Marlie, she half expected an attack. Kara was making moist circles on the little table with her glass. In little signals made up of moues and raised eyebrows, she was communicating her disapproval of Mrs Caulder to Joan. Mrs Caulder was shredding a paper cocktail napkin and chain-smoking, lighting one cigarette immediately after crushing out the one preceding it.

The men had gathered together in a huddle about ten feet away. Greg was leaning against the rail, idly turning the stem of a glass in his hand as he listened to one of Howard's fish stories. The others gave Marlie the impression they were only waiting for a chance to interrupt.

Bill Holmes was wearing a polite, patient attitude that left Marlie cold. Mr Caulder had finished assessing the cost of the boat and was inspecting the clothing of the others. Lyle Kearns was looking frankly bored.

As his eyes wandered, they met Marlie's. She gave a little shiver of apprehension when she realised she had caught his attention. She saw his face change from boredom to interest, to decision, to charm-boy on his way to make a conquest. She was reminded of the dial settings on a washing machine.

Lyle was weaving slightly as he crossed the deck and sat on the end of the chaise. Marlie drew up her feet to keep them from being trapped beneath him.

'You looked all by yourself, and I'm all by myself, so how about saying beautiful words to each other?'

'Sorry,' Marlie replied. 'There's no more room.'

He looked around, confused. 'No room for what?'

'No more room for words,' Marlie explained. 'Look around, words all over everywhere. Look at those long sentences from the fishing stores. See that marlin caught in that one?' If he thought she was a kook he might go away. No such luck. She could tell by the sudden light in his eyes he was in favour of a game, anything to break the pall of the evening.

He peered in the direction Marlie pointed. 'Yeah—but if we speak very low, maybe we can get our talk in under that group over there.' He waved a hand in the direction of an area on the other side of the deck.

'Oh, I don't think so,' Marlie argued. 'If they bunched up, ours would be pushed down into the bay, and if there is one thing I can't stand, it's soggy prose.'

Lyle nodded solemnly. Then he smiled. 'How about asking Henry to bring out a fan? We'll blow the pest away.'

'And have a breezy conversation?' Marlie asked. She gave herself ten points for a cliché.

'Fascinating!' the tall Kara said abruptly. She leaned forward, tapping Marlie on the shoulder with one long, perfectly manicured nail. 'Why haven't we seen you around before?'

'Oh, I'm around, I'm just usually busy—earning my living,' Marlie said airily. She expected that to take care of any further interest she might have received from Kara. Joan's smirk, intended to be an insult, was in fact a reward.

'Well, some people must do it, I guess,' said Mrs Caulder. She was quickly picking up on Kara's and Joan's attitudes, Marlie noticed. 'Tell me, dear, how do you occupy yourself?'

Marlie formed the words in her mind with exceptional clarity: I occupy myself by instructing the offspring of people who do not have yachts. No matter how she phrased it, she was still saying teacher. That was somehow too respectable an admission to the three snobs. They were ready to make fun, quite well-bred fun, of course, of anything she said. She wasn't about to give them her profession to shred with their perfect nails. She thought of saying she did night duty on the seamier streets in town, but that would be carrying things too far. That would embarrass both Greg and Howard. Then it occurred to her that the present truth might do as well. She looked them straight in the eyes.

'I paint ducks.'

Mrs Caulder and Kara looked blank. Joan snickered behind her napkin. Lyle parked his elbow on his knee and his chin in his hand. The alertness of his eyes proved his interest.

'How do you catch them?' he asked.

The explanation came from over Marlie's shoulder.

'With a duck catcher—it's a gun that shoots a lasso,' Howard said. 'Gal, I think we'd best be gettin' down the road a piece.'

Marlie, who was still nursing the cup of after-dinner coffee, nearly choked on a sip. Obviously from his countrified accent, Howard's reaction to the company was the same as hers. He was not the type to drawl, and he never sounded like a country bumpkin. He, too, was laying it on for their benefit. Fleetingly, Marlie thought she and Howard had a snobbery of their own. She felt justified since the others had started it, but she was willing to admit her own faults.

As she rose and turned, Marlie saw Greg standing by Howard. His mouth was grim.

'If you'll excuse me for a moment,' he said to the assembled group, 'I'll bring up Miss Richmond's bags. Miss Richmond, perhaps you'd like to come down to make sure you packed everything.'

The formality alerted her to his mood, even if she hadn't seen his grim expression. She had packed everything and she had no desire to be alone with him in his present mood. But short of refusing to go, there was little she could do. He looked angry. He didn't like the put-down she and Howard had given his friends, she was sure. But then neither she nor her uncle had asked to be included in their group. If he mentioned it, she would tell him so. She was primed for an argument when they entered the compartment.

In the stateroom she wordlessly swept her hand around to indicate nothing had been left. Then she nodded to the bags, which he ignored.

'Miss Richmond,' his voice was cold. 'I would advise you not to encourage Lyle Kearns.'

'What?' That was the last thing she expected.

'I am told I speak quite clearly. I would advise you, for your own good, to leave Lyle Kearns alone.'

A warmth spread into her cheeks, as she glowered up at him. She fought to keep her voice under control.

'Mr Alston, I have absolutely no interest in Lyle Kearns, nor in anyone else at the moment.' She paused and took a deep breath. She had a lot to say. 'If I did, I hardly see how it could be any concern of yours. You purchase a product made in my uncle's factory. Our responsibility to you stops with giving you a satisfactory product. Yours ceases with payment. If I choose to interest myself in anyone, including Mr Kearns, I need neither your advice nor your permission. Is that perfectly clear, Mr Alston?' Marlie took a deep breath. Under the circumstances, she was rather proud of herself.

Greg's answer was to step forward suddenly, catching her up in his arms. She was surprised into immobility as his lips came down on hers. Her first inclination was to fight, and she pushed at his shoulders, but his response was to hold her tighter. Her breathing became difficult, but the restriction was within her. She was aware of his strength, and his repression of it—it pulsed in his hands, and his heart within his hard chest beat against her as she was trapped by his arms.

His tongue, seeking entry between her lips, touched tender places, sending thrills racing through her. His hands, hot against her back communicated their own messages of desire.

Her mind fought his insolence, the arrogant supposition that she would welcome his advances, but her body instinctively recognised in him the source of a fulfilment long desired, and she warmed and trembled at his touch. She had ceased struggling, and her arms were moving to wrap around his back, when he suddenly released her.

She stumbled back against the bulkhead, staring at him.

'Miss Richmond—' His voice was maddeningly calm. 'Concerning those persons in whom I interest myself, both my advice and permission are needed.'

He picked up the bags and left her standing with her mouth open. He had disappeared down the hall when she closed it with a snap. Her eyes narrowed. Her voice was almost a whisper as she spoke into the empty passage way, but it held the emotions of a scream.

'You—you—oh, am I going to fix you!'

CHAPTER FOUR

As THE sound of Greg Alston's footsteps receded, Marlie stood in the stateroom. She could feel the warmth in her cheeks, the pulsing of blood in her veins. Desire and anger were both passions, and one, the other, or both would show in her face if she went on deck right then. She hurried to the small but well-equipped bath and dampened a face-cloth, holding it against her flaming cheeks. The mirror showed she had achieved some results, but not enough. There was nothing she could do about the sparkle in her eyes.

'Stop that,' she ordered, but the blue eyes that stared back at her showed an obstinate desire to retain the feelings she was trying desperately to hide.

Not wanting to face that mirror any longer, she went back into the stateroom and looked around. She had better make sure she had left nothing behind. No way was she coming back after any forgotten articles. The smooth spread on the bed, the top of the built-in dresser were bare of her belongings, but she was a creature of habit. Could she have dropped something in a drawer—a comb, a brush, the soiled clothes she had worn in the factory? No, she remembered packing them in a plastic bag to keep the sawdust from getting on her clean clothes.

Sure now that she had indeed packed everything, and hoping her experience with Greg would not show on her face, Marlie left the stateroom, closing the door behind her. Her thoughts were in a turmoil. She absently bid good night to the six people who were on the deck and hurried down the gangway and over to the car. Greg had been leaning over, his arms braced against the window while talking to Howard, who was already behind the wheel. Before he could come around to assist her, Marlie was in her seat with the door closed.

He returned to Howard's window, bending down to look in at her. 'I enjoyed our dinner,' he said with a half-smile. 'We'll have to do it again sometime.'

Was that a put-down for her rudeness? Marlie wasn't sure.

'The pleasure was ours,' she answered through lips unaccountably tight and pursed. Ordering herself to behave normally was becoming increasingly unsuccessful.

He stepped back away from the car as Howard gave a wave and started the engine. As Howard backed the car and turned it slowly, the lights illuminated the side of the yacht. The white hull and superstructure stood out beautifully against the starlit night, a vision from a modern fairy-tale. For the first time, Marlie noticed the name of the ship. The *Veronica*. Another woman in his life, Marlie thought.

Marlie noticed none of the traffic on the busy highway along the ocean. When they turned off on the series of country roads that wove through the back areas of Virginia Beach, she stared out into the darkness, not seeing the lights from occasional subdivisions that became less frequent.

Some miles farther on they left the suburbs behind and drove through farming country. The car lights showed long straight rows of growing crops. The green plants stood out against the rich black earth. Through the windows of the car came the scent of fertile black soil that had been recently disturbed by a cultivator, the summer scent of dust warmed by the sun and left to cool in the evening. Occasionally she caught the perfume of honeysuckle where the fast-growing blooming weed had begun to wind itself along a fence.

The lighted windows were farther apart as they passed farmhouses, each set back from the road, usually surrounded by huge dark trees whose size indicated how long those large farms had been in existence.

Howard turned off the state route and drove along the smaller, private road that led to the river. The Norvels, who owned most of the road had opted to keep the timber on their land in preference to farming. Instead, they sold off small portions to select people for the building of fishing cabins, and ran a large camp-ground and fishing dock.

The road was dark, overhung by the wood that encroached up to the pavement, and Howard slowed, careful not to drive too fast. Sometimes the children from the camp-ground wandered through the woods and appeared suddenly out of the darkness.

Marlie's mind was neither on the drive, nor wary because of the children. Her thoughts were still back aboard the yacht.

Veronica. The name was beautiful, musical, it rolled off the tongue. She was probably a beautiful woman, Marlie thought, if the yacht had been called after her. There would be a real Veronica somewhere. And whoever she was, Marlie thought, she was probably more important in Greg Alston's life than Joan Owens-Lane.

Marlie's cheeks began to burn again. Suddenly she wished she hadn't been in such a hurry to get in the car. She wished she had stood right there on the dock and demanded to know what kind of man he was. He had Miss White-and-bright on his arm one minute, was kissing her the next. Why the man was a Bluebeard!

She wriggled in her seat, angry with herself that she had wasted a single thought on him. Remembering how pleased she was that he had given so little attention to Joan on the boat was enough to make her anger flare up again.

Let that teach you, she told herself. Mind your business, and don't think about him any more.

Consciously, she gave herself a stiff lecture. Some perverse little thought kept trying to intrude, saying, now here's what we'll do when we see him again.

'Marlie Richmond, you're impossible.' She had spoken aloud before she realised it.

'I've known that for years,' Howard replied. 'What brought on that sudden realisation?'

'Never mind,' Marlie snapped. 'You can either pull in at Frank's, or you'll do without breakfast in the morning.'

'Oh, oh. Messed up your schedule, huh?' She saw Howard's grin by the light of the dashboard. Marlie turned her face to the darkness wondering why her uncle would find that so funny.

The flurry of grocery shopping in Frank's Grocery, the little back-country store, and the hurried activity in unloading the car at the cabin, pushed Greg to the back of her mind. Usually they arrived at the waterway early enough so that the weekly chore of moving in was finished before dark. In good weather they took the lawn chairs from the storage shed and enjoyed sitting by the water until time for bed. They maintained a schedule of early rising on the river.

Marlie finished her unpacking, pushing Howard to help, and was glad to crawl between the cool sheets of her bed. She seldom had any trouble sleeping because her days were full of activity. The difference in teaching and working with her hands left her with an almost pleasant fatigue. But that night sleep fought her. She tossed in her bed, knowing she was tired, but when that pleasant drowsiness stole over her, back would come Greg's face. Most often it was accompa-

nied by Joan Owens-Lane's platinum-blonde head at his
shoulder.

She turned over and mauled her pillow, not sure if she was
using it for an effigy of Greg or Joan. The socialite was
never going to be her best friend, but Marlie kept insisting
to herself that she disliked Greg just as much. He had one
woman clinging to his arm, and yet he was finding the
chance to kiss another in the stateroom. That was, she
thought, a little too much, especially when that second
woman was Marlie Richmond.

She was surprised by the effect of that kiss. The memory
of it was still on her lips, she could still feel his hands on her
back as if he had branded himself on her body, a body that
had turned traitorous in its desire, and was not obeying her
conscious commands to forget him. Marlie's mind fought
the war of her unbidden thoughts versus her common sense
until sleep came.

Even though she had been late getting to sleep, Marlie
awakened early the next morning. Before dawn she was up,
dressed, and had made a pot of coffee. As the light grew in
the sky she watched it from her favourite spot, a large stump
that had been carefully sawn to her specifications. Years
before, a huge old oak tree had shaded the cabin, but lightning had destroyed her tree, so the caretaker had the stump
cut at two levels. The lower one was two feet from the
ground, and the upper, eighteen inches higher, making a
chair that Marlie had painted to keep the raw wood from
rotting away. For the past three years she had made early
spring trips to the river, planting marigolds and zinnias
around the base. Her labours had produced a colourful
garden around the rustic seat.

To Marlie, the best part of the day was its beginning. She
preferred to come out to her stump while night still held
sway. At first, the world seemed not to notice the faint grey

streaks in the sky, but little by little it became aware. A faint breeze came alive. It brought movement among the leaves of the trees, the pussywillows on the river bank and the grass, as if the plants themselves were stretching towards the faint light.

She heard the flutters of little feathered wings and single uninspired chirps among the birds, as if they enjoyed their sleep and protested its end. The flowers at her feet were only shadowed caricatures of themselves when she first arrived, but they seemed to grow in colour as if freshly painted by the day. Then the birds, cheerful little fellows when once awake, flew down and hopped around, looking for their first food of the day.

As the light grew, she could see, along the river, the other cabins, and around the bend the dock where the campers could rent boats or launch their own. The camp itself was out of sight in the trees, The rustic cabins, set a good distance apart, and their mowed yards were all that intruded on nature. The waterway that lay dark and quiet in the growing light, was originally a river, and Marlie supposed it had been shallow at one time. Years before it had been dredged and was now a part of the inland waterway, where even some ocean-going ships could travel along its course. Her head was turned to watch the lightening of the water, so the voice startled her.

'Venus rose from the waves. I can't remember who rose from the flowers.'

Marlie looked over her shoulder to see Greg standing nearby, a fishing rod and a tackle box in his hands.

'A duck painter,' Marlie said, putting her cup on the upper plateau of the stump that served as both seat-back and table. She pushed down the elation that tried to spring up inside her and eyed his fishing equipment critically. 'You look loaded for—birdwatching?' There was no line on his reel.

He laughed. 'Howard said he could supply me with the right line to fish for bream. Not many sports shops open this early.'

'No,' Marlie bit back a laugh. His term, sports shop conjured up a vision of carpeting, fancy equipment, and enthusiastic clerks who sold specialised equipment at outrageous prices. In the vicinity of the waterway and back bay, he would find only general stores that sold everything from fishing equipment to eggs, milk and cornplasters. Two still had old-fashioned pot-bellied stoves. Her grin refused to remain hidden.

'No, our local—sports shop—doesn't open until seven.'

The flash in his eyes said he knew he had made a mistake.

Um-m—caught with your jet set showing, Marlie thought. But though he was casually dressed, everything about him said socialite, or that he was a step above the average. He was wearing what she thought might be termed designer jeans, the type never advertised on television. The pale grey knitted shirt needed no appliqué on the front to announce its quality. Such gimmicks only announced they sought the status Greg Alston took for granted.

He was wearing blue canvas deck-shoes and carried a denim jacket over his arm.

Still, he wasn't relying on his money to carry him through, she thought. She watched him strive for something to take her attention away from his thoughtless remark. He was saved by Howard who banged the door to the screened porch as he came out, carrying the coffee pot and two cups.

'Found the place, I see,' Howard held out a cup which Greg took.

'Either that, or he got lost in our direction,' Marlie said as she reached for her cup, irritated that Howard had said nothing about Greg's intended visit. Yet he had certainly known about it, if he had offered to supply Greg with a fishing-line.

Except for Marlie's stump, there were no seats on the lawn. Neither she nor Howard had had time to bring out the folding aluminum chairs they used in the yard. Howard squatted, one foot under him, the other slightly in front to balance himself.

'Pull up a chair,' Howard said. Knowing her uncle as well as she did, she knew Greg was being tested. The good opinion Howard had formed of the man in the shop had been offset on the boat by his choice of friends.

She returned to her seat on the stump, watching the wealthy socialite out of the corner of her eye. Greg imitated Howard, appearing to be as at ease as any farmer taking a seat between ploughing.

'You mean sit on my fist and rear back on my thumb?' Greg asked.

'Lord, I haven't heard that one in a hundred years,' Howard laughed. 'Had breakfast?'

Marlie knew Greg had passed with honours. She wondered if she was happy or sorry.

'Now why should I have breakfast?' Greg looked at Marlie over the top of his coffee cup. 'I thought I was invited for—let's see—it I remember right it was good Virginia ham, fresh tomatoes and the best home-made biscuits east of the Pecos?'

'Naw,' Howard shook his head. 'Don't give the girl a swelled head. Doubt if she could outdo anybody past the Mississippi.'

Greg sighed. 'Well, I'll just have to rough it, I guess.'

'Thanks!' Marlie leaned over, pouring her remaining coffee into a bare spot in the flower bed. 'That's why you made sure I bought that ham last night, but you didn't see fit to tell me we were having biscuits for breakfast.' She stood up, shoving both hands in the pockets of her jeans. 'You can forget the best fishing, I haven't turned on the oven.' She strode off towards the cabin, and not until she entered the kitchen did she remember the coffee cup sitting on the stump.

She called to Howard from the window.

'Bring in my cup and some tomatoes when you come!' She hoped there were tomatoes on the vines. But she wasn't going to be embarrassed if there weren't. Howard had promised them, not she. He sometimes forget the terrapins had a feast when they could reach a ripe one. Working quickly, Marlie flipped on the oven, set the table and laid out what she needed to prepare breakfast. She cooked the way she had been taught by her mother who had been schooled by her own mother, and she swiftly sifted the self-raising flour into a large bowl, putting in more than she would usually do for the bread she was making.

She had sprayed her bread pan, made a depression in the flour and was adding the milk, salt, baking-powder and shortening when Greg strolled into the kitchen. He was carrying the coffee pot in one hand, and the handles of the three cups were hooked over the fingers of the other.

'Howard went tomato hunting,' he said, putting his load on the counter. With his head cocked to one side, he watched as Marlie, using her right hand, mixed the ingredients for the biscuits.

He leaned against the counter, supporting part of his weight on his left elbow and forearm. He was too tall for his stance, so his left knee was bent, and Marlie was aware of its closeness. The faint elusive scent of his aftershave was a brand unfamiliar to her, but then it would be, she supposed. There was something persuasive about it, very understated, yet it created its own undercurrents. Was it the brand, or him? she wondered.

She was terribly aware of his closeness, his arm lying casually on the counter, the muscles of his forearm swelling slightly with the strain of holding his own weight.

His eyes were moving from her hands, working with the dough, to her face. She was aware of their gaze, and though she couldn't be sure, she felt a tingling along her side as if her body had been lightly touched by his appraising look.

What was he thinking? she wondered. After experiencing Henry's gourmet cooking, she thought he would probably find hers countrified. Worried about it, she jumped to her own defense before she was struck.

'Like it or not, I make bread by an old family custom,' she said airily. 'For more than a hundred years—I guess a hundred and thirty now—' She paused, wondering about the story and its age. 'Anyway, since my great-great-grandmother's time, we have always made bread the same way.'

'Sounds like some story,' Greg said, shifting his weight. Was it her imagination, or did he move closer?

'A family legend,' Marlie replied. 'Years ago, my great-great-grandmother's family had a small farm. The land wasn't too good, the crops had been bad, and they were very poor.' Her voice slipped into the dreamy tone she used with her class that kept them spellbound when she told them stories.

'Some miles away there was a very rich man who was getting on in years, and he decided it was time to take a wife. He was a very handsome man—he was said to ride a white horse.' She raised her eyebrows as she glanced at Greg.

'That may or may not be true about the horse. Well, he started visiting all the families in the area, looking for a young wife. Naturally she had to be able to cook, so he would arrive just before dinner-time and watch the noon meal being prepared. Oh, I forgot to mention that he was a man who hated waste.'

The dough was the right consistency, so Marlie, using a little of the excess flour, rubbed her hands to clean off the clinging dough and started forming the biscuits by hand. From long practice she knew just how much to pinch off each time to get them uniform. She was acutely aware of Greg's closeness as he watched. To take her mind off him she continued with her story.

'Most people roll their dough out on boards and cut their biscuits with a cutter, or, barring that, the top of a drinking glass will do. Then they take the scraps and reform, roll and cut again. But you can only reroll once and then the bread gets tough, so the last scraps are usually thrown away. Well, the wealthy old gentleman didn't like that.'

'He thought it was wasteful,' Greg said.

Marlie nodded. 'He kept riding his horse down the road until he reached my great-great-grandmother's house. I told you they were poor—so poor they didn't have a bread-board, a rolling pin, or even a biscuit cutter—'

'And they had no glasses, they were drinking out of Mason jars,' Greg added. Marlie gave him a speculative look. Was he making fun of her? No, he seemed to be interested.

'Exactly. So when my great-great-grandmother made her biscuits, she shaped them by hand. Of course there was no waste, and the wealthy man had found his wife. That's the way customs begin, I guess. Anyway, since that time we've always made our biscuits by hand.'

'Any white horses on the horizon?'

His question caught Marlie by surprise. She looked up to see his wide grin and the amusement in his eyes.

What have I done? she demanded of herself. How could she repeat that old tale to him, a wealthy bachelor, sought-after by women from all over the country? He had to be thinking Howard, too, was following in the old customs, bringing him home to see the daughter of the house at work in the kitchen.

Knowing what he must be thinking, mortification caused her to want to sink through the floor. She felt the scalding blush rise to her cheeks. She threw up a hand in an attempt to hide it.

Greg laughed and handed her a paper towel.

'You do wear the strangest things on your face,' he said.

Marlie looked down at her hands, covered with flour. She didn't have to see a mirror to know what she had done. She glared up at him, so perfectly groomed, his attire so spotless, and wondered what it was about him that made her seem so ridiculous in his presence.

The sheer impotency of her anger caused her to tremble. While he stood grinning she jerked the paper towel from his hand and threw it on the floor.

'Oh-h-h!' she squealed, stomped one plimsoll-shod foot and raced out of the kitchen.

Five minutes later, with clean face and hands, Marlie re-entered the empty kitchen. Had her outburst disgusted Greg Alston so that he had decided to leave? she wondered. Before she had time to worry or consider whether or not she was in favour of it, she heard his voice outside as he talked to Howard. The hum of the well pump and the splash of water accompanied their voices.

Marlie had the thick slices of ham sizzling in the pan, and was just sliding the biscuits in the oven, when Howard and Greg came in, each carrying two large tomatoes.

'Beefsteaks,' Howard was saying. 'You don't find them in the stores, they don't grow in the pretty shapes the housewives like to buy, but just wait until we cut into them.'

While Howard sliced tomatoes, Marlie heated another skillet and broke half a dozen eggs into the pan. By the time they had cooked to picture perfection, the ham, the tomatoes and the biscuits were on the table.

Marlie was anxious about how she was going to face Greg over breakfast, but with Howard at the table, she need not have worried. While she ate and considered what to put in their lunch, Howard swung the conversation over to where they would go on their day-long expedition.

The sides of the waterway were pocked with small widened areas where the current of the river had once meandered, creeks entered, and in many places the fish abounded.

Greg seemed to be giving Howard his entire attention, but twice she saw his gaze travel in her direction, and his knee, under the table, rested very close to hers. Twice she tried to move her feet, but that was a mistake. He shifted, too, and his leg came close again, not quite touching. She could feel the warmth, the brush of his trouser leg. He left her just that fraction of room to make any complaints foolish, yet he didn't allow her to forget his presence.

Marlie kept her eyes lowered to her plate, but she couldn't help seeing his strong arms as they moved at his side; his hands on the table when he paused to speak. The fingers of his left hand slowly rubbed the edge of the plate, bringing to Marlie the memory of those same hands as he had caressed her back the night before. She nearly choked on the ham and gave up trying to eat. She wondered if he had any idea what he was doing to her, but of course he did, she thought. Wasn't he supposed to have women up to his ears? She fought back her feelings and rose from the table.

'Excuse me, but if you're going fishing today, I'd better get your lunch ready,' she said. Efficiency, that was the game. Keep herself busy until he was safely away. She started taking bread, meat, tomatoes and lettuce from the refrigerator. She stopped to eye what she put on the counter. The one thing she was not going to do was touch anything that would get her hands dirty. Not while Greg Alston was in the cabin.

'You mean you're not going with us?' Howard asked, when she saw them off at the boat.

'That's exactly what I mean,' Marlie answered, looking back at her garden. 'There comes the time in every gardener's life when she has to weed, and this weekend is it. You have a good time, and I'll do my thing around here.'

Was that disappointment in Greg's eyes. She pushed down the little pang she felt in herself. All he wanted was someone to tease. He might be the great Greg Alston, but even he would think twice about trying to make a fool out of Howard. But Greg was used to having flunkeys around, someone who played the fool, to make him look good in comparison, she thought. Well, let him find someone else. She wasn't hiring on to be the crew and the joker.

'You have a good time,' she said lightly, 'and I warn you, I'm planning on having fish for dinner. If you don't bring it, you don't eat.'

She stood on the grass and gave the boat a shove with a pole they kept for that purpose. Before it had drifted out into water deep enough to start the outboard motor, she had turned back towards the cabin.

Behind her she heard a sputter and a roar. She turned to wave as the bow of the fourteen-foot aluminum boat rose. The seventy-five horsepower outboard motor brought the stern down almost to the surface as the propeller bit into the water.

The boat wasn't out of sight before Marlie regretted her decision. Why had she decided to remain on the shore, when she could be out with them, enjoying what she came to do? She loved to fish, she hated pulling weeds in the garden.

Greg Alston was the reason. If it hadn't been for him, she would be with Howard. In minutes they would be sitting in the shade of some overhanging tree branches, revelling in nature as it was supposed to be. Weeding around hybrid vegetables and flowers just didn't do it.

It was all Greg Alston's fault. She looked back at the river that was silent after their departure.

'Use him for the anchor!' she shouted after the departed boat.

CHAPTER FIVE

ONCE THE breakfast dishes were washed and dried, Marlie attacked the garden. Her mood required vengeance, and every weed became Greg Alston. She usually dreaded the chore of tugging them out by the roots, but with the socialite playboy in mind, she ran out of offending plants before she expended her energy.

Marlie's patch of garden would have fitted in a medium sized room. The purpose of the small plot was not principally the growing of vegetables, but to give her a use for other frustrations. She thoroughly enjoyed working with the soil in the early spring, and the planting. She came out on weekends as soon as the danger of frost had passed, using the labour as a release for the frustrations of a school-room full of active eight- and nine-year-olds. Third graders were rewarding to teach, but when the warm days began, and the youngsters were feeling they had spent half their lives in that classroom, they became restless and unruly. Marlie used the planting as an emotional release and spent the rest of the summer wishing she had taken up jogging.

To Howard's remarks that other emotional releases were less work and more rewarding, she turned a deaf ear. When he was persistent, she retorted that if he had wanted grandchildren, he was supposed to start with his own kids first.

'Rather have the fun and not the responsibility,' he always answered.

To her accusations that he set one standard for himself and another for her, he refused to listen. To him, women were supposed to be married to be happy. In his mind, the same wasn't true for men. When she reminded him that for every woman there had to be a married man, he usually remembered something that needed doing, and that something effectively removed him from the conversation.

Since she had her own apartment in the city, Howard was not aware of her romantic life. Most of it was too bland to make good conversation, she thought wryly. Thomas Carson, the new assistant principal had been very attentive, but she was aware that their relationship was, at best, just a convenient pairing off between two single people at social affairs involving the other teachers. Occasionally they went to a movie or a concert. The intervals between those dates had been lengthening since she had made it plain she had no romantic interest in Thomas.

That's what I need, she thought. I need a handsome hunk to build my ego after Mr. Corporation.

The weeding done, she marched in the house and turned out three cabinets, going from them to her closet which was almost filled with the debris of clothing she had ruined at the factory, or puttering around the outboard motors when she stood by as assistant for Howard's mechanics.

While she was packing some ruined shirts in a bag to use at the factory for paint rags, she looked in the mirror.

Greg was certainly right. She did wear strange things on her face. A smudge of dust or dirt ran down her cheek and across her chin. If Howard and Greg returned early from fishing he would be laughing at her again. She looked at her watch, unable to believe not only the morning, but half the afternoon had passed. She rushed the bag of old shirts out to the station-wagon so that they would not be forgotten in the flurry of Sunday night packing.

The next two hours she devoted to Marlie. A long shower, complete with shampoo and a home hair treatment, she followed by a manicure, sorely needed after her struggle with the weeds. She eyed her choice of clothes in the closet, settling on a pair of light blue gaberdine trousers and a silk shirt which was the same shade as her trousers with the darker flowers, cunningly appliquéd, matching her eyes. Her make-up was subdued, with only the faintest eyeshadow and blusher. In a spirit of fun, she put her hair up in the two cocker spaniel ears.

That, she decided, would offset any ideas Greg might have that she was interested in him. What female, when she was after a man, would risk looking like a kid, and an unfashionable one at that?

She surveyed herself in the mirror, liking the effect, but not quite satisfied. A slight darkening of the eye shadow, as well as a little blusher added to the chin, helped to bring her face into focus and detract from the hair flopping over her ears.

The general idea, she reminded herself, was to make him think she wasn't making herself attractive for him. If she could do it without his knowledge—she slammed her hairbrush down on the dresser. Why were thoughts about that man governing her every action? She stalked off to the kitchen, promising herself she was not going to think about him again.

After a few minutes of banging cabinet and refrigerator doors, she set out the ingredients for cornbread. If Howard and Greg came back with a string of fish—and knowing Howard, they would—her uncle was going to expect another family favourite. Greg's opinion of what they called 'fish bread' was not going to matter.

Fish bread was a misnomer. None of the ingredients had anything to do with fish. It was her standard recipe with whole kernels of corn cooked in the batter. The secret of making it the way Howard liked was in heating the heavy iron skillet on the top of the stove, adding enough oil so that the round flat cake would come out cleanly when done, and sprinkling a few grains of cornmeal into the greased skillet. The batter, when poured in the pan, sizzled, giving the bottom and sides a crust that could be achieved no other way.

With the batter waiting on the back of the stove, Marlie mixed up a crisp green salad and stored it in the refrigerator. Outside, she placed the folding aluminum chairs in the shade, and put fresh wood in the open fire pit that was surrounded by a low stone wall.

When the sun was out of sight behind the trees, she lit the fire and was relaxing with a glass of iced tea when the boat came around the bend in the river.

She raised her glass in greeting. She was ready for the fish fry, her preparations standing by. There was nothing else for her to do, and her hands were clean. This time she was ready for Greg Alston, and there was going to be nothing on her face but make-up.

Because of the large boats that travelled the waterway, and the experiences of their neighbours, Marlie and Howard had eschewed a dock. Instead they had installed a slip cut into the bank, and just large enough to hold their two boats.

When Howard cut the motor and let the boat drift into the slip, Greg jumped out and tied the bow line to the cedar post that had been driven deep into the bank for that purpose.

'Do we eat, or do we starve?' Marlie called out.

'We eat! Boy, do we eat!' Howard called back, holding up a string of fish, four of which were freshwater bass.

'Did you tell our guest the rules?' Marlie asked as they walked over to the chairs by the fire.

'Sounds like I'm in for something,' Greg commented.

'Oh, I don't know,' Marlie replied. 'The rule around here is, you clean what you catch. Are you responsible for much of that string?'

Howard laughed as Greg shook his head in defeat.

'Can't win for losing. Okay,' he got to his feet. 'I'm starving, so I better get to cleaning.'

Marlie sat back, watching the two men as they walked across the yard. Howard paused to pick up the end of the hose as they disappeared around the end of the cabin. While they were out of sight, she slipped into the kitchen, turned on the oven for her bread and gathered the plates, glasses and silverware to set the table. A table-cloth and a clear sheet of plastic completed her load.

When the men reappeared, she was again seated, but the battered round table was covered with a gay cloth on which daffodils rose from the circular hem. The bright yellow dishes and green glasses and napkins kept up the motif. Over the set table Marlie had spread a clear plastic cloth to protect it from dust and insects.

It was Howard's time in the kitchen. He had his own secrets for the fish batter, and Marlie was never allowed to watch the preparation. Since his recipe came from Marlie's mother, she knew exactly what he did, but it was their joke that he had a well-kept secret and she pretended to go to great lengths to discover it.

Greg had accompanied Howard into the cabin, but he came out first, carrying a pitcher of tea and the big old three-legged skillet that was the star of their outdoor fish fries.

Marlie sat back watching him as he put the skillet down by the fire and raised the protective plastic, putting the pitcher of tea safely in the middle of the table.

She found it amazing that he had been out in the small
boat all day, since not a wrinkle showed in his clothing nor
had he a mark on the white rubber that bordered his blue
deck-shoes.

Howard must have done all the work, she thought, and
decided that was uncharitable. After all, what had there
been to do? The boats were both watertight, the motors recently serviced, but it bothered her that she had had to work
at looking clean and fresh, whereas he seemed to stay that
way with no effort.

'How did you like our kind of fishing?' she asked.

'I didn't know you had a patent on it,' Greg raised his
eyebrows.

'I just meant, you usually go in for larger quarry,' Marlie
said. He was putting her in the wrong again.

'Anything can be a challenge,' he said. 'Some take brute
force, others require a more delicate touch.' Something in
his eyes told her he wasn't only discussing fishing.

Determined not to let him outpace her, but equally sure
she did not want to be the loser in a battle of wits, Marlie
sought an answer.

'I suppose you mean it's a matter of judgment, knowing
when all your resources will be needed, and when you're
having to limit yourself to the abilities of your adversary?'

His eyes flickered. She had put him in a dangerous position, and she knew it. With a smile, she sat back sipping her
tea. As if stalling for time, Greg rose and walked to the table, where he poured himself a glass.

When he returned to his chair, the slight lifting at the side
of his mouth caused Marlie to tense. He had worked his way
out of trouble, she knew.

'Is it the abilities of my adversary that keep me in place,
or how important I consider my goal?'

Marlie was glad Howard chose that minute to shout for help. As usual Greg had turned the tables on her, and it was she who needed the respite.

With his dish of batter, the plate of fish, and his cooking utensils, Howard had more than he could manage, so Marlie helped him carry his load. When they returned to the fire, his enthusiastic comments as he heated the skillet and battered the fish prevented Marlie from having to answer Greg.

Before long, the aroma from the pan was competing and winning over the pleasant smell of burning pine wood. Marlie sat back away from the heat and watched the two men as they argued over the best way to turn the fish, and how brown they should be allowed to get. They had developed a rapport during the day, and it was carrying over into the evening. No professional cook would give so much attention to each individual piece.

Marlie had put the bread in the oven when she had been in the kitchen, and her timing was perfect. The hot fish and bread, the cold salad and tea contrasted just enough for a delicious meal.

She polished off one small fillet of bass and next chose the bream. Fighting the bones of the small fish was a small price to pay for the succulent taste.

'Between the two of you, you really did a job on these fish,' she said as she wiped her fingers on her napkin. The platter that had been heaped with golden pieces was nearly empty. Both Greg and Howard had worked up an appetite, and Marlie had completely overlooked having lunch, which accounted for her hunger.

'No thanks to him,' Howard said, pushing aside a golden piece to look for one that had been cooked longer and was darker in colour. 'If I had let him have his way, they'd be raw.'

'He doesn't know the difference between browning and burning,' Greg retorted.

Marlie smiled at the camaraderie that had sprung up between them. With the difference in their backgrounds, they seemed unlikely to become friends, but apparently that hadn't stopped them.

Dusk was turning to darkness, and the glass-protected candles Marlie had put on the table were giving out a soft glow. From the marshy area across the river came the melody of the frogs. Each of the amphibians had a tone and rhythm of his own, and moved from chorus to descant in an ever changing symphony. From higher ground, the crickets added their share of sound. To the rest was suddenly added another, a human voice.

'I assume you're home, since I can see you— Should I ask if you're in to company?' Marlie didn't have to turn to know Doris Farmer was approaching. For as long as Marlie could remember, Doris and her husband had lived in a fishing cabin on the waterway. Sam Farmer had been dead for ten years, but she had stayed by the water, often fishing off the bank or taking her boat out alone. Though Marlie had known Doris most of her life, the older woman was principally Howard's friend. They were both in their fifties, both settled in their life-styles, and could be companionable without any emotional strings attached.

'You certainly should ask,' Howard called, rising from his place at the table. 'Come on over and have a glass of—' He leaned over, looking in the empty pitcher. 'Have a glass of fish.'

'Just the thing after a hard day,' Doris said as she strolled up. She gave Greg, who had risen at her approach, a critical once-over. Howard made the introductions, and Doris held out her hand. 'Well, thought we were never going to get you down here, young man.'

Marlie blinked with surprise. What was Doris talking about? Certainly they had not worked for months to bring Greg to the cabin, nor anyone else. Then she remembered that Howard had, in his efforts to push Marlie into a romance, often suggested that she invite Tom Carson out for the weekend. Possibly Doris had confused the names.

Howard was getting a chair for Doris, and she was turned away from the table, telling him some story, so neither of them saw Greg stiffen.

Marlie noticed, and wondered why it bothered him so much to be mistaken for someone else. Was it simply a matter of pride, that the great Greg Alston could not be mistaken for an inferior being, or did he resent being coupled with Marlie, even in an honest mistake?

She was still more concerned with Greg's reaction. He had said on the boat that he was interested, but what did that mean? Not much, she reasoned, not with glamorous women like Joan Owens-Lane hanging on his arm.

He was a man of pride, she knew, because she had pricked it a couple of times. That wouldn't account for his reaction. No, she decided, it was something else entirely. Doris had made the remark so casually that anyone who didn't know, would assume Marlie was involved in a lasting relationship. That was what had bothered Greg. Where he interested himself, as he had put it, he wanted unencumbered ground, but she reminded herself that he was just camping, not building.

The idea nettled Marlie. Well, here he would find a no trespassing sign, she decided. She pushed back her chair and rose.

'Fine thing, inviting someone to tea when there isn't any,' she said to Howard. 'I'll go make another pitcher.'

'Oh, leave it and let me do it,' Doris said as she, too, stood up. 'I've been sitting in my boat all day, and I want to stretch my legs. Come on, Howard, you and I will clean up and let the youngsters go for a walk.' She leaned over, giving Greg a broad wink. 'That little dirt road out there is pretty in the moonlight.'

'Then that's for me,' Greg said promptly. He took Marlie by the arm. 'The only thing wrong with your cornbread is where it will settle if we don't walk it off.' As he started around the side of the cabin, he propelled her along by his side.

'If there was anything wrong with the bread, you didn't have to eat half of it,' she protested.

'Oh, but I did. Mustn't let the cook think I didn't appreciate it.'

Once they reached the road, Marlie tried to steer him to the left, where a quarter of a mile away, the lights of Frank's Grocery seemed safe, if a little shoddy in comparison to the place Greg spent his time. But he had ideas of his own, and he turned right. Marlie tried to object. Doris Farmer's house was the nearest in that direction, and it was a good three miles away.

The full moon illuminated the hard-packed dirt road as it ran between the shadows of the overhanging trees. The air was warm and soft with the scent of life and decay that made up the woods. A slight breeze from the south carried the smell of fresh-cut grass and the aroma of a barbecue in progress.

Suddenly Marlie was half afraid of being alone with Greg. The night was out of a romantic novel, and he made the perfect hero. Unsafe, her conscious mind warned her. Delightful, her senses said in return. A good conversation was the least dangerous course, she decided. Keep him talking. If necessary, get him into an argument, but stay safe—enjoy. Marlie decided there was something wrong with her. All this splitting of thought was unusual for her. Something else for which Greg was to blame. She never argued with herself when she was with Tom.

'Pretty back in here,' Greg said. 'When you see it from the waterway, you have no idea what's behind those trees.'

'More trees, fields and houses,' Marlie replied. 'Our part of the country is not much different from the rest, I guess.'

Greg turned his head, looking down at her. 'There are differences,' he said. 'Every part of the country has its own speciality.'

By his look he was using double meanings again, Marlie knew. She rose to the bait, wondering if this time she could hold her own. She had been lucky so far.

'I guess connoisseurs are always on the watch for the speciality,' she murmured. She had put just enough slur on the words for him to get her meaning.

His lips twitched slightly. 'How not? And tell me, who else but a connoisseur would know a speciality when he finds one?'

'I see your point,' Marlie smiled up at him. 'And it takes genuine experience to gain that knowledge—or instinct.'

'Knowledge, by all means. Most instincts are inborn. Let's not make all that experience useless by calling it unnecessary. That's what makes finding that speciality, as we were calling it, so gratifying.'

Marlie was busy for a moment working that out. Since there seemed nothing to add, she tried a different tack.

'True enough, but tell me. If this—speciality—is capable of appreciating the compliment it's being paid, does it ever wonder if it is the ultimate discovery, or just another experience in the search for perfection?'

'Wouldn't that depend upon how it viewed itself?'

Marlie shook her head. 'Not at all, but how it was viewed. Nothing gives itself its true value, because nothing views itself objectively in relationship to its similarities.' Answering that should tangle his tongue, she thought smugly. But her smarting off could put her on dangerous ground too.

Greg's lips pursed thoughtfully. 'In that case the object, the—the—' His mouth pursed as he frowned down at her. 'Wait a minute! This conversation took a wrong turn somewhere!'

She threw back her head and laughed. Suddenly the night had increased in beauty as Greg laughed along with her. When he reached out, taking her hand, it was a natural reaction to wrap her fingers around his. They walked for some time, enjoying the night sounds of nature. Then the road began to rise and they climbed with it.

At the top of the low hill, by the edge of the road, the ground fell away sharply in the direction of the waterway. No trees blocked their view. Below them the channel stretched in a gleaming silver path, made all the more impressive by the surrounding darkness of the woods and marshes. They were barely sixty feet above the water level, but the land in the tidewater area was normally so flat that the little rise afforded a view that stretched for miles. Behind them a pine wood added a tangy odour to the evening air.

'A perfect place to put a house,' Greg said.

'Oh no!' Marlie cried. 'I would hate it if someone built up here. I like to think of it just as it is. I used to come here when I was a kid and this was my Everest, my Pikes Peak. It was the top of the world.'

Greg smiled down at her. 'Then you've been around here all your life?'

She nodded. 'Everybody has to grow up somewhere, and this is it for me.'

'Your parents?'

'My father works for the State Department. Right now he's with the Ambassador's staff in Italy. Mother is with him, of course.'

'Then you're not a poor little orphan?'

Marlie looked up, her expression blank. 'Did you think I was? I'm most certainly not an orphan, and I don't consider myself poor, though looking from your pinnacle of wealth I might be considered destitute.'

'Hey, peace.' Greg laughed. 'That was an expression—' He caught her by the shoulders and turned her around, gazing down on her face. His face held a serious expression. 'Did I come on as a snob? That's one accusation I'm not familiar with.'

'No, you didn't.' Marlie had to admit the truth. 'From anyone else I would have ignored it.'

'In other words, what's-his-name, who Doris mistook me for, could have gotten away with it.'

Marlie blinked. So that was still bothering him. 'If you mean we come from the same general background, the answer is yes.'

Greg's hands, still on her shoulders, gripped with more force. The firm line of his jaw seemed to become more prominent, the dark eyes, shadowed in the moonlight, were unreadable, but he seemed to loom larger, more threatening in Marlie's life. Without knowing why, she tried to step back, to fight against being drawn into the strength of this man who was enveloping her, though only his hands were on her shoulders.

'And that makes such a difference?' His face was drawing nearer to hers.

Hold on to your common sense, she reminded herself. Could the rest of her hear over the blood pounding in her ears she wondered?

'The similarities of background, of purpose in life—' Marlie's reasoning was inane, too often repeated, like a cliché, but with him so close she couldn't think.

'And that matters more than this?' His head bent, and his lips closed on hers. The desires he had aroused in her the night before were coming to the surface, flooding, eroding her thought, her strength. Some arbitrary part of her mind was still fighting him, the rest was yearning for the consuming fires.

His hands left her shoulders. One encircled her, drawing her softness against the bulwark of his chest. The other, cradling the flesh of her hip, lifted her nearly off her feet pressing her legs against his. She struggled and succumbed to the muscular strength that held her imprisoned.

Her mind was whirling in a dazed confusion of alarm and desire. A kaleidoscope of fears and hungers wove themselves into a pattern of frustration, fast being overridden by the waves of passion that rolled through her. With one hand she was struggling, with the other she was clinging when he raised his mouth from hers. He stepped back slightly, and his hands moved back to her shoulders, unwilling to release her. His breathing was slightly ragged as he looked into her eyes.

'And tell me. What background does that show?'

'The connoisseur.' The words came out of their own volition, based on the recent conversation and his ability to entirely sweep her emotions. She hadn't considered the effect it would have on him. His mouth tightened in anger. She could feel the pain in her shoulders as his grip tightened.

'Would you say the connoisseur is still in search for perfection, or has he found it?'

Marlie was half afraid of the intensity in his voice, his expression, in his grip, but that spark of independence that was within her would not be denied.

'As I said before, the speciality would always wonder, wouldn't it?'

With his intake of breath, he seemed to grow before her eyes. More than half afraid, Marlie tugged at his hold on her shoulders. Her fingers weak and useless against his, plucked at his grip. He allowed her movement but kept pace with her. In the moonlight, as she backed across the road, she saw the gleam in his eyes, the ruthless determination that had made him a power in the financial world, and was trapping her.

Her feet felt the softness of pine needles under the soles of her shoes. She looked wildly around him, seeing he had allowed her to back from the tenuous safety of the road to the depths of shadows beneath the pines. She tried to turn, but he forced her to continue for an additional two steps.

She halted, her back against the roughness of pine bark. Reaching behind her, she felt a huge pine, one of the grandfathers of the wood. Greg was inexorably drawing closer.

Her eyes wide, helpless to prevent him, she watched his face. His determination blurred into hunger. She watched the slight flutter of his thick lashes and the parting of his lips, just before they met hers.

Softly, almost hesitantly, his tongue trailed across the delicate skin, exploring, drawing back, waiting for her re-action. The fear, the refusal that would have fought his force, crumbled under the gentle treatment. Some slumbering creature within her awakened, shook itself, and pushed forward. Lulled by the lack of threat, it reached out, hungering after its long hibernation.

His hands, so gentle and feather-light, left her shoulders and moved down her arms. They travelled with agonising slowness, exploring her skin beneath the thinness of the silk shirt. Feather-light, his fingertips circled and encircled her upper arms, leaving her skin tingling with a new and wondrous sensitivity. She felt with amazement the sensuality within herself which had remained hidden until Greg had awakened it.

Behind her the tree, in front of her she could feel the masculinity of his wide chest, the light press of his muscular thighs against hers. She was trapped, not by his arms, his grip upon her, but by the strength of her desire, the longing that moved through her body in hot waves.

His hands, still exploring, moved down to her forearms, teasing the tender skin, bringing an ache to her muscles. Emptiness created pain. Her arms needed to be pressed against him, holding him, giving in return, but when she tried to raise them she met resistance. He kept them by her side, denying her that simple release of longing. When she ceased to struggle, his hands travelled down to hers, caressing her fingers, awakening them to the exquisite pleasures of a caress. She wanted to cry out her pleasure, her distress, but his lips, still exploring hers, blocked her efforts.

His release of her hands was like a reprieve from some heinous but glorious prison. Her arms encircled him, her fingers caressed the short hair at the back of his neck, pulling his head closer, demanding more of his kiss than an elusive exploration that pulled away, leaving her hungering for more.

She longed for his arms to encircle her, to pull her close as he had on the yacht, but while she was denied that forceful pleasure, she found another in store. His hands moved to her sides, gently touching, raising goose bumps of desire around the swell of her hips. As slowly, as thoroughly as he had awakened the sensuality of the skin on her arms, her body became alive under his gentle exploring touch.

Without recognising her own voice, Marlie gave a little moan. She was pressed against him, revelling in his strong hard body, the masculine scent, pulling him tighter and tighter against herself.

Fully awakened to what would satisfy her hunger, she was, in retrospect, a little surprised that she had fought so hard against Greg. Only a foolish and blind woman would not recognise her need and its source. What if he had known other women before? Did she expect his life to be cloistered until he met her?

Desiring more of him, she moved his hand that was still torturing her side until it was cupped around her breast, but before her arm had encircled him again, he had dropped his hand, lightly fingering the outside of her thigh, still keeping his touch so light that one moment he was igniting fires, the next she wasn't sure he was there at all.

Desperately, she pulled him closer. Was he never going to stop his teasing? Her urgency had grown beyond her patience. She wanted him, was he never going to realise that? Was he going to forever play the game as if he were only interested in tuning an instrument—holding a glass of fine wine only to enjoy the bouquet? The thought came unbidden, but like a lightning bolt. Like a connoisseur? The idea was a cold shock. Her very being drew away like warm flesh from an icy hand.

With a rage fed by frustration, she shoved away from the tree, flinging herself out of his arms. She dashed several steps away before she turned to face him, her blush hidden by the shadows under the trees, her eyes blazing.

'You—you!' she shouted.

If she had expected him to be caught off guard surprised enough to lose the Alston cool, she was disappointed. Instead of dashing after her, he leaned against the tree, his arms folded across his chest.

'You—you connoisseur, you searcher for—for—'

'The specialities of life?' he suggested.

'Thank you,' she retorted. 'Trust you not to lose sight of your objective.' She turned towards the road, marching through the trees, and nearly fell over a large fallen branch.

Before she could right herself she felt his hand on her arm, steadying her. 'Thank you, I can manage.'

'But surely you don't imagine such an experienced man with the ladies would leave one stumbling through the wood alone?'

His tone, so urbane, so filled with subtle humour, made her even angrier.

'Experienced is right!' she snapped as they came out on the road. 'You must have to keep a file cabinet on your search for perfection. I'm not sure even then how you manage to keep them straight. I mean, with one female on deck while you're kissing another in the stateroom.'

There was the slightest pause before he smiled. 'Nice little girls don't say such things.'

'Nice little boys don't keep harems,' she retorted. 'And get one thing straight, Mr Alston. This—speciality—is one of a kind. And that apparently isn't your type, so just forget you ever met me.'

Marlie stumbled as her foot came down in one of the dry ruts that ridged the dirt road. He reached out and caught her arm, preventing her from falling.

'Forgetting you is going to be difficult if you keep trying to fall in a hole.' His composure was insulting.

'Thank you, but I did learn to walk at the normal age, and have managed for years,' she snapped.

All her resentments, and their reasons, came pouring back at once, including their first argument. 'And another thing.' Her blue eyes flashed as she stumbled and caught her balance. 'I don't need your advice on painting ducks!'

CHAPTER SIX

LOOKING BACK on Saturday night, Marlie was ashamed of herself. That was a hard, cold fact that coloured the next two days, but the true reason behind it was hiding in the chaos of her conflicting emotions. One by one she ticked off the possible reasons, filing them away again for future consideration.

Part of her problem was her loss of temper. She was a rational human being, not given to childish tantrums. How could she lose her control, act so immature? How did the man bring out that hidden part of her nature? Still, that wasn't all she had discovered about herself when she was with him. The awakening of a flaming desire that no other man had even stirred left her shaken and wondering at herself.

By Tuesday morning her mood had begun to lighten. After all, she would probably never see Greg again, so what was the point in staying angry? Thinking he might be hundreds of miles away, never planning on returning to Virginia Beach, left her as depressed as she had been irritated.

Her thoughts were interrupted as Howard approached her worktable.

'There's a delivery for you up in the front office,' he said. His casualness was elaborate, forced.

'What—I haven't ordered anything.' Then it occurred to her that her mother might have sent her something from

Italy, not an uncommon happening. 'Just sign for it. I'll take a look when I've washed my hands.'

'Can't do it,' Howard replied. He was rocking back on his heels, his eyes focusing somewhere above her head. 'Man says he's instructed to leave it with you personally.'

'Of all the stupid—' Marlie rose from her stool, using a turpentine-soaked rag to wipe the paint off her hands. 'I hate to touch anything in this state, but let's see what's there.'

She entered the office to find a man in a delivery uniform holding a clipboard on which a pen was tied with a piece of cord.

'You Miss Marlie Richmond?' he asked.

'That's right.'

'If you'll just sign here, please, accepting delivery of that crate, the one sitting on the end of the truck, I'll bring it in.'

Marlie glanced through the dusty window, but she could only see an inch of what appeared to be a wooden crate. She took the pen and signed, handing the board back to the delivery man. The delivery would not be a present from her mother.

'Maybe someone sent me some oranges from Florida,' she said to Howard, who had walked into the office. Suddenly she was wary. Why had Fred, Norm and Paul followed Howard? Her eyes narrowed.

'What's going on?' she demanded. 'Are you pulling a practical joke?'

Howard raised his right hand solemnly. 'On our collective honour, we are not.' Was there the slightest emphasis on *we*?

Howard stepped over and opened the door as the delivery man came back, pushing a dolly. Marlie knew immediately that her first guess was wrong. Fruit came in smaller amounts. The crate was at least two feet high, with a length and width of approximately forty inches. Cardboard with evenly spaced holes an inch in diameter had been stapled to a wooden frame. She knelt by the box as the driver eased it off the dolly and made a hurried retreat. Through the holes she caught the silvery glint of wire. The unexpectedness of seeing a black eye appear at one of the holes made her draw back until she noticed the luminous green that surrounded it.

'There's a mallard duck in there,' she squealed, pulling away part of the cardboard.

Inside, she saw not one duck, but four. Closest to the wire screen was the mallard duck. His bright, metallic-green head was tilted, returning her inspection look for look. Behind him were two females, both drab in comparison. One was obviously his mate, and the other a female canvas-back. Her partner was standing in the opposite corner. His red-and-brown head was turned away, as if he disdained to honour the interruption with his attention.

'They're beautiful!' She waved Howard over. 'Look, aren't they gorgeous?'

'Sure are,' Paul answered, joining Marlie as she inspected the birds. 'Get a load of those mallards! Hey, that's some present.'

Marlie's eyes were wide as she looked at him. 'Who on earth would send me ducks? What am I going to do with them? Aren't they beautiful?' In her excitement her voice had risen, and she could hear it reverberating back at her from the walls. She lowered her voice. 'But where did they come from?'

'Maybe that will tell you,' Howard said, pointing to an envelope attached to the top of the crate.

Marlie grabbed and opened it, pulling out the single sheet of note paper. It read:

Dear Miss Richmond,

Thank you for a most enlightening visit to your factory.

I am sending you these four ducks, hoping you will benefit from having live models available.

Sincerely,

'Greg Alston!' Marlie wailed. 'That insufferable snob, that overtailored stuffed-shirt creep thinks I need models!' She jumped to her feet.

Howard retreated behind his desk. Fred slipped out of the office, followed by Norm and Paul, the latter unfortunate enough to let his smothered laugh be heard.

'Paul, you come back here!' Marlie shouted after him.

'Knew that boy was no fool,' Howard said as the doorway to the office remained empty.

'Fine,' Marlie stood with her arms akimbo. 'If you approve of his staying hidden, then you take care of these monsters.'

'Oh, no.' Howard leaned back in his chair, grinning. 'They're not my ducks, and I didn't hire Paul to look after livestock. Just wood-stock.' Howard chuckled over his own pun. 'And since when did they become monsters?'

'Well, they're not—' Marlie grudgingly conceded. 'But what am I supposed to do with them? The closest I've ever been to a real duck is at the meat counter in the supermarket.'

'Can't help that. You signed for them, you accepted them, they're your ducks.'

'But I thought they were oranges,' she insisted.

Howard leaned towards the crate. His eyebrows drew together, his mouth pursed thoughtfully. Marlie waited, hoping he had a solution. He slowly shook his head.

'No, don't think they're oranges.'

'That's just what I need—another jokester,' Marlie said with asperity. 'I want you to help me!'

'Okay, I'll help you.' He stood up and walked around the desk. 'Once again I will explain, they're not oranges, and they don't belong in my office. Now you get that end of the crate, I'll get the other. We'll take them back to your corner—one more word out of you, and you can manage by yourself.'

'Men,' Marlie said, after the crate had been lowered to the floor by her worktable. 'You're all alike, you all stick together.' She glowered at Howard, who was squatting by the pen. 'Next, you'll be telling me I don't know how to paint—hey, that's my sandwich you're feeding that duck!'

'I thought you wanted my help,' Howard said, standing up. Marlie could see he was hiding his grin. 'I guess I'll mosey back to the office. Happy farming.'

Marlie sat on her stool, watching him go. His enjoyment of her discomfort was adding fuel to her indignation. It was just like him to think his precious fishing buddy could do no wrong, she thought.

When he was out of sight, she frowned down at the cage. What did Greg Alston think he was doing? She told herself that was silly. He knew what he was doing. Deadly insults were seldom handed out by accident. No one stumbled and dropped four live ducks by delivery van.

'You'll just sit right there until he comes and gets you,' she growled. She knew better. Welcome or not, they were alive, they had to have water, they had to be fed. Did they have to have exercise? She shook her head at the thought of walking ducks through the business district.

But in the interim, something had had to be done for the birds. The weather man was predicting rising temperatures. The cardboard that had been fastened over the wire cage had probably protected the birds on their journey, but it cut

off the ventilation. She knelt on the floor and tried tearing
it away with her hands. After her second effort she sat back
on her feet and decided another method would do the job
with less wear and tear on her nails. From the painting table she took the screwdriver she used for prying off paint-
can lids and worked it under the board where it had been
tacked to the wood. Some minutes later she sat back, surveying Greg's gift. The sturdy wooden frame was covered
by a meshed wire, and inside, ducks tilted their heads, inspecting her in turn.

'My, you are beauties,' she said.

Her voice broke the spell. The bright, metallic-green head
of the mallard drake turned slowly, looking over the surroundings. His squawk was loud with more than a hint of
disdain. The female mallard stepped towards Marlie and
gave less raucous opinion.

Seeing the difference in the two birds of the same species, Marlie could feel a parallel between the birds and her
problems with Greg Alston. Even the appearance coin-
cided. The male mallard with his green head, the white band
around his neck like a white collar, and the perfect rows of
blue and white on his wings, looked as if he might have pa-
tronised Greg's tailor.

The female, patterned by nature to be camouflaged on the
nest, was drab in comparison. The irregular design of her
muted colourings gave a ragged, unkempt look. Marlie
readily identified with the hen after her experiences with the
king of the haberdasheries. She felt an immediate bond between herself and the female mallard.

'They do it to us every time,' she muttered. 'I bet that guy
you fly around with is a feathered beast.' Marlie chose to
accept the answering quack as an affirmative.

Further back in the cage a pair of canvas-backs were
watching. They stood feather to feather, and any curiosity

was satisfied from a distance. Marlie took exception to the complacency of the buff-and-grey female who was also paled by the presence of her more comely mate, but seemed not to resent it. Her drake was not as brilliant in his colouring as the mallard, but the dark brown on his beak, breast and top of his head was a strong contrast to the red on the back of his neck and under his eyes.

'I'll bet you catch his dinner,' she accused. Then she remembered that species ate only plants. She had forgotten what.

In the corner of the cage was a large, moulded, plastic dog dish. The two cuplike bowls were empty. One still showed moisture in the bottom.

'Not much hospitality on the delivery truck, I see,' Marlie said as she unfastened and raised the hinged top. She slowly inserted her hand and arm, poised to jerk back if one of the birds took exception, but while they quickened their interest, they made no offensive moves. Nor did they draw back out of reach.

When she stood up, she looked in the side of the empty container that had held food and wondered what in her lunch would appeal to them. While she thought it over she took the dish to the bathroom and washed it out, filling the water bowl. Back at the end of the paint table she looked at what was left of her sandwich and sighed. It wasn't much for four ducks, she thought, but it would stave off starvation until she could locate something more appropriate.

'Here you are.' She walked around the table to the cage and stopped. The wire enclosure was empty. 'What happened to the ducks?' she cried.

She whirled around in time to see Fred at the Howler. He was reaching for the switch to start the machine. Like a vehicle travelling too fast to turn suddenly, his hand, out of habit and its own momentum, hit the button. His expression turned from puzzlement to horror as the implication connected in his mind. The Howler roared to life only to be shut off immediately.

But the one roar had been enough to locate the birds. Quacking their fear, all four took wing. Like a covey of grouse rising from a bush, all four rose at once.

'Ya-hoo!' Paul shouted, his empty hands pantomiming a hunter sighting a quarry down the barrel of a gun.

'Stop that!' Marlie shouted, running around the end of the worktable. 'Help me catch them—umph!' Her eyes on the birds, she ran into Norm who was also watching their flight.

'They sure fly weird,' he said, dodging the female mallard who dived straight at him.

Marlie paused, looked up, and realised Norm was right. Not one bird could keep a straight course, nor did any fly well. Both drakes and the mallard female had crippled right wings. The canvas-backed female had been injured on the left side. She was the strongest flyer. Unable to keep aloft for long periods, they were rising, making short curious flights and landing on whatever happened to be handy.

'We've got to catch them,' Marlie cried, afraid they would be hurt in a collision with the machinery. She started after the brightly coloured mallard drake. He was the most erratic. After getting a running start along a table he was airborne, swooping in circles.

Fred, who had been watching open-mouthed, made a leap towards the bird and fell over a tall stool sitting by the belt sander. While he was spreadeagled on the floor, the canvas-back, who was just landing, planted his feet firmly on Fred's hips. He ran up the machine operator's back as Fred was trying to rise and took wing again.

'They don't need any assistance,' Marlie called to Fred as she jumped over his legs, still chasing the mallard.

'If I wanted to be a runway, I'd join the airforce,' Fred griped as he jumped to his feet and kicked the stool under the table.

Howard, just coming out of his office, let out a yelp as the female canvas-back appeared to be aiming for his face. His fistful of invoices went flying as both hands went up to protect himself. Almost without intention he clasped the feathered body. The female voiced her protest and continued to flap her wings.

'Hold on to her!' Marlie called to Howard as she scrambled on to the table, still trying for the mallard. He was circling just out of her reach. As she made a grab for him, he dipped, sailing under her arm. With the added momentum, he changed his course. Determined to catch him, Marlie ran to the end of the sturdy table, jumping from it on to the one on which she painted. As she landed her foot slipped, causing her to fight for her balance. In the process her foot struck the can of green paint, sending it skittering along her work area before it overturned.

'Oh-h-h,' Marlie sighed. Howard had rapidly crossed the room with the canvas-back female and was bent over the cage at the end of the table. Green paint dripped from his arms and down his trouser legs. Fortunately, he and the floor had taken most of the splash, but there were several drops of paint on the duck.

Across the room, Paul was stumbling across the top of a bin heaped with the three-foot lengths of wood that had been cut for carving. As the female mallard winged about erratically, lit and flew again, Paul tripped and staggered about, knocking wood from the bin.

'Hey, watch it!' Norm yelled as he chased the male canvas-back that had given up the air in favour of running between the bins and under the equipment tables.

Marlie shook her head as the chaos increased. A yelp from Fred caused her to turn. He was scrambling up from the floor again, swearing at the duck he chased and Paul, who had knocked the wood on the floor. Not content with them, he had a few choice words about the company for giving him a job, and the President, who should have passed a law against everything.

A swish of wings by her shoulder startled Marlie and she jumped back. The mallard drake made an awkward landing on the shelf where she kept the drying ducks. He turned an inspecting eye on his wooden counterparts. Then, stretching his neck, he nibbled at the sleeve of Marlie's blouse.

'Why, you faker! You're not wild at all.' The indignation that should have sent him flying again, earned her a loud, oblique reply. With the rapid thrust of his neck and bill, he caught the end of the red ribbon, tied above Marlie's ear, and gave a tug.

'Behave yourself!' she said, picking him up. 'You stay right here on the table until I get down—watch out, you're walking in that spilled paint!' Marlie scrambled down from the table, a task made more difficult by trying to keep the bird out of the cans that were still upright. By now Howard had closed the top of the cage, so Marlie stood the drake on the floor, and considering the perversity of the males in her life, wasn't surprised that he took the opportunity to step into the paint on the ground before him. His webbed feet left perfect tracks as he walked over to the stool. When he was out of reach, Marlie decided to forgo chasing him. There was an easier way to catch a tame duck. She picked up the dish of food and water, tapping on the side until he turned to identify the noise. He gave a loud quack and came, on the run.

His call for food alerted his mate and the male canvas-back. The red-headed male charged out from between two cartons, evaded Fred, and he, too, ran through the spilled paint. He was trying to climb into the wire enclosure before Marlie could put the mallard in and gave him a lift. The mallard female made the trip almost as quickly, taking long fluttering jumps.

'Why didn't you try that in the beginning?' Howard demanded.

'You needed your exercise,' Marlie retorted. She glanced around the room at the havoc and sat down on her stool, her chin in her hand. 'This isn't happening,' she told Howard. 'It's all a bad dream.'

'Such is real life sometimes,' Howard grinned suddenly. The paint on his arms and clothes seemed to be forgotten.

Marlie straightened and shook her head. 'Reality can't be like this, it has to be—what are you laughing at?' She needed no answer. Her right hand, the one that had been holding her chin, was streaked with green. It came from her handling the mallard duck who had struggled in his desire to get to the food in the cage.

'He's done it to me again!' she wailed. 'Greg Alston's not even here and he did it—' She started for the ladies' room, then turned back to Howard, her eyes flashing, her fists clenched in frustration. 'And if you tell him, I'll—I—I'll never paint another duck as long as I live!' Near to tears, she ran towards the front of the building, nearly tripping over Paul as he picked up the wood in the centre aisle.

Five minutes later, her face clean, her hair combed, and her shirt tucked neatly in her jeans, she marched back out to the production area.

In her absence, the cage had been lifted and placed on the packing table. Fred was busy with a hammer and some small nails.

'You pulled the wire loose when you took off the card-board,' he said, explaining how the ducks had escaped. Marlie stood gazing at the birds. They appeared none the worse for their escape and the chase. She wondered just how frightened they had been. Fred's hammering on the side of the cage seemed to be of intense interest to them. The can-vas-back hen was happy enough. The others were moving hesitantly, picking up their legs and shaking them because of the paint that coated the bottoms of their feet and the webbing between their toes.

Marlie wondered how to remove it. Did she dare use paint or varnish remover? She decided against it, not knowing how sensitive their skin might be. First she would try some-thing more soothing. She lifted the wire top and took the mallard drake under her arm.

'I shouldn't bother with you at all,' she told him. 'You're the one that caused me to kick over the can.'

Back in the ladies' room again, she took a jar of cold cream from the personal items she kept in the small cabi-net. She lowered the seat on the toilet and sat down, hold-ing the bird in her lap.

'Now this might work if you co-operate,' she told the duck. With the cream on both hands she started smearing his webbed feet. Either he was ticklish, or he objected to sitting on his tailfeathers, because he squawked and kicked. 'Wait just a minute!' she protested, trying to hold his slip-pery feet with slippery fingers. 'Be still, will you?'

He ceased his struggles, but not because of her com-mand. The jar of cold cream had arrested his attention. Be-fore she could stop him he arched his neck and stuck his bill in the jar. With a disgusted hiss he shook his head and wiped his bill on her cheek.

'Oh, you pest!' Marlie grabbed a handful of tissues from a box and wiped her face, his bill, and started on his feet.

The still wet paint had mixed with the cold cream and spread, in their struggle, from his webbed feet up his legs. He appeared to be wearing bright green boots.

'I've failed again,' she muttered as she took him back to the cage.

Norm and Fred, working together, had wiped most of the paint off the feet of the other ducks, but on all three, the stains would remain for some time.

'If Greg Alston sees that, I'll never live it down,' she muttered. There was no doubt in her mind that he would see them. She stood very still, her eyes narrowing. Then why not make it immediately, she thought. It meant hearing him laugh at her, but the ducks came from him, and he should be the one to take care of them. She certainly could not keep birds in her apartment nor at the factory. Maybe the yacht was still at the marina.

Paul had cleared the aisles and was preparing to clean up the spilled paint.

'Leave that for a minute,' Marlie told him. 'Get Norm, and the two of you bring the cage out to the station-wagon.' She wordlessly held out her hand to Howard, waiting for him to give her the keys.

He was reluctant. 'What are you planning? You can't drive to the nearest river and open the pen. They'd never survive.'

'No, but I can return a gift. Greg Alston can give them a stateroom or tow them behind his yacht—the choice is his.' Her harsh words caused her to pause, wondering if he would take proper care of them. She decided she was being unjust. He was not the type of man to be thoughtless of animals, she was sure. She held out her hand again and, with a sigh, Howard handed her the keys.

During the drive Marlie tried to rehearse her speech to Greg Alston.

'I thought it was a darling joke,' she experimented, checking her smile in the rear-view mirror.

A raucous noise interrupted from the wire pen. She glanced in the mirror again to see the birds looking in her direction.

'You're right. Maybe I should just kick him in the shins. That would be more in character, after the way I've behaved recently.'

The mallard drake gave her his opinion. His loud voice grated on Marlie's already tight nerves, not because of the volume, but his authoritative tone reminded her of the man she would soon be seeing.

'That's all you know about it. Just because you're a male, you're not guaranteed to be infallible, you know.'

The blare of horns brought Marlie back to reality. She slammed the brake pedal to the floor just in time to avoid a collision. She looked up at the light, which was a bright, glaring red. The following thunk caused her to think she had been struck by one of the cars that had also screamed to a stop. Then she realised the pen holding the ducks had slid forward. Startled by their collision with the cage and each other, they renewed their clamour.

Marlie waited until the light changed, feeling conspicuous as the wagon blocked the pedestrian walk and the cross traffic manoeuvred around her.

She felt like sinking in the seat as she watched the inconvenience she had caused. She was overcome by guilt because she should have been paying attention to her driving, not arguing with a duck. That admission left her slightly incredulous. The week before she had been a sensible schoolteacher on vacation. Five days of knowing Greg Alston had reduced her to blocking traffic and fighting with birds.

I should kick him in the shins, she thought. She savoured the idea as she drove to the marina.

Marlie wheeled into the sandy parking lot near the yacht and backed the station-wagon into a convenient position to unload the birds. The near accident as she came through town had erased from her mind all thought of trying to outwit Greg. She just wanted to deliver the ducks and escape without being embarrassed again.

She stepped out into the bright sunlight and closed the door on the vehicle, leaving the window down so that the birds could get the breeze. Henry was just leaving the boat with a suitcase. When he saw her he altered his direction to approach her.

'Miss Richmond,' he said in surprise. 'I'm sorry, but if you wanted to see Mr Alston, you are too late by a day. He will be in New York until Friday.'

'And you're joining him?' Marlie realised her question was prying, but she had been so disappointed at not finding Greg aboard, that she asked without thinking. But Henry explained willingly.

'No, I'm on my way to Baltimore. My brother is in need of assistance for a few days and Mr Alston has given me time off until Friday afternoon.'

Marlie looked at the large, well-kept boat. 'Surely there is someone aboard,' she said. 'I like the ducks Mr Alston sent, but there's no way I can keep them. One of the crew can feed and water them until he returns.'

Henry's good humour dissolved into resignation. 'I don't think Mr Alston would approve of that. I'd better stay. Our crew is made up of first-class sailors, but I doubt Mr Alston would trust them to care for his ducks. He's very particular about them.'

'I don't think that's necessary,' Marlie retorted. 'If Greg Alston thought they were too delicate for a sailor to feed, he wouldn't have used them for a silly joke, shipping those poor things around, probably scaring them half to death. That is not my idea of a compassionate man.'

Henry bowed his head in an unsuccessful attempt to hide his laugh. He gave up trying to be discreet and chuckled out loud.

'I wouldn't want to see anything that would scare them. They think they own the farm in Maryland.' His plump form shook as he tried to stop laughing. Then his eyes turned serious.

'I don't think you know Mr Alston well enough to understand, Miss Richmond. I wasn't privy to the arrangements, but I know he would never trust those birds to strangers. Because they're crippled, he takes a keen interest in their welfare. I'm not sure what you mean by insult, but I can assure you he would not honour many people with that much confidence in their character. Mr Alston has a great man's aversion to mistreatment of the helpless. I would say you've made quite an impression on my employer.' Henry's smile was kind.

Marlie's blue eyes sparkled with frustration. She stuffed her hands in the pockets of her jeans as she gazed at Henry. She was momentarily at a loss for words and was finding it difficult to give up her plans for revenge. Deep down, she knew she had been enjoying them. Henry was pulling away all her excuses for fighting with his boss.

'Greg Alston has a farm?' she asked, looking for a chink in the impression Henry presented of his employer.

Henry nodded. 'He breeds race horses. We're close to the marshes and occasionally an injured bird gets away from a hunter or is caught in a storm and hurt. I suppose we shelter at least thirty.'

Marlie caught the change in Henry's explanation that bared his pride in Greg, and his involvement in his job.

'I'll take care of them until the weekend,' Marlie said slowly. Half of her wanted to acknowledge the compliment Henry had suggested, but the other half was resisting. On the drive out to the marina she had been frustrated by not having a plan to outwit Greg. Now she would have more time. She threw a dark look at Henry.

'But he's not to know we had this talk.'

Henry's lips pursed; his eyes twinkled. 'Of course not.'

Before she left him, Henry had told her when he expected to arrive back aboard the yacht, in the event she needed to return the birds as early as possible to free her weekend. The information that Greg was due just an hour or so later than his employee, was, Marlie thought, volunteered with an air of anticipation.

As she drove back to town, she was certain Henry was looking forward to the weekend and its possible diversions.

CHAPTER SEVEN

MARLIE'S THOUGHTS were in a tumble as she drove back to town. Because of her talk with Henry, she had an insight into Greg Alston that was new and disturbing. She had thought of him as unfeeling with his joke, and yet, according to the picture Henry had painted, Greg was trusting her not to take out her indignation on the helpless.

She wouldn't, of course. She hoped she was more fair-minded, but how did he know that? Obviously he had read that part of her character, but how, what had brought him to that point? What had she done? A good feeling invaded her. In spite of their bickering, she had won his good opinion.

Hold it, she warned herself. Remember, he's not just any man, but Greg Alston. She concentrated on what she knew about him. A man successful with women. He had another on the string that she knew about—a beautiful socialite—and probably more, yet he was trying to add her to his harem. A man that experienced with women would know the science of compliments. How he knew this particular one would work with her, she couldn't imagine.

Yes she could. He was using that connoisseur's experience. Her cheeks grew hot as she remembered Saturday evening. She had considered herself worldly-wise after more than her share of struggles with amorous males. She was wary of their passes, games and tricks, but those of Greg Alston were entirely new to her. She was embarrassed again as she remembered how she had succumbed to his advances.

'He should be outlawed,' she muttered.

The answer from the wire pen startled her. For a moment she had forgotten the ducks. Reminded, she gritted her teeth and tried to think of some appropriate reprisal for his latest insult, but her mind balked. Intruding into her thoughts with growing regularity came the pangs of hunger.

No wonder, she thought, looking down at her watch. She was accustomed to having her lunch at twelve-thirty, and two o'clock had passed. Her favourite restaurant was two blocks away, but she was in her painting clothes, and she could hardly leave the vehicle in the parking lot. The ducks could succumb to heat prostration in the closed car, and if she left the windows open, they might end the day on dinner platters.

Three blocks farther on, she spotted a fast-food restaurant that had a drive-through lane for take-out orders. When she pulled up at the sign that displayed the menu and held the intercom, she saw a note.

Speaker out of order.

As she drove up to the window, she slightly misjudged her stop. She was too far forward. By the time she adjusted the rear-view mirror so that she could see over the cage to back up, two cars had pulled in behind her. The confusion involved in requiring them to move back was more than she felt she could handle after her day of upsets. She was close enough to pay and receive her order, but she had to turn in her seat to speak to the fresh-faced youth at the window.

'A cheese burger and a Coke, please.'

The birds had been quiet, but when she spoke the mallard drake started to quack, accompanied by the two females. Marlie eyed them, wondering how to prevent their noise. Of course, they could be hungry again. If they were fed maybe they would sleep. She knew mallards in the wild fed on insects and grain, and that could be loosely translated into meat and bread. Twice she tried to speak, but she was forced to wait until the birds finished their harangue.

'And give me two regular hamburgers,' she said, gazing back at the boy. His brows knotted together as he looked from Marlie to the ducks and back again. The mallard male quieted, but his lady still had a few comments.

Marlie, getting frayed nerves from the racket turned slightly, and considered banging on the cage. She decided against it. If she frightened them the noise could continue indefinitely. She waited for them to pause before amending her last request.

'Make those last two burgers plain,' she said, not sure if ducks liked mustard and pickles.

She wondered what was bothering the clerk. He stared from her to the birds and back as if he had never seen a duck. And his eyes were wary. Did he think they were going to get out of the cage?

The mallards had quieted, but the canvas-back started making himself known. His quacks were barely audible, and Marlie frowned. Was he hurt or sick? As she focused her attention on him, she remembered his normal diet was wild celery.

'And a salad, no dressing,' Marlie added. By now the kid was frowning, biting his lip. His eyes travelled in a circle, from the order to her and on to the ducks.

His attitude was puzzling. 'Is something wrong?' she asked. She knew better than to take an animal inside a restaurant, but surely there was no reason why they couldn't be in the car while she ordered. Possibly she was taking too much time, but while the birds were creating so much racket, she had trouble thinking or being heard.

He threw a furtive glance over his shoulder, then leaned forward, making sure his voice was inaudible to the others in the restaurant. He jerked a thumb in the direction of the cage.

'Did that one with the green head say anything about french fries?'

Marlie closed her eyes, trying to keep control of her temper. She had had as much of male superiority as she could stand. That kid was hardly old enough to shave, yet he was already trying to make a fool out of a woman. She was speechless for a moment. Turning, she looked into the cage. For once, the ducks were quiet. The male mallard, who could usually be counted upon to give out with a disdainful quack, was busy smoothing his feathers. When he looked up he sounded positively friendly.

She might have let Greg Alston get the upper hand, but no team of males made up of a duck and a smart-mouthed kid was going to get away with it. She looked the boy straight in the eye.

'He says "thank you, but he's on a diet."'

Once away from the restaurant, she pulled over in the shade of a tree. Two hamburgers were too much for the mallards, she decided, she tore one into duck-bite sized pieces and did the same with the salad before putting the food in the cage. She made a mental note to thereafter feed the ducks when she had her meals. Their table conversation left a lot to be desired, but they were reasonably quiet.

The birds were becoming accustomed to riding, and they were sound asleep when she pulled into the parking lot at the factory.

'You brought them back?' Howard frowned when she wanted Paul and Norm to bring in the cage.

'Temporarily,' Marlie sighed and told him why she hadn't left them on the boat. 'I can't take them to my apartment.

If we keep them here, we can't run the Howler, it's too loud—it scares them.'

'Then you're going out to the cabin?' Howard's question supplied the only answer, and they both knew it. He shrugged. 'Why not? You're caught up, and you should take some time off.'

'Great vacation, looking after a quartet of spoiled ducks.' Howard's sharp look brought out a desire to tell him about ordering lunch, but she bit back the impulse. He would tease her for years.

'I'll just leave them here while I do some laundry and pack. In this heat they'd be roasted in an hour if I left them in the car.'

Marlie was considerably more than an hour in her apartment. While the washer and dryer did their stuff, she searched her wardrobe. As she planned her packing, she removed several outfits from the closet, inspected, considered, and put them back. Many were too dressy to take to the cabin. The orange sundress was her favourite, but she had worn that when she had dinner on the yacht.

'I need new clothes,' she informed her reflection in the mirror. The blue eyes that gazed back at her were teasing, questioning, as if they heard something in that remark she had not considered. Well, why not, a part of her muttered. She deserved something new and she remembered reading that women won half their battles with the masculine sex by the appearance they made. She wasn't going to upgrade her wardrobe because of Greg Alston, however. What she bought, she would get because she needed it.

Sure, came a little voice from inside, but she firmly shut it away.

She refused to let doubts enter her head. The additional time she spent in the department store before she returned to the factory was, in her mind, well spent. She wasn't so sure about her depleted bank account.

But the new outfits were carefully tucked away when she arrived at the cabin. Greg would be out of town for the next three days, and she needed to turn her mind to her reprisal. The next move was hers, and she was determined to make it a good one.

Tuesday evening and Wednesday morning were lost because no brain would function over the racket of the ducks. Not until she threatened to drown the entire quartet did she realise their problem. They could see the water from their cage and were demanding a swim.

She felt guilty for keeping them penned up, but did she dare just turn them loose? She thought not. Perhaps a leash. On a duck? A strong cord knotted around the leather-like ankle would do, she decided. Ten noisy minutes later, she held four cords as the birds ran for the water. She frowned at the four men in a small boat who laughed as they passed.

The rest of the morning was peaceful. While the birds paddled about on their long leads, Marlie considered her problem. Greg could not be allowed to get away with his little joke. If she was to believe Henry, it was not the insult she had at first believed, but retaliation was necessary to her self-respect.

It still bothered her that he had been so trusting with the birds. Suppose he had been wrong in his judgment of her. She could have been the type to chop the heads off the poor creatures without a second thought. It would serve him right if she had. Of course, the ducks might have some objection, but Greg Alston needed to be taught a good lesson.

A glimmer of an idea lit the back of her mind, and was just shimmering into brilliance when Doris strolled around the side of the cabin. She raised her hand in greeting, but stopped with her mouth open as she saw her ducks and the confining cords that were tied to the nearest tree.

'Just the person I need,' Marlie jumped, jumping up from her chair. 'You've just been elected to entertain my guests while I make a dash for the store.' She left while Doris was still too stunned to object.

After her shopping, Marlie settled down to a peaceful afternoon. The birds were happy, and she spent the rest of the day, as well as all of Thursday, enjoying the river, planning her revenge, and chasing away a shivery tingle as her thoughts kept returning to Greg Alston.

Friday morning she awakened with the knowledge that Greg was due back that evening. She thought back on her conversation with Henry, who was planning to arrive at the boat just an hour before Greg. Marlie knew her plan would require perfect timing. She wanted to see and talk to Henry, but if Greg demanded a confrontation, he would have to drive out to the cabin. She had no doubt he would. He would be unable to resist, if her plan worked. If it didn't . . . she shuddered.

The morning passed quickly as she spent her time between cleaning the cabin and watching the ducks as they swam. At two o'clock she turned on the oven and removed the defrosted fowl from the refrigerator. She diced oranges, grated the peel and busied herself with the stuffing while the oven heated. Finished with that, she made her preparations for hers and Howard's dinner, knowing they might be having a guest.

She checked the clock as she straightened the kitchen and slid the fowl in the oven. Pleased with her arrangements she strolled into the bathroom for a leisurely soak. She gave particular attention to her hair, curling it so it fell in soft waves. Her manicure was time-consuming, but perfect. The new blue trouser-suit was darker than her eyes, giving them additional colour. She carefully applied her make-up, liking the new shade of lipstick. Her summer tan had given her a need for a slightly darker shade. Her new sandals were perfect with her outfit. When she was dressed, she approved of what she saw in the mirror. She had made her plans carefully; she should not see Greg, but it was wise to be prepared. If he had changed his schedule and she confronted him on the boat, it would be to her advantage to look her best.

Back in the kitchen, she wrapped a large apron around her new outfit and removed the cooked duck from the oven. If the taste matched the appearance, she would have nothing to be ashamed of. She slid it on the platter and covered it with foil. With a piece of scotch tape, she attached the note she had written that morning. If Henry was keeping to his schedule, he should arrive at the boat no more than ten minutes before her. He would not have had time to prepare dinner for his boss.

Marlie had timed her plans even closer than she had expected. When she brought the car to a halt in the parking lot, Henry was just crossing the deck, suitcase in hand. By the time she stepped aboard he was out of sight. An elderly crewman who appeared from the port side, took her message to Greg's personal servant while she waited in the lounge.

Henry was all smiles when he entered. 'Miss Richmond, did you bring the ducks?'

'Well, I brought a duck,' she replied, allowing him to read the attached note. In her best copperplate she had written: The others were delicious.

She felt guilty when he paled. Since he must have known she was planning her revenge, she had not expected a reaction from him.

'Now, Henry, how could I know they were pets?' she paused and gave him a broad wink. 'We did not have our little talk, remember?'

His breath expelled in a deep sigh as he grinned. 'You gave me quite a scare, Miss Richmond.'

Marlie laughed. 'I just wish you could have seen your face. If you could serve it with that expression, I would be grateful.'

Henry shook his head emphatically. 'It's impossible—I could never serve it—not if you want Mr Alston to believe it—' he hesitated, seeing her dismay. 'The far more effective route would be for me to show it to him with an attitude of outrage. He knows I would never put one of his pets before him on a platter.'

'Of course not,' Marlie cried, her eyes wide. 'Why didn't I think of that?' For a moment she was stunned by her lack of foresight. Then she nodded thoughtfully. 'Still, showing it to him as you suggested will do as well.'

Marlie left hurriedly, since as much as she would like to see Greg's face, she did not want to be on the boat when he arrived. Battles were always easier on one's home ground, she had heard, and if his wrath brought him out to the cabin as she expected, she could stop his anger at any time by simply showing him his pets were safe and sound.

When she arrived back at the cabin, the ducks were indeed safe and sound, but angry at her for leaving. Not that she blamed them. The afternoon was hot, even in the shade, and they wanted a swim. She hurried into the kitchen to start dinner and returned with a large apron to protect her clothing while she tied the cords to their legs. As she worked, she sighed. No matter what she did, nothing would prevent Greg from seeing the paint on the ducks' feet. She could imagine the remarks, and just thinking about them caused her to flinch. She finished tying a cord to the foot of the canvas-back drake and stood him on her lap, shaking her finger at his bill.

'I warn you—if you love your master, when he comes around, squat, because if he makes one remark about your feet, I'll—I'll kick him in the shins!'

As she followed them to the bank, trotting because of their haste, she was determined that nothing was going to ruin her carefully made up appearance before she saw Greg again.

The ducks weren't in the water more than five minutes before she realised she had made a mistake. Friday afternoons the traffic on the waterway was heavy. The centre of the channel was periodically being used by large pleasure boats and the smaller, faster craft were zipping in close to the bank. Over their objections, she brought the ducks back to shore, towing them in by the cord attached to their feet.

While they complained at the interruptions of their swim, she untied the boats moored in the slip and pushed them further out in the stream. No one would run into them, but few of the fishermen would pay attention to birds, thinking they could fly out of danger. After the trick she had pulled on Greg, if anything happened to one of his pets, she would never convince him she hadn't been careless.

Once in the water again, the ducks quieted. They had a new area to explore, and Marlie sat back, watching the river traffic. She was keeping a close eye on her watch as well. If Greg kept to his schedule, the earliest he could arrive to confront her was half an hour away. She wanted the ducks quiet and out of sight until she chose to tell him they were in their cage. After their swim, if they were well fed, they might settle down and doze, she decided. She filled their dishes and one by one, she towed them in, untied their cord leashes, and put them in the cage. She had three in the pen when she went back to the slip to get the mallard drake. His cord was still tied to the mooring post, but he was not at the other end.

'Oh, no!' she cried and ran around the boats. No duck. She looked up and down the waterway, half expecting to see him paddling out in front of a speedboat. She was only partly relieved by not seeing him in danger. Her big worry was that she didn't see him at all.

'You—male!' she muttered. 'When I find you, you may end up in the oven after all.'

She walked around the slip, checking to see if the drake had hidden himself between the boats or between them and the wooden sides of the slip. She even checked the yard, thinking he might have left the water to chase an insect, but no duck.

He had to be on the water, she decided. She untied the rope and jumped down into her ten-foot boat, glad she had put the motor on it only that morning. One push of the pole and the small boat floated out into the river. She lost no time in starting the engine, intending to search up and down the river. But the roar of the motor flushed her quarry. With a spate of frightened quacking, the mallard came out from under an overhanging bush and half paddled, half flew into the safety of the slip.

Marlie pointed the boat back towards its berth and cut the motor after one jog of the throttle. She drifted after the bird, blocking his escape by water.

'Now, you stay right where you are,' Marlie told him. She tied up the boat and jumped ashore.

The mallard floated close to the end of the slip, but when she approached him, he swam slowly out of reach.

'Now you stop that!' she demanded and circled to the other side, but he drifted off as she approached. He was casual to the point of insolence, staying just beyond her, moving so slowly he could have been pushed by the breeze.

'You green-headed monster,' Marlie snarled through gritted teeth. 'It's easy to see you've learned from your master, but if you think you can get away from me, you think again!'

Tired of chasing him around the slip, she stepped into her boat and moved up into the bow. By use of the emergency oar, she moved the craft slowly forward. When she was within reach, she dropped the oar and leaned over the side. As her fingers touched the feathers on his back he spread his wings and tried to fly. Marlie made a grab for an out-stretched wing and tumbled into the water.

She came up sputtering. While she was under the water, her head had contacted the wooden side of the slip, not hard enough to be considered a bump, she decided. As she stood, waist deep in the water, clouded by the muddy bottom, she put the fingers of her left hand to her forehead. The darkened fingertips, as she inspected them, looking for blood, told their story. She was wearing the mud residue that clung to the planking.

Ruined again, she thought. A strand of hair, stringy and dripping with muddy water, hung over her forehead and across her face. The new trousers and shirt were streaked with mud and plastered to her skin. She could feel the mud between her toes as her new sandals sank deeper into the soft bottom.

With no surprise, but with a sense of utter futility, she watched Greg Alston striding across the grass. A glance at her water-soaked watch showed he was on time to the minute.

'Wonder if I can drown myself,' she muttered. At that moment a watery death seemed preferable to facing him after her dunking. She held her nose and slipped under the surface, intending to make her way submerged to the shelter of the boats four feet away. She had hardly started when a strong hand grabbed her arm and pulled her upright. Still holding her nose, she looked up from under her wet brows.

He was glaring down at her, his face darkened with anger. His strong square jaw out-thrust, the cords of his neck standing out in tension above his white collar. That gleaming white collar! She hated that collar! What right had he to be so clean and shining? His perfection was suddenly past all bearing.

'How dare you eat those ducks?' he shouted at her.

'How dare you be so clean?' she shrilled. Without thought, with an instinct born of her frustration, she reached up, grabbed his arms, and planted her feet against the wooden side of the slip. Greg, half squatting, leaning over the water, was helpless against her sudden jerk. The surprise on his face as he sailed over her head, did wonders for Marlie's injured dignity.

Her heart sang when he stood up, his dark hair dripping muddy water, his white collar a mottled brown. He was still angry, but his shock at being pulled into the slip had taken precedence.

'You—you—' He tried a menacing step in her direction, but the muddy bottom was slippery and he nearly lost his balance. While Marlie faced him defiantly, out from behind the bow of her small boat swam the mallard drake. He silently moved up behind Greg and stretched his neck to nibble at his hand.

'Sick 'em,' Marlie ordered just as the duck's bill closed on Greg's little finger.

Thinking he had been attacked, Greg tried to jump away, lost his footing and went under again. Marlie had backed up to the edge of the slip and watched as he surfaced. He came up eye to eye with the mallard.

Even if he hadn't recognised the bird as his own, it was ready to take possession of him. After a casual glance at his face the mallard stretched his neck and tugged at a lock of Greg's hair. With a gentle but firm hand, Greg stroked and pushed the duck back away from his face as he stood, the water running down his shirt and arms.

'What are you doing, turning my own ducks against me?' he demanded.

'That one, at least,' Marlie retorted. She still wasn't ready to admit the others existed, but they had ideas of their own. They set up a clamour, and even though their pen was out of sight, there was no doubt about the source of the noise.

Greg looked at her blankly for a moment. His gaze dropped to the mallard who was busily trying to eat the large gold ring on his left hand. Marlie could see in his eyes his struggle to lay aside his anger, and knew the feeling. To build a rage on a premise that later proved to be false, required an emotional readjustment. But he was fast getting himself under control. His mouth, that had been tight, widened into an evil grin. His deep grey eyes gleamed as they narrowed.

'You devil,' he murmured and started in her direction. 'You are going to pay for that little trick!'

'You stay away from me!' Marlie cried. She grabbed the well-anchored mooring post and scrambled on to the grass. Her intention was to make a dash for the dubious safety of the cabin.

Greg scorned pursuing her across the slip. Instead he reached for a support on his side, and in one leap was on the grass and running. He was between Marlie and the cabin so, denied her refuge, she circled the flower bed, depending on his respect for the flowers to keep him on the border. Directly across from her he waited, giving her the right to make the next move.

The tailored perfection that had so irritated Marlie had been overcome by the muddy water. His hair streamed in his face unregarded. A smear of mud streaked down his cheek, another spotted his left arm, but he ignored them. Rather than detracting from his masculinity, his soaking clothes clung to his body, revealing his wide chest, his muscular arms and thighs. His dishevelled state accentuated that wild look Marlie had seen in the torchlight on the yacht. Like some magnificent savage, he was half crouched, balancing on the balls of his feet as he swayed back and forth, alert to every nuance of her movement.

The flicker of his eyes, as he took in her appearance, reminded her of her own state. The silk shirt was embarrassingly transparent, causing her to feel naked under his gaze. She desperately wanted to escape to her room and dry clothing, still his obvious appreciation gave her a thrill, reminding her of her own sensuality as well as his.

'You stay away from me,' she threatened again as she moved back and forth, seeking an escape. 'You deserved it!'

'And you deserve what you're going to get,' he answered, his smile turning satanic. With a sudden leap he cleared the flowers and jumped to the narrow cleared path between the plants and the stump that had been cut to resemble a chair.

Knowing she had to flee, and fast, Marlie turned and ran. Too late she realised she had trapped herself. Directly ahead was the river bank, barely two feet above the water level. As she tried to check her stride she was grabbed from behind, lifted and thrust forward. She could feel Greg's body against her as they splashed down into the water.

Although the middle of the channel was deep enough to carry ocean-going vessels, immediately adjacent to the bank a shelf less than two feet deep had been left by the dredging equipment.

Marlie and Greg floundered in a tangle of legs as they both sought to gain their balance. Marlie heard, but paid no attention to, the quacking of the mallard as he half ran, half flew across the yard in their direction.

'Oh, you asked for it!' Marlie sputtered. Grabbing a handful of bottom mud, she flung it at Greg, who wasn't quite fast enough to dodge. She missed his face, but did manage to splatter his neck and shoulder.

'You must feel absolutely naked,' Greg retorted. With his left hand he grabbed her shoulder, keeping her within reach. With his right, he smeared her cheek, then leaned back, surveying her appraisingly. His brows went up. 'Now I recognise you!'

'I hope so!' Marlie disdained to clean her face. Instead she flung another handful of the black bottom soil.

Greg, expecting it, successfully dodged. Marlie scored a direct hit on the mallard, who was preparing to join the swimming party. The bird gave an outraged squawk and staggered on the edge of the bank, shaking his head.

'You're taking it out on the duck?' Greg teased.

'Well, he started it,' Marlie muttered, sounding like one of her students. She was ashamed of having hit the poor thing, but it wouldn't do to let Greg know that.

They tactfully called a time out while Greg picked up the angry bird and dumped him in the water, head down. The bright green legs and webbed feet thrashed in the sunlight.

Just let him open his mouth, Marlie thought, her jaw tight, both hands full of mud.

He surprised her by not mentioning the paint, but while acting so concerned about the bird, he still managed to sling a handful of mud in her direction. Marlie was quick enough to turn her head, but felt the wet glob strike her hair.

'Never trust a man,' she cried, retaliating in kind.

The mud was flying fast and furious when a sardonic voice from the bank startled them both.

'Is this how the rich and famous play?' They looked up to see Howard, arms akimbo, looking down at them.

Marlie, with a handful of black goo, altered her swing without pause. She barely missed Howard, who made his retreat at a dead run. Greg came closer to the target, but Howard dodged just in time.

'Enough fun and games,' Greg said, climbing the bank. 'If you think you've worked off your childish energies—' He held out his hand to assist her, but she noticed his legs were braced. He was wary of her.

Marlie bit back a retort. That was exactly what he wanted.

'You're right, of course,' she lowered her eyes. 'I do let my enthusiasm run away with me.' She meekly held up her hand, accepting his assistance. Not until she was standing on the bank did she realise they had overlooked the reason she had first been dunked.

'We forgot the duck,' she objected.

Greg gave a whistle. 'Come on, Caesar.'

Obediently, the mallard hastened his speed, flapped his wings and landed on the bank.

Marlie's mouth dropped open. 'You mean they come when you call?' she demanded, incredulous.

Greg's look suggested she was demented. 'Of course! They've been tame for years. And they were born wild creatures, so we don't keep them penned.'

Marlie thought about the chaos in the factory, her problems with tying cords to their ankles and her fear when she thought the mallard drake had escaped.

'Oh-h-h,' she wailed in frustration. She looked down at her new outfit that had been, less than an hour before, so attractive. Her new sandals were ruined, and so was her perfect manicure. She wailed again. Then she glowered at Greg, her blue eyes flashing.

'Just don't speak to me ever again,' she ordered. 'At least not for the next five minutes!'

She stalked off across the yard, decided she could not enter the cabin in her condition, and turned towards the corner of the house and the hose.

Howard had anticipated her. He turned the nozzle to a medium-fine spray and caught them both unawares as they rounded the building.

CHAPTER EIGHT

MARLIE'S SECOND shower that afternoon was considerably more hurried. She dried her hair, and pushed it into a gleaming page-boy. Considering her record around Greg, she knew she was taking a risk by slipping into a pair of white linen slacks. But the blue-and-white sailor top was flattering to her figure and complementary to her eyes. The flat-heeled white sandals with tiny straps showed off her slender feet and ankles as well as the new shoes that were drying on the patio.

She applied her make-up with more than ordinary haste, but that evening she required less than usual. The exertions of scuffling with Greg in the river had brought to her complexion a glowing colour and her eyes sparkled. Was it the exercise? she wondered. She knew better, but decided she must not dwell on that. She was getting to know Greg too well. He had an uncanny way of finding the chinks in her defences. She needed to be on her guard every minute. She could imagine the string of broken hearts in his past, but when he sailed away on his yacht, she refused to weep for him. Wealthy men were used to collecting trophies, and not all of them with a gun, she surmised. This particular game was going to be completed without anyone being wounded, she determined.

While Greg showered, she joined Howard in the kitchen. He had already spread the table-cloth on the lawn table and had carried out the candles. While Howard arranged the dishes, glasses and flatware, Marlie diced garden-ripe tomatoes, cucumbers and onions, and washed lettuce for her salad.

From the oven, where they had been simmering undisturbed, she took the lima beans and combined the cream and mushrooms. While the last ingredients heated on top of the stove, she removed the stuffed pork chops, put them on a platter as she periodically checked the bread, and mixed her salad dressing. In that one field she could not outdo Henry, she knew, but she defied even him to improve on her mushroom stuffing.

When Greg strolled out into the yard, Howard followed him with the hot bread while Marlie checked the table for anything they had forgotten.

With his own clothing too wet and soiled to wear, he was dressed in a pair of Howard's cut-offs and a knit shirt. Greg was several inches taller than his host, but he was slim, and fitted the shortened jeans well. He more than filled out the shirt. Without the give in the material, he would not have been able to wear it at all. His broad chest, the muscles in his back and arms were outlined against the tight material. Below the frayed bottoms of the cut-offs, the dark hair curled on his tanned muscular thighs.

Wouldn't you know, Marlie thought. He could make even a ragged pair of old jeans look as if they were exclusively designed.

When Howard passed Greg the steaming platter of chops, he helped himself liberally and reached for the rolls. When Marlie had the time, she enjoyed making the cloverleaf clusters. That night they were golden and perfect.

'I'm getting to be a fixture at this table,' Greg said as he passed Marlie the limas with mushrooms. 'I may have to start paying board. Before I decide, what's for breakfast?'

'Duck.' She gazed at him solemnly over the top of her iced tea glass.

Howard grinned and bowed his head over his dinner. The gleam from Greg's deep grey eyes was ominous, but he made no reply.

'How long are the birds on vacation?' Howard asked.

'I'm having someone pick them up tomorrow at the boat,' Greg answered. 'That is, if they're not in the oven, and if I can get the cage in my car.'

'Why don't I put them in the back of the station-wagon,' Howard suggested. 'Doris and I are going into town to-night. I'll drop them off on my way.'

When dinner was over, Howard and Greg helped to clear the table. She was once again glad of the dishwasher. Several years ago she and her mother had threatened to hold cook's strike unless it was installed. A vacation cabin was no place to spend hours washing dishes, they insisted.

She and Greg loaded the appliance and stored the food. Howard, mumbling about getting dressed, hurried to his room. While Marlie tidied the counters, Greg helped Howard load the ducks' wire cage in the wagon.

She had enjoyed his help in the kitchen. His breadth and height caused the rather large area to seem small and cozy. She heard the slamming of car doors and either one engine had stalled and had to be started twice, or he was following Howard back to the boat. Over the noise of the dish-washer, which had started roaring in its age, she couldn't be sure.

Better that he goes, she thought. Having him around for an evening could be dangerous to her heart, she knew. Still she was disappointed. After all her work and plans, surely he wouldn't leave without a word. She bent her head and scrubbed at a spot on the counter, trying to submerge her emotions under physical effort.

The roar of the appliance masked his entrance, so that she was startled by his voice.

'If you think you'll hand me a dishcloth, forget it.'

Did the room suddenly grow brighter? Marlie wondered. Afraid to turn, to let him see how his entrance affected her, she leaned over the sink, rinsing out the sponge. She laid it carefully on the small rack at the back of the counter.

'I thought you had followed Howard,' she said casually.

He stood in the kitchen door until she turned, and then he stepped back into the dimness of the screened patio.

Am I being manipulated? Marlie wondered. She was, she knew, but they could hardly continue to talk if he was outside in the dimness and she was in the kitchen. She followed, seeing him only as a dark silhouette against the silver of the moonlit water.

'Henry can look after the birds for a bit,' he replied to her question. He was still facing the water, but her shadow as she passed through the doorway had advertised her presence. He came to meet her. Marlie was aware of his tactics, but only because she was wary. His movements were so casual it seemed accidental that, with his natural breadth and his right thumb hooked in the pocket of the jeans, he had successfully blocked her way to the chairs at the other end of the narrow patio. Unless she pushed by him, she was forced to sit on the nearer end of the redwood lounge.

He was offering a challenge again, she thought. Something in her wondered if she had not been waiting for it, expecting and ready to welcome another battle of wits. This time she would be on her guard. She was not going to be caught with her defences down as she had been the week before.

But in that past week she had considered the man. He was much like the river that flowed by the cabin. Unless one knew it was part of a vast complex of channels and dredged streams, its depth could be deceptive and dangerous. But Marlie knew the stream, and after her experience on her walk, she thought she could handle Greg Alston. If not, she was only a hundred yards from where the Billings, next door, were cooking on their outdoor barbecue. She could see the glow of the charcoal and Mrs Billings moving around the small portable table in the light of candles.

But once she thought of it, running to the Billings for help was silly. Greg was not a man from whom a woman would have to force an escape. Nor was she sure she would want to.

She took the seat on the end of the cushioned redwood lounger. Greg dropped down beside her, his face turned away, looking south.

From that direction the sound of marine engines carried over the water. They sat in a companionable silence for several minutes waiting to see what type of vessel appeared around the bend.

Their wait was worthwhile. As if teasing the eye, offering an appetiser before a feast, lights twinkled between the trees on the other side of the river. They were in sight in intermittent patterns only to be hidden again by the foliage.

Then the first boat came in sight. The nautical running lights, the square gleams from windows, and the torchlit decks alerted Marlie to the treat in store.

'It's that convoy of houseboats,' he said as the second vessel rounded the bend. 'They pass occasionally, but I've never seen them on the river at night. They're beautiful!'

She leaned forward slightly, watching the unhurried approach. Over the throb of the engines they could hear shouting and laughter. On the first boat, illuminated by the torchlight, two children were standing, waving towards the shore.

'Is it dangerous, running the waterways at night?' Greg asked.

Marlie was poised to say he should know, but she remembered he had a crew for his boat. With his busy schedule, he probably left the crew to move the boat from place to place. That's wealth for you, she thought with a tinge of contempt, and chided herself for being unfair. Rich or not, if he had no time to see the beauties of the waterway, he was to be pitied. She answered him with a genuine sympathy.

'I don't think so,' Marlie replied. 'The channel is well marked, and they travel through here often—see, there is the flash of his lights.'

From the first boat came a powerful beam of a searchlight. A long bright oval skimmed the surface of the water, pausing momentarily where the marker buoys indicated the channel. The light travelled quickly along the surface and was dimmed.

Both Marlie and Greg remained silent as the lights of the moving houseboats and their reflections on the water turned the silent river into a theatre for a light show. A quarter of a mile upstream several fishermen were trying their luck from the bank. Apparently, they gave up any idea of getting a strike while the boats were passing, so they abandoned their silence, calling out to the voyagers. The laughter and banter added to the party atmosphere.

Not until the nautical parade had passed did Marlie notice that Greg's arm was resting on the top of the cushion at her back.

'That looks like fun,' he said, his face finally turned in her direction. Until then she had not allowed herself to believe she had been waiting for his attention.

'Oh, I guess so,' she countered. 'It's a slow way to travel if you're going any distance. I doubt they have crew's quarters aboard.'

His expression was hidden by the darkness, but she saw the gleam of his white teeth as he smiled.

'Was that a shot across the bow? Have we broken the temporary truce?'

'Did we have one?' Marlie asked, surprised.

'I thought so, since we haven't had a pitched battle in ten minutes.'

Was that an attempt to start one? Marlie wondered. The darkness kept her from seeing his eyes. She tried to pick up his intent from his voice and failed. While he spoke with a pleasant inflection, his tone gave nothing away. A good negotiating voice, she thought. She leaned forward, picked up the matches she had placed on the table earlier, and lit the glass-enclosed candle.

His look, half amused, was slightly irritating to Marlie.

'If you think I was trying to start an argument, you're mistaken,' she said with unnatural primness. 'I've been aboard a few, and I hardly think they'd fit your lifestyle.'

He was very still, but Marlie sensed a withdrawal.

'I see. And you're convinced that I'm locked into my habits. I can't see past my nose, or enjoy anything different?'

'I hardly think you'd be comfortable without your crew and your Friday "gofor"—or whatever you call Henry. Slumming it around a cabin on the river and going fishing in a boat with an outboard motor is a novelty right now, but you'll tire of it.'

She was half surprised at the flatness of his eyes, the set of his jaw. He was angry. Forcefully angry, but holding himself in. Marlie wished she could have taken back her words, but they were said, they were the truth.

His voice was low, dangerous. 'I'm glad you warned me. Now, when I grow bored, I can look back and remember you told me I would.' He stared at her for a moment, then looked out into the darkness beyond the candle. 'You surprised me. I didn't expect you to be a snob.'

'That's an unfair remark,' Marlie retorted. 'I'm not a snob because I'm not blind.'

'No, but there's a difference between blindness and deliberately distorted vision,' Greg replied through tight lips.

'Thank you,' Marlie's voice carried a touch of ice. 'Call it distorted if you want, but when you tire of hobnobbing with the local yokels, you'll return to your friends in New York and Paris, or wherever you spend your time. You'll go back to the beautiful socialites—' Marlie could have kicked herself for sounding like a jealous female. She could imagine his scorn. She flinched, expecting him to come back with a scathing remark.

The tiny muscle under his jawbone was quivering again. She knew she'd touched a sore spot on his ego.

'What am I, in your opinion—' he asked, then shook his open hand as if erasing his words. 'Don't answer that, I can read between the lines. In your mind I spend my time running over people, getting my own way, and ravishing virgins, looking for—what did you call it?—a speciality? Perfection?' A heavy breath of suppressed rage hissed between his clenched teeth. 'Do we go on now to the wretched men I ruined in shady business dealings, or to the string of broken hearts that lie in my wake?'

His scorn, and his ability to know what she was thinking, sent Marlie's defences soaring.

'I don't know how many females you've left behind you in your search for perfection, or whatever the connoisseur's term is, but here you leave no broken heart. When you get back to New York and can't remember the name of that funny girl who painted ducks, you'll know she's one who has an equally short memory.'

'So I'll be forgotten before I'm out of sight?'

His face was flushed with anger, his eyes were narrowed to a dangerous gleam, but Marlie refused to be intimidated. Her chin came up.

She replied with an arrogance worthy of Scarlet O'Hara. 'You can believe it!'

In a sudden move, not taking his gaze from her face, he reached out and grabbed the candle. His piercing eyes, nearly black with rage, were the last she saw as he blew out the small flame. His voice cut through the sudden darkness:

'Like hell you'll forget me!'

His silhouette was a blur as he moved forward. His hands, hard and forceful, grabbed her shoulders, pulling her towards him until his lips found hers, bruising, bringing both pain and a demanding pleasure. Still holding her tight, he moved one arm around her shoulders and the other under her knees. She felt herself lifted and laid down on the soft cushions of the redwood couch.

In one fluid movement he was beside her, his long hard body pressed against her, trapping her with part of his weight. His hands, that less than a week ago had been so gentle in the awakening of her passion, were pressing hard against her flesh, kneading her side and leg, her arm, her breast.

Marlie gasped at her own reaction. She had been, that evening in the wood, like a sleeping thing slowly awakening to his gentleness. Now her body responded to his rough demands by flaring into an ecstasy of desire, into an urgency closely matching his.

No, she told herself, this is the very thing I must not do. In giving in to the desires of her body, in allowing Greg Alston to be the man to bring about that first unforgettable experience of true joining, he would gain a place in her life that could never be erased.

Her will struggled against her body but, even as she fought, her arms encircled his back, drawing him closer, joining him in his demands.

His lips left hers. His tongue found the secret tender places around her ears. His hand interrupted the torture of her breast to push back the boatneck collar of her blouse, where his tongue found the hollows of her throat, and travelled down towards her breasts.

She moaned as he teased her senses into a frenzy of desire. His hand moved down the outside of her thigh, and then started up again, caressing the more tender flesh on the inside of her leg. Still torn between her mind and her body, she knew her logic was losing the battle when, of their own volition, her legs parted to give access to his exploring hands.

Her body was an echo of her mind. So powerful was the passion he had aroused, that she was in terror of being drawn further into that strange territory. She felt as if she were on the edge of a strange and frightening sea. Something irresistible was pulling her forward, she could not withstand the beckoning, yet if she gave in, slipped into those unknown waters, would she ever leave them? The sea and Greg seemed to be demanding more than some bodily reaction—her heart and will were being pulled from her. Instinctively, she knew there was more involved than bodily lust, part of her would be consumed by him, and part of him would never leave her. Once she made that trade she was no longer a solitary being.

She mentally fought against him, terrified of unknown perils, yet physically she held tight, not daring to let go for an instant. Losing the promise offered by his growing urgency was a fear that loomed like a thundercloud of doom.

His hands stopped torturing her body and suddenly he pulled away from her, raising to one elbow as he tugged and worried with her blouse. He fumbled for buttons, and realising there weren't any, he was pulling it up when a laugh came from the Billings as they worked over their barbecued dinner.

His head turned in their direction for a moment. Then he was on his feet, lifting Marlie in his arms. He carried her into the bedroom and lowered her to the bed. Her arms were still around his neck, but once there he turned away. Shocked, stunned and disappointed, she raised on one elbow as she saw him outlined against the window. He was standing very still, looking out into the night. His chest still heaved with the ragged breathing of his passion. His jaw moved as if he were gritting his teeth.

'Greg?' she whispered, puzzled. He averted his face. She called his name again.

'You can call me what you will,' he rasped, 'but I've never taken any woman in anger.'

Marlie's mind was still spinning from his lovemaking. She had completely forgotten their argument. How did she answer him?

Before she could get her thoughts in order, he had left the window. She could barely make out the blur of the light shirt as he moved towards the doorway.

'This is not what I planned, not what I wanted,' he spoke through clenched teeth. 'And I won't let you goad me into it.' Open-mouthed, Marlie watched as he crossed the room, stumbling into a chair in the darkness. Then his tone changed. 'Tell Howard I'll be here in the morning.'

The white blur in the doorway was gone. Marlie sat up on the side of the bed. She wondered if she could trust her watery legs to follow him. She wanted to convince him that she understood.

Understood what? What had happened? Before she could make her mind and legs follow her heart, the engine of his sports car roared to life. The snarl that had been in his voice had been transferred to the car as he raced off into the night.

Marlie had never felt so alone. She had been right about that treacherous water. Only it had not taken the culmination of their lovemaking to rob her of part of herself. She felt as if she had lost something vital, something that made her a total person, and had been given nothing in return. Part of her was in that speeding car, it was with him, had melted into him. Though she could give it no name, it left a void that only part of him, left in return, could fill.

She collapsed on the bed, too miserable for tears. Her pain was too big for her—she was overwhelmed. It gagged her, blocking the release that might have lessened it.

Greg Alston had his souvenir. She could not name what he had taken. He might not remember the name of the duck lady in the boondocks, but he was too experienced not to know he had walked off with her heart. He had another trophy.

Marlie's misery was compounded by a difficulty sleeping. She was still lying awake when Howard came in. Several times during the night she awoke, weighed down under her misery. In her half-conscious state, she had trouble putting a name to it, but memory was never long delayed.

The next morning she was awake long before daylight. Knowing she wouldn't sleep again, she rose, and worked quietly in the kitchen preparing for breakfast. Greg would arrive too late to see her get flour on her face, but if she did it wouldn't matter to either of them, she thought.

During the night she worked out her own answer to what he meant by his cryptic remark. He said he neither planned nor wanted to make love to her, he simply was not interested. She had been a fool to think he was.

With wealthy and beautiful women trailing after him, he had no need to seek female companionship. Howard and a

new fishing ground was what drew him to the cabin, she
decided. She had been a recipient of his naturally charming
and flirtatious nature, but that was all. It had been her ego
that convinced her he would want, even as a trophy, the
heart of a woman who covered herself with paint and mud.

'So much for you,' she muttered as she took her first cup
of coffee out to her stump. The sky was just turning grey in
the east. She wished she had time to drive out to the ocean
and watch it rise. But sitting among her marigolds and zinnias, watching their colours emerging with the light, was a
pleasure denied her when she was on the beach. Sitting on
the stump was homy and safe.

Absently she ran her fingers over the rough wood. The
great Greg Alston would probably describe it to a group of
his cronies at a New York cocktail party, leaving everyone
wiping their eyes after laughing at the joke. But it was her
stump and she liked it.

She heard the throaty purr of the sports car. Greg was
early, quiet as he closed the door of the car.

Marlie kept her eyes on the river, not daring to turn
around. What would her face show? She had no idea if she
knew how to hide the feelings. A broken heart, if that's what
she suffered, was not in her field of expertise.

She heard Howard call from the kitchen window and
Greg answer. She still didn't turn as they came across the
yard. The lawn chairs were close to the flower-bed. Both
men sat. Howard poured Greg a cup of coffee and called to
Marlie to come for a refill.

She knew she had to go. Sooner or later she had to face
Greg, and the less light, the less he could see. She made up
her mind to stroll over, get the coffee and say something
casual, inane.

She strolled over, held out her cup to Howard and gave
Greg a nod.

'You're early.' That was inane.

'I am.' That was inane, too.

Glad of an excuse to get away, Marlie went to the kitchen. If Greg thought he was going to be surprised with something different for breakfast every time he showed up to go fishing, he was mistaken. Marlie liked to cook, she was imaginative in the kitchen, but never before ten in the morning. Breakfast was the same standby that had served her family for generations. The dieticians might frown on eggs, but nothing had more staying power. If the men were going to spend their day fishing, they needed food that would hold them through the morning.

The ham was sizzling in the pan, she had hulled some strawberries, mixing them with bananas and then adding the heavy cream. The farm-style biscuits were golden brown when she discovered there would be four for breakfast.

The put-put of outboard motors was no novelty in the early morning and she had paid no particular attention to the one that slowed and stopped in front of the cabin. But she smiled as Jonas Jones followed Howard and Greg into the kitchen.

'I haven't seen you this year, Jonas,' she said, handing him a cup of coffee. 'You'll have breakfast with us, of course.'

'Well, guess I could, no harm in one meal out—don't do it often, mind.'

Marlie nodded with forced solemnity. She was being afforded an honour, she knew. Jonas was by choice a hermit. His ragged clothing and torn sneakers made him appear a pathetic character, but he was proud and independent. Everyone on the river knew that few were considered by Jonas worthy of his conversation. If she could keep him for breakfast, she was sure his reaction to Greg would be interesting. Interesting to Greg, as well, if she knew Jonas.

They were halfway through breakfast. Howard and Greg were discussing the relative merits of various fishing spots when Jonas put down his fork, staring at Greg's shirt.

'Sell clothes, do you?'

Greg, who had just taken a bite of ham, nodded. Marlie thought his reaction was a little too enthusiastic. If he was condescending to Jonas, she would resent it, she knew, but his attitude seemed only encouraging. Jonas leaned forward, taking a close look at the shirt. Then he leaned back, frowning.

'Couldn't sell that one, I take it.'

Marlie glanced at the dove-coloured knit shirt, obviously tailored by a name whose very existence was a secret known only to the select few. Jonas wore a ragged green tee-shirt that had begun life as a respectable undergarment for a soldier. His trousers were a match, both in origin and wear. While Howard choked, she ignored him, holding her breath. If she dared breathe, her mirth would be hysterical.

Greg, stunned speechless, had shaken his head. Whether he was answering Jonas or expressing his wonder, she didn't know. But Jonas wasn't finished. He took another closer look and patted Greg on the shoulder.

'Good money in fishing.'

Howard left the table with a fit of coughing. Marlie expelled one breath and drew in another. Her face was beet-red from holding her breath, but she wasn't worried about her appearance, as long as she could keep from laughing.

Greg, with all his poise, his exclusive school training, his jet set aplomb, stuffed an entire biscuit in his mouth to stop any sound.

Marlie created a diversion by pouring more coffee. Greg kept his eyes on his plate, and she was grateful. The less eye contact she had with him, the more likely she was to control her mirth. She was just sitting down again when Howard returned to the table.

He tried to turn the talk into safer channels.

'What brings you out so early?' he asked Jonas.

'Trouble with my water pump,' Jonas muttered as he suspiciously eyed the dish of strawberries, bananas and cream. He had saved his fruit for dessert.

Marlie met Howard's eyes. The flat statement, lacking any emphasis, held a tremendous importance to the few who knew Jonas. He needed help. He had, in his own way, asked for it. Nothing else would be said. Either he received it or he didn't.

Marlie knew, too, that Howard felt he must assist old Jonas.

'Do you want to take my boat?' she asked her uncle casually.

'No, better take mine,' Howard replied. 'I'll take tools, but we may have to bring the pump back here to the shop. You and Greg go on with your plans.'

Marlie's question had been unnecessary. She was only letting Greg know Howard was going with Jonas. The first part of Howard's answer was expected. The second part was not. He was saying she was to take Greg fishing. He couldn't know about their argument the night before, or what followed. She tried to catch his eye, but he had turned his attention to the old hermit, completely ignoring her.

Greg had held a still, listening silence, taking in the undercurrents of the conversation, she knew. He was a man too used to nuances not to understand. He was giving his concentration to his plate, leaving her and Howard to settle the arrangements.

Jonas thanked Marlie for a 'tolerable' breakfast, and left the kitchen when they rose from the table. Howard helped

Marlie and Greg with clearing the table and fixing two large picnic lunches.

'Sorry, but I've got to go,' he muttered to Greg.

Greg nodded. 'We've got one just like him in Maryland,' he replied.

The sun was just up when they gathered at the slip. Jonas eyed the two coolers in Marlie's boat. The smaller one held cold water and canned drinks. The large had ice and was to be used for the fish they caught.

'Too many weekenders out this morning,' Jonas said. 'I'd go to the graveyard.' He looked at Marlie under his eyebrows. 'You could get in—' He looked Greg up and down, taking in the shirt again. 'He couldn't.'

Marlie beamed under the praise from the old man. She had manoeuvred the treacherous path many times, but to have Jonas recognise her skill with a boat was a compliment bestowed on few. In saying Greg could not, he meant a stranger could and probably would find himself in serious trouble.

Marlie waited until Howard and Jonas had poled out into the river, started their outboards and were out of sight before she stepped in her boat.

The Whisk was small, only twelve feet in length. The thirty-five horsepower Evenrude motor would take Marlie anywhere she wanted it to go. She could not compete with the speedboats, but with no more than three people aboard, she could make considerable speed. Then, too, she had advantages denied the more luxurious vessels. Her motor lifted off, and could be locked in Howard's workshop when she was away from the cabin. While she had the power and speed to travel distances in a short time, her motor could be released and tilted if she found herself clogged by weeds or suddenly in the shallows.

But at the moment she wasn't thinking about her boat. Greg was lifting the hawser off the mooring post. She dreaded the day in his company, as visions of the night before kept intruding into her mind. How could she blot that out? How could she even attempt to act natural? He would probably pretend the evening never happened—but in that she was wrong.

He stepped into the boat, picked up the pole to push them out into the stream, and hesitated. Moving easily, showing his familiarity with boats, he took a seat while they were still drifting in the slip. His eyes were soft. A half-smile played on his lips.

'Pax,' he said softly.

'Wh-what?'

'Peace. Truce. I can't apologise for my feelings, for wanting you, but last night was unfair to both of us. We deserve something better. Let's start this morning with a clean slate—okay?'

Marlie nodded. She was surprised, confused, and glad she need not pretend. She felt some effort was due on her part.

'Do you want to take us out?' She waved her hand at the motor.

Greg drew back, feigning dismay. His eyebrows were arched as he fingered his collar.

'In this shirt? We'd never make it.'

CHAPTER NINE

MARLIE WAITED until Greg had poled them out into the stream. As they drifted lazily on the water, she adjusted the throttle and gave a tug on the starter cord. The motor roared to life. After letting it idle for a few minutes to warm up, she readjusted her throttle. The stern dipped as the propeller bit into the water. The bow of the light fibreglass boat lifted as they sped down the river.

Ahead, the reflection of the trees and plantlife on the edge of the placid waterway created a double world. No breeze ruffled the surface, and the disturbances of earlier boats had disappeared. In some places the banks, left by the dredging equipment, were still sharp cut, as if they had been carved only the day before. But where the sharp knife-like blades of cattail grass rose three and four feet from the water, the mirror image of growth seemed to extend out into the river.

Behind them the wake of the fast moving little boat spread out to the banks, losing its force on the way. Lazy little waves splashed against the water plants and brushed against the river banks.

They had travelled almost two miles downstream when they rounded a slight curve. Ahead, and just coming into sight, was a small ocean-going freighter.

'Slight detour!' Marlie shouted to Greg and whipped the tiller around, abruptly reversing her direction. A hundred yards down their wake was a wide creek she knew well. With no loss of speed Marlie headed into the tributary. She travelled as far up the creek as she dared, dropped her forward motion to trolling speed and made another complete turn. When she allowed the motor to idle, the bow was facing the river.

Her straight look at Greg was half defensive.

'Call me coward if you want, but I don't cross the wake of the big ladies.'

Greg nodded. 'Narrow here.' She saw understanding in his eyes. He drew the sturdy pole from beneath the seats and held it as he waited.

That one action told her he knew what they faced and what had to be done. Not only would she be spared any teasing, but he would be a help in holding the small boat when the large ship passed. He moved up to crouch in the bow. The hand that held the pole was relaxed, but he had dropped one end off the right sight of the bow. He looked over his shoulder, and Marlie knew he watched her as she checked the catch that held the motor upright once it was attached to the boat. She reached under the seat, pulled out the emergency oar and laid it within easy reach, knowing she would need it later.

Satisfied that she knew her task, he turned back to watch for the bow wave. Few people ever gave a thought to the small disturbance at the front of the boat. Arching out from a small boat on the river, or a ship out in the bay, that white-topped curl appeared playful, lively, never frightening. But in those situations, the vessel was small in comparison to the surrounding volume.

What approached Marlie and Greg as they waited, bore no resemblance to a froth-capped wave. A good portion of the river water, trapped within its banks, was being pushed ahead of the ship. It piled and compounded upon itself, creating a visible hill of water, an artificial tidal wave. As it moved, the opposite bank disappeared under the rising tide.

When the sudden tide rushed into the creek, Marlie steadily increased the pressure on the throttle to keep the boat from being washed up among the trees. The banks, lower on that side of the river, were completely lost under the surging water. She kept her gaze fixed on two trees, using them as landmarks to stay in the middle of the stream.

She spared only a glimpse for the ship as the bow passed. She noticed the Liberian registration and heard the 'Halloo's' called in foreign accents. Had she been standing in the yard at the cabin, she would have tried to guess their nationality as she answered and waved, but at the moment she was occupied. Her next movement required all her concentration to achieve split-second timing.

Once the bow wave crested, the reverse flow would begin. Her gaze shifted back and forth between the trees that were her location reference and the bow of the ship. After years of watching such vessels pass she knew exactly when to expect the change in flow.

'Now!' Greg shouted to be heard over the ship's throbbing and the roar of the Evenrude, but Marlie had already cut the power. Working quickly, she released the catches and tilted the motor forward, bringing the shaft and propeller out of the water. She grabbed the emergency oar, thrusting it down and forward, ready to assist Greg in holding the boat against the pull that was coming.

As the bow passed, and with it the crest, left behind was an emptiness that showed the shallower original river bottom near the banks, left when the deeper channel was dredged. With the bow pushing water ahead, and the force of the powerful screws forcing water back behind the ship, the surface had visibly dropped several feet below normal.

The full creek emptied, its contents pouring into the emptiness that had only minutes before been a quiet river.

Greg threw his weight against the pole as he used his strength to keep the small craft from being swept forward. Marlie buried the tip of the oar in the creek bottom. Bracing herself, she held the stern in position, keeping it from spinning around on the pivot of Greg's pole. As the water rushed away, the small boat settled in the mud, tilting slowly.

Once the boat was grounded, Marlie was able to relax. In the bow, Greg's shoulders lost their tension, but he kept one hand on the pole.

'That's a weird sight, isn't it?' He spoke without turning around.

Marlie knew what he meant. For the water to suddenly drop several feet below its normal level was a departure from normal that upset the senses.

'It's not so spectacular where the river is wider,' she said casually. 'We are in a particularly narrow section.'

As the stern of the ship passed, the final step in the natural phenomenon approached. Some distance behind the ship, kept back by the powerful thrust of the screws, the river followed. A slope of water rolled over itself, filling the void the freighter left behind. Nature mending herself at the same speed as the man-made vessel, was in itself unsettling.

As the rolling wave passed, part broke away. Freed from the restraints of the propeller thrust, it rushed and bubbled in the creek bottom until the natural surface had been reached. Greg and Marlie, using the pole and the oar, held the boat to the centre of the stream until the peace of the quiet river was restored again.

Marlie pushed the motor up, lowering the propeller back into the water, and fastened the clamps. While she tucked the oar under the seat, Greg turned and did the same with the pole. His smile as he faced her was genuine. She was thrilled by the admiration she could see in his grey eyes.

'Hey, gal, you done good! Even Jonas would have approved.'

'You weren't so bad yourself—for a city slicker.' Her joking qualification of her compliment was an attempt to hide how deeply she had been affected by his praise and the way he offered it. He was generous, not begrudging her abilities, yet, by his actions in handling the pole, he had the knowledge to handle the situation as well, if not better, than she.

Marlie pulled the starter cord, adjusted the throttle, and ran the boat out on the river. After checking to make sure the way was clear, she swung out into deep water and increased her speed. Ahead, the leaves of the trees moved slightly in the light breeze, the waterbugs made widening circles as they moved along the surface, and the slanting rays of the sun added contrasts of shading to the reflection of the marsh growth and trees on the water.

Two miles further on, Marlie slowed her speed at what appeared to be the intersection of two rivers. Before the channel had been dredged, the original stream had meandered across the flat area of the tidelands, and some of the snaking curves had been ignored in favour of a less tortuous route.

Half a mile up the natural waterway, the river made a hairpin turn. To the left, the stream curved away, and three boats were anchored as anglers tried their luck. To the right, the water spread out into a small lake. Warning signs alerted fishermen to submerged obstructions.

Not all the obstacles were submerged. Rising from the acres of still water were the hulking shapes of rotting wooden barges. They created a nautical ghost-town of bows, hulls, and unsafe decking. Here and there a small cabin or pilot house tilted crazily, caused both by the cant of the half-sunken wreck, and its own rotting supports. As they approached, beneath the surface other wrecks were dimly visible in the murky water.

Marlie dropped back to her slowest possible speed and circled twice before attempting to enter the graveyard.

Greg, who had been twisting on his seat, inspecting the general area and the sunken barges close enough to see clearly, turned, grinning.

'That's a paradise.'

'If we get in,' she muttered, concentrating on locating her mental key. 'For me, getting started is the roughest part. Once I find the place I want to enter—there it is.' She sighed. To fail would be terrible, she thought, after bringing him this far.

Marlie had not been back to her favourite fishing spot that year, and during the winter storms or the autumn hurricanes, several of the wrecks had shifted. Once she located the barge that had once worn the name Old Sally, she knew her way. She was just relaxing when she saw Greg's worried expression. She wondered if he had decided not to trust her to take them through the obstacles, but he pointed behind them.

'I think we may have company,' he muttered. 'Those characters look like they want to follow.'

'Then they had better ride my wake,' Marlie replied, by now concentrating on her course between two submerged wrecks. Not until after she spoke did she realise how arrogant she must have sounded. Her words had held a literal connotation a local would have understood. She had first learned to manoeuvre a boat through the barges by following close to Howard's boat, but she wondered if Greg recognised that. Looking back, she was relieved to see the fisherman in the stern of the other boat was refusing to make the attempt.

But what did Greg think? An effort to justify herself would make the situation worse. She tried to lessen the distasteful impression she was sure she had made.

'Do you see a spot you'd like to try?' she asked.

'You do the choosing,' he remarked as he turned his head from side to side, getting a good look at the area. 'I'll take your word for it.'

Was there anything sarcastic in that remark? she wondered. No. His head turned slightly as they passed within inches of some jutting planking, and she saw his absorption. He was relaxed, interested, and enjoying the ride, letting her use her own judgment without reservation. She had wondered fleetingly, as they passed the other fishermen, how he felt about a woman running the boat, while he sat idle. But she decided she had done him a disservice in thinking about it.

Greg Alston was a powerful and successful man. Too powerful and successful to find any other person's abilities a threat to himself. That was for lesser men. She thought back to little over a week before, when he had run the carving machine at the factory, and his assistance with the boat in the creek. He was too big a man to limit himself to only the larger things in life. He encompassed everything he could reach.

She warned herself not to think about that. He was beginning to look too good in her eyes, especially after his last words to her the night before.

She concentrated on manoeuvring the boat through the narrow, twisting channel. Marlie didn't consider her ability to traverse the dangerous area anything in which she should take a particular pride. No skill was required. A modicum of common sense, enough to keep the speed down to a minimum, and a memory for the twists and turns were all she needed.

She cut the motor as the boat entered an open area, letting it drift until they were in the centre.

'This spot okay with you?' she asked.

'Fine.' Greg lifted the anchor and lowered it slowly by the rope. His movements were designed not to frighten away the fish.

They floated in the centre of the best fishing ground in the area. She could count on her fingers the people who knew the way into the less accessible sections of the graveyard, so the waters were neither overfished nor disturbed by speedboats.

The closest humans were the anglers they had passed at the bend in the river, and Marlie had travelled more than half a mile since passing the warning signs. To the left, and straight ahead, the green marshgrass and a few trees were visible beyond the wrecks, but no human habitation. Behind them and to the right, the old barges, some piled one on top of the other, created a peaceful, but eerie atmosphere, intensified by the reflection. Water spiders danced across the surface of the water, flying insects dipped to avoid the hovering dragonflies.

The busy world seemed many miles away. Even the barges, evidence of man's intrusion, had weathered until they too seemed a part of nature.

A sudden doubt shook Marlie. Would Greg understand her reason for bringing him to this particular spot, or would he think she had some other motive? After the incident the night before, would he think she was trying to regain ground that had been lost when he suddenly walked out?

Her cheeks were growing hot at the thought. She was wondering if she should make some excuse and find a less isolated spot when the peace was disturbed. Across the calm sheet of bright water, a silver flash broke the surface. A large bass gleamed in the sunlight as it arced at the top of its leap and splashed back into the water. Greg watched the widening ripples and spun around on the front seat.

'Why are we sitting here, doing nothing?' he lifted the two padded folding chairs and attached them to the wider, middle plank that served both as a brace and a seat.

'That's not going to give either of us elbow room,' she remarked, hiding her real objection. Sitting that close to Greg, with the memory of the night before still reeling in her head, would make it difficult to be casual. She felt a slight tremor course through her body as she thought about it.

But Greg was giving her no chance to put an alternate plan into action. He was shifting the coolers, the thermos of coffee, the fishing gear and tackle boxes. By the time he had finished, there was no place for Marlie except on the seat beside him. He held out a hand to assist her as she stepped over the folded boat seats and waited while he raised the padded back-rests.

When he sat beside her, necessarily close in the small boat, she knew she would be unable to keep her mind on her fishing. Looking sideways, under the brim of her fishing hat, she watched him as he seemed totally absorbed in checking his reel. His first cast was perfect, settling the fly directly over the spot where they had seen the smallmouth bass break the surface. Marlie was just raising her rod and reel, wondering if she could do half as well when Greg spoke.

'I'd take a cup of that coffee, if you're offering.'

'Sure,' Marlie laid aside her rod and turned to get the cups and the thermos. She filled two cups and sat back, feeling the warmth of his arm on the back of her seat.

'Your coffee, sir,' she murmured, waiting for him to take it.

At that moment his line gave a jerk, and he was all attention, playing the fish. Marlie put the coffee on the plank seat
in the bow of the boat and reached for the net. Then she sat
back, watching Greg play the fish.

He was using the special line Howard and Marlie kept on
their reels. To them, the fish deserved as much of a chance
as the man. Most mediocre fishermen could bring in a bass
or a bluegill with no trouble at all. Pitting a man's one hundred and seventy pounds against a three to five pound fish
was not sporting. They handicapped themselves by a light
line so that one false move on their part, and the fish
could—and often did—win the contest.

Marlie watched as Greg gave his complete attention to his
task. His strong brown hands seemed almost relaxed as he
held the rod in his left, his right on the handle of the reel. He
seemed to be caressing the equipment, concentrating on
every nuance of the fish's movement. Marlie watched him,
aware of how convincing those hands could be, how sensitive, how strong.

Poor little fish, you haven't a chance, she thought, but she
was wrong. In trying to out-think his prey, Greg mistook the
slackening of the line to mean the fish was tiring while it was
apparently playing him. The line snapped and lay slack on
the surface.

He hissed under his breath, stifling a swear, and Marlie
saw his gaze cut to the corner of his eyes, watching to see if
she would take advantage of the situation to tease him.

'Happens to the best,' Marlie said as casually as she could
manage. By his stiffening he had known she was hiding her
true thoughts. 'You wouldn't believe how many hooks
Howard and I lose,' she added, and knew, even as she said
it, she sounded false.

He thought she was laughing at him, but her mind had
been on whether one try and loss on the small line would

make him want to switch to the heavier tackle. She would be acutely disappointed in him if he did.

'As you say, it can happen to anyone,' he said grimly. He moved his coffee to the top of the cooler by Marlie's left leg as he opened the tackle box, reaching for another hook and leader. 'What about you? Aren't you going to put out a line?'

'I haven't had a chance,' Marlie objected. 'First I poured coffee, and then stood by with the net. You didn't bring Henry, remember?'

Greg raised one hand in surrender. 'I take it all back. But the coffee is poured, there is no fish on my line, and now it's your turn.' He cast again, took a swallow from his cup and leaned back, putting his arm around Marlie.

She followed his example by sipping her coffee, and sat back after picking up her rod. Her voice, as she answered him, was deliberately light. It would not do at all for him to know how she was affected by that arm so close around her shoulders.

'Yes sir, of course, sir, I will endeavour to join in the activity—sir!'

The last sir carried all the force she put behind her cast. She had never been an expert at casting over her left shoulder, and she proved it immediately. As her line flew out and settled on the water, Greg's hat was attached to the hook.

Not another dumb day! Marlie railed at herself. She thought of several things that might take his mind off her gaffe, such as tipping the boat or throwing the lunch overboard, but the consequences that could follow were as unattractive to think about as having to face him. To get the dread out of the way, she turned to meet his mockery.

His eyes showed his amusement, but the rest of his expression was carefully solemn. With deliberate slowness, he removed his arm from around her shoulders, and took his rod in his left hand. With his right forefinger he touched his tongue and made a score mark in thin air.

'One for you—' He licked his finger again and made another mark. 'And one for me.'

Marlie shook her head in exasperation. 'Losing a fish is not on a par with snagging a hat. You're at least half a point up on me.'

'Five points, but who's counting?'

'I'll reel it in, you get the net,' Marlie grumbled and carefully worked the hat across the water.

'I will admit it was entirely my fault,' Greg said when they had recovered his hat and Marlie had attempted to blot it dry with a wad of paper towels. 'It was ungentlemanly of me to take the right seat. Please change with me.'

'Oh, no,' Marlie demurred. 'You are my guest. You remain where you are.'

Her next cast was more successful. They settled down to await strikes and for a while they sat in a companionable silence.

Marlie was having difficulty concentrating on fishing. Greg's proximity, his arm thrown casually across the back of her seat, the occasional touch of his leg against hers as he shifted his position, all brought back with vivid clarity the incident of the previous evening.

He had declared a truce that morning, and by all apparent expressions, inferences and conversations, he was keeping it. Still, she was bothered by his closeness.

As if he had been reading her mind, and some perverseness in his nature had decided to put her to a test, he shifted so he was facing her at an angle. Under the brim of his hat, his eyes were shaded and dark, but glints of light reflected off the water made her wonder at the thoughts behind them.

'I like this place,' he murmured softly. His voice was like a caress. 'I like having it to ourselves.'

Was there some meaning behind the last remark? she wondered. The muscles in his left arm, resting partly on her shoulders and partly on the back of the seat, were moving slightly, as if his hands or fingers were in motion, but without turning, she could not see, and they weren't touching her. His left leg, bent slightly, brushed her knee rhythmically as the boat was rocked by a breeze.

Marlie was not sure how to answer him. There seemed to be a particular meaning behind his words and position, but what if she were wrong? The night before he had told her he had not intended to make love to her. She had been fooled and hurt by misreading him once, and twice would be too much.

'I like coming here,' she said. 'It's no fun getting settled to fish and then being buzzed by speedboats.' That, she thought, should keep the conversation on an even keel.

Greg reached for his cup again, leaning forward, his arm still around her shoulders, his face coming close to hers. She dropped her eyes, not wanting to see the golden-brown face, the strong jaw, the full, sensitive lips so near, yet so achingly far if she had understood his harsh words the night before.

She wondered if he could be playing some game, or if he had no idea of his physical attraction, but that was absurd. He was an intelligent person. It wasn't conceit to be aware of one's effect on others; only the very foolish or the coy pretended otherwise. But if he knew, then he was deliberately baiting her, as he had in the woods, as he had only the night before. But the night before they had both lost control of their emotions. Today she was on guard against that, and he seemed to be also. He had given her no reason for anger, just as she was giving him none. We're both walking on eggs, she thought.

Quite possibly, she would have felt better if they had stayed in sight of the fishermen at the bend in the river. They were so isolated, and his nearness was torturing her with memories of his caresses. She flicked the rod, watching the whip action as the line arced over the water. A strike would at least draw her attention away from him.

She kept a firm hold on the cork handle of her fishing rod and dropped her eyes. In front of her his long legs stretched out across the cooler, his left knee only a fraction of an inch from hers. She shifted, trying to relieve the tinglings his proximity sent coursing through her, while at the same time, afraid any movement might communicate to him her feelings.

He leaned forward again, drawing closer as if moving in for a kiss, but only reaching for the coffee cup. Marlie's nerves tensed and relaxed. He was aware of it.

'Was it a strike?' he asked lazily, a slight curl of amusement on his lips.

'I thought so,' Marlie answered, glad he had at least given her a plausible reason for her reaction, even if he didn't believe it. Then she asked herself what right he had to give explanations for her behaviour with that smug look on his face. She wasn't having that.

'It was just a feint,' she added. 'Nothing to get upset about.' If he didn't catch the double meaning, he was pretty dense.

'They can be irritating, getting you ready for a move and then finding nothing to fight.'

Was he talking about fish? Maybe he was playing a cat-and-mouse game again, but did she dare accuse him of it? What a fool she would look if he denied it.

He leaned close again, putting his cup down. Behind his ear, his dark hair curled slightly. The deep brown that showed beneath his hat caught the sunlight, showing up several strands that gleamed a dark auburn. The softness of the wave made her fingers itch to touch and smooth the few pieces that had been disarranged by the breeze.

As if he knew what she had been thinking, when he straightened, he removed his hat, reaching across her to put it within reach of his left hand. For a moment she had been within a loose embrace. She tensed and relaxed again, this time more visibly than before.

'Another try at the hook?' he asked.

'Um-m-m,' Marlie nodded, at first not sure she could trust her own voice, but the gleam in his grey eyes assured her he was not referring to a fish. Still, if she accused him of anything, he could laugh at her.

'That little fish had better be careful,' she said. 'If he keeps playing around that hook, he's asking for trouble.'

'Then you think he might get what he deserves?' Greg asked.

'Let's just say he might get more than he expects, and it might not be at all what he had in mind.'

Greg's eyes glittered with amusement, but at that moment a large bass struck his fly and the line zinged out. He was busy for almost quarter of an hour, working the three-pound bass in on the small line, but this time he made no mistakes.

Marlie had to admit she had never seen a fish better played. Once it broke water she had warned him he had little chance of getting it to the boat and netting it on the thin filament they were using, but his skill and delicacy won the contest.

The next strike was on Marlie's line. After a stiff battle that lasted some minutes her line fouled on a snag, and she lost thirty feet of line as well as her hook, fly and leader.

'Another for you,' she conceded to Greg as she reeled in her line.

'That one doesn't count—hazard on the field,' he said.

After the brief flurry of activity, quiet again reigned on the still water. Greg poured more coffee, putting the cup back on the cooler.

The fish had given Marlie a respite, but after the two strikes, nothing seemed awake beneath that sheet of still water. Only Greg seemed to be restless, reaching for his coffee, checking the anchor rope, taking his hat off, and putting it on, and every action seemed to be designed to keep Marlie on the edge of her emotional seat.

Her senses were reeling from having him so near. As he leaned forward and across her to pick up the coffee again, his aftershave was tantalising in its dry meadows freshness. His strong hand, encircling the fragile styrofoam cup, reminded her of the passion she knew was in him, and the urges he had raised in her kept fighting to come to the surface.

His lips neared hers as he put down the cup. They were shaped in a relaxed sensuality of enjoyment. Her own tingled with remembered sensations. She pulled them tight against her teeth, not wanting him to read her thoughts in their trembling.

Each time he moved, Marlie wondered if he were going to renew the advances of the night before. Her nerves were screaming when he suddenly sat up, reeled in his line and stowed the rod and reel under the seat. Propping his feet up again, he slid down on the cushioned boat seat and lowered the brim of his hat until it covered his eyes.

'Wake me by two-thirty,' he mumbled. 'We'll have to start back by then to get ready for the party.'

'Wake you? What party?'

'Oh, didn't I tell you? Kara Holmes is having a party aboard their boat tonight. I told her we'd come. If you'll excuse me, I'll get some sleep.'

Marlie's fingernails dug into the cork handle of her fishing rod. Either he was stark, raving mad, or she was. How dare he tell someone she would attend a party without consulting her?

And how dare he give her those sultry looks, those innuendoes, almost touching, almost embracing, bringing her emotions to screaming heights, and then just go to sleep?

CHAPTER TEN

'I AM not going!' Marlie said as Greg raised the anchor and moved to the back of the boat to start the motor. He had slept away the afternoon on the uncomfortable boat seat and was in no mood for an argument. Disdained to wake him, Marlie had allowed him to sleep until four-thirty.

She had to direct him out of the graveyard, but she sat in a stony silence until they were back at the cabin.

'I am not going to that party!' Marlie said as he strolled into her bathroom. She had to follow him since he had a firm grip on her hand. Luckily her make-up was confined to the one case she carried back and forth to town. He picked it up, marched her out to his car, and they sped away.

The louse! How had he learned her address?

'I am not going!' Marlie insisted as she stood in her bedroom while he sorted through her dresses and chose one. In self-defence she grabbed undergarments, shoes and stockings, and shoved them in a small carrying case. She knew he would choose for her if she didn't. By this time she was doubtful of winning the argument, but she kept trying.

'I am not going!' Marlie stood in the companionway on his yacht while he pointed imperiously into a stateroom.

For the first time he replied to that statement.

'Would you like some help with your shower?' The gleam in his eye, the determined set of his smiling mouth sent her scuttling inside where she slammed the door. She had lost this argument from the beginning, and she knew it.

THE ADAMANT objections she had repeated were only for
show. She was glad she was going to the party—not that she
cared about Kara and Bill Holmes, but Greg's insistence that
he was going to take her had to mean something. It meant
she was more in his mind than just a niece of a fishing
buddy—or did it? Was it more? He couldn't be pulling some
trick on her, could he? No, she wouldn't accept that.

She pushed the catch on the door and turned towards the
shower. After her day on the river, getting clean and fresh
again had definite attractions.

Marlie was just leaving the shower when Henry brought
her a tall glass of iced tea. She enjoyed the leisure of drying
her hair by combing it, since they had forgotten her hair
dryer. Her small amount of natural wave, unconfined by the
strictures of dryers and curlers, framed her face in tiny
waves of fine hair and fell to her shoulders in a page-boy.

Since Harry had told her dinner was still some time away,
she took particular care with her eyeshadow, blending white,
brown and blue in faint and subtle shadings. It took time to
achieve that perfection of enhancement and still keep a
naturalness to the blended tones.

She was glad she thought to bring her sheerest stockings.
But she wondered about her choice of shoes. They were
high-heels, and never intended to be worn aboard boats. She
slipped them on. Never mind, if necessary she would take
them off.

Her dress was perfect. Teal-blue silk, it brought out the
blue in her eyes, deepening the colour and showing off her
skin to perfection. Standing in front of her closet, Greg had
reached for it unerringly, as soon as he saw the colour. The
connoisseur, she thought, and pushed that unwelcome idea
away.

Since she was going to the party, and would be spending the entire evening in his company, it would be foolish to begin another fight.

When she was satisfied with her appearance, she packed away her fishing clothes and went into the salon.

Dinner *grâce à* Henry was superb. The conversation between Marlie and Greg was desultory. He complimented her on her dress, a praise she could believe was genuine by the light in his eyes. He was the epitomy of elegance in his white dinner jacket. His tall muscular figure, and his rugged, dark good looks were an asset no tailor could build in.

Marlie was sorry to be leaving his boat when they crossed the deck, preparing to make the short walk down the pier to the Holmes' craft.

She was just putting her foot on the gangway when she heard a familiar sound. She looked up at Greg in surprise.

'I'd know that voice anywhere! That's Caesar!'

Greg nodded. 'You have a good ear for ducks.'

'I thought you were sending them back to your farm.'

'Slight hitch in plans. Minor problems on the farm are keeping everyone busy right now. I may be too cautious of those birds, but I'm not sending them by common carrier.'

'Are they comfortable on the boat?' Marlie was concerned.

Greg laughed. 'Comfortable? Caesar's elected him admiral.'

Marlie had never considered herself particularly adept at eye measurements, but it was easy to see the Holmes' yacht was smaller than Greg's. Even from a distance the difference in the condition of the two vessels was apparent. Both boats represented a small fortune in teak alone, but aboard the *Veronica,* the constant care kept the surfaces a glistening gold. On board the *Windswept,* several spots of the decking showed a grey, weathered look. Marlie saw Greg's jaws tighten as he ran a hand over a wooden railing.

But the lack of care for the boat was not extended to the party. Lights were strung from the masts and yardarms, a red carpet had been spread out on the deck for better footing, and waiters were wandering about with trays of drinks and hors d'oeuvres. One glance at the trays of glasses showed her choice to be champagne, champagne, or champagne.

She was being put in her place already, Marlie thought. In her lack of sophistication, she had never acquired the taste for the effervescent wine. Greg lifted two glasses from the tray of a white-collared waiter and grinned.

'Carry this until I find the tea vendor.'

They had walked less than three paces across the deck when out of the crowd came Kara Holmes, a vision in silvery chiffon and diamonds at her throat, wrists and ears.

'So glad you could come, darling,' she said to Greg, linking an arm through his. 'How are you this evening— Marlie?' There was just the slightest hesitation before the name.

'Delighted to be aboard,' Marlie replied with a smile. The deeply veiled insult had not passed Greg, she saw, and his eyes sharpened.

Her next play will be to tell him there's someone he really must see, Marlie thought.

Kara, taking Greg's hand that held his champagne, lifted it, sipping from the glass. 'Darling, there is someone you really must meet, and here comes Lyle to entertain Marlie.'

Kara's hand raised, along with her voice, an obvious signal across the boat. Lyle's head came up as if he had received a stage cue, and he seemed to tilt as he came through the crowd. He had begun his partying early. Despite Greg's dislike of the man, Marlie saw no real harm in him. He was, she thought, one of those weak characters who seemed always to hang on around more energetic, successful people.

Remembering Greg's reaction the first time she met Lyle Kearns, she glanced at her escort. Kara had been as subtle as a raging bull, and Greg could hardly blame her because their hostess had called Lyle over. If he actually objected to the man she felt he was responsible for seeing to it that she was in other company, preferably his.

But his attention had been sought by two men. The first was slightly loud, a blustery character who managed to get an important name into every sentence. The second, smaller and nondescript in comparison to most on board, displayed a casual silence. By the genuine respect Greg afforded him, she knew she had been right to think he was someone above the ordinary.

Her idea of an enjoyable evening did not include Lyle Kearns, but the quiet man gave her pause. If Greg was attending this party for business reasons she could hardly hang on his arm. To stand in the way of a valuable contact he might make would be unthinkable. She resigned herself to being entertained by Lyle.

'Hel-lo,' Lyle flipped some inner switch, turning his smile on bright. He slipped an arm around her waist and bent to speak softly in her ear. 'Was there room for that one word?'

'Just barely,' Marlie replied. The rest of her quip died on her lips. Greg chose that moment to turn back to her. She saw his mouth tighten.

To her his disapproval was childish. If he wanted her by his side he could say so. Instead, he allowed himself to be led away by Kara. Disappointed, Marlie allowed her attention to be drawn by Lyle, who had snagged a full glass of bubbly from a passing waiter. He sipped and held up the glass, inspecting it critically.

'Ah, southern fried,' he murmured with appreciation.

'The secret is in the buttermilk,' Marlie volunteered.

Lyle cocked his head, looking thoughtful. 'A great mystery of life. How does one milk butter?'

'With both hands.'

Lyle took another sip from his glass and eyed her critically. 'I knew the moment you walked on board, the evening would come alive.' He took her arm and steered her to a pair of empty chairs on the fantail.

'You knew the minute I walked on board that Kara would snap her fingers and you were to keep me out of her hair,' Marlie retorted. Her remark was too blunt for good manners, she knew, but Kara's cavalier treatment still stung.

Lyle gave her a satanic smile. 'But did you ask yourself why it was necessary?' He seemed to find some secret amusement in his own words, but the meaning had eluded her. Then he shrugged.

'Hangers-on take orders,' he explained. 'They do their bit—that is, if they want to keep riding around on the boat belonging to big brother-in-law.'

'Then Kara is your sister?' There was certainly no family resemblance.

'Unfortunately.'

'I'm sorry, I—' Marlie halted in confusion, feeling her cheeks heat up in embarrassment. One did not commiserate with another because of the other's relatives. She stumbled for a change of subject and blurted out a question that could be as ill-mannered, but one that had been on her mind for some time.

'Why are you down here—I don't mean you individually, but Kara and Bill, Greg, and the other large yachts? We like our part of the country, but we're hardly the centre of elite society.'

Lyle shrugged. 'Yachts are social creatures; park two together and soon you have four. We're here because of Alston. Bill wants to interest him in one of his schemes.'

'And Greg?'

'Originally the shipyard. He's been in and out, watching some repairs on the *Veronica*. Since the work was finished a week or so ago, maybe you can answer your own question. Obviously he's given up any idea of going into the hotel business—no matter how things look at present.'

At first, the last part of Lyle's comment went right over Marlie's heard. She glowed inside at his hint that she could be the reason for Greg's remaining on the *Veronica*. But his eyes warned her.

She looked up as Greg came out of the salon with Joan Owens-Lane on his arm. Behind them, Kara Holmes looked smug.

Marlie gathered her courage and was about to rise, planning on brazenly joining the group, when she caught Greg's eye. His anger blazed as he looked in her direction.

How dare he, when he had another woman on his arm, she thought. To be truthful, she had to admit he wasn't hanging on to Joan, she was doing the clinging, but for him to give Marlie a hard look while he stood with Joan was just too much.

She turned back to Lyle, giving him an engaging smile. Out of the corner of her eye she saw Greg's glare, before he bent to hear what Joan was saying.

Marlie spent most of the evening in the company of Lyle Kearns. Joan and Kara seemed to be conspiring to keep Greg away from Marlie, and from her vantage point, they were getting little resistance from him. From time to time she let her eyes wander in his direction, but he was usually deep in conversation.

She was surprised, therefore, that while the party was still in full swing, he freed himself from Joan and came striding across the deck.

The anger she had seen in his eyes was still smouldering. He was curt with Lyle.

'Sorry to break this up. We have to be on our way.'

Lyle, who had been increasingly dull company after numerous glasses of champagne, nodded languidly, tried to rise and slid back in his chair.

'Come anytime, glad to have you,' he mumbled, staring out over the water with a glassy look.

With a firm hand on her elbow, Greg led Marlie down the ramp, along the pier and back to his car. He slammed both doors and spun the wheels as he left the parking lot. His hands were gripping the steering wheel, and his jaw was tight. Marlie could see that betraying little muscle as it quivered just below his jawbone.

He was out on the street when he made his first acid comment.

'I hope you thoroughly enjoyed your evening with Lyle Kearns.'

'Beautiful!' Marlie retorted, meaning his remark and not her evening. 'You spent all your time with your platinum girl-friend and ignored me completely. If you wanted to be with her, why did you invite me?'

'I wasn't aware she was in town,' he snapped.

Marlie jumped on that remark. 'But if you had known, you would have taken her, so I think you should be grateful I stayed out of your way.'

'That is an idiotic remark,' he growled.

'Then maybe I had better not make any more,' Marlie retorted.

As the low slung sports car sped around corners in the city and then on to the curving roads that led back to the waterway, Marlie sat tense. So much for hoping they would have a beautiful romantic evening. That had been a pipe dream, and she was foolish for letting it enter her head. Obviously she and Greg Alston were never going to spend more than a few hours together without friction.

She leaned back, turning her head slightly to watch him as he drove. He handled a car with his characteristic expertise. His strong brown hand lay on the gear shift. She could still see the tension in his fingers, but his driving was not influenced by his anger.

Could he really be jealous? she wondered. No, she decided. He had expected her to hang on to him as Joan had done. His ego was damaged because his friends discovered there was one female who wasn't falling all over him. An objection kept trying to creep into that line of thought, but she obstinately resisted it. He was an insufferable boor, she told herself, and held on to her thought. She waved it in front of her mind, like a cape in front of a bull. Better that than to be crushed by other considerations.

She had been so deep in thought she had not realised they were in familiar territory until Greg brought the car to a stop behind the cabin. He pulled up beside the battered stationwagon as Howard was opening the passenger door for Doris.

Greg threw her one last angry look.

'The next time we go out, I hope you'll stay away from Lyle.'

He was out of the car and walking around it before she could frame an answer. When he opened her door, she was ready.

'The next time we go out, volcanoes will be freezers,' she said, sliding away from his hand, held out to assist her.

'Nice party?' Doris called as Howard greeted Greg.

'Marvellous, but I've developed a headache and I'm going to bed,' Marlie answered. As she expected, Greg was about to accept Howard's offer of a nightcap, but under the circumstances he could only refuse.

She entered the house and was just switching on the light in her bedroom when she heard the sports car pull away. She had taken honours on that last round and kept him from staying. He had left angry. Would he ever come back? Do I care? she asked herself. No! she shouted her answer. Did she want to see Greg Alston again? No! No! *No!* She was lying to herself, and she knew it, but if she lied enough, it might become truth. At the moment that seemed the less painful course.

Sunday she moved listlessly around the cabin, taking care of small chores and making an effort to enjoy the beauties of the river. Somehow, with neither Greg nor the ducks sharing her afternoon, nothing seemed as vibrant, as colourful. Colour everything sad, she thought, then chased away that idea.

She hated and detested, simply loathed Greg Alston, and hoped she never saw another live duck! For the next half-hour she sat brooding on all the embarrassments she had suffered because of him and his pets. Feeling better, she went back into the cabin. But the lighter mood had been built on a false foundation. During the night, the rain, beating on the roof, seemed to add weight to her misery.

Monday morning Howard was getting ready to drive to the factory, and Marlie was planning to stay at the cabin. Howard was just leaving the kitchen when they heard the ragged put-put of Jonas's motor.

'That makeshift repair didn't hold up,' Howard said. 'We'll have to run over to Portsmouth and get a replacement part.'

'Want me to go in and open up?' Marlie asked, getting to her feet.

'Let me make sure I'm right first,' Howard grinned and went to meet Jonas.

Howard's assumption had been correct. In minutes Marlie was in the station-wagon, on her way into town. Fred had recently lost his key, so he, Paul and Norm would be standing on the pavement until she arrived.

The big push to get out the back orders was over, and that morning the three men were giving the small factory a good cleaning. Marlie helped move a few odds and ends, but her co-operation ceased when she walked over to the painting area. One look at the floor in front of her table, and she gave out with a spate of complaints against Greg Alston, Paul and Norm, who had cleaned up the paint spilled when the ducks escaped, and men in general. The boys had scrubbed and sanded until not one trace of the original spill remained, but they had worked with extreme care, leaving every little webbed footprint intact. She was still giving the grinning boys her opinion of their work when a big brown truck, bearing the insignia of the transcontinental package delivery service, pulled up outside.

'If that's more ducks—' Marlie growled and went to meet the driver. He entered without the customary clipboard.

'Returned shipment,' he said. 'It's a big one—no idea what happened, but two of the boxes are damaged.'

Marlie walked out with him, looking in the back of the truck, which was filled with boxes.

'The Alston shipment,' she said, surprised.

'We can fill out the forms, I'll take it back and have it shipped on if you want,' the driver said. 'But a couple of the boxes took a pretty good beating. You might want to look at them.'

'Yes, let's unload them,' Marlie said. 'We'll want to replace anything that's been damaged.' Marlie took a look at the address labels as the driver rolled them in. By some mistake they had been delivered to a Mrs Anne B. Franklin in Tallahassee, Florida. The mental picture of a startled housewife facing one hundred and eighty wooden ducks was mind-boggling.

Forty-five minutes later, the cleaned production area was a jumble of boxes, styrofoam peanuts and wooden ducks. Five of the boxes, each holding six decoys, had been crumpled in shipping, but none of the carvings had received a scratch.

Fred straightened, rubbing his back after bending over the boxes.

'No point in opening the others. These are okay, and those boxes weren't even scratched.' Norm laughed. 'I'm just glad these are the wooden ducks. I'd hate to have this many live ones here.'

Marlie was very still, both mentally and physically. In her fertile brain an idea was forming. Greg Alston liked ducks. Live ducks and wooden ducks. And, after all, these were his, he had paid for them. He had ordered them, at least. She imagined his salon on the boat, his staterooms, his dining room, all loaded with decoys. After their last argument, she might never see him again, but if he were forced to bring back the shipment—

'Open all the boxes,' she shouted, startling the three men. 'Norm, do you still have that van?' She saw his nod. 'Paul, I didn't see yours this morning.'

'I sold it to my younger brother.'

That was a foul-up in Marlie's plan. She needed another vehicle, one that would hold a number of large boxes.

'Well, hire it back! Him, too, if you can get him.' Fred was watching her warily as Paul rushed to the phone. 'What are you going to do?'

'Play boss for a while, so don't argue with me,' Marlie laughed. 'If Howard comes in and starts yelling, refer him to me. I'm getting good at ducking—no pun intended.'

CHAPTER ELEVEN

WHILE FRED watched, prophesying doom for the factory, the employees and particularly Marlie, the rest fell to with a will. They ripped open the boxes and pulled the carved birds from their nests of styrofoam and packed them closely together in other boxes.

By the time the station wagon and the van was full, Paul's younger brother, Sam, had arrived. Marlie led the way to the marina, driving the station wagon. Behind her, Norm in his van, and Paul, riding with his seventeen-year-old brother in the second, followed.

Luck was with Marlie. Greg was out on business. The elderly deck-hand who seemed to be the only member of the crew, recognised Marlie. He told her that since Mr Alston had taken the car, Henry had ordered a taxi and left to do some shopping. He eyed the boxes Marlie and the boys carried on board.

'I don't know about cargo,' he said, shaking his head. 'We've never carried cargo that I can remember—and I've been aboard the *Veronica* for forty-five years—'

'But he wants these, that's why he's been staying around this area,' Marlie said. 'And he wants to see them. It seems he doesn't care much for our new painter, and he insists on checking the quality for himself.'

'You know how he is about quality,' Norm, who was enjoying the joke, added his bit.

That decided the old seaman, who stepped back out of their path.

'The salon first,' Marlie called and led the way. With Norm unloading one box, and she another, they had already begun to cover the tables, chairs and couches with decoys.

'Can I put one here?' Norm pointed to a silver bowl, and suited action to words by placing a duck in it so it appeared to be swimming.

'Excellent,' Marlie replied, thinking of Greg Alston's face when he returned to the boat. She would teach him to make fun of her painting. She'd pay him back for all his smart insults. She'd also have to dodge his anger when he came around again. Remembering their arguments, and the result of one, she shivered in anticipation mingled with dread.

Paul came in, staggering under a large box, and behind him, his younger brother peered around the load he was carrying.

Norm, digging in the bottom of his almost empty box, looked up.

'Avast there, mate,' he said to young Sam.

'What's avast?' Sam asked.

'It means unload,' Marlie said, pointing to the dining room. She grabbed the edge of her empty box and rushed out, heading to the car for another load.

She unpacked hurriedly, removing the papers from the decoys. The boys were working just as fast. But when Norm disappeared with an empty box and was back almost immediately with a full one, she looked at him in surprise.

'That was quick.'

Norm grinned. 'I don't think that old guy trusts me. He's getting the boxes out of the vans, making sure we don't carry any away, I think. Or maybe he's just helping to be sure the boxes we take out are empty.'

Marlie paused, worried, but she couldn't stop her giggle. 'I hope he doesn't tell Greg he helped us.'

The *Veronica* was a yacht large enough to draw attention in any harbour, but like all ships, the living quarters were limited. One hundred and eighty wooden ducks, each nearly twenty inches in length, made a noticeable addition in the decor. Ducks sat on the dining room table, on the sideboard and nested in the chairs. Duck heads peered out from behind the throw cushions on the couches in the salon, perched on the footstools and wooden heads appeared over the top of the magazine racks.

In the staterooms they sat on beds, in chairs. Someone had been very creative, she thought. The upturned ducktails were just visible as they stuck out from beneath the bedspreads that came within an inch of the floor. In the bathrooms they sat in the sinks, looked out of the showers. When she went back up the companionway, Paul was clustering a few on the carpet.

'Migration,' he grinned as he stood up.

'Let's get out of here,' Marlie said. 'I wonder how soon we'll hear from the great Mr Alston.'

'I don't know, but I'm going to stay out of the way,' Paul chuckled.

They were still panting from their exertions when they walked down the gangway and over to the trucks. Marlie saw the taxi pulling away. Henry had returned. He carried two large bags of groceries, and had given two to the old sailor.

'I hope we're not in for it,' Marlie whispered to Paul. She could see the old seaman talking to Henry.

'Henry, I left your kitchen alone,' Marlie said, 'but I sincerely hope you'll allow Mr Alston to inspect his merchandise.'

Henry stood quite still for a moment, the concern and amusement striving in his expression. Training won out. His face was bland, unreadable.

'Very good, Miss Richmond, since I really must use my facilities. Mr Alston is at present at the airport, meeting a gentleman whose good offices are vital to a rather large business venture Mr Alston has in mind. They are due here for luncheon.'

'What!' Marlie cried out. 'Henry! Under all that gibberish, you're telling me he's going to be holding a business conference—'

Marlie wanted to sink in the sand. To play a practical joke on a man who was vacationing on a pleasure craft was one thing, but to risk making him look a fool when he was conducting a business deal was another and far more serious matter. She might storm and rail at his teasing her, but after all, he had done nothing to endanger her career or harm Howard's business. She had no right to treat him that badly.

She whirled to stop Paul and Sam before they closed the doors on Sam's van.

'Back to the boat!' she shouted, grabbing an empty box.

'I knew you would understand,' Henry murmured, trying to hide his smile.

Marlie dashed back towards the yacht, the box bumping against her leg. Behind her she heard other hurried footsteps and Sam's puzzled voice.

'I thought we avasted everything,' he panted.

'Now we unavast,' Paul retorted.

'Disavast, it's faster,' Marlie called, nearly falling over the box as she stepped just inside the salon.

Pulling the protective paper from the decoys had been a simple task. Wrapping them again was more difficult. In trying to hurry, Marlie dropped one duck twice, thankful that it fell into an upholstered chair. Norm, who was working in the same room, picked one up by the tapering tail and stared as it shot out of his hand like a bar of soap.

'Who greased them?' he demanded.

'We're just nervous,' Marlie said, biting her lip in an effort to grab a decoy, wrap it in paper, and lay it in the box, all in one smooth motion. She felt as jerky as a doll on strings, handled by a novice puppeteer.

From the dining-room, she could hear Paul exhorting his brother to more speed. Sam was retorting by saying Paul was doing no better.

Marlie looked up as she saw Henry standing in the doorway. His eyes were crinkled with worry as he glanced at his watch.

'Henry, what are we going to do?' Marlie wailed. 'We'll never get them off in time. We can't just throw them in the boxes, if we ruin them, my uncle will kill me!' She pushed a wayward strand of hair out of her face. 'And Greg will kill me if I don't,' she muttered.

'We could hide them and come back later,' Norm offered. 'If we put them somewhere just for the afternoon, we won't have to wrap them. That'll save time.'

Marlie felt a surge of hope. 'Henry, are the guests staying aboard?'

'I understand they will be leaving before dinner,' he replied.

'To the showers!' Marlie ordered, grabbing an armload of decoys.

After five minutes of running up and down the companionway, bumping into each other in their hurry, not a duck was to be seen. The boxes they had packed had been set out on deck until they had hidden the others. Panting from their exertions, they hurried off the boat carrying their loads.

Marlie was of the opinion that despite his unfailing courtesy, Henry would be delighted if he never saw any of them again.

Greg will probably feel the same way, Marlie thought as she started the wagon and led her convoy through the parking lot.

If she had been able to leave two minutes earlier she would have escaped notice, but just as she turned into the main driveway of the marina lot, Greg's car turned off the public thoroughfare.

'I am not going to face him now!' Marlie muttered to herself. Mentally setting her course, and making sure of the alignment of the steering wheel, she slid down in the seat. Her last view of the sports car gave her a memorable picture of Greg's astonished face as she slid out of sight.

Marlie had calculated her course correctly, but not her slide on the seat. For a moment she lost her balance, and grabbed at the upholstered handle of the door, then back at the steering wheel. Grabbing was her mistake. She missed the wheel and clutched the horn ring. The blare of the horn was deafening. She jerked her hand away. The noise continued. She wiggled the steering wheel, throwing herself into terror of hitting something, so she raised in the seat to make sure she had not aimed the wagon into a collision course with another car.

A quick glanced encompassed a group of fishermen who stared at the apparently driverless car as it crept along the driveway, blaring for attention. Behind her, Norm was frantically waving his arm, and the sports car had pulled over to the side of the road. Greg stood by the open door, wearing a puzzled, half-humorous expression.

'Drats and mice and little fishes!' Marlie muttered, wondering what to do. One thing was certain, she was not going to stop. All she needed was for Greg to walk over and offer assistance.

And he would, she thought, gritting her teeth. No matter how large that business deal was, he would not be able to resist catching her in a ridiculous position.

Raised just high enough to see between the steering wheel and the bottom of the windshield, she paused to look both ways, and pulled out on to the main road, ignoring the sign that demanded she come to a full stop.

She could feel the heat in her face as she drove at a reasonable speed up the street, inching her way up in the seat as she travelled.

Two miserable blocks later she flashed her right turn signal light and pulled over to the curb. Norm pulled in behind her, jumped from the van and came hurrying forward. He raised the hood on the wagon as she went to assist him.

Blessed quiet returned as he pulled at the horn wires.

'That's a botched up job of stopping it, but you don't want to wait two hours for a repair, do you?' He was still staring down into the engine compartment.

'Not two seconds. Let's get out of here,' Marlie snapped.

Paul came running up, followed by Sam. His grin spread all over his face.

'Boy,' he said, his voice full of admiration. 'You sure sneak out of place in style. But don't ever take up burglary—I don't think it would be your thing.'

Marlie's face, that had been fiery red because of her embarrassment, had lost some of its colour, but as her complexion darkened again, Paul backed away. Norm and Sam lost no time following him.

'Men!' Marlie stormed as she slammed the door of the wagon and turned the key. 'They're all the same!'

Some had a tendency to forget their sense of humour, too, she learned as she walked in the office of the factory after unloading the wagon.

Howard sat on the edge of his desk. The expression on his face meant trouble.

'Well, I hope you're satisfied,' he muttered.

Marlie stopped and stared. He would of course know what she had been doing. Fred would have told him. She had not asked the machine operator not to, it would have been an unfair request. But how did he know what the possible results could have been if they had not been off the yacht in time?

Had Greg called him? She wanted to ask the question, but shrank from it, fearing the answer. If Greg had called it could only have been because he was so angry he couldn't wait until after his meeting. If that were the case, what had she done to him—and what had she done to Howard?

Suddenly she saw her prank in an entirely different light. Was it just eagerness to get her own back at Greg—was that what she had been doing? She knew different. When Greg had driven away after their jealous argument, she had been afraid she would never see him again. Her entire plan had been to make sure she did. But would she? Had she been so wrapped up in herself that she had hurt Greg's business and endangered Howard's?

That little perversity that kept rearing its head, trying to force away the pain, was stirring again. She faced Howard with the determined attitude of a child who knows she deserves punishment, but hopes to avoid it.

'It was a rotten thing to do, but I didn't know he was expecting to hold a business conference there.'

'You should have expected it,' Howard snapped. 'Not everyone can spend their entire summer playing games.'

'Don't say that as if I do,' Marlie retorted, stung by his anger. Howard was usually on her side.

'I know I was wrong,' Marlie answered quietly. 'But I just thought he was out goofing off on his boat—I had no idea—' She let the words trail off. Everything she had done suddenly seemed so idiotic.

'Goofing off!' Howard snorted. 'Is that what you think I do when I come here every day?'

'I think that's a bit different,' Marlie objected. 'This is a business. That yacht is a very expensive toy. I don't know what it cost, but when someone spends that amount of money for a plaything, you have a tendency to suspect them of playing.'

Howard shook his head. 'I don't know how you could spend so much time around the man and understand nothing about him.'

Understand him? How could you love a man and not understand him? She had not believed that possible, but then she had never been in love until she met Greg Alston. She pushed that thought away. She didn't love him. She wouldn't allow herself to care about him.

'What is there to understand? He's a wealthy coupon clipper. He's rich, he's a socialite, and all he has to do is snap his fingers to have everything he wants. He leads a wasted life. I've no real use for a man like that!'

Keep saying that, the little voice said. Sooner or later you'll be convinced—maybe.

Howard snorted. 'Next, because I have a few coupons, you'll be saying I live a wasted life too.'

'You're different,' Marlie said. 'You keep something back to act as a safety bumper for the protection of the company. I know how you plan to make sure Fred, Norm and Paul will have work—if I've endangered that, I'll do what I can to straighten it out.'

'I'm not worried that Greg Alston is going to take his anger at you out on me,' Howard said shortly. 'He's not that kind of man. I just think it's interesting that you think it's right for me to protect my four or five employees, yet it's a waste of time for him to protect his hundreds. He works a lot harder than I do, and not entirely for himself.'

'I don't see that yacht as conclusive evidence of self-sacrifice,' Marlie retorted. She was continuing an argument that was pointless, but the pain in her heart seemed to demand a struggle.

'What do you know about yachts?' Howard demanded.

'Oh, not as much as you, dear uncle, but the difference in our experience with wealth wouldn't fill a coffee cup.'

Howard leaned back, humour playing around his mouth.

'Then you recognised the boat for what it was? A fifty-year-old craft? Prime condition, of course. And he didn't spend a penny on acquisition. It's been in the family since it was new. Named after his grandmother.'

'His what?' Marlie felt as if the floor had moved.

'And you didn't pay much attention to the crew, did you? You know how attached people get to boats. How could he sell it when the crew has been serving aboard it since before he was born?'

Marlie sank in a dusty chair. The old seaman had said he had been aboard for forty-five years. She had been so busy with her prank she had paid no attention at the time.

Howard was explaining away her every objection, but she still had one more that he couldn't answer, she thought.

'He certainly has enough time for Joan Owens-Lane,' she muttered, bringing out her last objection.

Howard laughed. 'Okay, green eyes, how would you treat the one and only daughter of a major hotel chain owner— that is, if you hoped to open exclusive shops on his premises? Most men would have paid more attention to her, and less to you, under the circumstances. It was my guess that she had hopes of making Greg part of the family. Since you've been on the scene, I don't think things have been going the way she planned.'

The telephone rang and Howard turned his attention to a sheaf of papers on the desk. Marlie strolled back to her painting table, her head lowered, her hands in the pockets of her jeans.

Had her judgment of Greg Alston been that far off? If Howard was right, she didn't know people as well as she thought.

She looked up to see Sam walking around, looking at the boxes that had been brought back from the yacht.

'I know this is the one I packed,' he was saying to Paul.

Paul was exasperated with his brother. 'What difference does it make?'

Sam rummaged in the box. He gazed at Marlie, his face showing all the misery she felt.

'It makes a lot of difference,' he muttered. 'There's a duck missing.'

'Now how could you possibly remember how many you put in there?' Norm asked with a trace of impatience. 'We were slamming them in the boxes almost too fast to count.'

Intrigued, Marlie walked over to listen.

'I didn't put it in there,' Sam argued, 'and I didn't take it out, but I had it when I left the boat and now it's gone. It was that big one.'

'Sam,' Marlie interrupted, touched by the boy's concern, 'They were all the same size.'

'No—this one was bigger—it wasn't a carved bird, it was stuffed, I guess, with real feathers, and it was in the box when I turned around—' He went back to rummaging in the box. His worry turned to amazement as he brought out a stained and damp wrapper. 'No wooden duck did this,' he said.

'Green head?' Marlie demanded.

'Yeah,' Sam seemed surprised that she would know. 'It sat so still I thought—I didn't know it was real! I just shut the box and carried it to the van.

'Oh, I hope he's here,' Marlie wailed. In addition to everything else, if Caesar were lost because of her joke, she'd never forgive herself.

'Caesar,' she called, looking around the boxes and under the tables. 'Someone check outside—we left the doors open—Caesar!' Marlie tried to whistle, but that was a talent she had never acquired. Paul, Norm and Sam made up for it.

Since no one else was following her orders, she left the rest to search the factory and hurried outside, around the building. She checked the street, but nothing indicated the bird had wandered in that direction. As she turned back she noticed the puddles of water that still remained in the uneven back driveway. Thinking the water might entice the duck, she walked back.

Caesar was not in any of the puddles, but just as she was completing her search, Marlie saw a pair of green legs and black and white tailfeathers, twitching with anticipation. The duck was standing very still, his long neck stretched to reach under a pile of timber. He had cornered a beetle, but couldn't quite reach it.

'Why eat bugs when you might get another hamburger?' Marlie asked him as she picked him up.

The duck made strenuous objection to being deprived of his quarry, but when Marlie sat on a low pile of wood and placed him on her lap, he found a satisfactory substitute for the bug. Sliding his bill beneath the gold band, he attempted to eat her watch.

'You're a spoiled character,' she told him, running her nails lightly through the metallic-green feathers on his head.

'You know, after they took you back to the boat, I missed you.' She sat stroking his feathers as he gave up the watch and turned to give her face an examination before deciding to pull the collar off her blouse.

'But I'll have to take you back,' she sighed. 'As much as I like you, you belong on your owner's farm. You probably shouldn't have hamburgers, and he has everything you like up there.'

'At least until his owner goes bankrupt.'

Marlie jerked around to see Greg standing behind her, his arms folded over his chest. He was wearing the same pale blue outfit he wore the day he came to the factory, only he had left the jacket behind and his long sleeves were folded back to his elbows. His dark hair and golden skin added a vividness to precise well-tailored cleanliness. Once again she was struck with the surrealistic picture he made in the shabby but respectable surroundings of the factory.

She was dressed much as she had been the first day she met him. The main difference was her hair that was being rearranged by Caesar, who had decided to remove the ribbons that held it tied above her ears. She lowered her head, staring down into the buff-and-brown feathers on Caesar's back.

'I'm sorry if I ruined your meeting,' she said. 'I had no idea you were having it, or I wouldn't have brought out the decoys. We did try to get them out of the way.'

'Yes, that helped enormously,' Greg said. 'No one would have known they were there if Trent Owens-Lane hadn't decided to check out the facilities aboard the *Veronica*. The last thing he expected was to open a shower door and be caught in a rain of wooden ducks.'

Marlie clapped her hand over her mouth to prevent a laugh. The visual picture was humorous, the probable results horrible.

'He wasn't hurt, was he?'

'Just his poise—crushed.' Greg's eyes were narrowed as he tried to keep his mouth straight. 'I'll never forgive you for taking Caesar. He should have been aboard. He'd have been the final insult to push that ass over the brink.'

Marlie's mouth formed an 'O' of surprise. Her blue eyes widened.

'You mean you didn't mind? But it must have ruined the deal you were working on—surely you're upset about that.'

Greg gave a shout of laughter. 'You can't imagine how glad I am to be out of it. I think it was worth every dime I would have made, and I include the—fringe benefit that went with...'

His face had hardened at his last words, and he stopped abruptly. He stepped forward and sat by her on the stack of lumber, his face and apparently his attention turned to Caesar.

Marlie knew he had said more than he thought was proper under the circumstances. She might have misjudged Greg in many ways, but she had learned for herself that he was a gentleman in the old-fashioned sense. He had proved that in her bedroom, though at the time she had misunderstood even that.

She had found nothing in Joan Owens-Lane to like, but still she felt pity for the woman. She was so beautiful, with social advantage and wealth behind her. Why had she found it necessary to try to buy a husband? She had not known Greg Alston either, if she thought he could be purchased as if he were some article in his chain of stores. But maybe Joan had loved him, though Marlie doubted it. If she did,

Marlie was sorry for her. Greg took a large space in her own heart, too large an area to be filled by anyone else.

She kept her eyes down, not wanting him to see the schoolgirl happiness that filled her.

'I've been miserable, thinking I'd ruined things for you,' she said. She felt his arm slip around her shoulders.

'You failed this time, but I have no doubts you'll ruin me sooner or later,' he said.

Marlie looked up in surprise. How could he possibly think that? He was looking solemn and thoughtful as he met her gaze.

'I'm sure, with you around it won't be long before I'm on welfare and Caesar's in the bug line. The only man I know that can protect himself against you is Howard. I suppose the best thing for me to do is apply to him for a job when you've bankrupted me.'

He raised her chin so that she was forced to look him in the eyes. She was overcome with confusion. What was he saying? She dared not let her hopes rise, just to have them smashed again. Better to stay with the game, the thrust and jab of wit. That was what he liked. She cocked her head, giving the idea some thought while she retied one of the ribbons that Caesar had pulled free.

'Quite possibly Howard would give you a job,' she murmured as if she were giving the matter serious consideration. 'You do know how to run the Howler. That reminds me of a question. Why did you want to run the machine? You said you would tell us after you worked out your idea.'

'I'll never tell,' he said, his chin thrust forward with playful hauteur.

Marlie lowered her brows in a mock frown. 'Just as I thought! You came to steal our industrial secrets.'

'Of course,' he sounded surprised. 'Didn't you know that was my main occupation? By tomorrow the entire world will know your mallards have green heads.'

Marlie laughed at his remark, her heart filled with love and happiness simply because he was with her. At the moment she felt life could hold no more happiness.

'Seriously, what was your idea? Perhaps Howard and Fred could lay it out for you.'

'I don't need their help.'

His answer had been so short it shocked Marlie. She wondered if she had stumbled on sensitive feelings. The flicker in his eyes, and a change of expression told her he had noticed. He put his arm around her, his hand on her shoulder.

'It's too late, you see. After my trip to Norway, I had a terrific idea. Bureau valets in the shape of viking long-boats. Totally new concept.'

Marlie's frown was genuine. Which would be best, she wondered. Should she flatter his ego or tell him the truth? The idea was far from original. She decided the truth would be best. Even if he were disappointed, that would be better than letting him bring out a well-used idea as his own. That could be embarrassing later.

'It's a good idea, but there have been some on the market,' she said slowly. 'In fact, I gave my father one two years ago.'

'And probably bought it in Alston's,' he said, laughing. 'The next how-to book on spying should include a chapter on not stealing from yourself. When I saw one in my own store, I felt like a fool.'

Her heart skipped a beat as she saw that engaging, almost childlike smile appear again. At that moment he resembled a little boy, caught in a foolish prank. She wanted to put her arms around him, reassuring him his next idea would be the greatest ever, but she was committed to the game. She shrugged.

'Then I don't know how Howard could hire you. You're obviously not original in your thinking. Your only talent seems to be making millions. We make ducks.'

'I see what you mean,' Greg appeared thoughtful. 'Do you think I'd have a better chance with him if I married into the family?'

Married? Into the family? Marlie's gaze flew to his. There was no mistaking the laughter, mixed with tenderness. Her lips parted to answer but at that moment her view of Greg was blocked as Caesar stood up, putting his head between theirs.

'You and your ducks!' Greg growled in impatience. He pushed Caesar off Marlie's lap, sending the bird off in his lopsided flight. Caesar gave an angry quack and went back in search of the beetle. As he waddled along, his green legs and feet were brightened by the summer sun.

'Mine?' Marlie cried. 'Caesar is your duck!'

'And that's another thing,' Greg eyed her sternly. 'I know you have this problem with paint, but when I feel like an explanation, I want to know why my ducks have green feet.'

Marlie opened her mouth to tell him, but she was interrupted by his lips on hers. As her arms encircled him, she decided she could make her explanations later. Then she'd kick him.

THE AUTHOR

Dixie McKeone, when she isn't writing romances and mysteries, can be found designing subdivisions and streets. Her background includes twelve years in civil engineering and surveying, and she has worked on designs for bridges, superhighways and dams. Her vivid imagination, combined with her unique background and experiences, brings a freshness, an edge of excitement to her writing. She has two grown daughters and lives in La Mesa, California.

Fire and Steel

Mary Wibberley

No ordinary man could transcend humble beginnings to become a millionaire so quickly. But then, Garth Vanner was no ordinary man.

Arwenna was aware of his magnetism the moment they met, and she knew her life would never be the same. Her folly was to fall in love with him....

For he was like the irresistible force; she, the immovable object. And that explosive kind of relationship could only destroy them both!

CHAPTER ONE

'MY DARLING sweet,' said James, looking at Arwenna with some amusement, 'the man's not all that bad.'

Arwenna gazed calmly back at him, not amused at all. 'You expect me to believe that you're having him to dinner simply out of neighbourliness? Come off it, James, since when have you been concerned about anyone who moves into the village? There's another reason you're not telling me—and until you do, my answer's no.' She stood there, tall and straight, and lifted her hand to her hip. 'I'm waiting,' she said.

For a moment his mask of amusement slipped; she saw the sulky boy underneath. But it was only for an instant, and she knew him too well to let it annoy her. 'All right,' he said. 'It's business. Dad's keen to get in well with Garth Vanner—'

'Your father is?' She lifted her eyebrows in disbelief. 'Why?'

He shrugged. 'I don't know. He doesn't tell me everything.' There was a slight trace of annoyance in his words, and she hid a grin. That was true.

'And your father wants me to come to dinner as well? He's chancing it a bit, isn't he? Doesn't he remember what Garth was like fifteen years ago when he left the village?'

'He remembers him as a tough young man who vowed he'd return one day as a millionaire—'

'And the rest? Has he forgotten? I haven't,' she cut in.

James laughed. 'You were only eight when he went. How can you remember?'

'I remember what I heard off *my* father—'

'That's all history. Okay, so your dad and his had a standing feud. So what? It was over twenty years ago—'

'And now he's come back, the new owner of Raneley Hall, and all of a sudden, because he's rich, he's made stacks of money, he's socially acceptable—'

'That's a foul thing to say!' James cut in, face pale.

Arwenna laughed. 'It's true. Twenty years ago your family wouldn't have given him or his family the time of day, and you know it. And you were only ten when he left, so you don't know the half of it either.' Her cheeks were pink. She waved her hand in a dismissive gesture. 'I'm not keen to have anything to do with him, you know that. Why me?'

'You're my fiancée,' he said, 'that's why.'

'And?'

'And Dad thought—' he hesitated.

'Yes?' she said silkily. 'Dad thought?' She paused. At last she might hear the truth.

'Well, he's supposed to have an eye for a pretty face—er— if you're here, he might be more—amenable.'

'Thanks!' She looked at him, wide-eyed with amused disbelief. 'You mean I'm a sort of decoy, is that it? A pretty face to soften him up over the hors d'oeuvres? Hah! I've had some left-handed compliments from you, James, but honestly, this takes the biscuit! And what will you do if he starts ogling me over dessert? Tell him to keep his eyes to himself?'

She turned slightly and looked into the ornate mirror over the sideboard. Her face looked back at her, a rounded, striking-looking face with long dark-lashed beautiful eyes that were usually laughing. They weren't now. She turned away and towards her fiancé.

'Please, Arwenna,' he said softly. 'Please, don't be angry. I thought you'd be pleased.'

'Pleased? I'm not. I feel as if I'm being used, if you must know.'

He closed his eyes, and Arwenna went towards him, soft-footed, graceful, and touched his arm. 'Don't you see?' she said. 'How can I be nice to him? I love you, James, you know that, but you're asking the impossible.'

'Do you?' he said bitterly. 'I sometimes wonder—you're in no hurry to get married.'

'I've told you why,' she said softly. 'Until you can break free of your father's domination.'

'He's not as bad as he was. He admires you tremendously.'

'I know. And I'm learning to get on with him, but it's an uphill battle. He doesn't actually like people who speak their minds.'

'He's accepted you,' James pointed out.

'Accepted? Yes, I suppose he has. Admires? Yes, I know that too—but only because he had no choice. Only because for the first time in his life he met someone who wasn't frightened of him.'

'You're not. You're not frightened of anyone, are you? That's what I find so—so—unusual about you, Arwenna.' James sighed. 'God, you're the most unusual, *wonderful* woman I've ever met.'

'Is that why you came chasing after me to France?' she asked mischievously.

'That's only one reason, and you know it, you little minx,' he growled, taking hold of her. 'How could you travel all over Europe, working for all those greasy foreigners?'

'I went because I wanted to,' she said, and there was a slight reminiscent smile touching her lips. 'And they weren't "greasy foreigners," they were decent families.'

'You know what I mean,' he groaned, and kissed her. 'Say you'll come tonight. Please—for me.'

She was about to open her mouth when the door to the drawing room opened and Colonel Rhodes walked in. White-haired, white-moustached, tall, erect, he was, every inch of him, the country squire, the gentleman.

Arwenna turned towards him, disengaging herself from
James' suddenly embarrassed arms. Poor James, she
thought, terrified of his father. How he ever plucked up
courage to pursue me half across France, I'll never know.

'Hello,' she said. 'James has just been telling me you'd
like me to come for dinner tonight, to meet Garth Vanner.'

Henry Rhodes coughed and looked at her. She knew that
she threw him completely, and she had no compunction
about speaking her mind to him. He was so hidebound by
tradition that he found it difficult to talk normally to anyone. Yet between them had grown a kind of mutual respect. 'Er—yes,' he admitted. 'Lends a bit of—er—
femininity, you know. Jane is—um—rather shy at meeting
strangers, and I thought—'

'Garth Vanner is hardly a stranger,' she said, as he hesitated. 'Considering he lived here with his family until fifteen years ago. You did know, didn't you, Colonel?'

'Well—um—yes, of course.' He looked uncomfortable.
'But the past is past, Arwenna. He's now a successful businessman. I think it's important to welcome him back here,
don't you?'

She smiled, meeting the Colonel's blue eyes with her own
hazelly blue, beautiful ones. 'If you say so,' she said slowly.

James spoke for the first time since his father had come
in. 'Arwenna doesn't particularly like the man,' he said. His
father looked at him as if he had crawled out from under a
stone.

'Really?' he queried, voice cold.

'Yes, really,' Arwenna added, sensing the latent hostil-
ity, never far away, between the two men, and hating it. 'But
don't worry, I'd be delighted to accept your invitation.
James persuaded me.' She smiled at the younger man,
knowing that this was important to him, knowing...

James grinned in relief, and his father unbent sufficiently to smile. 'Ah, splendid,' he said. 'Splendid.'

She didn't know why she had agreed, except that the atmosphere was so tense, the minute the older man had en-

tered, that she had felt a strange pity for James. It was an uncomfortable feeling to have. She shouldn't feel pity for the man that she loved, only warmth, and love...

'I'll go and see Mrs Rhodes,' she said. 'If you'll excuse me?' and she smiled at them both and walked towards the door. 'What time do you want me?'

'Seven?' said James, with a look at his father, who nodded. 'I'll pick you up.'

'Seven will be fine,' Arwenna agreed. 'I'll be ready.' She went out, and heard Colonel Rhodes' voice as she closed the door. She couldn't hear the words, but the tone was hard and angry. She sighed, shook her head, and went towards the kitchen to find James' mother.

IT WAS seven-thirty, and they were waiting for the visitor. Jane Rhodes, James' mother, a tense bundle of nerves, fluttered anxiously in from the dining room, a smudge of mascara beneath her eyes, lipstick slightly askew. 'All ready,' she said. 'Oh dear, I do hope—'

'Don't be stupid, Jane,' her husband said sharply. 'Relax.'

It seemed to Arwenna, sipping cool champagne by the window, to be a wasted admonition. There was no way Jane Rhodes would ever relax when guests were expected. Her whole life was geared to pleasing her husband, and she never fully succeeded, for how could anyone please a perfectionist? She was never able to behave as other women. Arwenna had always liked her, felt sympathy for her, and occasionally wished that she knew her well enough to tell her to tell her husband to go to hell, and walk out. She went over to her now and put her hand on the older woman's arm, sparing Colonel Rhodes, stiff and formal in black tie and evening suit, a brief glance as she did so. One more word from him...

'I'm sure everything's perfect,' she said, smiling soothingly at Jane Rhodes. 'There's a glass of champagne I've been keeping for you,' and she led her to the leather-topped table by the window. It was light outside, cool, with a slight breeze coming in through the open windows, welcome after the heat of a July day. 'Here you are. A couple of these and nothing will matter.' She raised her glass. 'Your health.'

'And yours.' Mrs Rhodes sipped, flicking a brief glance at her husband, who stood by the fireplace. Doing his lord of the manor bit, thought Arwenna wryly, while the serfs look on admiringly.

'He said he'd be here at seven-thirty,' she whispered, so that the Colonel couldn't hear.

'It's only just—' As Arwenna said it, the door chimes went. Henry Rhodes stiffened, adjusting his tie, Jane Rhodes nearly dropped her glass, and James darted towards the door. Arwenna was the only one who made no move. I wonder what he'll look like now, she thought. I wonder. After fifteen years away from here...

She hadn't long to wait. There were voices from the hall, and then the door opened and the man she had thought she would never see again walked in. She had heard so much about him that she felt as if she knew him. She had only a hazy recollection of him, as an eight-year-old—a vague memory of a dark, shaggy-haired youth with wildness in his blood and lightning in his fists, a young troublemaker who had hurt her parents and caused trouble wherever he went, and now she was seeing him properly for the first time, and it was such a shock that she found herself catching her breath. She didn't know what she had expected. But not this. Not this.

Garth Vanner was bigger than she had remembered. Big and dark, sleek and bold. His eyes came to hers, right across the room, and she experienced a shock that went right through her, as though the look was charged with electricity. For an instant of time it was just the two of them in the room; everything else faded away. He stood and looked at her, and she was naked, her whole being revealed to him in that moment.

Then the spell was broken, Colonel Rhodes spoke, walking forward, hand outstretched, and all was normal. The civilised preliminaries began; that primitive moment might never have been at all. 'Welcome, Mr Vanner,' said Henry Rhodes, 'nice to meet you.'

'And you, Colonel.' The man shook hands, and Henry Rhodes turned.

'My wife, Jane, my son, James—and his fiancée Arwenna.'

She was the last one with whom Garth Vanner shook hands. She stayed where she was, her glass now in her left hand, and held out her right as he walked towards her. 'How d'you do, Mr Vanner,' she said pleasantly. It had not gone unnoticed by Arwenna that the Colonel hadn't said her surname. She had no intention of telling him. Once having agreed to come, she would play her part well, be the pretty decoy for this man. For this one evening, no more. She wouldn't let any of them down, for that was not her way.

'How do you do, Miss—er—?' He raised a polite, questioning eyebrow. It was a thick, dark eyebrow, above dark grey-blue eyes that were as strong as the rest of his face.

'Call me Arwenna,' she answered, and heard the imperceptible sigh of relief from behind Garth.

'How kind. Thank you.' He turned slightly, and released Arwenna's hand. His hand clasp was cool and very firm—and totally impersonal. 'It's very nice to be here, Colonel, Mrs Rhodes.' He smiled at his hostess, and she managed a smile in return.

Henry Rhodes handed him a glass, murmuring: 'Champagne,' as he did so, and Garth Vanner raised it.

'Your good health,' he said, and drank.

Arwenna watched him, her eyes shrewdly taking in every detail of his appearance. The evening suit he wore was expensive, the shoes handmade, and if his haircut had cost him less than ten pounds, Arwenna thought, I'm a Dutchman. So this was the return of the prodigal, the local boy made good. She wondered why he had come back, after all this time. What had he done in the last fifteen years? He had made a fortune, if rumour was to be believed, and he had bought the dilapidated Raneley Hall—fact, not rumour— and Colonel Rhodes wanted something from him. And now he was here, in Grey Gables, drinking the Colonel's champagne, about to eat his food, and looking perfectly at home, as if he belonged, had always belonged, to places like this. He turned, as the conversation ebbed and flowed, and looked at Arwenna, and it was as though she had been waiting for him to do just that. His mouth twitched slightly, and he inclined his head, as if in acknowledgement of her expectations, and said quietly: 'This is a lovely house, isn't it? Do you live locally, Arwenna?'

'In the village,' she answered. 'Just a couple of miles away.'

'I see. Have you lived there long?'

'All my life,' she answered, softer, so that he had to lean his head forward slightly to catch the words.

'Really?' The bland grey-blue eyes were expressionless. 'I lived here, years ago.'

'Did you?' She put her empty glass down. 'I think dinner's ready. Mrs Rhodes is—'

He turned, nodded. 'Of course.'

They all went in, Mrs Rhodes leading their guest, the others following. Arwenna was seated opposite Garth at the beautifully laid table, the Colonel to their left at the end, Mrs Rhodes beside Garth, and James opposite his mother and beside Arwenna. Their daily housekeeper, Mrs Hedges, came with the soup, and Arwenna thought, it'll be all over the village by morning, if not tonight. The little woman's bright button eyes never left Garth's face. Arwenna wondered how much she remembered.

The dinner passed pleasantly. Whatever Mrs Hedges' faults, she was an excellent cook, and the conversation was easy, facile, due to Arwenna's efforts mainly. She had agreed to come, to help James, and once committed threw herself into the task whole-heartedly, asking Garth about Raneley

Hall, the work that would be needed in it, and gradually she sensed the others relaxing, and taking their part.

There was eventually a lull, and as they waited for Mrs Hedges to bring in the dessert, Garth looked directly at Arwenna and said: 'Tell me, Arwenna, do you work nearby?'

'In Raneley itself. My aunt has a small café—but I only returned last year, when I got engaged to James. My aunt's not in very good health.'

'Ah. You'd been away?'

'Working abroad, yes.' She gave him a pleasant smile as Mrs Hedges wheeled in a trolley holding the most mouth-watering-looking confections of meringue with marron glacé purée on it, and plates of cheese and biscuits. There was silence for a few moments as they were served, the cheese and biscuits were left on the sideboard, Mrs Hedges murmured something about coffee following soon, and left them.

'This looks quite delicious,' said Garth, as they began to eat.

The Colonel beamed as though the sweet had been all his doing, although Arwenna was willing to bet he hadn't a clue until that moment what they were going to eat. He was about to say something when Garth spoke again. 'Where abroad?'

'Italy, France, Germany, Spain, Greece,' said Arwenna.

'Good heavens!'

'I was nanny to two families over the last five years,' she explained, 'and both travelled a lot, the first in Italy and France, the second in the other three countries. It was marvellous work and I had a wonderful time.'

'I'm sure you did,' he answered. The others listened politely, as if they hadn't heard it before. The Colonel heartily disapproved of Arwenna's having worked abroad, although he had never said so directly to her, preferring to express his opinions via James. He should have been alive in Victorian times, she had often thought. He would have been extremely at home in a time when women were vigorously suppressed. It prompted her, mischievously, to say:

'I think everyone should travel when they're young, don't you? See how other people live, learn their languages, etcetera.' She gave the Colonel a warm smile. 'Don't you agree, Colonel?'

He nodded, nearly choking on his meringue. 'Indeed, yes, most interesting.'

'You learnt a language?' Garth enquired gently. 'Which one?'

As if he cared! But perhaps he had picked up something of Colonel Rhodes' unease at her account of her travels. Garth was a shrewd man, far shrewder than anyone there, save Arwenna herself, she realised. She had seen his eyes resting on the Colonel several times during the course of the conversation, and the looks had been far-seeing.

Arwenna raised her beautiful eyes, now bright with innocence, to him. She was going to enjoy this. 'All of them,' she answered gently, modestly.

The dark lashed grey-blue eyes met hers coolly. No surprise—merely amusement, as if he were far ahead of her in any games of words they could play. He gave a slight nod, as if of acknowledgment of her enjoyment, and she felt a small irrational flash of anger, which she hid successfully. Damn the man!

'That's most interesting,' he conceded. 'And you mastered the Greek alphabet?'

'No,' she admitted. 'But it didn't seem to matter. I mean, I was able to communicate verbally most places we went,' she shrugged delicately. It seemed to be one all, the score so far.

'Of course.' He nodded politely. 'A gift for picking up languages is to be admired indeed. It seems coincidental, but I'm looking for a translator at the moment, so I've got an interest, naturally.'

'You don't speak any languages yourself?' she queried. The others had abandoned any attempts at joining in. They all three wore polite, listening faces which didn't deceive Arwenna, nor, she suspected, Garth for a moment. As soon as decently possible, the Colonel was going to get Garth on his own, she surmised, for otherwise why would he have invited him for dinner?

'Alas, no. A smattering of French is the extent—' He gave a mock-rueful smile that managed to convey that he didn't really give a damn. Languages were for peasants. He was too busy making millions... She wondered if she had an over-active imagination, or could really read his mind. Now she was being fanciful.

'Oh, shame. Still, never mind. I'm sure you can always find employees who're bi-lingual, can't you?'

'Indeed yes, usually.' There was a delicate pause while everyone digested the meaning of that last word, then he turned to James' mother. 'I really must congratulate you on the meal, Mrs Rhodes.'

'Thank you—Garth,' she answered. 'Some cheese and biscuits?'

'I'm not sure if I could manage—' he half stood. 'May I get them for you?'

The Colonel rose instantly. 'Stay where you are, dear fellow,' and he fetched the plates from the sideboard, giving a baleful glance towards James which was unseen by Garth.

The coffee arrived moments later, was drunk amid desultory talk regarding varieties of cheese, and personal preferences—Garth confessed a weakness for Camembert, and was persuaded to take a morsel—and then they drifted back to the drawing room, replete, whereupon the Colonel said, before Garth could sit down: 'I believe—er—Garth, that you're interested in philately?'

Garth looked faintly surprised. 'Yes, I am. I've a modest collection, but how—'

The Colonel smiled mysteriously. 'Ah, just something I read once. Got a good memory. Come into my study for a moment if you will, I've a couple of stamps you might like to see.' It was a ploy, and obvious to everyone, to get him away privately, and Garth put an interested look on his face as if he wanted nothing more than to see his host's stamp

collection, gave an apologetic smile to James' mother, and
went out, followed by the Colonel.

Jane Rhodes collapsed on to a settee, and Arwenna
poured her a stiff brandy, whispered: 'It went off beautifully,' and sat beside her.

'Did it?' Jane Rhodes eyes were anxious and vulnerable.

'Yes, super. Didn't it, James?' Arwenna looked at him.
His mother needed reassurance. She never got it from her
husband.

'It seemed to. The meal was fine.' James looked levelly at
Arwenna. His cheeks were slightly pink. 'You got on like a
house on fire with him. Or did you?'

Arwenna's mouth twitched. Dear me, was James jealous? 'What do you mean—"or did you?"' she countered.

'There seemed to be the slightest touch of aggression flying about to me,' he responded.

Jane looked anxiously from one to the other, clearly
puzzled. Arwenna wished James would shut up. 'Don't be
ridiculous!' she said, laughing merrily. 'We were having a
lovely chat about languages.'

'Mmm, yes—so you say.' He shrugged. 'However—'

He had picked something up after all. Arwenna was very
determined not to cause Jane Rhodes any distress, and patted her arm. 'I love your dress,' she said. 'Blue suits you.'

'Thank you, my dear. And yours is lovely too. Those
gorgeous flared gypsy dresses do suit you so much.' She
sighed. 'Ah, what it is to be young!'

All was safely steered away. Arwenna would talk to James
later, when he ran her home. Only he didn't, so she
couldn't—because shortly afterwards the two men returned, looking very casual as if stamps had occupied their
entire conversation, and everyone had a few drinks, and
Garth concentrated all his attentions on Mrs Rhodes, until
she was pink-cheeked, laughing and relaxed, and then announced, regretfully, that he would have to be leaving
shortly and had had a simply splendid evening. Then he
looked across the room at Arwenna and said: 'I'm going

through the village, Arwenna, I'd be delighted to give you a lift home—if you need one,' and he then regarded James, who had drunk several too many glasses of port and was sitting talking to his father, next to Arwenna on one long settee. 'It would save you getting your car out again.'

James opened his mouth to speak, and Colonel Rhodes said, too quickly: 'That seems a damn good idea, eh, Arwenna?'

In an odd way, she had expected his words. In an even stranger way, she had sensed that the Colonel would reply as he had. What she didn't know then, was why. It might be interesting to find out, she thought, and lifted her eyes demurely. 'That's very kind of you,' she said. 'I am rather tired, and it's a busy day tomorrow at the café.'

Garth looked at the watch on his wrist, and stood up with a regretful smile at his hostess. Ten minutes later, farewells said, Arwenna was in his car.

CHAPTER TWO

HE DROVE swiftly down the long drive from Grey Gables, the door closed softly in the distance, and the three people who had stood on the steps were gone. Arwenna wondered what the atmosphere would be like; James was most definitely not pleased. She sat back in the seat, then looked at the man driving the black Lotus, hands steady on the wheel.

'Why are you going through the village?' she asked. 'Your new house is the other way.'

'You get right to the heart of things, don't you?' He stopped at the end of the drive and glanced at her. He looked as faintly amused as he had all evening, which Arwenna realised, belatedly, she had found slightly annoying.

'Yes. And so do you. So—where are you going to in the village at this time of night?'

He started up without answering, then, as they drove along the narrow country road, said: 'I'm not. It seemed a harmless enough white lie in order to give you a lift.'

'And why should you want to do that?' she asked calmly. 'James was all set to take me home. He's not pleased.'

'I could see that. I could also tell that he'd had too much to drink.'

'*That's* really none of your business,' she answered.

'True, it isn't. But I wanted to talk to you alone, and this seemed as if it might be the only opportunity.'

'Oh, I'm sure we'll meet again—some time,' she answered. But not if I see you first, she added mentally.

'Do you?' he laughed, as though he had heard those unspoken words. As if he knew that she disliked him—perhaps even why. 'I don't wait for "some time." I'm a "now" man.'

'So I've gathered,' she said dryly. 'Okay, you want to talk. Here I am, a captive audience. Fire away.'

'You're very direct.'

'You've already said that in another way. So I am, I don't believe in wasting time either—Garth.' She hesitated deliberately before saying his name. 'So what do you want to say?'

'I want you to work for me.'

She hadn't expected that. Not that. 'What?' she laughed. 'You're mad! Work for *you?* Why?'

He slowed the car down and stopped at the side of the road. The village was in sight, about a quarter of a mile ahead, street lamps shining high and yellow in the one main street. If she wanted she could get out and walk. If she wanted. She didn't—yet. She wanted to hear more about his preposterous suggestion. She was going to enjoy turning him down flat. There was no way she was ever going to work for him.

Engine off, the car silent, he turned to her. 'Mad? Tut, tut—strong word to use! You haven't heard what the job is yet.'

Arwenna too turned to face him. The interior light off, the only light was that from a high clear moon, and the car was shadowy, his face a blur.

'I don't really care what it is,' she answered. 'I don't want to work for you. I'm quite happy working for my aunt.'

'After travelling round Europe, seeing life in the big cities? You're happy here?'

'Yes. I'm also engaged to James—or had that slipped your mind?' she asked, with a touch of asperity.

'No, it hadn't. He's a fine young man—and after you'd been married to him for six months you'd be bored to death.'

Arwenna froze, shocked. She turned to open the door and he put his hand out to stop her. 'Take your hand away!' she

snapped. 'I don't have to sit here and listen to your insults—'

'I'm not trying to insult you.'

'You might not be trying,' she snapped, 'but you're
damned well succeeding!'

'Come off it!' he said, voice mocking. 'Do you think I'm
stupid? James is scared to death of his father, his mother is
equally scared—you're the only one who's not—'

'You've seen a lot of things on one visit, haven't you?' she
said angrily. 'How dare you say such things!'

'I do because they're true. And you know it.' He took his
hand away. 'You can't open the door anyway. There's an
automatic lock. Only I can open it.'

'You've no right—'

'Maybe not. There's not much you can do about it. When
we've finished our talk, I'll run you to your home, and you
can get out.'

'As far as I'm concerned our talk is already finished,' she
said, icy cold with anger.

'No, it's not. I've not told you about the job yet.'

'There's no point. I'm not taking it.'

'I need a secretary who's competent in several languages,' he reminded her.

'I can't type.'

'You can learn—in any case that's not the important part.
The languages are—'

'Rubbish! You can employ who you like. You're loaded,
aren't you? Or *supposed* to be,' she added scathingly.

'Oh yes, I'm loaded all right,' he agreed, infuriatingly
calm. 'Absolutely rolling in filthy lucre—quite disgustingly
so, actually.'

'God!' She turned her head away in contempt. 'You are
absolutely—'

'It's what you expected me to say, so I did.' Garth put his
hand to her cheek and forced her to face him. 'But I haven't
finished yet.' His eyes were cold and hard, that much she

could see in the dim confines of the vehicle. 'You don't like me, and I think I know why.'

'You don't,' she grated, and pushed his hand away with an abrupt, jerky movement. She didn't want to touch him; she didn't want him to touch her.

'I know your surname. It's Holmes.'

That shook her. 'How did you know?' she asked.

'I did.' He shrugged. 'I know everything I want to know— I make it my business to find out. So I know why you think I'm the loathsome creep who's come back flashing his money—the only snag is, you don't know as much as you think you do, not by a long shot, Arwenna. You were how old when I left Raneley? Five—six?'

'I was eight.'

'Then you know nothing. You were a child. You heard only what people told you.'

'And that was enough,' she said. 'Let me out here,' she added. 'I'll walk home.'

'I've not finished.'

'I have. I don't want to see you again.'

'But you're going to. If you love James you're going to work for me, and, incidentally, one day learn the truth of what actually happened years ago here.'

'Love James?' Arwenna seized on the words because they were so totally alien to the subject he had been discussing; what could James have to do with him? The evening was still warm, but Arwenna had gone cold, and pulled her black stole closer round her. It was as though everything wasn't quite real. She felt deathly cold. It was like a nightmare, a bad dream from which she had no escape. 'What do you mean? What has James got to do with—'

'Listen,' he said. 'Just listen to me. What do you think Colonel Rhodes took me off to his study for? It sure as hell wasn't to admire his stamp collection, and I'm sure you knew that as well as I did.' He tapped his finger on the wheel. 'He wants me to invest money in his clothing firm— he desperately wants that. What he didn't know is that *I* know all about his factory just the other side of Raneley. He's damned near bankrupt—but I'll bet you didn't know that, did you?'

It was a nightmare. What he was saying couldn't be true. James' father was wealthy. Not as much as Garth, obviously, but extremely well off. Everyone knew that. She shook her head. 'You're lying.'

'I'm not lying, and I can prove it. In another year he'll have to close the place, and several hundred people will be out of work. He's heavily in debt—has been for years, and now everything's catching up on him. I can save that place, and he knows it. You don't think he'd have invited me to dinner otherwise, do you? I wasn't born yesterday, Arwenna, and I haven't made my money by being taken in— I'm meeting him tomorrow, doing a tour of the place, and then we'll talk. And how those talks go depends on you.'

It was not only a nightmare, but he was mad. His words weren't making sense. She shook her head, almost dazed with disbelief. 'How—what—' she began.

'I've told you. I want you to work for me.'

She lifted her eyes then. 'You mean if I agree to work for you, you'll agree to save his business?'

'More or less,' he agreed.

'Why? Why *me?*'

'Because, when I saw you this evening, I realised you were different from anyone I'd ever met. You've a strong, decisive personality—I need people like you on my team, and I always get what I want,' he laughed.

'You—that's blackmail,' she said with contempt.

'Yes, it is. I told him in his study that I could do with someone like you working for me. I said it quite casually, almost as an afterthought—but he got the point.'

She shivered. 'You bastard!' she whispered.

'Yes, possibly. Well, what's your answer? You do love James, don't you?'

'Of course I do,' she said. 'What are you trying to say?'

'Nothing. He must love you very much to have defied his father sufficiently to chase all over Europe trying to persuade you to come home and marry him.'

She took a deep breath. 'How did you know that?'

'I told you, I know everything I want to know.'

'You don't. There's something you don't know. And it's one reason—though there are dozens of others—why I can't work for you, despite your blackmailing efforts. I despise blackmailers, and I despise *you*,' she snapped, stiff with anger.

'Your aunt?'

'My *God*—don't say you—'

'Yes, I do. She's ill, you said. She's got gall-bladder trouble, and is working in almost constant pain, and has to be on a strict, fat-free diet—not easy when you're running a busy café. And, the hospital situation in this area being what it is, there's an eighteen month waiting list for her to have her gall-bladder removed. Unless she has it done privately, which you can't afford.'

She was silent at last. Shocked, shaken beyond words, Arwenna put her hands to her face and covered it. It was as though he were revealing her life to her, peeling away the layers of privacy until there was nothing left.

'I have a friend who runs a private clinic in London. She *needs* that operation, not constant pain-killing drugs to enable her to get through each day. She would be inside within two days, back home next week, and within a month she could be leading a near normal life—with help.'

Arwenna slowly took her hands away from her face. The palms were damp with tears. '*If* I agree, *you'll* pay for her operation?'

'Yes. And for someone to help her in the café for as long as she needs help.'

'And in return, all you want is for me to work for you. Where? In London?'

'No. Here at Raneley Hall—and abroad.'

'Here? But the place isn't habitable yet. It'll take months.'

'Weeks. I've a team of workmen starting in two days. Next week there'll be two rooms ready at the back of the house. It's all planned. I have a lot of work to do here—I intend to do it, and to make this my base for all my future work. You can live at home—you'll just have changed your place of work, that's all.'

Arwenna sat very still, turning Garth's words over in her mind. It was all so simple and clear-cut, the way he put it. She worked for him, he would put money that was urgently needed into Colonel Rhodes' business, and he would enable her aunt to have her operation within days. There was really no choice to be made. He had successfully blocked all her escapes, literally as well as figuratively. She had the oddest feeling that if she had said no, he would just drive on, and on, and never let her out. She shivered. She wasn't normally fanciful, but she sensed that with a man as ruthless as Garth Vanner, anything was possible—and probable. He had said that she was a strong personality. She was as nothing compared to him. She had never, in all her travels, met anyone like that, and she had mixed with so many people when she had worked abroad. Wealthy people, kind, ruthless, charming, selfish—all kinds.

Never had she seen anyone remotely like Garth Vanner. He was unique, he was steel and fire, forged from humble beginnings into the person he had become. She despised him, yet at the same time she knew that he was fascinating—in a similar fashion that a snake was fascinating to a rabbit. She was no rabbit, she was a fighter, and she knew it, knew that she was capable and intelligent—and not being tried to the full, helping her aunt in the café. She loved her aunt dearly, for she had brought Arwenna up since the age of twelve, when her parents had been killed in a car crash, and she owed her much, for Aunt Daisy had the streak of independence and the adventurous spirit that had encouraged Arwenna to work abroad, 'see the world' as she had put it, at the age of eighteen.

It was one reason Arwenna had returned the previous year, when it had become increasingly obvious that her aunt wasn't well, had accepted James' fifteenth proposal of marriage, and settled back in the village life as though she had never been away. She had no regrets about returning, for her life had been rich and full on her travels, and she had many memories, and many friends, with whom she regularly corresponded. She had also worked hard, as she did now, in the café, for her aunt could do less as the time passed, and on to Arwenna the burden had fallen—a burden she shouldered willingly, and with love.

'Well?' he said, after several minutes of silence.

She looked at him, and nodded. 'I'll work for you, Garth, and I'll work hard, but only because you've made me accept. But you'll not be disappointed—because once I agree to do something, I do it to the best of my ability. You'll get your pound of flesh.' She gave a little, contemptuous smile. 'There is a time limit, though, surely? I mean, you don't expect me to work for the rest of my days for you, do you?'

'No. You are, after all, getting married soon, aren't you?'

'Don't you know? Dear me, I thought you knew everything!'

'I can hardly know something that isn't fixed up, can I?' She saw his smile in the shadowy greyness. 'Let's say eighteen months, shall we? After that you're free.' He touched her left hand, touched the ring she wore. 'Free to marry James.'

She snatched her hand away. 'I might marry him before that.'

'Really? When? You've been engaged nearly a year already. I thought the fashion nowadays was for short engagements.'

'I don't follow fashion,' she said tartly.

'You follow your heart instead. How wise! Foolish to rush into things without being sure.'

'I am sure,' she insisted.

'Of course,' he said soothingly. 'Forgive me, I should have worded it differently. It's sensible to wait until James is fully independent. He works for his father, doesn't he?'

'You know everything else, you should know that.'

'Of course I do. But he'd like to change.'

'How do you—' she began.

He smiled. 'I didn't. It was a guess. But I do now.'

Arwenna turned away. 'Drive me home, please.'

'Certainly.' He switched on, and the powerful engine roared into life. Five minutes later he had stopped outside the café door, and turned off the motor. He looked at her. 'Are you going to invite me in for a coffee?'

'No.' She turned the handle, then looked at him. 'Will you unlock this door, please?'

'Yes, when you ask me in.'

'What for?'

'I'd like to meet your aunt, tell her about my friend's clinic.'

Seething, she said: 'All right, if you must. If she's in bed, though, I don't want to wake her.'

'Of course not. However, there's a light on. Is that the sitting room or bedroom?'

She looked up through the front. 'Sitting room,' she answered.

There was a click, and the handle turned, and the door opened. Arwenna found her key and went inside, followed by Garth. She didn't switch on the light, and didn't care if he fell over one of the chairs. He didn't. He followed her closely, and up the twisty staircase at the top of which Arwenna shouted out: 'It's me, Aunt Daisy. I've got someone with me. Are you respectable?'

'As much as I'll ever be, love—come on in,' her aunt's voice floated back, and Arwenna grinned. She never moaned or complained, even when it was obvious that she was in pain. She opened the door to the sitting room and Aunt Daisy, cosily clad in warm red woollen dressing gown, feet up on a pouffe, was watching a horror film on television. Her bottle of pain-killing pills on a little table told their own story. She tried to move them, but knocked them over instead.

'Oh, Aunty, why didn't you phone?' Arwenna asked in distress, going over to pick them up.

''Cos it was only a twinge, that's why,' her aunt retorted with spirit, and looked over to the doorway where Garth stood watching. 'Come in, Mr Vanner, and sit down. My niece forgets her manners sometimes!' She grinned at Arwenna to show that she didn't mean it, her rosy-cheeked round face belying her health. As she had once complained to Arwenna, she had never received any sympathy as a child, because even when at death's door from 'flu, she always looked rosy-cheeked and blooming.

'And talking of phones, before I forget, James rang about ten minutes ago. Sounded surprised when I said you weren't back.'

There was a sound that might have been a small cough from Garth, and Arwenna looked round. His face was expressionless, polite. Aunt Daisy had never once mentioned his name, or the events of fifteen years before, and Arwenna was never sure if she had even heard of them. She had only moved in from London to look after Arwenna eleven years previously, and was still classed as a newcomer by older villagers.

'This is Garth Vanner, Aunt Daisy,' said Arwenna. 'Garth—my aunt, Daisy Holmes.'

He came forward, hand outstretched. 'I'm pleased to meet you, Miss Holmes.'

She looked at him, bright blue eyes searching his face. 'James said the name when he phoned,' she said. 'Do sit down, dear, it's a long way for me to look up. My, you're very tall, aren't you?'

He laughed and sat down next to her on an easy chair. 'Is that better?' he asked her.

'Much. How tall are you, then?' Arwenna left the room and went into the small kitchen next door to it. Aunt Daisy would have his sock size before she was finished! She heard his faint answer, her aunt's reply, and pushed the door closed. After putting on the kettle she picked up the telephone carefully and dialled James' number.

'Hello, James love, it's me—' she began, to be interrupted by his furious voice.

'Where the hell were you? I thought he was giving you a lift?'

'Hold it!' she cut in. 'What's with you? He did—'

'Yes. An *hour* ago—' she looked at the kitchen wall clock. It was nearly eleven. They had left at ten. Surely they hadn't been talking for nearly an *hour?*

'Well, we were talking,' she said, and at James' snort of disbelief, her temper rose swiftly. 'And he's offered me a job—and if you want to know why, why don't you ask your father?'

James suddenly became contrite. More quietly he said: 'Okay, simmer down. I'm sorry. Job? A *job?* What do you mean?'

'It's a long story,' she said wearily. 'And I'm supposed to be making coffee for him. I'll ring you in the morning.'

'Is he there *now?*'

'Yes,' she answered dryly. 'Talking to Aunt Daisy. Why? Do you want him?'

'Why did he come in?'

'To talk to her. He's going to pay for her to have her gallbladder operation. Anything else you want to know, James, or can I go? I'm tired.'

'I don't understand—' he began, confused.

'Nor do I—look, we'll talk tomorrow.'

'Arwenna—he didn't—er—make a pass?'

'No, he didn't!' she answered. 'I wish he had, I'd have enjoyed punching him hard. But he didn't, I promise.' He's a blackmailer, she could have added, and a swine, but he didn't make a pass at me, not once.

'I'd better go, darling,' said James, 'just wanted to make sure you were home. Can I call in the morning?'

'Yes, of course. See you then. 'Bye, darling.' She re-placed the receiver, saw that the kettle was boiling, and made three cups of coffee. She frowned thoughtfully. James had been understandably angry at first, then calmed down. She would tell him as much as he ought to know when she saw him. She went into the sitting room. 'Black or white, Garth?'

'White, please. No sugar.' He turned back to her Aunt.

'Have you told her?' asked Arwenna.

'No.'

'Told me what?' Aunt Daisy looked indignantly from one to the other. 'What's going on?'

'Garth has got rather a nice surprise for you,' Arwenna answered gently. 'I'll bring the coffee in. Just a moment.'

She handed them their coffees, black for Daisy, and sat down on the little stool. 'Well, go on,' she said to Garth. 'Tell her.'

He grinned at Aunt Daisy. 'You'd better put your cup down,' he said, and took it gently from her. 'How would you like to have your op within two days and be back home next week, a new woman?'

For a moment her face registered stunned disbelief, fol lowed by shock, followed by a kind of pity. She shook her head. 'I'm sorry, Mr Vanner, I don't think that's a very funny joke,' she said. She looked at Arwenna and her eyes were sad, as if someone had let her down.

Arwenna felt her own eyes fill with tears. For this, this alone, it would all be worth it. To see Aunt Daisy's face change, as it would do in a moment, for her to *know*—it would be worth her sacrifice.

'Believe me, Miss Holmes, I wouldn't make a joke about a matter like this,' said Garth. His face was serious. 'I have a friend who runs a clinic in London—it's a private clinic, and I have his card here,' he felt in an inside pocket and handed her a small business card. 'I shall phone him in the morning, once you've given me the go-ahead, and arrange for you to go in immediately and have your operation. I can assure you that he's an excellent surgeon who treats very important people—Members of Parliament, actors, those in the public eye who need quick treatment or operations with the maximum care and minimum of waiting. And you won't have a penny to pay.'

Aunt Daisy looked absolutely dumbfounded. Her mouth opened once or twice, then she managed to speak. 'It isn't a joke, is it?'

'No, Aunty, it's not a joke,' said Arwenna, and leaned forward to clasp the other's trembling hands.

'Oh, my! But how—why—' She turned to Garth, a small smile growing bigger as she began to accept the unbelievable.

'I've blackmailed Arwenna into working for me,' he said, as if confessing something. 'She speaks several languages, and I desperately need someone to help me—and I used a little gentle persuasion, I'm ashamed to say.' He didn't look ashamed; he looked very calm and completely assured. 'I'll also arrange for help in the café, so you needn't close at all. Well, have you got used to the idea, or do you still not believe me?'

She sighed a deep sigh. 'I believe you,' she said quietly. 'And I can't even begin to thank you.'

'Then don't try.' He finished his coffee and stood up. 'If I may come over tomorrow and see you—say in the morning?'

'Yes.' Her eyes shone.

'And I will, of course, drive you down to London—I suggest you begin packing your things, Miss Holmes. They'll obviously want you in for a day before the operation for rest. I'll also have arranged, by the time I arrive tomorrow, for a couple of staff to take over the café.' He extended his hand, and Aunt Daisy took it. Her eyes shone with bright tears.

'You're so very kind,' she said. 'So very kind.' Arwenna, watching, had to harden her heart. He wasn't kind at all, he was ruthless. Her aunt would never know that, though.

'I'll see you tomorrow,' he said, then to Arwenna: 'I'll see myself out.'

'I have to bolt the door anyway,' she said, opening the sitting room door, 'so I'll come with you.'

'Goodnight,' called Aunt Daisy as he followed her out.

'Goodnight,' he answered. 'Sleep well.'

Arwenna led him across the darkened empty café, the tables and chairs silent ghosts waiting for morning. 'You can be a real charmer when you want, can't you?' she remarked softly as she opened the outer door.

'Yes,' he agreed, 'I can. Don't forget to phone James and let him know you're home.' He smiled blandly at her from the doorway.

'I already have,' she answered.

'I thought I heard a telephone ring from somewhere when you went out to make coffee. Was he annoyed?'

'No. Why should he be? He trusts me,' she said, as bland as he.

'Foolish man!' He turned, was walking away before she could reply. 'Goodnight, Arwenna.'

She closed the door and bolted it, and then, standing back in the deeper shadows, watched him get into his car. As he started the engine and began to move, he looked right into the café, raised his hand as if in salute, and drove away. Furious—he couldn't surely have seen her, could he?—Arwenna turned away and walked straight into a table. 'Damn!' she muttered, and kicked the leg. Then she went upstairs to settle her excited aunt down for the night. She felt very tired.

THINGS MOVED fast the next morning. No sooner had James been, been soothed, and left, than Garth appeared. If Arwenna hadn't suspected that he didn't give a damn about people's feelings, she would have thought that he had remained tactfully out of sight for James' visit. His car rolled up as soon as James' had disappeared.

There were three customers in the café, drinking coffee with scones, three village women waiting for the bus to the nearest big town, Radford, and their weekly shopping trip. They had paid, and would leave when the bus appeared, so Arwenna took him up to her aunt who was waiting in the sitting room. It was only ten-thirty, and they would be busy in another hour until about two.

'Good morning, Miss Holmes,' he greeted her as he went in, Arwenna following. She hadn't spoken on the stairs, and given him only the briefest hello as he had entered the café. 'Are you packed?'

'Yes,' she nodded. 'You told me to.'

'That's good, because we're leaving this afternoon, after lunch.' He turned to Arwenna. 'There are two very capable women driving up from London now. They should arrive in'—he glanced at his watch—'um, an hour or so, say twelve to be on the safe side. They'll take .over the running of everything for the next few weeks. You'll have an hour or more to tell them everything they need to know before you leave.'

Arwenna looked at him. Had she misheard? 'Before I leave?' she queried.

'Why, yes. You're coming to London, of course, with your aunt and me.'

'I am?' It hadn't occurred to her, but of course, how sensible it was. She would be there to help her aunt settle into a strange place. She could even stay there a couple of nights, and be at her side after the operation—if she had somewhere to sleep. She looked at her aunt, sitting so patiently and calmly there.

'I'll stop in London a day or two,' she said, 'seeing that Garth has two women coming to take over.' She went and knelt by the old woman's side. 'Would you like me to?'

'Bless you, love, it's still like a dream to me! I keep pinching myself to make sure it's real. I'd love you to stay— do you know any hotels, Mr Vanner?'

'Garth, please,' he answered. 'It's summer, a difficult time. But no problem, I know a place literally within five minutes' walk of the clinic for you, Arwenna. Hadn't you better pack as well?'

She nodded. It was all happening too fast. She must let James know, that was the most important thing. 'Yes. I'll phone James first,' she said. 'if I'd known before, I could have—'

'I've seen his father this morning, just before I came. We had one or two things to discuss, and I mentioned that you were both going to London, so he'll know later today anyway,' Garth answered. A shiver ran down Arwenna's spine. It was as though—and it was ridiculous—she was being taken over by this man.

'Nevertheless, I'll call him,' she said pleasantly.

'Then, if you'll excuse me, I have one or two things to do before we go. I'll see you in an hour. Au revoir.' He went out, leaving a small, full silence behind him. It was broken by Aunt Daisy.

'My word,' she said admiringly, 'he doesn't waste time, does he?'

Arwenna nodded. She couldn't trust herself to speak. The sensation she had, of helplessness against an over-whelming force, was totally alien to her independent spirit. But even worse was the realisation that it was only just beginning. She had met him only last night, less than twenty-four hours ago, and already her life was being organised for her. And this was only the start of it.

CHAPTER THREE

JAMES WAS puzzled, angry, and hurt. He too seemed to think, like Arwenna, that Garth Vanner was coolly taking over in too many areas of their lives. She hadn't told him about the blackmail over his father's firm. She hadn't told any direct lies, either, but implied that her aunt's health had been the overriding factor that had persuaded her. He looked at her in disbelief. They were in the kitchen of the flat over the café, and it was nearly time to leave, and two very capable and very charming middle-aged women from an agency were already taking over downstairs, under the guidance of a still bemused Aunt Daisy.

'You said something last night about asking Dad,' he said, looking at Arwenna accusingly.

She sighed. She'd said that in temper, and she shouldn't have done. It wouldn't help James to know the truth about everything. 'Did I?' She smiled. 'It seemed as though your father wanted him to give me a lift home—or didn't you think so? Perhaps I was imagining it.' She touched his cheek. 'I'll not be away long, love. I don't mind working for him, honestly. It'll be a challenge, I suppose, using my languages, and it won't be for long.'

'How long?' he demanded.

'Let's say until I feel I've worked off the fees for the operation.' She kissed him, and he drew her into his arms and held her tightly.

'I'll get a job away from here—I'll be independent soon, I've made up my mind.'

'Have you? Good. Best thing.' Her voice was muffled, because he was holding her so closely against him—and it was at that moment that Garth walked in. Arwenna knew even before he spoke, because she felt James relax his hold, then tighten it again.

'I'm so sorry.' Garth's voice was quite unmistakable. 'I'll wait in the living room.' The door closed very firmly.

Arwenna looked up, shaking with laughter—and saw James' furious face. 'Damn the man,' he muttered, his eyes narrowed with temper. '*Damn* him!'

'He wasn't to know,' she said mildly. 'Anyway, it'll do him good—let him see who belongs to whom.'

He relaxed slightly and gave a wry grin. 'I suppose so. Just watch him though—'

'What *do* you mean? I wouldn't touch him if you paid me. I'll be working for him, that's all. I don't like the man. You don't need to worry.'

'Sorry.' He ruffled her hair. 'I don't like you out of my sight. And you'll be in London with him.'

'Oh, no, I won't,' she answered. 'I'll be staying at a hotel. I probably won't even see him, once Aunt Daisy's settled in the clinic, don't *worry.*'

'Okay, I won't. You'll phone me?'

'Of course. Soon as I'm settled. Promise.' She kissed him. 'See? I'll unpack my case, find a phone, and give you my address.' It was all arranged in her mind. If the hotel Garth knew was too expensive-looking, she would tell him so, and find a cheaper place. In the unlikely event of not finding anywhere, Arwenna had a couple of numbers to ring, one the phone of two students she'd met in Paris, and of whom she was very fond, who shared a flat in London, the other the female Dutch cousin of her last employer abroad, a pleasant little woman, rather old-fashioned, who had assured Arwenna that she had a spare room any time she was in London. Arwenna was totally confident that either contact would provide an answer, and had copied the numbers and put them in her purse. But she didn't know then of the arrangements that had already been made. She didn't know until it was too late...

ARWENNA KISSED her aunt's cheek. Daisy was sitting up in a neat bed, in an attractively furnished room which had a colour television with a remote control switch, a huge vase of exotic flowers, and a view over London's rooftops. The curtains stirred faintly in the breeze from outside, and a pretty nurse walked over and closed the window, turned and smiled at Arwenna, and said:

'Miss Holmes will be well looked after, you can be sure of that. And you may visit her any time. I'll let you say your goodbyes now, and I'll come in again when you've gone.' She beamed at them and went out, closing the door softly behind her.

'Well!' said Aunt Daisy. 'I'm here, am I? Can't believe it. Look, my own telly—I'll be able to watch Coronation Street, and all those lovely Christopher Lee films—'

'Oh, Aunt Daisy, you're a T.V. fanatic!' Arwenna laughed, and hugged her. 'You'll get spoilt here.'

'So I will—and I'll love it. Off you go, dear, Garth will be waiting for you. Come and see me tomorrow, any time now—but you go and do your shopping first, and have a look around. Do you good.'

'Window-shopping more like.' Arwenna pulled a face. 'Still, I'll go to Fortnum and Mason's and buy you a pretty jar of marmalade or something, then I can go swanking round with the bag. Goodbye, dear. Don't be watching T.V. too late.' She kissed her aunt goodbye and went towards the door. As she opened it her aunt called out:

'Thank him from me, won't you?'

'I will. Sleep well. See you tomorrow.'

The pretty nurse was waiting outside. 'Mr Vanner's downstairs talking to Mr Chisholm, Miss Holmes. He's given us the number where we can contact you if necessary.' She smiled warmly. 'And he has this number, of course.' She touched the door handle of the private room. 'I'll get your aunt settled down for a rest before dinner.'

'Not with a television in the room you won't,' said Arwenna, grinning.

The nurse laughed. 'Thanks for the warning. We'll see. We have our methods.' She produced a bottle of pills and shook them. 'One of these—she'll drift off nicely.'

'Thank you, nurse. I'll be in tomorrow. Goodbye.'

'Goodbye, Miss Holmes.'

Arwenna took the lift to the ground floor, and Garth was waiting, alone. He walked towards her. 'Ready to go?'

'Yes. But before you take me anywhere, I must make something clear,' she began, and he opened the doors and led her out as she spoke.

'We'll talk in the car,' he said. 'I need a drink.'

He had found a space nearby and as they walked towards it he said: 'Aren't you hungry?'

'Not particularly. Are you?'

'Starving!' He unlocked her passenger door and she slid in. Moments later he was weaving a way through traffic, round a corner, along a few hundred yards, and then they were going down a slope beneath a large block of flats that had a sign by it saying:

'Frensham Mansions. Car Park for Residents Only.' Garth drove into a corner by a lift, leaned over to open her door and said: 'Out you get, Arwenna.'

Obediently she did so, faintly puzzled, and he took her arm and led her to the lift. 'Where are we going?' she asked, as it rose swiftly, the small lighted discs flashing with a rapidity that left her even more puzzled.

He looked at her as he opened the door, as though his thoughts had been miles away. 'Sorry? What did you say?' he asked.

They were in a small wide corridor, thickly carpeted in a soft green. The wall lights shed a golden glow on the passage. He took some keys out and opened a door, and they were in a huge room with a picture window that stretched from one side to the other, and looked out over a rooftop view of the most exciting city in the world. Arwenna stood transfixed. The room was furnished with antiques that must have cost a fortune. Exquisite settees—three of them—covered in old gold velvet, and a deep red carpet, and two long low tables, and further away, a dining table and chairs with the rich patina of age. The velvet curtains were of matching gold to the settees.

'I said—never mind. Where *are* we?' she asked.

'My London apartment. I told you I knew a place round the corner from the clinic. This is it,' he answered, and walked down from the steps, across the carpet, towards a heavy rosewood sideboard, and opened it. 'What will you drink?' he asked.

'Something for shock,' she answered dryly.

'Ah. Cognac, yes. Do sit down.'

She went over to the window instead, and looked out, trying to place landmarks. The Post Office Tower was visible in the distance, but the rest was unfamiliar to her. She needed a map. 'We've come for a drink, right?' she said.

'Right.'

'This is a simply beautiful place. Is the hotel I'm going to stay at near here too? Only I want to talk to you about that before we leave. If it's a large expensive place, I'd rather not. I may stay quite a few days, you see, and I can guess about prices. So, if you know of anywhere—em—small—'

'You're staying here, of course,' Garth cut in, and handed her a balloon glass of mellow gold liquid. 'Cheers.'

Her eyes met his as she raised the glass to her lips. She drank. 'No,' she said. 'Not here.'

'Don't be silly, Arwenna,' he said, in patient tones, as if addressing a small naughty child. 'It's highly practical. Literally a five-minute walk from your aunt—' He pointed out of the window. 'See that cream stone building? That's the clinic. I'm not even sure you can't see her window from here. You'll have to drape a towel on the window-ledge next time you—'

'No,' she said, not sure whether she was more amused than annoyed, but quite decided. 'I wouldn't dream of it.'

'Why not?' Hard dark eyes looked into hers.

She shrugged. 'I would think one obvious reason would occur even to you, Garth.'

'A man and a woman alone in a flat? Mmm, the conventions? You're afraid of what people might think? Or of me? Or of—yourself?'

'None of those things,' she answered promptly. Her clear, beautiful eyes, dark-lashed, looked back at him, totally unafraid. 'I'm independent—oh, I'm beholden to you already over my aunt's operation. This is a god-send, I won't deny it, but I'll pay you back eventually, never fear.'

'You will? I thought I'd made it clear—'

'You have, and I accepted, but I've had time to think about things since yesterday. I'll work hard, as I said, and—'

'But we haven't discussed your salary, have we?'

'No. Why? Are you going to pay me a pittance so that I'd never manage to be free?'

Garth laughed. 'That's a thought! You'll get good money for what you do. You've said you'll work hard, as I said, and—'

'But we haven't discussed your salary, have we?'

'No. Why? Are you going to pay me a pittance so that I'd never manage to be free?'

Garth laughed. 'That's a thought! You'll get good money for what you do. You've said you'll work hard, and I believe you. You'll earn your money. In fact, you can start immediately—which is one reason you're here. Some papers are highly confidential, and I wouldn't chance them being left in a hotel room.'

'You really do think of everything, don't you?' she said in reluctant admiration.

'Yes, I do.' He raised his glass. 'And I'll also tell you this. You'll see very little of me over the next few days—I'm a very busy man. This bringing your aunt down has been ideal for me, actually I'd have had to come down anyway tomorrow or the weekend. So you see,' he shrugged, 'it's worked out nicely.'

Arwenna was silent, pondering his words. So logical, eminently sensible, practical—and a mere stone's throw from the clinic. There was no argument she could put up against his.

'All right,' she said at last. 'But—'

'No buts, please. Can't you just accept things?'

She took a deep breath. 'You're taking over my life, and I don't like that.'

'Arwenna, no one can do that to you. Only if you let them.' His words were softly spoken, strangely the more powerful and decisive for that, and she realised the truth of them even as she heard them. 'I'll ring down for someone to bring up your case,' he added, 'then we'll eat.'

'Do you live here alone?'

'Yes, most of the time,' he smiled faintly. 'There are three bedrooms, and two bathrooms. Any more questions?'

'Yes. Where do we eat? Here?'

He nodded. 'I'm a fair cook, and the fridge is full. Come and see what there is, and we'll decide what we'd like.' He put down his glass on a table and walked towards the far end of the enormous room, up the steps, and opened a glass door. They were in another, wide corridor with several doors leading off. He opened one, and they were in a long, superbly fitted kitchen, with rich dark wood louvred cupboards, and tiled walls, and dark brown tiled floor. In addition to the usual fitments there was a microwave oven. Garth opened the door of the refrigerator and peered in as if not sure what he would see.

'Did you stock it up?' queried Arwenna, amazed at the variety of food within.

'No, this is a service flat. I phoned this morning when I knew we'd be coming, and had them fill it.' He gestured. 'What will it be? Steak, scampi, Dover sole, chicken—name it.'

'Steak and salad?' she suggested. The compartment at the bottom was crammed with greens.

'As good as done. I'll show you your bathroom and you can wash while I work. How do you like your steak? Rare, medium or burnt to a frazzle?'

'Medium, please.'

He led her to a door opposite the kitchen and opened it to reveal a fair-sized bedroom with fitted wardrobes in cream, a large picture window, and a large bed. The walls were white, and had several pictures on, modern but not unpleasing to Arwenna, who preferred traditional paintings. She looked around her. 'Very attractive,' she commented.

'Thank you. Your bathroom is there, by the window,' he pointed to a door that she would have mistaken for a closet door if he hadn't told her. 'It's all yours while you're here. I have my own. I'll have your case put just outside here.' He walked out and left her alone to look round. The bed had a white woven coverlet that touched the floor all round, and had a dark grey fringe and a faintly defined flower design on it. Arwenna went over to the window and looked out on to a quiet grassy square with trees and benches. An old man sat on a bench feeding pigeons, a newspaper by his side. Beyond that more flats on three sides, as though the garden was a private one. It was very quiet, with no sound of traffic, or only distantly, when she listened. She couldn't begin to imagine what the apartment cost, but she had never in all her life seen such luxury, and she had been in some extremely costly homes on the Continent.

Shaking her head in disbelief, she opened the bathroom door and went in. When she came out refreshed after a good wash several minutes later her case stood by her bedroom door, which was ajar, and a succulent smell drifted in. Arwenna combed her unruly curly hair, smoothed on a trace of pink lipstick, and went to find her host.

A small white-topped table in the kitchen was laid for two, and he was lifting the steaks on to the plates as she went in.

A bowl of mixed salad stood in the centre of the table, and a crusty French loaf cut up, and beside it a bowl of butter.

'Sit down,' he said, 'and eat. Then I'll show you your work.'

She looked at him. 'You're like the irresistible force, you know that?' she said calmly. 'I met you twenty-four hours ago—give or take a few minutes—and I'm here in London with you, and I'm not sure how it's all happened.'

He smiled slightly as he seated himself. 'And what are you? The immovable object? You know what's supposed to happen when an irresistible force meets an immovable object, don't you?'

'Trouble?' she queried dryly, and began to eat.

'Disintegration.' He helped himself to a piece of bread as Arwenna took some salad on to her plate. 'Bang! Nothing left.'

'I must remember that,' she answered calmly. Something was happening, and she wasn't sure what it was, and she certainly wasn't sure if she liked it, and it was an atmosphere in the room, a beginning of a kind of subtle tension, an awareness, a sharpness to the air. Garth Vanner was a powerful animal, sure and magnetic, and he exuded a kind of force. It was in everything he said and did, and in the way he moved. She knew why he was successful, and rich beyond a normal person's understanding, and the more time that passed, the more Arwenna realised the truth of her thoughts the previous evening, when she had known that she had never met anyone like him in her life. He gave off a kind of energy that must surely communicate itself to everyone with whom he came into contact. She shivered slightly at the knowledge, and he noticed, and asked:

'Are you cold?'

'No. You're a strange man, aren't you?'

'Am I?' He smiled.

'You know you are. You're well aware of it.'

'Are you always so outspoken with people you scarcely know, Arwenna?'

'No,' she answered promptly.

'Oh. Should I be flattered, then?' He bit into a piece of the crusty bread with strong white teeth.

'Not necessarily.' She bent to her plate and sliced a morsel of delicious steak, and ate it. He watched her, eyes unfathomable, expression serious.

'That's no answer.'

'It's all you're going to get for now. May I get myself a glass of water?'

'I'll get it.' He stood and went to the sink. 'Or would you prefer wine?'

'No, thanks. Water will be just fine.'

Garth handed her a glassful and sat down again. He was about to speak when a buzzer sounded in the kitchen. 'Damn!' He stood up, went over to a wall phone, and picked it up. 'Vanner,' he said. He looked across towards Arwenna as he listened to whoever spoke, then he said: 'All right, send her up. I'll open the door. Thanks.' He hung up and walked back to the table and sat down. 'That was the hotel porter. A friend has arrived.'

'So I imagined. A woman friend?'

'Yes.'

'Do you want me to stay in my room while she's here? If you do, will you give me some folders to look at?'

'No, you can meet her. I wouldn't dream of shutting you away.' He shook his head reprovingly. 'That wouldn't be very nice, would it?'

'I thought you were going to open the door?'

Garth finished his steak. 'First things first. Come out when you've eaten.' There came an important buzz from somewhere distant, and he laughed as he rose to his feet. 'I'll let her in before she breaks the bell.' Then he was gone. Arwenna finished her steak and carried her plates over to the sink. She would give them a few minutes and then go in. She looked down at the blue cotton dress she wore. It was one she had bought in Greece, square-necked with gorgeous embroidery at the wrists. It was her favourite dress, washed

like a dream, and always made her feel good when she wore
it. It was also James' favourite—which reminded her that
she hadn't telephoned him. She would do so as soon as
possible, or he'd be imagining all sorts of things. She went
into her bedroom, combed her hair again, put on more lipstick, frowned at herself in the mirror, and went out.

Garth was standing by the window talking to a tall blonde
who stood beside him. He turned at Arwenna's entrance,
and, a moment later so did the woman. Arwenna found
herself being stared at by the blonde, who was very attractive, dressed in a breathtakingly slim-fitting dress in some
swirly flame-coloured material. The look was a rather puzzled one, but it vanished a moment later as Garth said: 'Arwenna, meet Lucy Moore. Lucy—Arwenna Holmes.'

'Hello, Arwenna,' said Lucy, in a voice that matched her
face. Very attractive, slightly husky.

'Hello.' Arwenna walked slowly down the steps, and towards them. Lucy half turned towards Garth again—not in
a rude manner, but as though continuing a conversation.

'So Rollo persuaded me, as I was passing, to call in. He'd
been trying to get you all day, darling.'

'We only arrived here half an hour ago. Sorry, Lucy, but
I think I'll give this one a miss. I've got a heavy day tomorrow.'

'He said he asked you weeks ago and you said yes.'

'Did he? So he did. I simply forgot. In fact if it hadn't
been for bringing Arwenna's aunt here to Bob's clinic, I dare
say I'd still have been in Raneley.'

She made a small moue of exasperation. 'Really, Garth!
You know Rollo wants you to meet his Dutch chum—'

'Damn! So he does. Look, Lucy, let me get you a drink,
and I'll call him now. I dare say I can squeeze a meeting in
tomorrow. Sit down and talk to each other. What'll it be?'

'Got any champers?' asked Lucy, with a winning smile in
the vague direction of Arwenna, and seated herself nearest
the window. 'I had a heavy night last night—you *know* how

it is. Couldn't touch anything stronger.' She passed a delicate hand across her forehead.

'There's a bottle in the fridge. Be back in a moment.' Garth strode away, leaving Lucy and Arwenna alone.

'Are you an old friend of Garth's?' asked Lucy, with an innocent look at Arwenna—taking in the engagement ring in passing.

'No,' conceded Arwenna, wondering what Lucy would say if she told her the truth, 'I've not known him long. But he drove my aunt down to his friend's clinic today, and we came back here for a meal.'

'Oh, shame. Nothing serious, I hope?' Lucy spoke politely, but distantly, as if her mind was on other matters.

'Gall-bladder.'

'Dear me! Has he known your aunt long?'

Garth returned as Arwenna answered that no, he hadn't really, and he opened the bottle and poured out three glasses. 'I'll phone Rollo,' he said. 'Take your time. Help yourself to more.' He went to a telephone by the window, picked up the receiver, and dialled.

'Rollo gives *the* most *fabulous* parties,' said Lucy, as Garth began to speak. She kept her voice low, and Arwenna, sitting beside her, had to lean forward to catch the words. 'He'll be *furious!*'

'You're going, I take it?' asked Arwenna.

'Wouldn't miss it!' was Lucy's cheerful answer. Her eyes were a bright blue, heavily made up, and Arwenna suddenly felt as if the other's face was familiar.

'Have I seen you somewhere before?' she asked.

Lucy smiled. 'I dare say. I've been in several adverts on T.V. Nothing spectacular, but—' she gave a modest shrug.

'Good gracious! You're the girl in the Verini Vermouth ads!'

'The same. How clever of you!'

'How fascinating,' said Arwenna. 'I've never met anyone from television before. My aunt will be green with envy!'

Lucy laughed. Arwenna sensed a slight thaw in her manner, though it had been pleasant enough all along. 'It's a job like any other,' she said casually, 'but still, it's nice to be recognised, I must admit. And what do you do, Arwenna?'

'From today, I'm working for Garth. I speak several languages, and he needs a translator.'

'He does?' Lucy's beautiful face registered blank surprise. 'But he—'

'All settled,' said Garth, as he put the telephone back and walked over. 'We're all going, but I'm not staying late. You don't mind, do you, Arwenna?'

Lucy's face was a sight to see. Several things appeared to be in her mind, and uppermost was—could it be anxiety?—Arwenna wasn't sure.

'Of course not,' Arwenna answered. Why not? Lucy, despite her slight agitation, was pleasant enough, and Arwenna enjoyed meeting people, and it was certainly a better alternative to spending the evening alone with Garth.

'That's settled, then.' He looked at his watch, poured out more champagne for them all, and added: 'We'll all go together from here. Where's your car, Lucy?'

'Outside.'

'Give me the keys, and I'll get Fred to put it in the car park. You won't want to drive home after you've been drinking, will you?'

'No, but I was going to go home and then get a taxi.'

'Save time. He says to go now, before it gets too crowded.'

'But I must change—' began Lucy.

'Rubbish! You look gorgeous as you are, and you know it. Besides, if I know Rollo's little do's half the guests will be wearing jeans and tee-shirts!'

Lucy gave Arwenna a helpless look. 'There's no point in arguing with him, as you'll find out if you're going to work for him, darling.'

Arwenna gave a noncommittal smile, and Garth went on: 'I'll have a shave, change my shirt, and we're off.' He finished his glass, and Arwenna stood up.

'May I phone James before we go?'

'Sure. There's one in your bedroom.' He walked out. Arwenna turned to Lucy, about to excuse herself, and saw a look of stunned disbelief on the other's face. Lucy's eyes were wide.

'Are you *staying* here?' she asked.

'Yes.' Arwenna sat down slowly. 'Why?'

Lucy shook her head. 'Oh!' was all she said. Arwenna felt an irrational flare of annoyance, but hid it. It wasn't after all, *her* fault that she was staying.

'Why?' she demanded, and Lucy looked at her, perhaps sensing Arwenna's impatience.

'Has he mentioned Marcia?' she said.

'No. Who's she?'

Lucy gave a faint smile. 'An—acquaintance of mine, and a very good friend of Garth's.'

'A—*very* good friend?' queried Arwenna with delicacy.

Lucy nodded. 'Mmm. And she'll be there tonight.'

'Which is why you looked rather anxious when you knew *I'd* been asked to the party.'

Lucy's mouth twitched. 'Did I? You're very quick, aren't you?'

'Yes. So are you.'

They looked at each other, and there was a sudden mutual understanding. 'You'd better tell me,' said Arwenna, 'before Garth gets back. Is Marcia the jealous type?'

'You could say that.'

'And she's a friend of yours?'

Lucy laughed. 'We're both models. We both do T.V. work. I've known Marcia for a couple of years.'

'Doesn't she mind you coming here alone?'

'Not a bit. Garth and I like each other, but we don't fancy each other, and she knows it. I've got a special boy-friend, so as far as Marcia's concerned, I'm no threat. But, oh *dear,* she won't like you.'

'Lucy, I'm engaged, and I love my fiancé. I have no interest in Garth at all, I promise you,' Arwenna assured her.

'I believe you, ducky. But—as they say—try telling that to Marcia.'

'Is he in love with her?'

Lucy frowned. 'I don't think so. She'd like him to be, but he's an elusive bird, is our Garth. She's good company, fantastically witty, beautiful—got loads of men after her, but only wants one.'

'Well, the party should be interesting,' said Arwenna, 'if nothing else.' She stood up again, and Lucy said quickly, quietly:

'Arwenna, a word of advice—'

Arwenna paused, half turned away. 'Yes?'

Lucy pulled a face. 'Be careful.'

'You mean—keep out of her way?'

'Something like that.'

'Thanks for the warning. But why?'

'Why what?'

'Why tell me? She's your friend—I'm nobody really. I shouldn't even be there.'

'She can try and make you feel small—she would spoil your evening. It's just a friendly warning, no more,' Lucy explained.

Arwenna nodded. 'Then thank you, Lucy. I'll remember your advice.' She gave her a reassuring smile. 'If you'll excuse me, I'll go and phone my fiancé.'

Lucy watched her go, then she bit her lip and shook her head. Arwenna wondered fleetingly, as she went into her bedroom, if Garth had made sure she was invited, knowing what Marcia's probable reaction would be. It seemed likely. Perhaps he enjoyed playing people off against each other. If so he would be disappointed. They seemed, from what she had just heard of Marcia, an ideally matched pair, well suited in every way. Even Lucy's suggestion, that Marcia would be jealous, was preposterous. She began to laugh softly at the thought as she picked up the telephone receiver from the bed-side table, and started to dial.

Three hours later, she wasn't laughing.

CHAPTER FOUR

THE ROOM in which the party was being held was so crammed with people that it was a simple matter to avoid anyone. Arwenna had been introduced to so many that she had forgotten half the names instantly, had been chatted up by four good-looking men—not all at once—and plied with drink until she was pleasantly muzzy; and was thoroughly enjoying herself. She had seen little of Garth since arriving, had managed a brief conversation with Lucy, and their host, Rollo, a slim middle-aged man with silvery over-long hair and delicate manner who went around kissing everyone indiscriminately, and was extremely tipsy, and she had seen Marcia twice, in passing. She was stunning-looking, and always at the centre of a crowd of admirers, and Arwenna began to think that Lucy had overdramatised everything— even though with good intentions—until she went to the bathroom which led off a main bedroom and when she came out Marcia was waiting for her.

She noticed two things straightaway. The bedroom door was closed, and Marcia was icily, coldly, angry. It was such a contrast to the laughing, beautiful face that Arwenna had glimpsed before that it was almost as though this were a different woman. 'Are you Arwenna?' Marcia asked.

'Yes, I am,' Arwenna smiled, only slightly puzzled. She had, after all, been warned. 'And you're Marcia.'

'And I want a private word in your ear, dear,' said Marcia silkily.

'Fire away. We're alone—but not for long, I should imagine,' Arwenna answered cheerfully.

'What I have to say won't take long. What's your little game with Garth?'

'Game?' Arwenna laughed. 'What do you mean? I'm working for him—hasn't he told you?'

'Yes, he has. But he doesn't normally have his employees living at his apartment.' Marcia's eyes glittered coldly.

'Oh, I wouldn't know about that. I only met him yesterday,' said Arwenna, hearing the other's indrawn hiss of breath with some satisfaction.

'You little *tramp!*' spat the other. 'There's only one woman stays there—and that's me. I don't know what the hell you're thinking of, but *you* can leave tonight, do you hear? *I'll* be going back there with him after the party and we won't want you.'

'Where do you suggest I go?'

'I don't give a damn, quite frankly. Just go.'

'And what would I tell him?'

Marcia moved nearer to her. She was as tall as Arwenna, dressed in a shiny cat-suit in pink, and very high heels. She should have looked ridiculous, but she was very elegant. 'That you can't stay—what else?'

'Suppose I tell him you've threatened me?' asked Arwenna.

'He wouldn't believe you—and I'd deny it.' Marcia smiled slowly, cat-like. 'He'd want to believe me, anyway—if you see what I mean.'

'Oh, I see all right. You're his mistress?'

'And don't intend to be usurped by some country yokel. You get my meaning?'

'I think so.' Arwenna widened her eyes innocently. 'And I suggest you tell him so yourself, because I have no intention of leaving until I'm ready. You get *my* meaning?'

Marcia reached out and slapped Arwenna's face hard. It hurt. Arwenna caught her breath in shock, and the other said, low and shaking, 'You'll regret it—I mean it! He won't always be there—'

Slap! Arwenna stepped forward, lashed out with all her strength, and caught Marcia a stinging blow across the cheek. She moved even faster then, reached out and grabbed Marcia by the shoulder and shook her hard.

'Don't you ever dare hit me again,' she said furiously. 'And don't threaten me. I'm not in the least bit interested in your lover—as far as I'm concerned, you're welcome to him!'

Marcia wrenched herself free, gave a cry, and launched herself on Arwenna. Without even thinking about it, Arwenna twisted round, bent, caught the other's arm, and sent her sprawling. Before Marcia could get her breath, Arwenna was standing over her, and said: 'I warned you—*dear*—I'm a damned sight stronger than you, and I'll finish what I have to say, and you'll damned well listen, you vicious bitch. I'm going to tell him what you've done, and if he wants me to leave, I will—but only if *he* wants me to. Not *you*. Do I make myself clear?'

Hate-filled eyes glared back at her. Arwenna pulled Marcia to her feet as a pounding came on the door, and a voice: 'Hey, what's going on?'

She opened the door, which Marcia had bolted, and Lucy stood there, eyes horrified. 'Hi, Lucy,' said Arwenna. 'Marcia's in there,' and she walked out and back to the party. The first person she saw, waiting at the end of the corridor, was Garth.

'What's the matter?' he demanded, face hard.

'Don't you know?' Arwenna asked. She suddenly realized that she was shaking, and rubbed her bare arms. 'I've just been threatened by your mistress, who seemed to think I was after you.' He glanced along towards the closed bedroom door. A raised voice could be heard from behind it.

'You're joking,' he said.

'Don't be stupid,' she snapped. 'If I was going to make something up, it wouldn't be that. She slapped my face, if you must know.'

He started to walk towards the door, and Arwenna caught up with him and held his arm. 'Just a moment,' she said. 'You'd better hear the rest of it. I hit her back harder—and if she tries anything with me again, I promise you she'll be sorry. You can tell her that. I'll wait here. If you want me to leave your flat you'd better find me a hotel.'

Garth looked down at her. 'There's no question of that,' and he pushed open the door and went in. Arwenna heard Marcia's loud sobbing, and the next moment Lucy came out. The door closed, and Lucy looked at Arwenna.

'My God!' she whispered. 'What happened?' Her face was white with shock.

Arwenna shrugged. 'You were right. I apologise—I thought you were exaggerating. She told me she wanted a word with me, and then told me to leave Garth's flat—I refused, so she hit me—I hit her back—and she came off slightly worse in the fight that followed.'

'Stay there, and I'll get you a drink,' said Lucy. 'There's a loo at the end of the corridor. If anyone else comes along, direct them there. There's a big scene going on in the bedroom.' She pulled a face. 'Won't be a moment.'

She came back a minute or so later holding a glass. 'Brandy,' she said. 'Drink that. I'm sorry, Arwenna, I saw her go after you, but I waited a while—I should have knocked sooner. She'd locked the door, you see.'

'Yes.' Arwenna shivered. 'I'm sorry. I don't like unpleasantness, but she got me so mad—'

'She's had it coming to her for a while.' Lucy shook her head. 'She's always had her own way, always—I suppose she imagined you'd meekly take everything from her, as most people do.' She looked at Arwenna with sympathy-filled eyes. 'I did try. She's always been so careful not to let Garth see her temper, but now—' she shrugged.

'I hope she won't take it out on you,' said Arwenna.

Lucy grinned slightly. 'She'll be sorry if she tries! I'm not a shy little creature myself, believe it or not.'

'I'm sure you're not.' The door opened, and Garth came out. He looked at Lucy.

'Lucy, do you want to stay, or would you like a lift home? I think it's time we left.'

Lucy grimaced. 'Hadn't I better go and pick up the pieces?'

He shook his head. 'Marcia has a—headache. She'll come out when she's ready. But it's up to you.'

Lucy nodded. 'Give me a minute.' She left them alone. The noise of the music was loud, the voices nearly as much so.

Garth looked at Arwenna, and a muscle moved in his jaw. 'I'm sorry about this,' he said.

'Don't apologise. You could have warned me it might be hazardous working for you, though. I'd have been more prepared.'

'It won't be in future,' he assured her.

'I hope not. I'm not used to being physically assaulted.'

'But you gave better than you got.'

Arwenna smiled slightly. 'I've worked in Italy and Greece and I've learned how to look after myself.' Sudden, raw tension sparked between them, and she saw his face change, was aware that her own had too. She felt lightheaded, almost dizzy. Nothing had prepared her for this.

'I was right about you,' said Garth, as if choosing his words carefully. 'You are unique.'

'What did you say to her?' she asked breathlessly. She wanted to move away, but couldn't. She wanted to escape, but there would be none.

'Not a lot. I told her we were through, then I came out.'

She shivered. That was it, with him. Finish, the end. She was glad she didn't love him; to do so would be to become vulnerable. 'You are hard,' she whispered.

'Yes, I am.' He took her arm as Lucy came out, alone. 'Let's go.'

They were driving away before Lucy spoke. 'Marcia was crying,' she said. 'I didn't like leaving her.'

'Marcia will recover. She's going away to Malta on a job in a couple of days, and you can bet she'll be all right for that.'

'I didn't think you could be so hard, Garth.'

'I didn't realise that Marcia had such a temper until now. I'd never believed the things I'd heard, and I thought it was jealousy because she's so successful, but now I realise it wasn't.' He turned and grinned at Lucy as they drew to a halt outside a block of flats. 'Thanks for breaking it up, Lucy. What time do you need your car for tomorrow and I'll see you get it?'

'I'll collect it in the morning.' She slid across the back seat to the pavement side. 'Thanks for the lift. Goodnight, Garth, Arwenna.'

'Goodnight.' He waited until she had gone inside the main entrance and drove on. Fifteen minutes later they were entering his apartment.

ARWENNA AWOKE from a deep sleep to see the sun streaming in through the open curtains. Someone was knocking at her door.

'Come in,' she said, and Garth came in with a cup and saucer.

'Good morning. I've brought you coffee. I'm going out in a few minutes.' He put the cup down on her table, and beside it, a key. 'I don't know when I'll be back. There's a key for you to let yourself in. Tell the hall porter your name and he'll let you up in the lift. If you want to go shopping, get a taxi—he'll call one for you. It goes on my account. If you want to phone anyone, feel free. I'll phone if I'm any later than you. Oh, and there's toast ready in the kitchen. Want some?'

There was no tension now. He was being polite, the perfect host, in fact. 'I'm rather hungry,' Arwenna confessed. 'I'll get my robe on and come out.'

'Okay, I'll take this coffee back and have one with you before I go.' He took the cup and went out, closing the door after him. Arwenna picked up the key, looked at it, and put it down. Then she got out of bed and padded barefoot to the bathroom.

In the kitchen Garth had set out her toast with butter and marmalade, and two cups of coffee. He was dressed in a very conservative charcoal grey suit and tie, and a white shirt.

'Sit down and eat,' he said.

Arwenna obediently sat down and began to butter toast. 'Want some?'

'No, thanks, I've eaten. Are you all right? Did you sleep well?'

'Yes, thanks—and yes, like a log. I always do.'

He gave a faint smile. 'Good. Will you see your aunt today?'

'This morning, if I can.' She had no intention of taking a taxi anywhere.

'Give her my regards when you do.'

'I will.'

Garth finished his coffee and stood up. 'I'll see you later. Goodbye.'

'Goodbye.' She waited, and heard the outer door close. She was completely alone. It was a strange feeling, to be in his apartment alone. She hadn't even seen all round it; there had been no time after her arrival. It seemed to Arwenna that he must trust her to leave her there when he scarcely knew her.

That was an odd feeling to have. She finished the toast and went to shower and dress. Afterwards she walked round the huge main room, just admiring, not touching anything. The view drew her to the window and she looked out to see rooftops gilded in sunlight, and tall buildings, and people and cars far below. All was so silent, as if she watched a film, and she saw that the window was double-glazed. A flash of movement caught her eye, and a pigeon flew past, shadowing the sun for an instant of time. Arwenna looked round again, and wondered why Garth should want to return to Raneley when he had this. She had met many of his friends the previous night, before her regrettable encounter with Marcia, and they were a world away from the people of Raneley, like a different race. She hugged her arms to her sides. He was one of them, no longer the village boy. He was worldly, hard, quick-thinking. Why then return? The slower pace of village life would not be for him, surely?

She might as well go out. The key was safely in her handbag, and she had sufficient money for small purchases, as well as her banker's card, which she didn't intend to use at all, but it was nice to have, in case... She grinned to herself. Time to go.

Ten minutes later she was walking into the clinic, and two hours after that was gazing round Fortnum and Mason's in wide-eyed wonder.

SHE RETURNED to the apartment at three, with a small stack of books from a secondhand shop, and a jar of strawberry jam from Fortnum's. Her legs ached from walking, and she had been lost more than once, and had to ask until she had bought a map. She put them down in her bedroom and went to make herself a cup of coffee in the kitchen.

Now what? Did she wait for Garth to return, like an obedient employee—or slave—or did she go out again? She sighed, took her coffee into the large room, sat by the window, and drank it slowly while she thought about it.

The shrill of the telephone startled her, so loud was it in the silence. She picked it up and gave the number.

'Hello, Arwenna, it's Garth. I've tried several times to get you.'

'I've only just got in,' she answered.

'So I guessed. Look, I'm tied up in a meeting for an hour or so. Do you want to do some work for me?'

'Yes.'

'My study's two doors along from the kitchen. Go in, and on the desk you'll find several folders relating to property abroad. Read them, but don't bother to write anything down yet, just translate mentally. See how you go. If you see anything you feel I ought to know, jot down notes—you'll know what I mean. There are several foreign dictionaries on the study bookshelves. You can practise typing as well. Paper in a drawer—'

'I don't like going through drawers if you're out,' she protested.

'Anything that's open isn't private. Feel free. If you need me, call me at this number—got a pencil?' Arwenna opened the small notepad at the side of the telephone. There was a pencil attached to it.

'Yes.' She wrote the number he gave her and closed the book.

'Only phone if it's important. If the phone in the study goes, you needn't touch it. It's on the answering machine, and is a separate line. Any questions?'

'No.'

'Right. Goodbye.' The line went dead. No, you certainly don't waste time—or words, Arwenna thought, and pulled a little face. At least her problem was solved.

Feeling not a little curiosity, she pushed open the door next but one to the kitchen, and went into a large room. It was full of bookshelves, filing cabinets, a huge desk with an electric typewriter in the centre, several folders neatly beside it, and a desk calendar.

The walls that weren't lined with books were poster-filled, pictures of large villas and houses and castles. There was also a large wall calendar, with the whole year spread out at a glance. She looked round her, taking it all in. A telephone was on a table by the window, attached to a machine. Arwenna went over to the desk, sat down, picked up the top folder, which was labelled, 'France', and opened it. She was confronted with a thick wedge of papers, illustrated brochures of property in France, of all types, and all in French. She put it aside and opened the next folder, marked, 'Italy'. The same type of papers, but now, not surprisingly, in Italian. There was a week's work here alone.

Arwenna opened a few desk drawers, found a notepad and ballpoint pen, carried the two folders with them back into the main room, settled herself down by the window after first making a cup of coffee, and began to read. She started on the French papers, found that the mental effort of translating as she went along tiring at first, then, as her mind adjusted, becoming easier until she was skimming quite rapidly over each separate brochure.

She laid each one neatly face down when finished, on the table, and that pile grew, and the unread one got smaller, and a pattern was beginning to emerge, which she found intriguing. She picked up the pad and started making notes.

Time passed, but she was scarcely aware of it, until she heard the door open and footsteps. She looked up to see Garth coming in, then at her watch.

It was past seven o'clock. He flung his briefcase down and walked over to her. 'Busy?' he queried.

She stretched. 'Yes. I'd lost count of time. I must have been sitting here nearly four hours!'

'There's dedication.' He seemed amused about something. 'Anyone ring?'

'Not in here. The phone in your study went several times, but I left it.' She blinked. 'I'm hungry—I've just realised.'

'Did you have any lunch?'

'A couple of sandwiches in a snack bar while I was shopping.'

'We'll eat out. Go and do your hair, or whatever it is you women do.'

'No, I'll stay here, thanks all the same.' She picked up a brochure in danger of sliding to the carpet. 'I've nearly finished the French folder.'

'Well? Anything strike you?'

'Yes. I've made notes. Want to hear them?'

Garth sat down. 'Fire away.'

She looked at him. 'Is there something you find funny? Have I a smut on my nose or something?'

He peered closely at her face, and Arwenna felt vaguely annoyed. 'No, all's clear. I don't find anything funny—I was just surprised at your dedication. Have you been through all these?' He tapped the larger stack.

'Yes. It's what you asked me to do.'

He shook his head. 'You're a quick reader.'

'I know. Once I'd started it all came back. The first couple were a strain, then it was just like reading English.'

'Amazing! I chose right, picking you to work for me. You're going to be very valuable. How do you feel about going to France in a week or so when your aunt's recovered from her operation?' He said it as casually as if he'd asked her if she would like a drink.

Arwenna dropped the papers on the table. 'What?'

'France—next week—once Aunty's home?' he repeated in abbreviated form, face expressionless.

She shook her head. 'But—Raneley Hall—James' father—' then belatedly: 'James—'

Garth held up three fingers and pointed to the first. 'There's a team working from tomorrow at the Hall, under the supervision of a very competent foreman. Two—I'll see James' father immediately we return to Raneley next week. It's Wednesday today, your aunt has her op tomorrow morning, and all going well, should be out by a week on Friday. We'll fly to Paris a week on Monday, by which time all will have been arranged with the Colonel. Three—James. Well, what about James? He knows you're working for me, doesn't he?'

'Yes, but not going abroad with you.'

'You object?'

'He might—he will—' she began.

'That wasn't my question. I said, do *you?*'

It was there again, the indefinable blurring of the senses in his presence that made Arwenna feel as if she was being swept along with a tide, helpless, unable to resist anything. 'You don't understand,' she said feebly.

'It's quite simple to me—it seems it's you that doesn't understand,' he answered.

'No. You said—when you *blackmailed* me into this job,' she added, emphasising that important word, 'that you'd be working from Raneley. You never said anything about going abroad with you.'

'True, I didn't. But flexibility is the key word for my staff. My plans are changing all the time. It's now rather essential that I go, and I want you with me. I've got some important deals lined up that will mean a lot of money. I don't have to remind you that your aunt is in the clinic, and the operation goes ahead tomorrow—so it's a bit late for you to back down out of our arrangement now.'

Arwenna jumped to her feet. 'That's—'

'Blackmail? Can't you find another word for a change?'

'No, damn you, I can't!' she blazed, suddenly angry, and he stood up and grabbed her arms.

'Calm down! You'd think I was going to torture you— I'm offering you a chance to go to France, travel round with me visiting beautiful places—a chance which, I might add, any one of a number of my staff would give their eye teeth for—and you're throwing a tantrum fit to—'

'I'm not!' she stormed, and pulled herself free. 'Anyone who doesn't agree with *you* is childish. Hah! That's typical male logic. I don't buy it, so don't try it again. You've led me into this gradually and cleverly, haven't you? One little step at a time and she won't notice. Well, I'm not as stupid as you think, Mr Vanner—I'm supposed to be terribly flattered and honoured. I'm not—I'm engaged to James, and I'm going to marry him, and *that's* all I want. Your money and your power doesn't impress me *one bit*—so why don't you take one of your starry-eyed secretaries or whatever, and do them, and me, a favour?'

'For one very obvious reason,' he said, apparently unmoved by her tirade. He looked her slowly up and down. 'Because you've got more personality in your little finger than most of them have in their whole bodies. Because you're different—and because you're bloody well wasted working in a café and I suspect you know it.'

'That's a horrible thing to say!' she burst out. 'Aunt Daisy—'

'Aunt Daisy is a lovely gentle person whom I respect and admire, and she's happy and content to run her café, and that's as it should be. But you've no place there, and you know it. The world can be yours, and all that's in it—yet you go and get yourself engaged to a young fool like James—'

He got no further, Arwenna stepped forward, incensed, and struck out at his face. But her hand never connected. He gripped her wrist, swifter than thought, and held it away from him.

'You don't like the truth,' he said harshly. 'But don't go and hit me because I tell you the things you deny. We are two of a kind—'

'Never!' she spat, eyes narrowed.

'Two of a kind,' he repeated relentlessly, still holding her as though she had never interrupted. 'Fighters, both knowing what we want out of life, although you've missed your way lately.'

'You're talking rubbish,' she cut in. 'And let me *go!*'

'When I choose to,' he answered. 'When I've finished what I'm going to say.'

'You've finished already as far as I'm concerned,' she snapped, and tried to pull her hand free of his. 'I'm *not* like *you*. You're ruthless, hard—'

'Perhaps. Not in that sense. You're neither of those things—but you have other qualities that we both recognise in each other, whether you choose to admit them or not. I saw them in you straight away, as soon as I met you—which was when I knew that I wanted you.' His eyes were dark and serious, strangely so, as he looked at her, and the last six words that he had said seemed to stay there, echoing and re-echoing in Arwenna's mind, double-edged, and meaning more, much more than what had gone before. She was still, no longer trying to free herself from his grasp, and it was as if in a strange way she knew that everything had been leading up to this moment. As if something had been said which would never be taken back.

She could feel Garth's hand clasp on her wrist, feel every inch of his skin on hers, and his hand was warm and strong, and the touch was an electric current that coursed through her very blood and made her temples pound and the pulse beat rapidly at her throat. Everything about him became etched sharply in her awareness. It was as if she saw him with all her senses, as if she could touch him, hear him, with her eyes. The tall powerful size of him, the smooth tanned face, not quite as hard now. The eyes, a clear grey-blue, dark-lashed, his mouth wide, sensual, full-lipped, nose straight, big, not too big, dark hair that was smooth and healthy-looking, a thick powerful neck on equally powerful shoulders. All this she saw as if seeing him for the first time, and she couldn't look away, couldn't move.

'I—don't—want—you,' she managed to say, and it was as if she had to force each word out separately.

'But you will,' he said softly, insistently.

'No!' The word was jerked from her.

He smiled, then he released her hand, and she rubbed it as if to erase his touch. 'We'll have a drink,' he said. 'Then we'll go and have a meal.'

'I don't want to go out with you,' she answered. 'I don't want to go anywhere with you—'

He walked away from her, poured two glasses of brandy and brought them back. 'You've just had a shock,' he said. 'Drink that, and you'll feel better, Arwenna. We'll talk about France and the folder, over our meal.'

'Don't you ever listen to me?' She swallowed some brandy and gasped as it went down, warm, soothing—and made her feel a little better.

He looked at his glass, held it up to the light, sipped a drop. 'Cheers,' he said. 'What did you say?'

'Damn you! You *don't* listen. I'm staying here. I'll cook something for myself—'

Garth sighed. It was quite a patient sigh as though he was prepared to humour her. 'I've a table booked for eight o'clock at a delightful Italian restaurant not ten minutes from here. We'll walk if you like. I've had a hellishly busy day and need a break. I do not want to eat in. Do you understand? We'll have a pleasant meal and return here, then I will go into my study and work for a couple of hours, then go to bed. I've been working hard so as to keep my morning free tomorrow so that I can wait with you for news from the clinic. Now, am I asking too much?'

Arwenna's resistance had been gradually crumbling away as he spoke, and his last words clinched it. Why hadn't he said that before?

She nodded. 'You—you've done it again, haven't you?'

'I always do.' He finished his brandy. 'I'll go and change. We'll leave in twenty minutes. Can you be ready for then?'

'Yes.' She put her glass down. Then, because it had to be asked, and while there would never be a right time, because she didn't really want to hear the answer, the sooner she asked it the better, she said: 'Before you go—what did you mean when you said, "I knew that I wanted you"?'

'I thought you'd never ask. Don't you know?'

'I want you to tell me,' she answered very quietly. Her mouth had gone dry.

'How does any man want a woman? I want to make love to you—to be with you, to know you in the fullest sense of the word—'

'And is that why you brought me here?' she gasped, shocked, even though it was the answer she had sensed she would hear.

'No. What do you take me for? That would be crude in the extreme, to put you in the difficult position of having nowhere to stay.'

'Then France? Is that what you expect?'

He smiled slightly. 'I'm not a fool, Arwenna. Nor am I impatient—about some things. You'll be as safe in France as you are here. When I make love to you, it will be because you want it as much as I do.'

'Then that will be *never!* You'll be wasting your time,' she cut in swiftly, but even as she said the words it was as though she was only saying what she felt she must. The strangest things were happening to her—a fine inner tremor, a warmth she didn't understand, a sense of weakness in her legs, as though she could hardly stand. She didn't like this man, because of all he was, and had done, but never could she deny his power to manipulate. She felt, for the first time in her life, frightened.

He looked at her, and there was much in that glance she didn't understand. She went on quickly: 'You said once, when I accused you of taking over my life, that no one could do that, only if I let them—yet it's what you're trying to do now, isn't it? You're telling me what you're going to do—and it's—' She stopped, overwhelmed by the strength of her own emotion. She felt breathless, and vulnerable, and helpless. She shivered and rubbed her arms, and looked at him, and there was nothing of laughter or amusement in his eyes or face now, he was deadly serious. 'W-why don't you leave me alone?'

'Because something began when we met, something I don't understand either. But we both know it. Life changes all the time. We meet people, we travel, we talk, links are made, and broken, nothing remains static. For us, for both of us, nothing can ever be the same again. There's no going back. There never will be.' White-faced, she listened to his words, and when he had finished speaking he added: 'Now you know.' He turned and walked away from her, out of the room, and there was silence.

Arwenna put her hand to her mouth and pressed the knuckles against her lips. She tried desperately to think of James, but nothing came. She couldn't picture his face at all. She wondered if she was going mad.

CHAPTER FIVE

THE CONVERSATION might never have been. Garth's behaviour when they went out was different again. Impersonal, businesslike, he asked her what she had thought about the contents of the French folder, and she told him.

'Very astute,' he said, when she had finished. 'You must know France well.'

'Enough to see, once I'd made a few notes, that these properties more or less stretch in a curving line from Paris to Nice, but none of them on the main routes—the Routes Nationales.'

'No. Tourists miss a lot of the old France, the real country, in their efforts to get from A to B—or in most cases from Paris to the South.'

'But I'm still none the wiser as to why,' she said. 'I mean, you can't be planning to buy a whole series of châteaux and hotels in a line.'

Garth laughed. 'No, I'm not. But I'm going to look at as many as I can when we go. We'll drive from Paris and follow the old trails, and visit the hotels particularly, not as a prospective buyer but as a guest. A business friend of mine is planning a book of alternative places to stay in France, small, out-of-the-way places off the beaten track for the more discerning tourist. I can see his point, and it's a damned good idea, and it'll work.'

'One snag. If everyone starts to go to these places, they'll no longer be out-of-the-way and ''off the beaten track'' as you put it. *They'll* become the in-places.'

'Not quite. It's a large country, and the scope is enormous. I'm just taking one aspect of it this time, but imagine a spider's web spread all over France, with small hotels all over the place, linked by minor roads instead of major ones—no, it'll work.'

'Is that what you do? Buy property?'

'Mainly. It's what I started out in when I was twenty, when houses were cheap. I worked up from a few to many— with a lot of hard work, and a stroke of good fortune at the right time.'

He looked at her across the dimly lit table of the small Italian restaurant. It was a corner table, in an alcove screened by trailing plants on a wooden trellis wall, and a red candle flickered in the Chianti bottle on the table, and they had eaten a delicious pasta, and were drinking a rosé wine. The restaurant was fairly crowded, but their corner was a quiet oasis in the desert of sound that swirled around nearby, not too near. It was nearly nine o'clock, and Arwenna felt tired after the events of the day, but she didn't want to go back, to be alone with Garth. 'You mean you just decided to go into property—why?'

'I'd worked on a building site for two years, and saved all I made. I'd also learnt plastering, carpentry, how to put in windows—' He held out his hands. 'Look at them. You can still see the scars—faded now, but there.' She looked. His hands were powerful and big, and she saw the old scars of callouses and cuts, marks that would probably never vanish, and he wasn't ashamed of them; he didn't need to be. 'So when I'd saved enough I bought a little terraced house in an unfashionable part of London—I'd studied the trends, and it seemed logical to me that the area was ripe for a takeover from the smart set—and I did the house up so that it was like new. The first couple who saw it when it was done bought it. I made enough on that one to buy two, equally derelict, in the same area. I worked an eighteen-hour day and slept in one of the houses, and paid a friend who was equally hard up but a good electrician to do the re-wiring.

By the time I was twenty-four I'd renovated ten houses and was looking around for more, in areas where prices were right. I'd got three men helping me, all damned hard workers who were prepared to do a good day's work for their pay—and then I bought a semi-detached in a bad state, and set to do it myself.

'There was an old chap living in the attached house and he did nothing but complain about the noise and the dust. He took me in to show me one morning after I'd spent a couple of days knocking out rotten cupboards, and he was quivering with indignation as he showed me the dirt my work had brought into his house.' He touched his glass thoughtfully. 'God, his house was a mess! How he could have told the difference between the dirt of years and the stuff I was supposed to have knocked through, I don't know. I was about to tell him so—fairly politely, when something made me stop. I looked round his living room. There was no carpet on the floor, just lino—worse than some I'd ripped out next door. He had a bed in one corner, no fire—and it was a bitter November day, and on the table were what looked like the remains of his breakfast, a stale crust and some margarine in the paper.

'I looked at him, and he wore gloves with no fingers—and he looked grey with cold. Only his indignation was keeping him going. I apologised profusely, assured him I'd do something about it, and the next day I went in just before lunchtime and told him I'd come to clean up. I took my Thermos of soup with me and my sandwiches—Bovril, I think they were.' He grinned very faintly at her. 'I spent as little as possible on myself in those days. I also took in a bucket of coal I'd dredged from my coalshed next door. I lit him a fire, asked him if he'd like to share my lunch, and began to sweep up. The poor old devil was desperately lonely. He told me his life story over the next two hours. Not a relative in the world, no hobbies—there wasn't even a book in the house—and only his stamp collection to look at. I expressed an interest in it, and we sat by a good fire and I looked through his album, and made him a cup of tea, and talked. I could have been working—I should have been getting on with repairs, but I didn't have the heart to leave him. Then I found a stamp that I thought might be valuable, and told him. You could almost see the suspicion flaring in his eyes, as though I was going to pinch it from him, so I suggested he write to any large philatelists and get it valued—in fact, I'd do it for him, I said.' He paused.

Arwenna, enthralled with the story, said impatiently: 'Was it valuable? What happened?'

'They gave him a fair price for it, about sixty pounds if I remember. I got to know him well in the weeks that followed, took him something to eat every day—it was the only hot meal he ever had, I suspect—and kept him going with fires. Then, when the job next door was nearly done, I felt a sense of obligation. He wasn't cantankerous when I got to know him, just old and lonely and poorly nourished. I got him fixed up with meals on wheels, left him with a good supply of coal that I'd bought, and promised to go and see him once a week. Then, one day in February, another bitter cold day, I went in and he was lying on the floor. He'd fallen and broken his hip. I got him into hospital and two months later he died there.' He gave a deep sigh. 'It was such a waste, a damned waste! If only I'd known before—'

'Known what?' she asked, disturbed by his words, and saddened.

Garth looked at her, eyes bleak. 'A month after he died I received a solicitor's letter, asking me to call in. When I got there, they told me that old Mr Simpson had left everything to me in his Will.' He took a deep breath. 'Do you know what I thought? I thought it would be his stamp collection—I—' he paused, and closed his eyes, as though in pain. 'God, what a *waste!*'

'*What?*' she demanded urgently.

'He'd left me eighty thousand pounds. *Eighty thousand.* It was all in stocks and shares that he'd accumulated over the years and never touched, and the money had grown and grown—and he'd lived like a recluse, not touching it. He could have lived in luxury, with good food and heat—but he hadn't. I felt ill at first. The money just didn't sink in at all until later. Then, when I realised that I actually possessed that amount, I vowed I would make use of it—as a sort of tribute to him, if you like. I didn't feel as though it belonged to me—I'd done nothing to deserve it.'

'You'd befriended an old man, fed him, helped him, talked to him—'

'But not for that. I thought he was penniless. I felt sorry for him.'

'You were the only friend he had,' she said softly. 'That must have meant a lot.' She was seeing another aspect of Garth, a side of him that wasn't all hard and decisive. He was a man who had taken pity on a fellow human being, and in so doing reaped a reward far greater than anyone could have envisaged.

'That's what I told myself, and so I went ahead and did all the things I'd imagined would take me years to do. I took calculated risks, studied the trends in house moving, bought a block of flats—and never looked back.'

'The men who worked with you at first, what happened to them?' she asked.

'Mike, the electrician, is a director in one of my companies up north. The other two, Bob and Eddy, are here in London. You'll probably meet them soon. I never forget those who've helped me.'

Arwenna smiled faintly. 'I'm sure you don't.'

A waiter was hovering respectfully near, and Garth beckoned him over. 'Do you want anything else to eat?' he asked her.

She shook her head. 'No, thanks.'

'Then I'll have the bill, please.' The waiter beamed and vanished, and Arwenna regarded Garth steadily.

'Are we going back to your apartment now?' she asked him.

'If you don't mind. I've a lot to catch up on.'

'Can I help you?'

'Do you want to? You don't have to work all day *and* all evening.'

'I'd like to.'

'Okay, fine.' He paid the bill and they went out into a cool summer's evening. It was still light, and the roads were busy. 'Shall we get a taxi or walk?' he asked her.

'Walk,' she answered promptly. The wine had left her rather lightheaded. She wasn't used to drinking much, and they had somehow consumed two bottles of a delightful rosé wine that had seemed very innocuous at the time, but whose effects she was now feeling.

'I don't want to worry you, but you're weaving about slightly,' said Garth, and took hold of her arm.

'Am I?' The pavement had seemed a little uneven to her sandalled feet. 'It was that wine. I thought it was harmless.'

'It is. At least,' he corrected himself, looking down at her, 'I thought it was.'

'It's not—you're not—trying to get me drunk, are you?' she asked suddenly.

He burst out laughing, a hearty laugh that made an old woman walking her dog look round, shocked-faced, and sniff disapprovingly before pulling her dog's lead sharply and moving away. 'To seduce you?' he said, when he could speak. 'You've been watching some corny old films, haven't you?'

Arwenna tried to pull her arm away, affronted at his laughter, but he tightened his grip. 'That's not my way,' he said quietly, and steered her towards the curb ready to cross.

'Then what is?' she demanded, still annoyed.

There was a gap in the traffic, and they walked quickly across. 'I've never needed one,' he answered.

'Implying that women fling themselves at you?'

'I didn't say that,' he chided. 'You mustn't read things into what I say.'

'Well, they would, wouldn't they?' she said tartly. 'You've got pots of money.'

'Thanks.' His voice was dry.

'I'm tired of this conversation,' Arwenna sighed.

'You started it, accusing me.'

'Can I phone when we get back?' she asked.

'Of course. Let me guess. James?'

'Yes, my fiancé.' She stressed the last word.

'You've told him where you're staying? In case he wants to phone you,' Garth added delicately.

'I—er—gave him the number. He didn't ask—' she swallowed.

'Oh, would he be annoyed?'

'What the hell do *you* think?'

'He'd be annoyed,' he said gently.

'I'll tell him tonight.'

'Just as long as you feel strong enough—'

'What does that mean?' she asked crossly.

He shrugged. 'You know him better than I do. Do you ever have rows?'

'That's none of your business!'

They were rounding the corner, nearing the block of flats in which Garth lived, and a Rolls-Royce was just drawing away from the front entrance.

The driver tooted, and Garth raised his free hand in salute. It vanished round the corner. 'I should imagine you do, myself, being of such different temperaments.'

'I didn't ask you,' she said pertly, and ran up the steps of the main door. He followed her in, towards the lift, and the hall porter came out from behind his counter, waving two envelopes.

'Mr Vanner, sir,' he called. 'Couple of messages for you.'

'Thanks, Fred.' Garth took them from him, and put them in his jacket pocket. The lift shot upwards, and Arwenna realised something rather belatedly. The lift had only one button: it said 'Penthouse'. It hadn't occurred to her before, because the doorman had ushered her into it when she had come in that afternoon, and pressed the button for her. There were two other lifts in the spacious hall, and she could easily have got in one of those.

'Is this your private lift?' she asked.

'Yes.'

'Just for *you?*'

'Yes. The other lifts finish at the floor below.'

'Good gracious,' commented Arwenna. 'That's a bit posh, isn't it?' They had come to a halt, and the doors slid open. 'What happens if there's a fire?'

'Sensible question. You obviously haven't looked round. I'll show you.' He took her down the private hallway and opened a door. 'Stairs, leading directly down to the hall, bypassing the other floors. There's also a fire escape from outside my bedroom.'

'Burglars? If you can get down, they could get up,' she pointed out.

'Not with the alarms, they couldn't. I've got the latest electronic system installed. As you may have noticed, I have some antiques—I don't intend to let anyone help themselves. I've worked for all I have.'

'You let me into your apartment—and left me alone there. Weren't you bothered?' she asked, as they went into the apartment.

He looked at her as if faintly shocked. 'I didn't think for a moment about it.'

Which meant that he trusted her. It gave Arwenna a warm feeling. But would she have trusted him if the positions were reversed? She suddenly thought, *I would trust him with my life.* And it was a strange thought to have, in the light of their previous conversation. She watched him as he walked away from her towards the drinks cupboard. With my life, with my life—the aftertaste of the realisation lingered, and it was true. It was also very disturbing. Something was happening to Arwenna that she didn't fully understand.

Garth had his back to her, at the cupboard. 'Why don't you go and telephone James while I'm fixing a drink?'

'Yes, I will. Nothing strong for me, please. Not if I'll be working. I need a clear head.'

He didn't turn around. 'A lot of orange juice and a little gin?'

'Perfect.' She ran up the steps, went through the doorway, and into her bedroom. She took a deep breath before dialling James' number. It was quite clear, when he answered, that he was annoyed, but was trying hard to control it.

'Where've you been?' he asked. 'I tried you last night— I've tried you half a dozen times today and again this evening and there was nothing, no reply—what kind of hotel is this, for heaven's sake?'

'Ah!' Now was the time for the truth, and it suddenly wasn't easy. 'I'm not at a hotel, James darling,' she said. 'Actually, this is Garth's *huge* apartment, and—'

'What?' His voice quivered. 'His *apartment?* You mean you're staying with *him?*'

'It's only round the corner from the clinic, love—hotels are hard to—'

'You're staying there with *him?* Who else is there?'

This was not going easily. 'No one,' she answered. 'Don't you trust me, James?'

There was such a long pause that she thought they had been cut off, then: 'I don't trust *him,*' he snapped. He wasn't annoyed any more, he was furiously angry. 'How the hell do you think I feel?'

'I know how you feel,' she answered. 'But let me remind you, it was your invitation to dinner that started all this.'

'I wondered how long it would be before you threw that at me,' he snapped. 'It didn't give you a licence to share his flat—and his bed, for all I—'

'Take that back!' she cut in. 'How *dare* you!'

'I dare. He's a real smoothie, right? And worth pots of money—'

Arwenna slammed the receiver down furiously, shaking with anger. 'Damn, damn, damn!' she muttered, and stood up. Still furious, she stalked into the main room and glared at Garth, who was holding a glass out.

'Your drink,' he said. 'Everything okay back at the ranch?'

'Cut out the sarcasm,' she snapped. She gave him a look that should have withered him, and he winced.

'Ouch! Something wrong?'

'Nothing's wrong. Everything's *perfect*. Why should anything be wrong?' she demanded.

'Because you look to me as though you'd like to stick a knife in someone—preferably me. Or could it be James?' There was no trace of laughter on his face, but it was in his eyes; amusement glinted, betraying him. He handed her the glass, not standing too near, as though frightened she might hit him.

She drank it all in one go, then gasped. 'Ah,' said Garth. 'I was just going to tell you—I'd only added a little orange. I was going to ask you to say when with it.' He produced a small jug of orange juice as if to give truth to his words, and managed to look apologetic. It didn't fool Arwenna for one moment. If he dared even smile, he'd be sorry. Just the merest flicker.

'Very amusing,' she said, when she had drawn a much-needed breath. 'Very, very fun—' The shrill ring of the telephone cut off her words. Garth looked at her, one eyebrow raised questioningly.

'James?' he queried.

'Most likely.'

'Do you want to?' He gestured towards the ringing telephone. Far better that she should answer it than he. She walked over and picked it up.

'Hello,' she said. A woman's voice came, not James'.

'Hello?' It was a puzzled word. 'Is Garth there?'

'Yes. Just a moment, please.' Arwenna held out the receiver. 'For you,' she said.

He took it from her. 'Hello, Vanner here,' Then, after a pause during which Arwenna could hear the faint voice at the other end: 'A friend. Yes, staying here. Yes. No, I'm sorry, Paula, not for several days—yes, fine. I'll ring you as soon as I—' There was another long pause as he listened. Arwenna added orange juice to her glass and sipped it slowly. She was gradually calming down, not sure whom to be more annoyed with, James, Garth, or herself for slamming the phone down before. He had every right to be furious. She probably would have been, in his place.

The call was over. He replaced the receiver, face expressionless. 'Another lady friend?' she enquired sarcastically.

'Yes.' He picked up his glass. 'Ready for work?'

'There's nothing else to do, is there?' she answered.

'You could phone James back. You did hang up on him, didn't you?'

'How did you know that?'

'I went to the kitchen for the orange juice. I couldn't help overhearing it slam down.'

'I suppose you were listening as well?' she accused.

'I wouldn't dream of it,' he replied blandly. 'Mind you, now you mention it, I did hear you demanding that he take something back.'

'My God, you must have walked quickly to get back here after—'

'True.' He gave a modest smile. 'I'm a very fast mover.' He paused, as though to let the double-edged words sink in, then added: 'Had he insulted you?'

'Not so's you'd notice. Just accused me of sharing your bed,' she snapped.

Garth poured some gin into her glass, almost absentmindedly it seemed, and Arwenna watched him do it without realizing fully what he *was* doing. 'Good grief. That wasn't very nice—'

'Perhaps he knows you better than I,' she said.

'Perhaps. But he should also know you far better than he knows me. He should surely trust you—'

'He does!'

'It doesn't sound like it. Tell me, when he was pursuing
you hotly all over Europe, proposing to you, did he have any
cause to worry then?'

Arwenna really didn't know why she was standing here
talking to him. The subject should have been closed before—but it was difficult, with him. 'You mean was I running round with Frenchmen and Italians?' she said
scornfully. 'Don't be ridiculous! I was working, remember? I'd not have kept my job long if I'd been gadding
about.'

He regarded her very levelly. 'You must have had time off.
And I did see you at the party last night. You weren't doing
so badly for yourself.'

'I didn't think you'd noticed.' She laughed. 'Being chatted up, you mean? Mmm, that was fun—before that green-
eyed bitch of yours tried to assault me.'

'She's not my green-eyed bitch any more. I already apologised for that. Do you always have men following you
wherever you go?'

'All the time,' she answered. He'd be sorry he'd asked in
a minute. 'All right, I admit it. I had a *marvellous* time
abroad. Of course I had time off, and I made the most of it.
Do you want a list of my lovers?' She frowned. 'If I can remember their names, that is. Let's see, there was Henri, he
was a Belgian diplomat in Paris, very charming, we had a
glorious weekend in Brussels—'

Garth wasn't looking amused any more. His eyes were
very hard and cold. 'All right,' he said. 'Joke's over—'

'It's no joke,' she said, enjoying herself. 'He proposed to
me in bed! Now there's an original place for a proposal, isn't
it?' It was true—but not in the way she intended him to take
it. Henri had indeed proposed, and *he* had been in bed with
'flu on a very respectable visit to his family in Brussels. 'And
then there was Philippe—French, very wealthy—let me see,
we had a super fling when my family went off for a few
days—' She gave a throaty chuckle. Philippe had indeed
been French, and wealthy, and he and Arwenna had spent

several days in the same house when the family who employed her had gone away to visit a sick grandmother—
leaving their children with Arwenna. And they had had a
glorious, fun-filled time, because Philippe, a cousin of Madame la Roche, her employer, was fantastic with the children and had tired them out all day, devising new and
original games for them to play. He was also only twelve,
and his mother had left him in Arwenna's care while she too
visited Grand'-mère.

'I get the picture,' said Garth dryly. 'Please spare me
any—'

'You asked,' she countered.

'True.' He took a swallow of his vodka and tonic as
though he needed it. 'But I didn't want a blow-by-blow account of your affairs.'

Arwenna began to laugh, glorious deep-throated laughter. If only he knew the truth! 'Then shall we begin work?'
she suggested.

'Perhaps we'd better.' Garth put down his glass. 'I'll go
and get the papers I need.' And he walked away. Arwenna
watched him go. Something had annoyed him. Why she had
spoken so outrageously, she would never know. It was totally out of character for her to do so—yet it was all a part
of the other things she didn't understand about herself—and
equally disturbing to her.

She bit her lip, suddenly unsure of herself, and went to the
table near the window, and began to tidy the folders there,
ready for Garth's return.

IT WAS morning. She had slept dreadfully, and awoke with
the sensation of having a terrible hangover. Groaning, she
sat up in bed and put her hand to her head. Then, realising
the time, she jumped out, pulled on her dressing gown, and
went into the kitchen.

Garth sat there, eating toast, fully dressed. 'It's after
nine,' she gasped.

'I know. Good morning, Arwenna,' he responded calmly.

'Good morning.'

'Do you want toast?'

'Yes, I'll do it.' She found the bread and popped two slices in the toaster.

'There was no point in waking you before. They're not operating until nine-thirty. I've been on the phone to Bill Chisholm, and all is fine. Your aunt had a comfortable night. They'll phone us when she comes round, and tell you when you can visit her.'

Arwenna took a deep breath. 'Thanks,' she said. 'I know it's silly, but—I'm shaky, now that it's going to happen—' She bit her lip. 'She's very dear to me.'

'I know, and she's in excellent hands. She's also a remarkably fit woman for her age, Arwenna. There's nothing to worry about. Sit down, I'll butter your toast. Pour yourself a cup of coffee.'

She obediently sat, and a few moments later Garth handed her her toast. 'Now eat up, then go and get dressed, and we'll do some more work. Easy stuff. You worked damned well last night, no wonder you slept on.'

She *had* worked hard the previous evening, they both had. Until past midnight, and the time had passed incredibly swiftly once they had begun. With Garth's words still resting uneasy in her mind, and her own confusion about her reaction, Arwenna had found it far easier to concentrate on the folder in French, and in the translation of it, and her mind had been sharpened accordingly, while he had made notes, asked pertinent questions, until there was another detailed folder, in English, on the table. He wrote quickly, and his sharp brain had stimulated Arwenna's, had exhilarated her. He was a challenge in himself, and when the work was done at last, and he had gone to make them both coffee, she had sat back and thought about the evening. She was tired, but it was the satisfying tiredness that comes only after stimulating work, and it had made her realise something about herself. She had never been so mentally pushed before, in any of her jobs. Some part of her had come alive.

She had known then that in spite of everything, Garth's 'blackmail', his reasons for getting her to work for him, she was going to enjoy her work for him.

She looked at him now. 'The Italian folder?' she queried.

'No. There's much more planning to be done for our French trip—or had you forgotten that?'

'How could I?' she countered.

A slight twitching of his mouth betrayed amusement. 'Then you can plan our itinerary, where we'll stay, etcetera. You've read enough to know which are the places that should be most interesting to me—or should do. It'll be interesting to see if our ideas coincide.'

'You're putting a lot of confidence in my judgment, aren't you?' she answered. 'I'm not a property expert.'

'You're a woman who's travelled a lot. So see yourself as a holidaymaker, a tourist. Base your plans on those lines. It is, after all, the tourists *I'm* concerned about. I work on a different wavelength—you will be my link, if you like.'

'With ordinary people? Thanks!' she said dryly.

'You *know* what I mean.' His voice had a sharper edge to it. 'We don't need to beat about the bush with each other any more, Arwenna. Not after last night.' His eyes were dark upon her and she couldn't look away. 'I told you, we're two of a kind. And after several hours working with you, I was even more convinced of it. Don't underestimate yourself—'

'I don't,' she cut in sharply.

'Then don't pick me up on words when you know damned well what I mean.'

She accepted the reprimand with a slight smile—a rueful smile, and Garth stood up. 'I'll go and get everything ready. Do you prefer to work in the lounge, or in the study?'

'The lounge.'

'Right. I'll be ready when you are.' He walked out, leaving her to finish her coffee.

Fifteen minutes later they had begun the morning's work, and it was different, but connected with their previous night's work, and gradually a picture began to emerge of what would soon be happening, and Arwenna found herself so totally absorbed in the plans that she was scarcely aware of the passage of time.

The telephone shrilled, and she dropped her pen and looked at him.

He stood up. 'I'll get it.' Arwenna looked at her watch. It was nearly twelve, and she heard him speaking, heard his voice, and her mouth was dry. Then she saw him nod, look across at her, and he raised his hand and gave her the thumbs-up sign. He was smiling.

She stood, suddenly shaky, her eyes filling with tears, her mouth quivering. Garth put the telephone down and walked across to her, and held her arms with his strong warm hands. 'She's fine,' he said. 'Fine and dandy. Came round from the anaesthetic about half an hour ago and went straight to sleep again.'

Arwenna tried to laugh, and it came out as a sob. Garth put his arms round her, gently, but very decisively. 'Don't cry, you cuckoo,' he scolded. 'We can go and see her soon.'

'I'm not crying,' her voice was muffled, leaning as she was against his chest. She felt her hair being stroked, and she felt very safe and sheltered, and warm. There was no question of her trying to move away. Just for the moment it seemed right for her to be there. 'I'm just so—happy and relieved that it's all over. Thank you Garth.' She lifted her face to look at him, and gave a tremulous smile. 'Thank you.'

She saw his eyes darken, felt his hold tighten fractionally, saw his mouth, and it was a warm, sensuous mouth. He had probably kissed, and been kissed by, many women, and she knew why, and she wanted him to kiss her, and suddenly it wasn't right for her to be there any more. She moved; she made a little sound in her throat and tried to move away, only she couldn't.

Then he put his hand at the back of her head, his fingers pressing into the tumble of deep auburn curls, and his mouth came down on hers in a long, lingering, beautiful kiss.

CHAPTER SIX

THEN IT was over, and Arwenna wasn't sure whether it had lasted a second or a lifetime. She only knew that no kiss had ever been so complete and wonderful. Shakily, as Garth released her—reluctantly, it seemed—she stepped away from him, eyes bright now not with tears but with something else, and he reached out and touched her under her chin, lifting her face slightly, making her look at him.

'Thank *you,*' he said softly. 'It was just as I imagined it would be.'

'You shouldn't have—' she began.

'No, how true. You're an engaged lady. Very naughty of me, I know.' His eyes held hers, and there was a depth of excitement there. Not laughter, not any more, but something so different that the very air in the room seemed to shimmer with an unknown brightness, and everything else was very still. 'But you see, I've been wanting to kiss you for a long time—and I always do what I want, sooner or later.' He took his fingers away from beneath her chin, not abruptly, but with the trace of a lingering caress. 'And I took advantage of you too.' His mouth was touched with the faintest smile. 'I shall apologise to your aunt when we visit her—mentally, of course, because she wouldn't understand why—but I won't apologise to you.'

Arwenna took a deep breath, but before she could speak, he added: 'And now I'm going to order some flowers for us to take. Will you be good enough to make us both a cup of coffee—or tea—whichever pleases you?'

She turned away and walked from him, released, and heard him pick up the telephone. She was supposed to be annoyed, and she didn't know why she wasn't. She didn't know what she felt, but she was faintly disturbed, and much confused.

When she returned with two cups of coffee Garth was sitting down by the table again. He looked up at her. 'Thanks, we'll leave when the flowers arrive,' he told her. 'We'll walk there. Then, after our visit, we'll come back here. Any questions?'

'Then what? Are you going out or working here?'

'What do you prefer?'

She shrugged, watching him light a thin cigar. He smiled. 'Sorry. You don't mind me smoking, do you?'

'Of course not.'

'I said, what do you prefer?'

'You must know what you have to do today,' she retorted. 'I don't. There's quite a lot for me to do here, as you know.'

'Yes, I know. I think we'll take a trip to my office after visiting your aunt, collect some papers I need, then work here for the rest of today. It's sensible, for if your aunt needs you, and we can visit her later, when she's fully recovered. They did ask me to tell you that you may find her very sleepy when we go—but it's perfectly natural.'

'Yes, I'm prepared for that,' she nodded. Perhaps she had imagined the kiss. She began to wonder if she had. And what was a kiss, after all? Nothing of any sort of significance.

The telephone shrilled and Garth rose to answer it, spoke briefly, and put it down.

'The florists have just delivered downstairs,' he said. 'When we've finished our coffee, we'll go.'

ARWENNA KISSED her aunt's cheek. The old lady lay in bed with eyes closed, but she stirred slightly at Arwenna's movement and murmured something unintelligible.

'The nurse says we can only stay for a moment or two,' she whispered to the sleeping woman, not sure if her words could be understood or not. 'But we'll call again later to see you.'

There was no response, save a slight sigh, and Arwenna kissed her cheek again and tiptoed to the door.

Outside, Garth was talking to a tall grey-haired attractive man who smiled warmly at Arwenna and shook her hand as he introduced them. 'Hello, Arwenna,' said Bill Chisholm. 'I was just telling Garth that your aunt's fine. The operation was quite straight-forward, and all being well, I'll have her home in a week.'

'Thank you very much, Mr Chisholm, we're very grateful.' She smiled at him.

'Anything for Garth.' He grinned at him. 'I've told him, any time he needs his appendix whipping out, he's only to ask.'

Garth laughed. 'Thanks. I'll keep what I have. I know you butchers!'

'Ssh!' Bill Chisholm looked around in mock alarm. 'Don't let the patients hear you. *They* trust me.'

Garth clapped him on the shoulder. 'Only because of your smooth bedside manner, you old fraud—' Arwenna listened, amused. The two were clearly old friends. There was a camaraderie about them that came only from mutual respect and affection.

She suddenly realised that she was being spoken to. She had, for a brief moment, been remembering a kiss...

'Sorry?' she said.

'Bill's asking us if we'd like to go round tomorrow evening for a drink?' said Garth, looking amused, as if he guessed her thoughts.

'Oh, how kind.' She looked at Garth for guidance, and he nodded.

'We'll be delighted. What time? Eightish?' he said.

'Yes, fine. Anne will be glad to see you again. Lovely. See you then.' A bleeper sounded from his pocket, and he pulled a face. 'Duty calls. You can find your way out?' He took Arwenna's hand and shook it. 'Nice to have met you, Arwenna. Don't worry about your aunt. Despite Garth's vile slanderous remarks, for which I shall possibly sue him, she's being very well looked after, I promise you. See you tomorrow evening?'

'Yes, I look forward to it. Goodbye.'

Walking out into the warm summer's day, she asked: 'Have you known him long?'

'About eight years. I sold him his house—I think you'll like it. His wife's very charming, and they've got three kids, the youngest of whom I'm godfather to.' He looked at her. 'He doesn't invite just anyone round for drinks, either. You must appeal to him.'

'I liked him very much,' she said, warmed by the compliment.

'You'd get on with most of my friends, I imagine,' he went on. 'Do you get on with James' friends?'

'Of course I—' she stopped, and looked sharply at him. 'What do you mean?'

He shrugged. 'It's a perfectly simple question. Do you?'

'Yes, of course.' She was suddenly annoyed at the implications. And oddly, more so because she couldn't stand some of James' friends—but had no intention of telling Garth that. She added, with a touch of asperity: 'And none have ever attacked me.'

'I asked for that, I suppose.' He took her arm as they dodged across the busy road. 'Aren't you ever going to let me forget it?'

She smiled sweetly. 'I don't know. It all depends—'

'On my questions about James? Okay. I don't like him and you don't like Marcia. And I got rid of Marcia—' the rest of the sentence didn't need to be said. Arwenna shook his hand off her arm as they neared the car park beneath the flats.

'So you did,' she said softly. 'And you have no reason to dislike James—'

'I have plenty,' he cut in. 'But there's only one reason that counts.'

'I don't want to know what it is,' she said, and walked on, sandalled feet clicking over cement, walking towards his car. Garth caught up with her and took hold of her arm.

'Because you already know,' he said.

Arwenna turned to face him by the car. No one else was about. There were few cars in, and vast empty spaces. It was a lonely place, a quiet place, and she wouldn't like to be alone there at night. 'Because I'm engaged to him, and going to marry him,' she said.

'You're engaged. You're not going to marry him,' he answered. They were standing only a foot apart, and it was shadowy there, away from the light slanting in, and there were solid concrete pillars near them, and a silence, the distant traffic muted, and there was a fine thread of tension reaching out to touch and fill them. Garth seemed, because of the shadows, to be even bigger and he wasn't laughing; he wasn't even amused. He was dark and serious—and his face was very hard.

Arwenna felt herself shiver slightly, and it seemed to have gone cold. 'Yes—yes, I am,' she said, and her beautiful eyes, so dark-lashed, normally so calm, were angry. 'Yes,' she repeated, 'I love him.'

'Love? You don't know what love is,' he grated. 'You were attracted to him, and he pursued you, made you feel wanted—'

'You're a liar,' she snapped, wishing she didn't feel so very cold. 'You have no right to say things when you know nothing!'

He suddenly took hold of her hand, not gently, and shook her as if angry. 'I don't have to know *him* to know that,' he said urgently. 'My God, you'd waste your life if you were fool enough—'

'I've *heard* enough!' Incensed, she struggled to free herself from his grip. 'How dare you hold me—talk to me like—'

She was silenced by his mouth as it came down on hers, blotting out her words in a savage kiss that was raw in its intensity and deep in its excitement. Her senses swam, reeling under the strength of it; she would have fallen had his hands not held her so firmly. She fought blindly to free herself, and then—and then suddenly she wasn't struggling any more, but finding her treacherous body responding against her will to the drugging sensation of overwhelming, trembling sensuality. As his hands moved, one across her back, the other to her waist, to secure his hold, she knew an all-encompassing inner warmth that she couldn't any longer deny.

Sensed blurred, completely overwhelmed, she gave herself up to the moment, and their bodies, touching so closely, were almost as one. She could feel Garth's heartbeats, rapid and strong, and was aware of her own heart hammering in unison. It was as if nothing else existed, and as if time had ceased to her. There was no cold any more, only a fire which swept through her.

'Oh God,' whispered Garth, and he was trembling as he held her, and she realised that the kiss, the love-making in an embrace, was over. He held her still, as if he was never going to let her go, and he was like a man with a fever, an uncontrollable surging fever that filled him too. His mouth was touching her hair. His warm breath teased it, his arms had a fine tremor that filled her because of the strength of him, and because it was in her too. She couldn't have moved even had she wanted to, and she no longer wanted to. There was no strength in her, no resistance at all, and she realised that her arms were around him, clinging to him, yet she was not aware of having put them there. Then at last, after eons of time, Garth moved, opened the car door, pushed her in, got in the other side and closed the doors, and reached towards her blindly.

Some slight vestige of reason remained. The seconds of moving into the car had allowed her a breathing space, literally and figuratively, and Arwenna made a slight sound of

protest and tried to lift her hand to push him away, but it
was not enough, and she was not strong enough—Gently,
this time, like a man for whom there is nothing save one
thought, he kissed her again, and held her face as he kissed
her eyes, her cheeks, her nose, then, at last, her mouth.

This time, lost to all reason, Arwenna gave herself fully
to the sweet heady sensation of his seeking mouth, and the
kiss was like none she had ever known before in her life. It
was unutterably beautiful, and it was gentle, and they were
in a dark, shadowy, wonderful place where no one existed
save them. Garth's hands, warm and equally gentle, traced
the soft contours of her body in featherlight caress that only
served to give the kiss an added dimension, a depth. There
was no reason in her any more. All was touch, and sensation, and a deep, deep warmth, and a knowledge that went
beyond time, beyond anything she had ever known before.

Then, gradually, and because perfection must be brief, or
it is no longer perfect, they drew away from each other, and
he looked at her, and there was an urgent tremor that still
touched him, but she couldn't see him properly because she
was too dazed, and for a few moments they were motionless, and silent, because no words could be said. He reached
out to stroke her cheek, and his hand was trembling, and she
made a soft murmur as he touched her mouth with his fingers, and closed her eyes.

She heard him take a deep breath, heard his sigh. She
couldn't move. She didn't want to open her eyes, she was
still drugged, almost drowsy, but she did so, at last, and he
was still watching her. It was very shadowy in the car, but
she could see his face, dark, tanned, and he had what
seemed to be lines of pain, a drawn look, and his mouth was
slightly open, and he ran his tongue over his lips as she
looked at him. Then he reached up and rubbed his face, as
if waking up from a deep sleep.

Arwenna felt her strength returning, and with it came a
realisation of what had just happened, and that was fol-

lowed by a kind of self-loathing, a contempt for her own weakness.

She had just allowed—not only allowed, revelled in— Garth's embraces and lovemaking, and she had responded to him with shameful abandon, all thoughts of fidelity to James completely forgotten as though he hadn't even existed. And this was the man who had told her he would make love to her, a man who had forced her to work for him, a man of strong personality and now, apparently, equally strong passions, who always got what he wanted— and he wanted Arwenna. If she hadn't believed it before, she did now. She sat there very still, as the deeper realisations and implications of what had just taken place washed over her. If Garth had decided to test her loyalty to James, he had chosen his method very carefully, and with great skill. He had told her that she was safe, staying in his flat with him, but how could she be sure of that now? She couldn't. She had betrayed not only James, but herself, and she wasn't sure which was worse. She only knew that she felt dreadful—as though she had been used. She turned to look at him, and she saw him clearly now, and it seemed to her that there might have been a faint look of triumph in his eyes, a sureness, a knowing. She felt sick.

'I hope you're pleased with yourself,' she said, and her voice held all the bitterness she was feeling.

'Pleased?' He repeated the word as if he didn't understand it.

'You—you—' She had to pause to calm herself. 'You did that deliberately!'

'Kissed you?'

'Made me respond,' she answered. 'My God, you must have had lots of practice!'

He hit the steering wheel hard with the edge of his hand. 'What the hell do you want me to say? That you're the first woman I've kissed? No, you're not. Did I *imagine* that you enjoyed it? What's the matter? Suffering pangs of conscience? I won't tell James, if that's what you're worried about.'

'No, that's not what I'm worried about,' she shot back. 'I'm staying in *your* flat—sleeping there—' She was shaking.

'And you think that after this, I'm going to be creeping into your room?'

'Yes, damn you! Do you blame me?' She flashed, eyes shining with unshed tears. 'And we're going to France—'

'I've already told you, you're safe.'

'And I don't believe you. Not after that skilful piece of—' she stopped, bit her lip.

'I kissed you because I wanted to kiss you more than anything else,' he answered, and the air crackled with tension. 'Not because I'd plotted to do so—what do you think I am? A bloody computer, working out every move? I'm a *man*—'

'I know that!' she interrupted. 'You made that very clear. And you want to make love to me—yes, you've made that equally clear—well, I don't want to make love to you!'

'That wasn't the impression I had five minutes ago,' he said, and his eyes were dark and angry, and a muscle moved in his jaw, and he searched her face as if not believing what he was hearing.

Arwenna struck out blindly at him, fist clenched, sobbing, and caught his cheek a hard blow, but he took her wrist and held it, and pulled it away from her face, then caught her other hand roughly. 'You'll hear me,' he grated, voice shaking with anger. 'You wanted me—'

'*No!*'

'You wanted me,' he went on relentlessly, 'and you know it. And, if we hadn't been here it wouldn't have stopped where it did.'

He pulled her hands as she struggled, shaking her head, crying: 'No—no!'

'Oh yes,' he said. 'So why fight your own instincts? You *want* me as much as I want you.'

She was sobbing helplessly, hurting, aching, knowing the truth of his words, and because they were true, frightened. 'Leave me alone!' she cried, when she could speak. 'I hate you—I *hate* you!'

'And yourself, for being a woman,' he said. 'If you hate me, you must hate yourself as well, because I didn't mistake your response.'

He let her go, and held the steering wheel tightly as if he would like to break it, as if he would like to break her. Arwenna sat very still, exhausted, frightened at the controlled violence she sensed in him that filled the car. Garth turned to her, still holding the wheel as if he didn't trust himself to let it go. She saw a mark beneath his eye, a swelling of the skin, the beginning of a bruise, and she had done that, and was filled with a kind of horror at her own violence. He touched it, as if sensing her eyes on it, and said: 'I'll have a black eye tomorrow. I hope that pleases you.'

'I'm sorry,' she began. 'I didn't mean—'

'Think nothing of it,' he said crushingly. 'I'm sure it gave you some satisfaction to hit me—if only to stop me saying what you couldn't bear to hear. I'm tired of this discussion. Are you ready to leave?'

'No, I'm not. I don't want to go to your office. I want to go—' She stopped. Where did she want to go? To his apartment? Where could she go? She was tied to him as though with invisible cords, her obligations too great to be broken. There was no escape from him. Not yet. Not until her debt was paid.

'I don't feel well,' she said, and that was no lie. She didn't want to face anyone, she felt weak and sick with all that had happened.

Garth opened his door, got out, closed and locked it. Then he walked round, opened her door and said: 'Get out, Arwenna.'

Silently she obeyed. He locked that too, then he took her arm as though she were a child and walked across towards the lift with her.

Minutes later, in his apartment, he said, 'Sit down. I'll make you a cup of tea. You'll feel better then.'

'But I don't want—'

'Sit down,' he ordered, steely, cold, hard. 'Please don't argue. I am not a patient man, and I don't feel very kindly towards you at this moment, owing to the fact that I have a headache, and a pain in my face, from your ladylike fist, and I would appreciate it if you just sat quietly for a while.' And he walked away from her and towards his kitchen.

Arwenna sat by the window, and looked out towards the clinic where her aunt lay recovering from her operation, blissfully—and fortunately—unaware of what was happening.

He returned with two beakers and sat down near her on the settee. 'Drink that,' he said. 'I've got the mother and father of a headache, and I'd prefer not to have any more arguments with you at the moment. I hope I make myself clear?'

She nodded. He hardly needed to tell her that he wanted no more argument. She was in no state to do so either. She was tired; she was tired of being independent, and strong, looking after everyone with whom she came in contact. She wanted to be cosseted and protected: she wanted someone to look after her. On her shoulders rested the responsibility for Aunt Daisy's operation—that was a burden she accepted willingly, and with love. But there was the other, greater one. If she backed out now, James' father would almost certainly go bankrupt. She leaned back into the cushioned comfort of the settee and looked blindly at the ceiling, seeing nothing save blurred white.

I'm tired, she thought, weary of the responsibility, and he—Garth—is ruthless, wearing me down, giving me nowhere to turn, nowhere to go to be safe, and free. She knew there was an element of self-pity in her thoughts, and it was alien to her, but just for the moment, she was incapable of doing anything about it. There was work to be done, much work, waiting for her; and travel abroad—a chance she knew many would be delighted to have. She had no illusions about that. Garth was an attractive man, wealthy, with a strong decisive personality; none of those things could be denied. And he had taken over her life, subtly and gradually, and was still doing so. She resented the fact, and him. She wanted to be cosseted, yes, but not in this way. Not in the way that said, look at me—do as I say or else. She wanted James to do it, to phone her, to say, never mind Garth and my father, let *them* sort it out between them, it's nothing to do with you. She wondered what she would do if he rang now, and told her that, and at the thought she almost smiled. Almost, not quite.

Her head ached too, a dull persistent throbbing that was getting worse. She sat up and drank her tea, then realised that Garth had been sitting still, watching her.

'What have you been thinking?' he asked.

'You said you didn't want any more arguments,' she answered.

'Would it cause one?'

She nodded, winced as her head throbbed in protest, and said: 'I'm afraid so. I'm sorry, I'm not strong enough either. Let's leave it. Why did you ask, anyway?' She didn't really want to know, but she said it.

'You had a whole range of expressions chasing across your face,' he told her, and his voice was taut. He sat, not relaxed, not tense either, but watchful, wary, and she sensed that he had spoken the truth before. He was not a patient man. Something had happened to him that was as alien to him as self-pity was to Arwenna. Perhaps he found it as difficult to cope with as she did.

'I was just thinking—about life,' she answered. 'I've a headache too.'

'Mine's gone.'

'Well, bully for you!' She finished her tea and put the beaker on the table. 'Haven't you got lots of things to do? I'll work here while you're out. I will work, I promise.' *Please go*, she added, beneath her breath. *Please go, because I don't know what's happening to me and I wish I did. I wish I could go to bed and lie down and cover my head and let the world pass by without me for a day or two.* She wanted to cry, but she wasn't going to do that.

Garth lit a cheroot. 'I told you, I thought—that I'd deliberately kept this day free of outside work.'

'Oh. I'd forgotten.' There was a tiny thread loose in the heavy gold of the settee, and she picked at it with her nail; she didn't want to look at him any more.

'What are you doing?'

She looked up then, because it sounded from his voice as if he might be frowning, and he was. 'I'm sorry, it's just a thread—' She patted it back into place, and he stood up.

'For God's sake, don't start apologising every time I speak!'

'I'm not. What do you want me to say?' He was standing there, towering over her, but she wasn't going to jump to her feet. 'That I'm pulling your stupid settee to bits?' She shook her head. 'I thought you didn't want any more arguments. It does seem as though that might be slightly impossible, though, doesn't it?' She glared at him angrily, and had a feeling almost of satisfaction at the darkening bruise beneath his left eye. 'Just tell me what you'd like me to talk about and I'll try and oblige. I am, after all, an *employee* of yours—and I'll try not to forget that.'

Garth pulled her to her feet, reached forward, jerked her upwards with both hands and held her, his face dark with anger. For one moment it seemed that he might strike her, but she stood her ground, unafraid, ready to give as good as she got, weary of him, and of nearly everyone—even James.

Her eyes flashed angrily. 'Go on,' she snapped, 'I dare you!' Her body tensed.

'Dare me to what?'

'Hit me. It's what you want to do, isn't it? It's what you've been itching to do ever since I struck you in the car.'

'Don't be stupid!' he snarled, took his arms from her arms, and turned away as if disgusted. 'Is that what you thought? Is that the kind of man you know—the sort that knock women about?'

'No, but you're different from any man I've ever met. I've never known anyone with such explosive violence inside them.'

'I don't hit *women*,' he grated. 'I never have. I certainly don't intend to start with you. What do you mean—*violence?*' He turned his head, tilted it slightly as if not believing what he had heard.

'It's there, in you—I can almost see it, feel it—crackling tension—frightening—' She shivered, and held her arms to her as if for protection.

'Then if you see it, it must be because *you* bring it out. I am not a violent man.'

'You *were!* Years ago, you were,' she shot back, and realised, too late, that she had said what should never have been said. Garth went white, as if she had struck him, wounded him, and she wanted to take the words back, but it was too late for that. Perhaps it had been too late during that moment of their first meeting.

Then suddenly the air went very still, as if waiting for what was to come. In those next few moments Arwenna saw everything around her with great clarity as if it might be etched on her brain for ever.

She wanted to cry out, no, no, let me take it back, but it was too late. It had always been too late...

'I see,' he said. 'Perhaps you'd better finish what you started.' He spoke softly, almost sadly it seemed. 'Perhaps you'd better tell me exactly what you mean.'

She shook her head. 'I can't.'

'Then *I* had better tell *you*. It concerns when I lived in Raneley, years ago, as a young man, when you were a child.'

He walked slowly away from her, towards the window. Then he turned. 'Doesn't it?'

'It's over. It was—over—long ago,' she faltered.

'No! It's not. Not as long as you remember—or think you remember—and you were a child, and believed only what you were told. You think I didn't know who you were that night at James' house? You think I didn't know that you'd gone under protest, to please them?' His voice was filled with contempt. 'Answer me, Arwenna. At least do me that courtesy.'

'All right. Yes! I did go "under protest", as you put it. I didn't want to meet you again. I didn't want to have anything to do with you.' She lifted her head. 'Does that answer satisfy you?'

'No, not yet. I want to know exactly what you heard.'

'You must know what you did—'

'No. I said what *you heard*. There's a vast difference between the fact and the fantasy. Why do you think I vowed to come back one day? Why do you think I'd vowed to show everyone I wasn't afraid?' He looked at her across the room, across time itself, and he was like a giant, tall and unafraid of anything. She couldn't imagine he ever had known fear.

'You're going to hear the truth at last. You're not going to like it, so you'd better sit down, Arwenna.'

'No, I'll stand.' He began to walk towards her. The time for fear had passed. There was an inevitability now to everything. Arwenna remained standing where she was, and when he was a foot or so away he stopped. They faced each other.

'Very well,' said Garth. 'Like this. So be it.' He took off his jacket and tie and laid them down on a chair. Then he began to undo his shirt. Disbelieving, rooted to the spot, Arwenna could only stand and watch. She didn't believe it, but it was happening. She looked as he took his shirt off, and he was deeply tanned, and muscular, and broad-shouldered. She wanted to look away, but she couldn't. With his eyes upon her, grim and cold, he said: 'Now look at my back,' and as he said it he turned away from her, so that she was staring, transfixed, at the broad back—the back that had a long, ugly, livid scar running diagonally from his left shoulder to his waist. 'You can see that,' he said, and picked up his shirt again. Turning, he began to put it on. 'But you don't know who gave it to me, do you?'

She shook her head, unable to speak. But in a dreadful way she sensed what his next words would be, and she wanted to stop them, but there was nothing she could do that would make this happen. Nothing.

CHAPTER SEVEN

'Before I tell you,' said Garth, 'I want you to tell me why you hated me, what you were told, years ago. Don't be afraid. I'm not going to get angry—or more angry than I am. I'll listen without interruption, and then I'll tell you the truth of the matter.'

She decided that it might be better if she sat down, and he followed suit. Then Arwenna looked at him. 'My father said that you were a troublemaker, a liar and a thief, and that Raneley was better off without you and your family. He wasn't the only one—when you were eighteen or nineteen you'd stolen some money from old Farmer Miller's home—and—beaten him up— She paused. This was horrible. This was something she had buried at the back of her mind as being so awful that it should never be said, and Garth was making her say it, but now, looking at him, it seemed impossible that she was talking of him fifteen years ago. She saw his face, bleak, hard, implacable, and a shiver ran down her spine. She had always accepted what she had been told as a child—had always believed, because the grown-ups believed it, and they were always right. Yet she had just seen his back— She held her hands tightly clasped together, and was silent.

'And old Farmer Miller was a friend of your father's, wasn't he?' His voice was taut, tense.

'Yes, he'd helped father out occasionally when the shop wasn't doing well.'

Garth nodded.

'Kind old Farmer Miller was a liar—and a hypocrite. The only difference was that he was respected in the village—and he had money. I was from a poor family, and I was young.' He stood up and paced the room as if he could no longer remain still. 'I did beat him up, as you put it, but I never stole from him. And the reason I beat him, and the reason I got this memento'—he gestured to his back—'was because I had seen him beating—with a whip—the poor simple lad who worked for him on his farm, and I stopped him.' He came over to her. 'I used to go swimming with my friends in the pool near his farm, and sneak home that way, taking the short cut. I was alone that day, it was Sunday, and as I passed the farmyard I heard the cries of pain, looked over the wall to see him lashing the lad—you won't even remember him, I don't suppose—because he'd obviously just upset a churn of milk. I leapt over the wall, and he saw me coming. If I hadn't turned at the right moment I'd have got the whip across my face.' He paused. 'Farmer Miller was a big strong man, about fifty then, big, red-faced, beefy. The youth he was beating was about your size.' He paused, to let the words sink in. 'That moment is etched clearly on my brain for all time: the look on the man's face—he was enjoying what he was doing—and the look of sheer terror on poor Ned's. I didn't even feel the pain at the time—not until afterwards. I took the whip from him, flung it away, and punched him as hard as I could. I was as tall then as I am now, but thinner, and Miller was as tough as old boots—but I gave him a thrashing, while Ned crawled away, then took to his heels.

'I left Miller in his own yard, sprawled in a heap of manure, and went home. Within an hour the village bobby arrived. Miller had told him he'd caught me breaking in, had tried to stop me, and got beaten for his pains. Who do you think the policeman believed? I was nineteen, I worked on a building site, I came from a poor family, and I drove a motorbike that had cost me all my carefully saved up money—but I was branded as a troublemaker because I was young, and because I couldn't prove my story. Ned had gone, run off. Miller's wife—as I found out afterwards, when it was too late—was too terrified of him to do anything else but corroborate his story of the break-in.

'My parents believed me, but that wasn't much help to me. Miller then announced that he wouldn't charge me, and everything was dropped. He was a clever man. Had it come to court they would have had to find Ned, and the real truth would have come out. He was the noble farmer—and I was a young thug, best avoided. My parents became ill with the shame of it—mud sticks, you know—and we moved away. That was when I vowed I'd return one day, with money, and show them. I wanted my revenge on Miller for the unhappiness he'd caused my family—but I never got the chance, because he died of a stroke two years later, when I was just beginning to make money.' He stopped, looked at her. 'There's one person knows the truth—his widow. She still lives at the farm. She's about seventy now. I went to see her a month ago, when I was negotiating for Raneley Hall, and she recognised me. After all those years she recognised me, and I think for a moment that she honestly thought I'd come back for revenge. She's a frail, timid creature, who's lived with the knowledge of her husband's lies all these years. I told her simply that I had no quarrel with her, that I just wanted to let her see that although I was coming back to live in Raneley, I bore her no ill will. Then I left her.'

Arwenna sat, tense and shaking when he had finished. There was the ring of truth to his words that no lies could ever have. There was one question she had to ask however.

'Why, if you had so many bitter memories of Raneley, did you still want to go back there to live?' she asked.

He walked to the window and looked out. 'I'll tell you that some other time,' he said. Then he turned round to her. 'You're not ready to hear it yet.' He looked at his watch. 'I'm hungry.'

Arwenna stood up. 'I'll go and get some food for us.'

She went into the kitchen, and there she leaned against the sink for a few minutes before moving. There was much more that Garth hadn't told her, some deep instinct within her was sharply aware of that, but he had told her all that he intended to for now. She felt the strangeness of the day's incidents, and they seemed to crowd in on her, and she was as exhausted as if she had run for miles. This deep, complex, fascinating man was like no other. Nothing was ever what it seemed—or was it? She was confused, bewildered, no longer the self-assured person she had been only days ago. Could there be a deeper, subtle reason for his return? Could it be that when he helped Colonel Rhodes, he would take over, cleverly, as he seemed to do in everything else? She stood very still. And after he had taken over—what then? Closure?—people out of work—people from Raneley—the townspeople who had turned their backs on him years before. And she might be helping him to do just that. By her agreeing to work for him, everything would go ahead as planned.

She turned sharply, hearing him come in. Eyes wide, she looked at him. 'What is it now?' he asked, voice hard.

'Colonel Rhodes—you're going to help him?'

'You know I am. That was agreed,' he answered.

'Yes, but I didn't know then about—what you've just told me. Is that what you plan? To close the place? To take over—then to—to—'

'Have my revenge at last?' he laughed. 'There's a thought!'

'Is it?' she demanded.

Garth looked at her, eyes narrowed. 'Is that what you think?'

'I think—anything's possible—with you.'

'Very true. And what do you intend to do about it? That is—of course—if that's what I plan.' And he smiled.

'Tell James' father.'

'And what do you think he could do?' He crossed the floor to her. 'He has no money, it'll close anyway, and he'll be bankrupt in a year if nothing's done.'

'Yes, so you say—but how much cleverer if *you* do it!'

'Is that how your mind works?'

She shivered. 'I don't know. I feel confused. All I wanted was yes or no—'

'Not from me. You intrigue me, Arwenna.' He put his hands on her bare arms. 'You intrigue me very much. Would it matter so terribly to you—'

'Of course it would.' She looked at him, calmer now, her strength and natural resilience helping her to cope with this powerful force of him.

'Yes, I see that it would. You care for Raneley, and its people, don't you?'

'Of course, I do! I can see that, for you, it's different—' She stopped.

'Very,' he said dryly. 'How much do you care?'

'What do you mean?'

'I'll tell you in a moment. First, I'll tell you that I'm planning to buy other businesses in and around Raneley. The large store there—it's for sale, but you wouldn't know that—the row of shops and houses on the main road—'

'Where our café is?'

Garth looked faintly surprised. 'Why, yes, so it is.'

'But it's rented. The landlord is—'

'A company in nearby Chesterfield, Green & Dutton, acting for an elderly gentleman who wants to sell.'

'Oh, my God!' she whispered. 'You're planning a take-over?'

'Not necessarily. And why should that be a bad thing?'

'Because of what I know.'

He released her and turned away, and opened the refrigerator door. 'What do you want to eat?'

'Nothing. I'm not hungry.'

He looked at her. 'Were you before?'

'I was—'

'But not now?'

'No.' She shook her head.

Garth fetched out a carton of eggs. 'I'm sure you could force an omelette down, couldn't you?'

'No, but I'll make you one if you want,' she said dully. There was a heavy weight in her stomach, almost a pain. How could anyone fight a man like this? She took the carton from him and began to search for a pan.

'Thank you. This is all supposition on your part, you know,' he told her, watching her break three eggs into a basin.

'Then your motives are all good?'

He shrugged. 'Are anyone's?'

'It doesn't answer the question.'

'It's not intended to. Perhaps you should work things out for yourself. Think. Think hard—and see what you come up with, Arwenna.'

'You're talking riddles.' She beat vigorously at the egg whites with a fork, and he began:

'There's an electric mixer—'

'I don't need one. I make a better omelette my way,' she answered, and redoubled her efforts. It saved her from screaming. The sheer physical exercise helped her.

'You know what I want,' he said, and she knew his words didn't refer to omelettes, or mixers. She knew, suddenly, what they meant. She poured the mixture into the pan with the heated oil in it, and it bubbled up instantly; she added salt and pepper, and reached over for the spatula. But everything was automatic, she was numbed with the sudden realisation. And he turned her round to face him, and held her there, and said: 'Yes, I can see that you know.' He said it very softly.

'You want me.' Garth nodded. 'No,' she said. '*No.* You've done enough already. I'm working for you. It was to help—James' father—to help him. Yet now it seems I've landed him further in it.'

'But it needn't be that. And I needn't buy those other places—'

'If I sleep with you?' she demanded.

He gave her a crooked smile. 'Would that be too high a price to pay?'

'I wouldn't even consider it,' she said coldly, and, freeing herself, turned away from him.

'You've had lovers. You're not a naïve virgin.'

'You believed that?' Her eyes flashed angrily.

'Wasn't I expected to? The Belgian who proposed in bed—'

'He had 'flu. *He* was in bed, *I* wasn't. We were at his family house, and they were there as well.'

'Ah!' Garth seemed amused. 'And the wealthy Philippe?' He held up his hand. 'Wait—let me guess. You didn't mention his age. He was about ninety-seven?'

'The other end—twelve. I was looking after him with the other children.'

'So I was right,' he drawled.

'Meaning?' she snapped. She turned away, tipped out the cooked omelette on to a plate and banged it down on the table, suddenly angry.

'I knew,' he shrugged. 'No, I *guessed*—that you hadn't—and James? You've never—?' he paused, mouth twitching delicately.

'No, never,' she said flatly. 'Satisfied?' She glared at him, at the darkening eye. 'I wish I'd blacked them both while I was at it!'

She was interrupted by his shout of laughter, and he caught hold of her, and he was shaking. 'Let me go!' she snapped furiously, and stamped hard on his foot. 'Just let me— Mmm—'

Garth kissed her, stopping her words, blotting them out in mid-sentence; he kissed her hard and long, and held her tightly to him, and looked down at her when he had done; his eyes were dark and intense, and his face was not smiling now, not at all. 'I want you,' he said, 'more than I've ever wanted any woman—'

'Only because you can't have me. You're like a child trying to get a toy that's out of reach—you expect me to fall into bed with you just because you're *you*,' she said, breathless after the kiss, and trying hard not to let him see the effect. 'But I've gone as far as I'm going with you, do you understand?'

She tried to push herself free of him. 'Let me go, please.'

'Make me,' he said softly.

'I can hurt you. I know how to hurt a man—'

He released her, and she thought her threat had frightened him, and she managed to smile—just before she was twisted round so that he was behind her, and now holding her, and there was no way that she could fight that. 'Now,' he whispered, 'let's see—'

Arwenna twisted, she tried to turn, she reached up her one free hand and tried to grasp hold of his hair, but he laughed, and evaded her, then caught that hand, and she was totally helpless. Exhausted, she gasped: 'What are you trying to prove? That you're smarter than me?'

'That I can kiss you any time I want,' he said, and eased her slightly round, and then did so. It was strange, being held like that, so helpless and secure, and being kissed, sideways on, as it were, and it was oddly exciting. Her heart began to thud, and she tried to free her lips from his, but only because she knew she should, not because she wanted to.

Garth's mouth left a lingering trail of fire across her cheek, then he kissed her hair, then the back of her neck, which made her shiver all over, so sudden and unexpected was it. Then he said: 'See?'

'Your omelette's getting cold,' she said shakily, and he released her, looked at her, then sat down.

Arwenna remained standing where she was. She wondered if her face was pink. It felt warm, she felt warm all over. 'You're a swine,' she muttered.

'This omelette is good,' he answered. 'Sure you don't want anything?'

'No. I said—you're a swine.'

'I heard you. What do you want me to do? Burst into tears? I've been called worse.'

'That I can believe.' She wanted to hit him, to hurt him, and she didn't know how—or why.

'Will you make me a cup of coffee?' he asked.

'No! Make your own.' She whirled away and then filled the kettle.

'Changed your mind?'

'No. I'm making myself one,' she snapped.

'Leave enough water for me.'

'Go to hell!' She switched on the kettle and fetched a beaker from the cupboard. Garth finished his omelette and took the plate to the sink, then got a beaker for himself. He stood beside her, and when the kettle had boiled, and she had poured the water on to the instant coffee, he followed her. She walked out into the main lounge and went over to the window. There she stood looking out over the buildings, seeing the traffic passing below, the busy hubbub of daily life, everyone going about their business unaware of her watching, not caring anyway, then she looked over to the clinic, imagining her aunt resting, perhaps sleeping now, but recovering. She wished it was all over and she was back in Raneley, with James, living a normal everyday life, helping her aunt, planning her wedding to James, looking for somewhere to live, saving up—and it suddenly seemed wrong. She frowned. James—she loved James, he loved her. But she hadn't really given him a thought since yesterday. He seemed very far away, distant, almost a stranger. She tried to conjure him up in her mind, and all she saw was the mocking face of the man she had just told to go to hell.

'James,' she whispered, and a voice from behind her said:

'Why don't you phone him?' She whirled round, spilling some coffee. She hadn't heard Garth approach.

'Do you always creep around?' she demanded angrily.

'I walk quietly. That's not creeping,' he answered mildly for him. 'I didn't want to interrupt your reverie.'

'Well, you did,' she snapped. 'You nearly made me spill my coffee.'

'That's your nerves to blame, not my fault.'

'There's nothing wrong with my nerves—or wasn't before I met you, thank you,' she retorted.

'Really? Is that the effect I have on you? Shame! I'd hoped for something different.'

'Why don't we get on with some work?' she sighed. 'At least you're fairly normal then.'

'That was the idea, I thought. Work, I mean, not me being normal. That's something I can't comment on. I consider myself perfectly normal.'

'You're about as normal as—as—a bulldozer in a—' Arwenna sought for words—'in a sweetshop,' she finished.

'Surely you can do better than that?' he commented, amused, smiling broadly. 'Never mind. Sit down, drink your coffee, and think about it. Incidentally, I'd better give you some money. What salary did we agree on?'

'We didn't.' She wished he wouldn't keep switching the conversation around, as though nothing was wrong.

'Ah, no, we didn't. Will a hundred do you?'

'A hundred a month?'

'A week.'

'A hundred pounds a *week?*' she gasped.

'Not enough? A hundred and ten, then.'

'That's ridiculous! I've never earned that much in my life!'

'Don't look so startled,' he grinned. 'A good secretary can earn that, and more.'

'I'm not a secretary.'

'A translator, then. And you're a good one.'

'You're not joking? You mean it?'

'I'm not joking.'

Arwenna sat down. Now was the time to tell him. 'I'm going to pay you back for Aunt Daisy's operation,' she said.

'I was going to save up as much as I could of what you paid me but I didn't think it would be that amount. I'll be able to repay you sooner than I thought, if you'll tell me how much, roughly—'

'I thought that was already settled,' said Garth. 'I undertook that responsibility. It was part of our agreement.'

'Part of the blackmail, you mean,' she said. 'No. That's *my* responsibility don't you see? She's my aunt. The other—Colonel Rhodes—that's different—'

'Different? They're family too—or going to be—aren't they?'

'*Yes!* But—' She stopped. What's the matter with me? she thought.

'But?' he enquired.

She shook her head. 'It's different, that's all.'

Garth sat down beside her on the settee. 'Let's get to work,' he said. 'I'll give you your money later. You'd prefer cash?'

'If possible.'

'It's possible.' He picked up a sheet of paper she hadn't seen before, and handed it to her. 'Read that, and tell me what you think.'

Work was resumed. Gradually the atmosphere became normal, her jangled nerves were soothed; she concentrated on what they were doing. Garth too was different now. It was like seeing another man in action. Incisive, cool and logical, still forceful, but in a different way. Arwenna could always appreciate a brain such as he possessed. She felt as though she was learning something from him all the time, and when he fetched in balance sheets and a calculator, and asked her how she was on maths, she told him that she was quite a whiz with these too, and he laughed and said he'd thought as much, and gave them to her to do, and the atmosphere was as near pleasant as it could ever be, with them.

When the telephone rang she left him to visit the bathroom, and looked at herself critically in the mirror as she washed her hands. Her face glowed, her eyes were bright and sparkling. She felt more alive than she had ever done in her life. She felt vibrant, alert—she pulled a face at herself and went back to join Garth. He was still talking, but it was about money and didn't seem to concern her, so she went back to the kitchen, made coffee, and feeling very hungry, found a tin of biscuits and ate three.

He hung up as she went in. 'Sorry about that,' he said. 'Ah, coffee! Good.'

He sat down. 'Let's have a break. What are we doing to-night—after visiting Aunt Daisy, I mean?'

'*We?* Don't you have friends to see or anything? I'm quite happy to watch television sometimes—please don't feel—'

'There's a good film on at nine. Okay, that's settled. We'll visit Aunty, call in at a little Indian take-away I know—er—you do like curry, I hope?'

'Yes, but—'

'Bring a curry back here and watch the film.'

He watched her face, apparently puzzled, frowned, and added: 'Don't you want a curry? We can get a Chinese—or eat out, of course.'

'No, it's not that.' But what was it? Arwenna didn't know herself.

'Look,' said Garth, 'I'd like to make a few phone calls, and I was going to go to the office to collect some things. It's nearly four now, I'll phone them and get them dropped off. I think we'll call it a day with this lot for now. Do you want to do any shopping?'

Arwenna was feeling more confused by the minute. It was like standing on quicksands—although she never had—but she was beginning to know what it might feel like. She nodded. It seemed easier to agree with him.

'Good. I'll get your money, phone for a taxi. It'll take you and bring you back. Where do you want to go? Oxford Street—Piccadilly—?'

'I don't know.' She looked up at him as he went towards the telephone.

'Better decide. Why not call at Harrods, buy some clothes? I've got an account there.' He turned round and regarded her gravely. 'Buy something to wear tomorrow night.'

'Tomorrow night?' she queried.

'We're going out, remember? Bill Chisholm?' he explained.

'Oh, yes, of course.' She had forgotten.

'Get yourself a nice dress. Please,' he added.

'I can't afford it—'

'On my account.'

'Oh, no!' She stood up and went over to him. 'No, I'd rather not. I don't have to explain why, do I?'

'It's not buying you, if that's what you mean. Call it a bonus, a perk, for working so hard.' He smiled. 'And you do. Besides, you'll need clothes for France.'

'You don't understand,' she said fiercely. 'You said you can't let anyone take you over, but you're doing it now. Clothes—what next? It's not—it's not—'

'Right? Of course it damned well is. You've got to dress the part if you're working for me. We'll be travelling incognito, don't forget, next week, as ordinary tourists, not prospective buyers. I want to see how those hotels are run, without them knowing who I am. Now, I insist you buy some clothes, anything you like—you've got good taste— and we'll talk about payment later, when we return.'

'And do you think James will appreciate your reasoning?' she asked.

'He doesn't have to know.'

'He's not stupid. He knows what I can and can't afford.'

'The last time you spoke to him he accused you of sleeping with me. Why haven't you rung him to get that little matter sorted out?'

'I—' she began, and stopped.

'Why?' he asked.

'I don't know,' she whispered. She looked at the silent telephone. It seemed very accusing.

'Phone him now. From your room, if you like.'

'He'll be at work.'

'Phone him there.'

'We were talking about clothes a moment ago—' she began feebly.

'So we were. Well, are you going to call him—or shall I?'

'No.' She shook her head.

'I have to phone his father,' added Garth. 'That's one of the calls I must make when you go out. There's nothing wrong with me talking to him as well, is there?'

'Yes, there is. I don't want you to.'

'Very well. But you should.'

'Why are you so concerned all of a sudden?' demanded Arwenna. 'You don't give a damn about him.'

'I wonder if *you* do,' he said, and the words hung in the air, and she turned away because she didn't want him to look into her eyes and know the truth, and he said softly: 'Look at me, Arwenna.'

'No,' she said. 'No—' But she knew what he was doing, even with her back turned, sensed his movement behind her, then his hands, drawing her round to face him, and she stood helpless before him, unable to look away again.

Garth didn't speak. He looked deep into her eyes for an endless, shimmering moment, and then slowly, reluctantly, it seemed, he released her.

'Phone him,' he said at last. 'Tell him you don't love him.'

Her mouth trembled. 'How do you know?'

'I know.'

'You're wrong—'

'I'm not wrong. I know. You don't love him now, you probably never have. Isn't it kinder to tell him?'

'We're engaged to be married—'

'Engagements can be broken off. That's the whole point of them. A testing time, a period of waiting before total commitment.'

'It will hurt him—' she began.

'Not as much as if you waited until after you were married—'

'It's what you want, isn't it? For us to finish?'

'Yes, it is.'

'So that *you* can have me? Is that it? Do you think I'm going to fall into your arms once he's safely out of the way?'

'There's certainly more of a chance of it.'

'There's no chance,' she said, voice husky with emotion. 'Not with a man like you—not for me—don't you see? You'd take over my life, tell me what to think, to eat, to wear—you're doing it now, and, God knows, we don't even love each other!'

'But we are attracted to each other.'

'Perhaps. I don't know. But you said it yourself. We're two of a kind—The irresistible force meeting the immovable object, then—bang! Nothing. No, thanks. Not me. Not me—ever. ' She was shaking, her voice was husky, quiet, so that he had to move near her to hear. His face was grim, and his voice, when he answered her, was harsh.

'There's no way I can change,' he said. 'Not for you—not for anybody. I am as I am.'

'You're powerful, you're almost overwhelming, you could be dangerous—I know that, I saw that the first moment I met you at James' house—yes, I admit it, I was as aware of something—I don't know what, the minute we looked at each other across that room. I still don't know what it is. I only know you've turned my life over, perhaps made me see some things more clearly—you've forced me to work for you, and I'm doing so, and I'll work hard, for the time we have together—but then, when it's over, when the year has passed, that's it. You may still live in Raneley, I don't know. I don't know how long you intend to stay—I don't know much about you at all, and I'm not sure if I want to. I've never met anyone like you before, and I may not again, but we have no real part in each other's lives, because we would eventually destroy one another.' She finished, and she was shaking like a leaf, and only her determination had carried her this far. 'Don't you *see?*'

'Oh yes, I see,' Garth said softly. 'And of course you're right. We both know the truth of what you say. There's only one thing you seem to have forgotten.'

'And what's that?' she whispered.

'We've neither of us ever loved. You've never loved James, nor, I suspect, any other man. Am I right?' Arwenna nodded slowly. 'And I've never loved any woman. I've made love, I've had affairs, yes, that—but I've never fallen in love with any woman. Perhaps, then, neither of us is capable of it. Doesn't that worry you?'

'No. Does it worry you?'

'No.' They looked at each other across an unbridgeable gulf, and the physical attraction was an almost tangible force, touching them both. It was Arwenna who looked away first. The tension was unbearable. 'So it might be better for us to work it out of our systems,' he said. 'Then we'll be free.'

'Have an affair? That's what you mean, isn't it?'

'What else do you think I mean?' he asked, and took her in his arms and held her to him.

CHAPTER EIGHT

SHE WANTED him—that was the awful thing. She wanted him to make love to her. She gently disengaged herself from his arms and looked at him, seeing him more clearly than she had ever seen any other man. Now was the time for her to be strong. Now, not later, when it would be too late to see clearly any more.

'Thanks, but no, thanks!' she said. 'I find your offer almost irresistible. You certainly have a charming—and direct—way of expressing your desires. Work it out of our systems, indeed! You talk as if we have a dose of 'flu—' She turned away. 'Will you please call me a taxi, I'll go and leave you to your phone calls, and then we'll talk about this evening.'

She walked steadily away from him, and heard him pick up the telephone as she went out of the room. She combed her hair vigorously, looking at her face in the mirror, wondering if it betrayed her to him. If he knew—if he ever guessed, she would be lost. If Garth even had the faintest idea that she wanted him to make love to her she would have no chance of getting away. That consideration was so strong that it was several minutes before she remembered the other shattering realisation that had come to her. She had known, in an instant of time, when he had said those fatal words: 'I wonder if *you* do.' She had seen everything so vividly that it was as if her life for the past year had flashed in front of her. No, she didn't love James. She never had, not truly. She had imagined herself to be in love with him, and that was a world away from what she knew now.

He would be hurt. That was one reason why she would not ring him at work. He would be angry as well, but how angry she was not, fortunately, at that moment able to imagine. She sighed, put down her comb, and went back into the main lounge. Into her bag she had put her banker's card. If she bought a dress, it would be with her own money, not Garth's. The only money she would take from him would be for work.

He was waiting, and he had an envelope which he handed to her. 'Don't get mugged,' he told her.

'I'll try not to. Thank you.' She put the envelope into her handbag. 'Shall I go down?'

'The taxi's on its way. I'll be here when you get back.' Garth went to open the door, and the lift was waiting, and he watched her into it. 'Think about what I said,' He looked at her very directly as he spoke, and he wasn't smiling any more.

'I already have.' Arwenna closed the lift doors and pressed the button, and twenty minutes later she was wandering round Harrod's, and had managed to put both James and Garth from her mind.

She didn't, after all, have a lot of time to shop there, didn't see anything she fancied—or not at the price she could afford—and was on her way out when a voice hailed her, an unmistakable loud, cheerful voice, 'Hey, Arwenna!'

She turned, on the pavement, nearly caused a minor traffic jam as the hurrying crowds swerved to avoid her, and saw a tall lanky bearded figure loping towards her from the roadway. He was waving and grinning all over the little of his face she could see, and he scooped her up in his arms and hugged her delightedly.

'It *is* you! I thought I was dreaming! What the heck are you doing in London? Why didn't you phone?' he asked, and Arwenna, laughing, said:

'Put me down and I'll tell you.' She looked into the blue eyes of Steven Marshall, the student she had met in Paris a

couple of years previously—the one with whom she would
have got in touch if accommodation had been difficult. He
looked delighted to see her, and kept hold of her arm as if
she might run away if he let go. 'I'm staying here for a few
days while my aunt has an operation,' she answered. 'It's
good to see you, Steve. I was going to phone you. Are you
still at the same place?'

'Yes, four of us now, in a grotty flat. I'm just on my way
back there now.' He gestured towards a crammed plastic
carrier bag he had put on the ground, much to the danger of
passers-by, and scooped it up. 'My turn to do the shopping.' A long French loaf peeped out, and the bag seemed
otherwise to be full of vegetables. 'Come on, let's have a
coffee somewhere.'

'I haven't got time—' Arwenna began weakly, and he
took her arm firmly and began steering her along the
crowded pavement.

'Yes, you have. I want to hear what you've been doing.'
He opened the glass doors of a small café and found a table, then loped off towards the counter, leaving Arwenna
with his shopping bag.

'Right,' he said, and sat opposite her, after depositing two
cups of espresso coffee on the plastic-topped table. 'My
treat, you notice.'

'Thank you. The last of the big spenders,' she grinned,
and he raised his fist in mock threat.

'Watch it, half pint, I'm bigger than you,' he answered.

'You're bigger than everybody,' she conceded. 'Look,
we've exchanged insults now, so how are you, and what are
you doing? And how's Zack?'

'I'm fine—I'm taking a post-graduate course in econom-
ics—and Zack is still pining for you. Any more questions?'
He took hold of her left hand and grimaced. 'Hmm, still
engaged. Zack won't like that.'

Arwenna took her hand away. 'Actually, I'm not—' She
had forgotten the ring.

'Then why are you wearing it?'

She sighed. 'I—I only decided this afternoon.' She looked at him. He was a whole world away from Garth, he and Zack, in age, temperament, background—he was refreshing to see. She was glad she had bumped into him, for it would have been so easy to forget to telephone him.

'Well, that calls for celebration—or does it?' He looked at her shrewdly. He was easily as intelligent as Garth. She had known him and Zack for only a matter of weeks, when they had been in Paris, but she had spent a lot of free time with them, and had established an easy-going relationship that would endure, as some friendships did, for ever. She liked them both equally, and knew they were fond of her, and though their letters had been spasmodic, there had never been a shortage of things to say. James had never understood the friendship, so she rarely mentioned them to him. Now it wouldn't matter anyway...

'Neither. I'd rather not talk about it, Steve,' she answered gently.

'Fair enough. What are you doing tonight? We're having some friends round for a spaghetti supper—you know what a whizz I am at the old spaghetti Bolognese—' he kissed his fingers, eyes closed in ecstasy, and she laughed.

'I'd love to, but I've got to see my aunt.'

'After then? I'll pick you up. Where are you staying?'

She looked at him. That was too long a story to tell. But why not go? Why *not?*

'All right,' she answered. 'What do you mean, you'll pick me up?' Her eyes gleamed with mischief.

'I have a *car,* my dear girl,' he said proudly. 'I *did* tell you, in one of my many *long* letters which I don't suppose you bothered to read—'

'I did, I did,' she protested. 'I'd forgotten, that's all. Anyway, you shouldn't be able to afford a car.'

'Daddy's softened up in his old age,' he answered. 'Gave me a Mini for my last birthday, but I'm not mad enough to drive it into town. Okay, give me your address.' He whipped out an envelope and stub of pencil from the pocket of the faded and well patched denim jacket he wore, and held the pencil poised expectantly.

Arwenna sighed. 'Look, Steve, can I make a phone call first? I'm staying at a man's flat'—he raised his eyebrows, but said nothing—'and if I phone him and tell him first I think it would be better.'

'A man? You naughty thing! And here was I thinking you'd kept yourself pure for me all these years—' Steve gave a disappointed sigh.

'Believe me, it's platonic, *and* it's a long story, which I'll tell you later. Okay?' She stood up. There was a pay telephone at the rear of the café. 'Got a five?'

He handed her one. 'Don't be long, we've got a lot of news to catch up on.'

'I won't.'

The first time she rang the line was engaged. She put the phone down and waited; looked back to see Steve sitting sipping his coffee and watching her. She dialled again and it was answered immediately.

'Vanner.' The familiar voice sounded almost staccato over the line.

'Garth? It's me, Arwenna. I've met an old friend who's asked me round this evening, so I said I'd phone you first to check if it was all right. He'll pick me up in his car—'

'Where does he live?' he cut in.

She frowned, trying to remember. 'Oh, Hampstead way—why?'

'I'll take you. You're coming back here first to visit your aunt, aren't you?'

'Yes, of course. I'm on my way now.'

'Where are you?'

'In a café near Harrod's.'

'Have you ordered a taxi yet?'

'No. I was going to get one when I bumped into Steve.'

'I'll pick you up there if you like in about half an hour. I have to go out—what's the name of the place?'

'I haven't a clue.' She felt faintly annoyed. 'Look, I can get myself home quite easily—'

'Just tell me the name of the café. You'll not get a taxi at this time of day.' Garth sounded impatient. Arwenna turned and looked at the counter. Over it was the name, which she told him. 'I'll see you outside. Half an hour from now. Goodbye.'

'Good—' The line went dead. Arwenna hung up and walked back to Steve and sat down.

'Wow!' he exclaimed. 'Had a row? You look good and mad.'

'Do I?' She simmered down immediately. 'Sorry. He says he'll bring me to your place. And he's picking me up from here in half an hour.' She sighed. 'He's a very busy man.'

'Hmm, sounds it. Who is he? Or is that none of my business?'

'Of course it is. You won't know him. His name's Garth Vanner, and I'm working for him, and he's paid for my aunt to have an operation at his friend's clinic, and as he lives literally only a short walk from the clinic, I'm staying there at his place.'

'That's put it in a nutshell. Vanner? I've heard of him— who hasn't? He's a real whizz kid, isn't he? Property millionaire?'

'That's the one.'

'How on earth did you get to work for him? I mean, living in a godforsaken little place like Raneley—'

'How dare you!' She slapped his hand. 'It's a lovely town!'

'Sorry, course it is, my sweet, but you know what I mean. It's hardly the hub of the universe.'

'He comes from there, and he's just bought a house there,' she explained. 'That's how I came to meet him, through James—'

'With whom,' Steve cut in, 'you have just severed relations.' He leered amiably at her. '*Vairy* interesting,' he drawled, in a heavy foreign accent.

You don't know the half of it, she thought wryly, and smiled at him. 'Oh, Steve, I'm so glad to see you, honestly. You're like a breath of fresh air.'

'Is this Vanner revolting or something?' he asked.

'No, he's not. He's a very attractive man—hard, ruthless, but very attractive—'

'And lusting after you?' he asked, too shrewdly by far.

'What makes you say that?' But her telltale colour gave her away.

'Come on, ducky, it's obvious, isn't it? You're a damned attractive wench, and *I've* been lusting quietly after you for two years or so, and so's Zack, and any other red-blooded male you set eyes on.'

Arwenna grinned impishly. 'You do me good!'

'I love you, Arwenna, you know that. I wouldn't want to see you hurt, ever.' Steve's eyes told the truth of his words, and he took both her hands and held them, oblivious to people sitting at the other tables. 'I don't love you in a possessive way, but in that special way that good friends will always have—and I want you to be happy.' He gave a rueful grin. 'Hell, I never thought I'd sit in a café with you making this kind of speech, but I care for you very deeply, and I always will, whatever other relationships we might have.' His face went serious. 'If anyone ever hurt you badly, I think I would want to kill them.'

'Oh, Steve!' His words had a curious effect on her. He was normally so lighthearted, walking through the world with an easy grace and charm, living life fully, one of nature's genuinely well balanced people who attract others like magnets, that his words were all the more moving. 'I love you too, in a special kind of way. And don't worry, no one's going to hurt me. I'm quite tough, remember?'

He grinned. 'You're all woman, too. Have we time for another coffee? I need one after that speech.'

'Why not? My treat.' Arwenna picked up her bag and went to the counter. They had another twenty minutes or so, no more. Garth wouldn't be able to park outside. She took the coffees back to the table, then asked Steve to tell her about his flat. He wrote down the directions how to get there, and she heard all about the other two flatmates, and the time passed swiftly and easily.

Then it was time to go. As they went outside Steve took her hand and kissed it. 'See you later, Arwenna. About eight—eight-thirty?'

'Yes, I'm looking forward to it. Off you go. Give Zack my love.'

'I will. He might even shave for you, who knows? Miracles have happened before.'

He stooped to kiss her cheek as a sleek Daimler purred to a halt at the curb. Arwenna saw it out of the corner of her eye and quickly turned her face and kissed Steve. 'He's here,' she whispered. 'Goodbye.'

She ran towards the car, and Steve watched her go with a strange expression on his face, a very sad expression that vanished as he waved to her, then turned away.

Garth drove on. For a few minutes the traffic occupied him fully, then, when they had turned into a comparatively quiet street, he asked: 'Was that your friend?'

'Yes.'

'And you have his address?'

'Yes. In my bag, with directions.'

'That's good.' Nothing more was said. Garth didn't seem annoyed at having to meet her. He didn't seem curious about Steve. He seemed just like a stranger. They drove straight back to his flat, and when they were in he commented: 'I see you didn't buy any clothes.'

'No. I didn't see anything I wanted.' Arwenna flung her bag down on a chair. 'I'd like to have a shower now if I may.'

'Of course you may. After we've visited your aunt I'll take you to your friend's flat. Give me the address and I'll check if I know where it is.'

She handed him the envelope in silence. He *was* like a stranger. She felt as if she couldn't talk to him at all. It was as though some shutters had gone down. He was remote, polite, and his face was expressionless. He read the address and the directions, in Steve's careless scrawl, then looked up. 'I'll find it,' he said.

'I'd like to phone James before we go.'

'If you must.' His eyes, as he looked at her, were like stone. 'I've made all my calls. What time are you planning staying on until?'

'I don't know. About eleven—' Damn the man! Did he think he could make her feel guilty at wanting to go out? 'I can make my own way back here, so please don't worry about that.'

'On your own? At night? Don't be stupid, Arwenna,' he said dismissively. 'You're not in Raneley now—'

'Not on my own,' she interrupted. 'I'd get lost anyway. Steve's got a car.'

'Oh, has he? And will he have been drinking?'

'He's not a teetotaller, if that's what you mean. Yes, probably.'

'Then I'll pick you up.'

'And aren't *you* going to have a drink all evening? How *noble,*' she said sarcastically.

'Probably not. And if I were to, I'd come in a taxi. I'm not stupid.'

'Oh, no, you're not. You're just bloody perfect, that's all,' she snapped. 'And I am over twenty-one, you know, and not entirely helpless. I'm quite capable of phoning for a taxi for myself, you know, if necessary, so don't think you have to be nursemaid!'

'I'm responsible for you being here. And while you are here I'll see that you don't get lost, or have to wander the streets at night. That's common courtesy, not "nursemaiding",' he retorted. 'And as I'm not doing anything particular this evening it's no trouble to take you and bring you back.' Said logically and sensibly as his words were, they made Arwenna feel as though she were childish. This was the man who had held her in his arms and told her he wanted to make love to her. It was quite hard for her to believe. He had never loved any woman, he had told her. She could easily believe that. He probably didn't know what love was, and never would.

'Then thank you,' she answered, 'I accept.' She left him standing there and went to her bedroom, closing the door firmly after her. Time to telephone James. It was something that had to be done, and the sooner the better. There was a heavy sick feeling inside her as she picked up the receiver and began to dial. Surely it would be better telling him in person? She hesitated, misdialled, and put the receiver down. Perhaps—now she would prepare him, tell him she would see him when she returned—she picked up the phone again, slightly easier in her mind. She owed him that, at least. The telephone at the other end began to ring.

ARWENNA STOOD by the window of her room and looked out at the gardens, but she saw nothing of them. Her eyes were blurred with tears. Twenty minutes had passed since the call to James, but she stood there oblivious of time.

He had known that something was wrong as soon as she spoke. He had also been waiting for her to telephone since his accusations, and her hanging up on him, and clearly during that time his jealous anger had been silently growing. It had been far more difficult than she had envisaged—and it had ended with him saying, in shaking, bitter tones: 'I don't want to see you when you get back to Raneley—there's nothing to say, is there? We both know we're through— Let's leave it at that. My God, I've been wasting my time, haven't I? You're welcome to him, and he's welcome to *you!*' and he had slammed the receiver down.

Arwenna had tried to call him back, but got the engaged signal. Now she wasn't trying any longer. He had made his opinions clear—that he thought she was having an affair with Garth. He would never have believed the truth. There had not only been anger in his voice, but spite in his words. That had upset her more than anything else, yet in a strange way it had helped her to realise that there could have been no future for them together.

She was cold, deathly cold, and she didn't want to go to Steve's flat. She didn't even feel like facing her aunt. She put her hand to her aching throat, raw with unshed tears, and prayed for strength. She didn't hear the knock at the door, and only turned when it opened and she heard Garth's voice: 'Are you ready?'

She blinked hard a few times and he came across to the window. 'James?' he said. Arwenna nodded, unable to speak. 'I see. You've—told him?'

She didn't answer; she didn't need to. She wanted someone to hold her, and comfort her, but not him. Not him.

She cleared her throat. 'I'll be all right in a minute,' she croaked.

'No, you won't. Not to visit your aunt, you won't.'

She brushed her cheek. 'I *will*. Leave me for a minute. I'll wash my face—'

'You're coming to have a good stiff drink first, then we'll get you looking human. For God's sake why didn't you ring him after?'

'I didn't know it would be that bad,' she retorted, regaining some of her spirit. If anything would cure her, it wouldn't be Garth. She'd get no sympathy from that piece of granite. 'And a drink doesn't solve anything—not for me. It might for *you*.'

'That's it,' he mocked. 'You're doing fine—getting some of the fire back, instead of standing there looking as though you'd been kicked.'

'Why don't you leave me alone? I don't need *you*,' she snapped.

'Leave you to wallow in self-pity? We don't have time for that. You're going out after, remember? Or had you forgotten?'

'No. Thank God I am,' she said fervently. 'I'll be with human beings.'

'And I'm not. Thanks!' His voice was caustic.

'No, you're not,' she answered. She could see him clearly now, not blurred. 'But don't let it worry you. I'm sure it never has. You've probably got a cash register where your heart should be.'

'Then I must need somebody to teach me how to be human, mustn't I?' he grated, not seeming angry at all, although he ought to have been. He suddenly took hold of her hand and held it to his breast. 'What do you feel? Don't you feel anything beating there?'

Arwenna tried to pull her hand away, and instead Garth pulled her nearer to him. 'Well?' he demanded. 'I'm waiting for an answer.'

He had her hand over his heart, and the beat was strong and steady. 'Let me go,' she whispered.

'No.'

'Yes! Let me—*go!*' She made a superhuman effort to be free, and he began laughing softly.

'You're doing fine,' he said. 'Keep fighting!'

She kicked his leg and twisted herself sideways, but he caught hold of her hair and pulled her to face him, and kissed her very soundly.

'*That's* for kicking me,' he told her, when he had done. 'Got any more little tricks?'

His eyes gleamed darkly. No longer the cool stranger, but a strong man holding her, taunting her, maddening her— holding her very tightly, but not brutally, and knowing his strength, and using it to keep her where he chose, until he was ready to let her go. Knowing the futility of trying to escape, Arwenna stopped struggling, but her eyes blazed defiance.

'I wouldn't waste them on you,' she breathed.

'Pity. I enjoy a good fight, now and again, as long as it doesn't get too rough—and you wouldn't, would you?' He smiled. 'You know what would happen if you did.'

'You're not a man, you're a brute!'

'Well, at least that's one step up from a walking cash register,' he mocked. 'Keep going.'

'Go to hell!'

He let her go, turned away, looked back from the doorway, gave a curious half smile. 'If I do, I won't go alone,' he
said. 'Rinse your face and comb your hair and we'll go.'

Arwenna watched the door close after him and clenched
her fists. Then she went to wash her face. The strange thing
was—and she didn't realise why until much later—that she
felt much better. The shattering numbness that had taken
her after her call to James had completely gone. She felt
alive again. She felt cured.

Five minutes later they were on their way by car to visit
Aunt Daisy. She lay in bed, still sleeping, but with more
colour in her cheeks than that morning. At Arwenna's kiss
she opened her eyes and said sleepily:

'Mmm—' Her voice trailed away. Arwenna sat at the
bedside and held the old lady's hand. There was silence for
a few moments, then Aunt Daisy said, 'Where's Garth?'

He walked over to her. 'I'm here,' he said, taking her
hand.

'That's nice.' Her voice was slurred, and she tried to give
him a smile, but it was an effort. 'Black eye?' she said, as if
faintly surprised—no more than that.

He laughed. 'I walked into a door.'

'Oh dear.' She had closed her eyes again, as if the effort
of speaking had tired her. 'Put on a grated apple poultice—
or potatoes—don't forget—' She stopped, and they both
realised that she was asleep. The visit passed in no time at
all.

Garth was driving Arwenna towards Hampstead then,
and remarked dryly: 'I must make a note of those cures for
black eyes, they'll probably come in useful. I found your
aunt's comment about your mild temper most interesting. I
thought she knew you well?'

'She does,' she answered shortly.

'Ah. Meaning that it's I who bring out the worst in you?'

'Got it in one.'

'How strange. Perhaps not, though,' and he smiled slightly, as if something funny had occurred to him.

'What does *that* cryptic remark mean?'

He glanced briefly at her. 'What do you think it means?'

'I don't know. I'm not a mind-reader.'

'Then think. You accused me of being violent, beneath the surface. I told you we were two of a kind—perhaps we are. Perhaps it's all simmering inside with you and you keep it well in check with others.'

'I've never heard anything so ridiculous in my life!' she retorted.

'It's not ridiculous, Arwenna, it's the truth, and you don't like it.'

'Just because you say something it doesn't make it gospel, you know.'

'Perhaps not. But I know you already better than James ever did. That's a fact.'

'You're wrong—' she began, but the words died in her throat. No, Garth wasn't wrong. What he said was true. She closed her eyes briefly, and felt the car slow to turn a corner, and when she opened them again she looked at him.

'Yes,' he said softly. 'And you know it. We're nearly there, Arwenna. Better start looking for the number.'

She gazed out of the window at the endless-seeming row of large old terraced houses on either side of the street. Cars were parked on both sides, and most of the houses were shabby and in need of paint, with scraggy front gardens. She pointed. 'There it is.' The front door was open, and as Garth opened her door, they could hear music drifting down from a wide open attic window. Steve appeared, leaning out, waving. 'Hi! Come on up, both of you.'

Arwenna hoped Garth hadn't heard, but he had. 'Tell him thanks,' he said softly. Steve's head had vanished, to be replaced by Zack's, who nearly fell out of the window as he waved, and Garth turned away towards his car. Arwenna waved back and blew a kiss, and as Garth was about to walk round to his driver's door Steve appeared, ran down the steps, and whirled Arwenna round, hugging her so tightly that she was breathless. Then he looked at Garth and grinned broadly. 'Thanks for bringing her,' he said, and stuck out his hand. 'Steve Marshall.' Garth shook hands with him, and Steve said: 'Would you like to come up for a drink? You're most welcome, honestly.' Garth looked at Arwenna, still within Steve's embrace, then he too smiled— a brief polite one, but a smile, nevertheless.

'Thank you, I will,' he answered, and began to lock the car.

CHAPTER NINE

ALL THE furniture in the huge attic room had been pushed
back against the poster-filled walls, leaving a large clear area
in the centre. A table was filled with cans of beer and bottles, a record player was on full blast in one corner, and the
room had about a dozen people in, standing or sitting,
talking and drinking. A young bearded man sat cross-
legged on a bed, strumming a guitar in silent competition to
the music, and seemingly oblivious of it. Steve switched the
record player off and clapped his hands loudly, as Zack, as
tall as Steve and even more heavily bearded, hugged Arwenna delightedly, declaring his undying love in tones that
became very clear as the music stopped.

'Right, everyone,' said Steve. 'Cut that out, Zack, we've
got other company. This is Arwenna, and Garth. Arwenna
is our one true love, Zack's and mine, so it's hands off,
everybody else, and what are you having to drink, Garth?
Beer, or cheap disgusting red plonk?'

A roar went up from the others, and a man's voice said:
'It's not plonk. It's best supermarket *vino,* man—' and Arwenna found herself greeting, and being greeted by, the rest
of the party. There were only three other girls there, students from the look of them, long-haired, pretty, two in
jeans, one in a long flowing flowered skirt and blouse. The
guitarist, now able to be heard, struck up a pleasant ballad,
and the atmosphere in the room was one of complete accord and harmony.

Garth and Steve stood talking, Garth with glass in hand
filled with something that looked like diluted Ribena, while

Steve opened a can of beer, and Zack pulled Arwenna away
from them into a kitchen overflowing with food and opened
tins, and said: 'Let me look at you. God, it's good to see you
again!' He grinned down at her. Zack, half American, with
dark flashing eyes, and olive skin, who looked more Span-
ish than anything else. He gave a long sigh. 'It's *good* to see
you, honey, really *good*. Even if you had to bring a man
with you.' He glanced through the open doorway to where
Garth and Steve stood. Both were of the same height, and
both, incredibly to Arwenna, seemed to be getting on well.
'You're working for *him*?'

'Yes, Zack, you're looking absolutely splendid. How long
has it been? Two years? I can't believe it.'

'Yes, well, I always was a handsome devil. And improving with age.' He forgot about Garth as he gazed fondly at
her. 'You too—improving, I mean. You look quite edible.
Quite, quite *delicious*.' He bent and kissed her. 'Mmm, taste
nice, too. Is *he* staying?'

'I doubt it. Steve asked him up for a drink.'

'I'll get him for that afterwards. I may kill him for it.
Here's me, been waiting for this moment for two years, and
we're surrounded by people. It's not fair,' he groaned. 'How
long are you in London?'

'Only about a week.'

'Hell! Never mind. We'll go out when we can. Does
thingy—*him*—let you out alone, or does he have to trail
along everywhere?'

'Of course not.' She laughed. 'I'd love to see you, Zack—
both of you—any time.'

'Okay, it's a date.' He was about to hug her again when
Steve pushed his way in.

'Break it up, you two,' he said. 'Come and join the party.
Someone's thundering up the stairs now.' He lowered his
voice. 'He's not all that bad, Arwenna—quite human.' Arwenna looked past Steve. Garth was talking to—or rather,
being talked to, by two of the girls, who clearly found him
an interesting animal in his sober grey suit. He was laugh-

ing at something one had said, and the next moment she was refilling his glass. He didn't seem to be protesting.

Two couples burst into the room, and voices were raised in greeting. ''Scuse me,' said Zack. 'Got to go and say hi to this lot. I'll be back.' He slid past Steve and left them.

'Is Garth stopping?' Arwenna asked.

'I dunno. Liz and Jo seem to have nabbed him for themselves. Come on, let's go and get the music going and have a dance. He's a big boy, Arwenna, I'm sure he can take care of himself.'

'You wanted to have a good look at him, didn't you?' she accused.

'Of course!' He grinned down at her. 'Did you give him the black eye?'

She looked at him, her face telling him without words, and he gave a low whistle. 'You did, you little minx! What had he done? No, don't tell me, I'd rather not know.' He took her round the waist. 'Come on, I'll get you sloshed first, then dance.' Someone had started up the record player, and the new arrivals were doing a fair imitation of disco dancing, urged on by whistles and claps, and the outer door opened again, and the room was suddenly full.

Arwenna found a glass in her hand, and the liquid that looked suspiciously like Ribena was not unpleasant, rather sweet, but clearly harmless. She danced with Steve, then Zack had joined in, and she looked to see Garth having his glass taken from him by Liz—or was it Jo?—and he seemed to be protesting, but laughing as he did so.

The room was very warm. The guitarist had abandoned his efforts to compete with the Bee Gees, and was doing a take-off of John Travolta in a corner, oblivious to the cat-calls of his friends. There must have been twenty or more there now, and the noise was unimaginable, and more seemed to be pouring in every moment. A few friends, Steve had said. Arwenna, laughing, realised that she was enjoying herself immensely. She wondered if Garth was, or even if he were still there, because she couldn't see him. As she whirled past the kitchen doorway—she saw. He wasn't alone. Liz—or Jo; Arwenna never had found out who was whom—had her arms round his neck, was standing on tip-toe, and kissing him. He didn't seem in any hurry to escape. And at that precise moment, as she halted with shock, he lifted his face from the fervent embrace and looked directly at her. Arwenna turned away. Garth had taken his jacket off, and his sleeves were rolled up, and his tie was undone.

Steve too had seen. He whirled her away into a dim corner and said: 'He's not doing too badly with Liz, is he? Better watch it, he may not get out of there alive. Liz is quite a girl.' He laughed. 'Anyway, I can have you to myself now.'

Arwenna didn't know why she was furious, or why the party should suddenly have changed. She glared at Steve, who looked wounded and said quietly: 'Hey, what's the matter?'

'He's disgusting!' she said fiercely.

'You're kidding!' Steve's face was stunned. He put his arms round her, soothing her, holding her tightly. 'It's only a party. I thought he'd be a stuffy bastard—okay, I admit it, I asked him up because I wanted to see his reaction to our little crowd. I've never met a bloated capitalist before—I thought it'd be fun—but he's the one having the fun.' He chuckled, his eyes alight with pleasure. 'He's not bad, honestly.'

Arwenna felt her temper subside. Steve would see good in anybody. And how could she tell him the truth anyway? Garth was even cleverer than she had imagined. He would know what Steve had done, and why. He could have easily refused the invitation. No one would have expected him to fit in with a crowd of students, all in their early twenties, yet that seemed to be precisely what he had done. 'Sorry, Steve,' she said, and smiled at him. 'Can I have another drink?'

'Sure, anything for you.' He kissed the tip of her nose. 'Stay right there. I'll be back.' He returned with two glasses filled with wine, they found a corner of a bed to sit on, and then began to catch up on mutual news. Arwenna put Garth out of her mind.

IT WAS midnight when they left, and the party was beginning to break up. Garth gave four people a lift home, and after he had dropped them off and he and Arwenna were alone in the car, he said:

'That was a very pleasant evening.'

'There's no need to sound surprised when you say it,' she answered. 'Anyway, I didn't think you'd stay. I wouldn't have thought a students' party was *quite* your scene.'

He laughed. To her sensitive ears, the laughter seemed to hold mockery. 'Oh, I don't know,' he mused. 'It was *very* interesting.'

'So I noticed. I didn't know you went in for girls of twenty,' she said, trying to control her sudden fury.

'Is that what's bothering you? She was a nice girl.'

'It doesn't bother *me,*' she snapped. 'Not one bit. If you want to make a fool of yourself—'

'You weren't doing so badly,' he remarked, with irony. 'Two devoted swains anticipating your every wish—come on, Arwenna, you loved every minute of it.'

'They're old friends,' she retorted, seething.

'Oh, I know. I had Steve telling me all about it. I got the impression that anyone who hurt you would probably get a knife in his back—he thinks the sun shines out of you. As your Aunt Daisy does. Mild-tempered indeed! God, they've not seen the temper in you—and before you cut in, look at you *now.* You're fuming. And why? Because I didn't stand there being stuffy and patronising and looking as though I'd a bad smell under my nose. That's what you'd have liked, isn't it? For me to fall flat on my face—well, I didn't. I know how to get on with anyone I choose, when I choose, and if I happen to want to go and kiss a nubile young woman in a kitchen, or anywhere else for that matter, I won't have *you* telling me what I should be doing instead.' And he switched

on the car radio, effectively silencing anything she might
have been about to say.

The rest of the journey was accomplished to the sounds
of classical music, the kind Arwenna loved, but which had
no power to soothe her now. When they reached Garth's
flat, she said: 'Thank you for taking me, goodnight,' and
stalked off to bed, a bundle of quivering fury. She slammed
and locked her bedroom door, not sure if he had been
laughing or not, and not wanting to know.

SHE SLEPT until nearly midday, and was only wakened by
the telephone shrilling loudly by her bedside. Fumbling for
the receiver, she managed to pick it up, and said, very
sleepily: 'Hello?'

'You *are* available? Good.' Garth's voice dripped sarcasm. Arwenna sat up. What time was it? Where was he?
Not that she cared, but . . .

'Yes, I'm available.' Her head ached, and she thought she
had slept badly, but wasn't awake enough to be sure. 'Aren't
you here?'

'If I were, I wouldn't be phoning you,' he answered. 'I
went out at ten and I shall be out all day. There's a message
for you from Zack by the phone in the lounge. If you want
to work I've left some letters out for you to translate. I'll be
in about six. Any questions?'

'No.' She put her hand to her aching forehead. 'Oh—
where are you if I need you?'

'I doubt you will, but I've left my number by the phone.
Don't call unless it's important. Goodbye.' The line went
dead, and the dialling tone began. She replaced the receiver. She supposed she had better get up. She could hear
a distant hum, and when she had put on a dressing gown
and gone into the kitchen, found a middle-aged woman
there doing the floor with an electric polisher.

'Good morning, madam,' the woman, said, switching off
the machine and smiling at her politely as if she was quite

used to seeing strange young women appearing at midday clad in nightclothes. 'I hope this didn't wake you?'

'No.' She probably *was* quite used to it, thought Arwenna. The woman had a pleasant face, grey hair, an efficient manner. She wore a blue nylon smock with 'Frensham Mansions' embroidered on the top pocket.

'I'm Mrs Holt,' the woman added. 'Would you like me to make you a drink, madam?'

'That's very kind of you, Mrs Holt,' Arwenna answered. 'I'd love a coffee. Are you having one as well?' She sat down at the table. 'I'll keep out of your way.'

'I've done in here, anyway. The other rooms are finished. There's only your bedroom, if you wouldn't mind?'

'No, of course not. I'm sorry, I—' Arwenna smiled at her. Mrs Holt was filling a kettle, getting out two cups and saucers, moving quietly and efficiently. The kitchen shone with cleanliness, everything neat and tidy.

'I will have a coffee if you don't mind, Madam. Mr Vanner never minds, but I do try to keep out of his way, of course.' She looked at Arwenna. 'Would you like something to eat as well?'

'No, thanks. I've some clothes I must wash. Is there anywhere to dry them?'

'We have a laundry room, madam. Just leave anything out and I'll see they're returned today.'

'Oh, I can do them. It's only lingerie—I just wondered about drying.'

'No trouble at all, madam,' the woman insisted. 'I'll do them personally.' She made the coffee and put it on the table, then went out, to return with a blue plastic bag. 'Pop them in there, and I'll bring it back later.'

'You're very kind. Do sit down.' Arwenna sipped her coffee and Mrs Holt sat down at the table and picked up her cup. 'How often do you come here, Mrs Holt?'

'Three days a week, madam, Monday, Wednesday and Friday. Two other women come as well, and we generally

have everything done about noon. But I stayed on to do
your room when you'd woken.'

'You should have knocked!' protested Arwenna, dis-
mayed.

'Oh, no, Mr Vanner said not to disturb you.'

'But I wouldn't want to delay you. I'm awfully sorry.'

'Not at all, madam, there was plenty to do in here anyway. You haven't delayed me at all. I believe there's a message for you by the phone,' added Mrs Holt.

'Yes, Mr Vanner called me just now to tell me, otherwise
I'm afraid I'd have still been asleep.' She gave a wry grin.
'But I don't make a habit of oversleeping, I assure you. It
won't happen again.'

The woman thawed slightly. Her manner had been very
formal, but it was as if Arwenna's natural warmth had
reached her. 'It's quite all right,' she said. 'Really, it is. And
it's no trouble to me. I'd have come back later if necessary.
We'd all do anything for Mr Vanner.'

'Are you employed here at the flats full time?'

'Yes. But Mr Vanner gets special treatment, of course.'

Arwenna didn't understand the 'of course'. Why? 'Oh,
why? Because this is the penthouse apartment, you mean?'

'Why, no, madam,' the woman looked faintly surprised.
'I mean because of him owning the flats.'

It was Arwenna's turn to look more than faintly surprised. 'Owning? You mean—the whole block?'

'Yes, madam. Didn't you know?'

Arwenna shook her head. She couldn't believe it. 'No. I
thought—just this one,' she said at last, stunned.

'Oh, no, it's owned by one of his companies. We're all
employed by him. He's a real gentleman too.'

She could have been saying that simply out of polite-
ness—and a shrewd desire to keep well in with the boss—but
Arwenna sensed the genuine respect in her voice. 'I'm sure
he is,' she said, because there was no way she could say
anything else. She had finished her coffee, and it was obvious that Mrs Holt wanted to get on with her work. Ar-

wenna stood up. 'I'll get my things to wash, then I'll work in the main lounge while you do my room.' She picked up the plastic bag.

'Thank you.' Mrs Holt stood as well, and took the cup. 'I'll be done in half an hour.'

Minutes later, Arwenna was sitting in the lounge going through the work that Garth had left. The surprise was fading. She wondered why he hadn't told her. Perhaps he assumed she knew—perhaps he didn't care, either way. But it made her realise something very sharply: how far apart their worlds really were. She had always lived a life where luxuries were to be saved for—never poor, but never rich. She had never wanted more, never felt deprived, and was happy thus. She wondered if Garth was happy, despite all his vast riches. She didn't envy him his wealth; she had never envied anyone anything in her life. There seemed something wrong to her about one person having so much, but she had never really considered it before. There were other things far more important in life than the pursuit of wealth.

She sighed, then dismissed the subject from her mind and got on with the work before her.

When Mrs Holt had gone, she showered and dressed in her most feminine dress, an Indian cotton with swirling design, soft and full; telephoned Zack, who was having a day off to revise for exams, and arranged to meet him the following day, Saturday. They discussed the party, and he made her laugh, and he was warm and caring and human, and she loved him like a brother. She had a brief moment of feeling sorry for Garth, who didn't love anybody, then remembered something. 'Zack,' she said, 'I know you know everything about London. I'm going out tonight with the man you fondly call Thingy—and I'd like to get a nice dress to wear. Any ideas?'

'From me? You're kidding! When do you think *I* last bought a dress?'

'I didn't mean that, idiot. Come on, you know loads of girls. Where's the in place for super dresses at super cheap prices?'

'There's only one girl in my life, honey, and I'm talking to her now. You're serious?'

'Yes, I'm serious.'

'Okay. Get a pencil and paper.' He gave her directions, the addresses of three shops in the Hampstead area, off the beaten track, asked her if she wanted him to go with her, and she thanked him and said no, he'd got work to do, and anyway, she didn't have much time and they'd be talking too much and she'd see him tomorrow anyway. They said their goodbyes and Arwenna hung up and looked from her list to the work she had to do.

If she went now, and took a taxi, she could be back in a couple of hours; it was nearly two. She would work hard from four to six, then be able to get ready. She had already done a lot, and there wasn't much left to do. She wanted to look nice for their evening out at Bill Chisholm's, though she wasn't sure why it seemed so important, except that an intrusive and annoying memory kept coming back, of a girl flinging her arms round Garth's neck and kissing him, in a tiny kitchen, and it refused to go away.

Decided, she picked up the telephone and rang down to the lobby of the flats. Ten minutes later she was on her way.

THE DOOR opened, and Garth came in. Arwenna looked up from her notepad, smiled a cool little smile and said hello— then caught her breath.

He nodded. 'Any messages for me?' He looked tired, in need of a shave, and he wore an eye-patch over his left eye, which shocked Arwenna immensely. She stood up and walked towards him, face anxious.

'What's the matter?' she asked.

'You should know. You did it,' he answered, and lifted aside the patch and took it off. 'I got fed up with people asking if I'd walked into a bloody door, if you must know.'

She closed her eyes, seeing only too clearly the glorious hues of the fully developed black eye that stared back accusingly at her. 'Let me do something,' she said quietly. 'Please.'

'Such as? Giving me another one to match? Thanks. I'm sure that'd help a lot.'

'No. I meant—well, what Aunt Daisy said. You've got potatoes, and apples—'

'It's a black eye, not a fruit salad,' he snapped, and sank down on to the settee.

'Let me get you a drink,' she said, and went to the cupboard.

'That's a better idea.' He flexed his hands. 'Make it a whisky—straight.'

She poured him one and handed it to him, and he drank it down in one. He looked as though he needed it. Arwenna's calm, contented mood vanished. She had worked well, and done all he had left, and she had bought a beautiful matching skirt and a blouse top that hadn't cost the earth, and she had been feeling good, and happy. Now she felt wretched instead. She felt guilty and unhappy, even as though she were to blame for Garth's obvious tiredness. She wanted to soothe and comfort him, and was disturbed at her own reaction. It was six o'clock, and they would probably leave about seven, to visit Aunt Daisy—on whom she had found time to call that afternoon, having found the clothes in the first shop on Zack's list—and she was going to help Garth in some way, if only to assuage her guilt. She took his glass from him, poured in some more whisky, but not much, and gave it to him, then knelt at his feet. 'Please. Just let me try,' she said. 'You look tired.'

'I am tired—I've been working hard. I'm also quite tough, Arwenna. After a shave and a shower I'll be fine. I'll still have a black eye, but we can't have everything, can we?' His voice was hard. She stayed where she was, and looked at him.

'If you want to insult me, go ahead,' she answered. 'I deserve it.'

'You mean you'll *let* me! *Thanks.*' His tone was heavy with irony. 'I wouldn't know where to start, would I? We'd never get out. All right, go and grate an apple, or whatever you want to do. I'll be in my room.' He finished the drink and handed her the glass. Arwenna took it into the kitchen and rinsed it, found an apple, peeled it, then grated it into a cereal dish. She paused outside Garth's door, hearing a shower running, then knocked. She had never ever been inside it.

'Come in, I'll not be a minute,' he called. She opened the door and went in. His bathroom door was closed, and the water stopped as she entered. She looked around. He had a large antique wardrobe and matching chest of drawers, beautifully polished and old. The bed was large and had a deep brown bedspread over it, matching curtains and furniture. There were several prints on the walls, of vintage cars. It was a very masculine room. Garth walked out wearing only trousers, a towel draped round his shoulders. 'I'll lie on the bed,' he said, 'and you can do your stuff. And while it's setting, or whatever it's supposed to do, I'd appreciate it if you'd make me a cup of coffee. Black, strong, no sugar.'

'Yes,' she answered. He lay down and she sat beside him. She had mashed the grated apple as finely as she could and it was turning faintly brown. Garth closed his eyes and she leaned over and applied the mushy mixture carefully round his eye. He didn't move a muscle.

'And how long,' he asked, when she stood up, 'do I have to stay like this?'

'About ten minutes.' She fled. She was mad, she knew she was. She made his coffee and took it back. Garth lay perfectly still, eyes closed. He could have been asleep.

'Do you want to drink it now?' she asked quietly.

'How? On my back?'

'No, I'll lift your head. Look, let me put this towel round you—' she did so, 'then if any mush falls off it won't go on the bed. There now.' She reached over and slipped her hand behind his head. 'Gently does it.' He let her. He suddenly seemed to be quite pliant and unresisting. He opened his good eye as she eased his head quietly up, and gave her a baleful glance. Ignoring it, she put the coffee cup to his mouth. He drank some, then said:

'That's enough.' Arwenna eased him back again and looked at her watch. Ten minutes were nearly up.

'I'll go and get a washcloth and a dish,' she told him, and went to get them.

'How does it feel?' she asked when she returned. 'Any better?'

'No.' She sighed and began cleansing the poultice off. What had she expected? A miracle? Two minutes later all was cleared and she looked closely at his eye as he sat up. It looked very much the same as it had before. He touched it carefully. 'Mmm,' he said. 'Soothing. It's not gone, has it?' This in dry tones.

'I'm afraid not. But I'll do it again later.'

Garth swung his legs over the side of the bed and she moved away. 'I shouldn't bother,' he remarked. 'It'll go, eventually.'

'Garth,' she bit her lip, 'I'm—sorry.'

He removed a minute portion of apple from his arm. 'Yes, I know. You already said.' He looked at her. 'You're quite something, you know that? Really something. I've never had a black eye in my life before, and I've been in some scraps when I was younger. And you come along into my life and put your mark on me straight away. I must be mad!'

'So you must. You talk as though I forced my way in. Listen—it was you, not me, remember?'

'I'll never forget,' he retorted dryly. 'I'll certainly never forget you as long as I live. And don't start with the smart answers. The new you—the one I met fifteen minutes ago with an anxious face, who couldn't do enough for me—"let me get you a drink"''—he added, in fair imitation of her tones, 'is okay for a while longer. It's quite a change from the firecracker I've come to know and love over the past few days—' He stopped, as if suddenly aware of what he had said, but the words didn't register with Arwenna, not then. She was too incensed at his mimicry of her voice at that moment.

'Firecracker!' she exploded. 'Me? If I'm a firecracker, what the hell are you?' She put her hands on her hips. 'I've been working hard all afternoon for you, *and* I nipped out and bought a dress because you wanted me to for tonight *and* I paid for the taxi myself, *and* bought the dress with my own money, and I've already said I'm sorry for hitting you, and you deserved it anyway. You seem to forget *that,* and I don't intend to go on apologising for the rest of my life, and you make me sick—' She stopped. What was that he had said? 'The firecracker I've come to know and love—' 'And *love?*' Him? What a stupid, ridiculous thing to have said!

Garth sat down suddenly again on the bed and put his head in his hands, leaning forward as if in pain, and Arwenna's anger faded away as quickly as it had come. She knelt down, heart beating fast at the sight of him, suddenly so still, as if ill. 'Garth?' Then, as he didn't answer, she put her hands out tentatively and touched him on the shoulders. 'Garth, are you all right?' she asked anxiously. Her heart hammered in sudden fear, and her mouth was dry.

He nodded, and made a sound, more like a groan, but stayed where he was. Was he ill? 'Please speak,' she whispered.

'Just go away and leave me alone,' he said, very quietly, but with intensity.

'No. Not while you're like—are you in pain?' She sat beside him on the bed. She was shivering.

'No. Leave me—' He seemed to be trembling.

'Garth—'

'Get out. For God's sake—get *out,*' he muttered, and there was such terrible violence in the words that she jumped to her feet as if to escape him, and stood there poised, torn with indecision. Then he looked up at her, and she was frightened at what she saw. She didn't understand it, and that was worse, and she couldn't move. Then he got to his feet and put his hand out to her arm. His fingers, when he held her arm, were hard, almost biting into the flesh. 'I want you out of my room,' he grated. 'Don't you understand?' He took his fingers away as if she had burned him. Sure that he had some sudden, awful fever, Arwenna took a step forward to him and held out her hands.

'I can't leave you—' she began, 'not like—' He swung his left arm out, striking away the hands she was holding towards him, to help him, and, stunned by the violence, she staggered back, clasping her wrist where his hand had struck her, gasping with the shock of it. Then, turning, physically frightened, she ran out, and along to her room. Inside she stood shaking by the door, rubbing her wrist. Garth had landed out blindly, and she felt the burning sensation where his hand had met her wrist, and felt almost sick with shock.

The door opened and he was there. She whirled round, hand going to her throat in an instinctive gesture of self-protection. 'Arwenna,' he said, 'Oh God, forgive me Arwenna—I didn't mean—'

'Don't touch me again,' she whispered. 'I left—I got out—'

'I didn't know what I was doing—I didn't intend to hurt you, I swear it. I only—' he stopped. There was agony on his face, and in his eyes. 'I couldn't see—I was telling you to go—' He walked slowly towards her, hands held out, palms upward. 'Dear God, I wouldn't strike you—I wouldn't ever *knowingly* hit *you.*'

'You did,' she gasped. 'You hurt my hand—see?' She held it up, and he took it, and bent his face to it and kissed it. Then slowly, as if compelled by a force stronger than he knew, he put his arms around her, trembling as if indeed he were in the grip of a fever, and held her to him tightly.

'Please forgive me,' he said, and his voice was broken and husky. 'Please forgive me—I didn't intend that—'

'All right, I forgive you,' she whispered. 'I know you didn't mean to hit me—I know it was accidental. I only thought you were ill, that's all—I only wanted to help.' She felt the tremor of his body against hers. 'Are you sure you're all right?'

'I am now.' He put his hand up to her chin and tilted her face slightly upwards, and she knew he was going to kiss her a moment before he did so. It was a strangely gentle kiss, a kiss that followed on his asking for forgiveness; it had neither passion nor excitement, but a longing for reassurance, and she had never known anything so very beautiful in her life. She responded to it, putting her hands behind his shoulder to hold him to her. They blended, they melted as though become one, and in his great strength was a gentleness she had also never known.

When the kiss was over, Garth held her against his heart, so that she felt the beats in her head, and heard, over that sound, his voice as he said: 'We'd better get ready if we're to leave soon.'

'Yes, I know.' But she didn't move, and neither did he. There was no explanation for her wanting to stay in his arms after all that had happened, but she did.

'Your aunt will be expecting us.'

'Yes, she will.' But neither moved. Garth wasn't trembling now, neither was Arwenna. She felt only a great welling of strength from him, as though her whole body was getting a charge, almost like electricity. It was wonderful and very satisfying, and she wanted it to go on and on...

She heard his deep sigh, almost a groan, but not of pain. They stood there in the sunlit room, and it might have been for seconds or minutes. There was no count of time at all. She only knew a complete and utter sensation of well being and happiness. At last, and as if by mutual consent, and at the same moment they moved slightly away from each other, and looked into each other's eyes. Garth gave a faint smile. 'If you feel like I do,' he said, 'You'll feel ready for anything. I feel as though I've just had my batteries recharged.'

'So do I,' she admitted. He touched her face with the back of his hand.

'I'm sorry, I should have shaved first. Your cheeks are very pink.'

'Are they? Never mind.' It seemed an inane conversation, but some things can never be said. 'They'll match my outfit. Which reminds me, I'd better get it on.'

'Yes,' he said. 'Let me see it.'

Arwenna walked away and opened her wardrobe and took it out.

CHAPTER TEN

IT WAS as though a truce had been declared, and one that was to be scrupulously observed by both sides. Arwenna held out the skirt and slim-fitting blouse in pale pink, silky material, fine knit, and was pleased herself with it. Garth touched the pleated skirt. 'Very attractive,' he commented. 'Harrod's?'

She smiled. 'No. A little shop—a boutique on the borders of Hampstead. I saw it, tried it on, and bought it. Twenty minutes and I was on my way back h—' She was about to say 'home' and substituted, 'here.'

'Clever. And quick. I approve.' The atmosphere, over the last few moments, had completely changed. As though something was safely locked away inside them both, hidden, both aware—the awareness was in the air—but calmness on the surface. For how long? thought Arwenna. It must stay like this, like it is, civilised and pleasant, or we will destroy each other—or he will destroy me.

The explosive, devastating scene of before, which had led to the embrace, which in turn had led to this safe haven, had been too shattering for words. Life could not hold too many of those, and there had been enough in just a brief few days to last nearly a lifetime. She took both skirt and blouse off the hanger and laid them on the bed. 'If you'd be kind enough to unbutton me at the back before you go,' she told him, 'I'd appreciate it. I can do it—but only with a bit of arm-stretching.' And I don't feel strong enough, she added, but silently.

'Of course. Turn round.' She did so and he unbuttoned the dozen or so tiny buttons with care. 'Okay?'

'Yes, thanks.' She turned to face him again.

'Sure you can manage now?' A slight smile, no more aggression, just a mild joke that she could appreciate.

'Oh yes, I think so.' A little smile back, just to let him know.

He shrugged. 'Well, I tried.' He went towards the door. 'Fifteen minutes enough for you?'

'If you go now.'

He went out. Arwenna let out her breath in a silent and deep sigh, and took off her dress. Let the truce continue, she thought. Please let it continue.

THEY SPENT a pleasant evening at the Chisholms' elegant house, after visiting Aunt Daisy, and it was nearly twelve-thirty when they arrived back at the apartment. There had been only the four of them, and Ann Chisholm had prepared a fantastic buffet supper that had made Arwenna realise, belatedly, that she had eaten very little all day. Garth was as much at home in their house as he had been the previous night at Steve and Zack's party, and had moreover, been charming and considerate to Arwenna. The truce continued and flourished, and on the way back she dozed off in the car, so totally relaxed and exhausted was she.

She was awoken by his voice: 'Wake up, sleepyhead, we're home,' and opened her eyes to see they were parked by the lift.

'Good heavens, did I fall asleep?' she gasped.

'You did.' He leaned over and opened her door. 'Out you get.'

Waking up rapidly, she stumbled out and stood on the hard concrete, waiting while he locked the doors, then led her to the lift. 'Straight to bed for you,' he said.

'Are we working in the morning?' she asked, as they sped upwards. 'I'm sorry I overslept today, truly. I'll make up for it over the weekend.'

'We'll talk about work in the morning, not now.' He closed the lift door behind them, then they were inside his apartment. Garth loosened his tie and yawned. 'I'm pretty tired myself,' he said. He had switched on only one lamp, and the soft light was sufficient.

'I had a lovely evening,' she told him. 'Thank you for taking me.'

'So did I. You looked very elegant in that outfit.'

'Did I? Thank you.' She slipped off her high-heeled sandals and gave a sigh. 'That's better.' Carrying them, she walked towards her bedroom. 'Goodnight, Garth.'

'Goodnight.'

Arwenna fell straightaway into a deep sleep the minute her head touched the pillow, and woke several hours later, wide awake, alert, as she heard a faint sound from somewhere near. She looked at her bedside clock, which showed nearly five-thirty. It was just getting light outside, and very early bird sounds came faintly through her open window. Arwenna sat up in bed and threw the covers aside and crept to the door. She opened it very quietly, then heard the noise again. It seemed to be coming from the kitchen, although the door was closed. The faintest bang, as of a cupboard shutting. She waited a moment, and heard a strange fluttering sound which sent a chill up her spine.

Quickly, quietly, she ran into Garth's bedroom, put her hand to his mouth, and shook him. As he woke up she leaned over, keeping her hand pressed over his mouth, and whispered:

'There's someone in the kitchen.'

He was instantly awake. He nodded and sat up, grabbing a dressing gown as he did so. Arwenna turned her head away, just in case...

'Stay there,' he whispered, and went out. There was no way she was not going with him, and she crept out after him, saw him open the kitchen door and switch the lights on. She nearly collided with him as he turned in the doorway and started to laugh.

'What—' she began, and peered round him to see a very frightened blackbird scrabbling frantically up the window trying to get out. 'Oh!'

'Someone left the window open,' he said, and she remembered opening the small top window that afternoon. 'Shut the door. I'll get it out.'

She did so, and Garth went and opened the larger window below, and the grateful bird dived out and vanished. He closed them both firmly.

'I'm sorry,' she said. 'It was me.'

'No great harm done. Well—' as he looked around, 'not much.'

'I'll get a cloth,' she said, and opened the cupboard beneath the sink.

'And I'll make coffee. Want one?'

'Please.' She began busily wiping away at the various small souvenirs of the bird's visit. 'Poor thing must have been here all night.'

'Weren't you scared when it woke you?'

'No.' She looked up at him. 'I thought it might just be you at first, until I heard a fluttery noise that sent a shiver right through me. Then I woke you.'

He produced two beakers and made the coffee. 'Most women would have screamed for help.'

'What, and frighten the burglar away? I thought you'd rather catch him.' She sipped her coffee. 'I'm wide awake now.' She sighed. 'With oversleeping yesterday I won't get to sleep again. I might as well stay up and do some work.'

'You've got to be joking!' said Garth, and looked at her as though she was mad.

'No, I'm not.' She smiled. 'Honestly. I often used to get up at home about six and go for a long walk.'

'You're *quite* mad!'

Arwenna had a sudden surge of pure, undiluted happiness. It was one of those rare flashes that come totally without reason or warning. It was a good-to-be-alive sen-

sation, filling her, making her face glow, and she saw his
eyes change as he watched her, and laughed.

'I'm *not!* In fact, I think I'll get dressed and go out and
walk for miles!'

Garth drank his coffee much as he had done the whisky
the previous night—as if he needed it. 'The door's double
locked. I won't let you out.'

'Try and stop me! Get dressed and come with me. Go on,
it'll do you good.'

He gazed at her as though he wasn't believing what he was
seeing. 'You really mean it, don't you?'

'Yes.'

'Then so help me, I must be crazy as well.' He stood up.
'Go on, then.'

'You'll do it?'

He nodded. 'I want my head examined, but yes, I'll do it.'

'See you in five minutes.' Arwenna ran to her room,
stripped, washed, dressed in comfortable jeans and sweater,
grabbed her coat, and went into the lounge to wait. All was
still outside, the city about to wake up, but not yet ready. It
would be an interesting experience, to see it when everyone
was still abed. She turned as Garth appeared, wearing jeans
and dark blue sweater. He scowled at her. 'Change your
mind?'

'No.' She shook her head. 'Come on.'

He took his key out of his pocket, muttered something,
and unlocked the door, carrying a dark suede jacket.

They crept out of the car park like two burglars, and set
off walking down the silent street. Garth put his jacket on
when they had rounded the corner, and Arwenna slipped her
arm in his. 'Smile,' she said.

'Later I might. I'm not awake yet,' he responded. There
was a distant whine, and an electric milk float appeared,
crates rattling on the back. It stopped, and the milkman
jumped out and vanished into the doorway of a block of
flats, and they walked past, and on to a main road. Cars
were passing, not many of them, but a few; two men were

cycling to work, one whistling as they passed. A cat dived down basement steps when it saw them, and watched them suspiciously from the door at the bottom.

They passed banks, and travel agents and shops, most with faint lights burning inside, and in the distance was the sound of heavier traffic and a train from far away. After they had walked for what seemed like miles they were nearing Euston Station and Arwenna said: 'Come on, let's go in and see what's happening.'

Garth looked at her, and shook his head as if he wasn't sure what was happening to him; they ran up the steps at the side, and along, and into the main entrance. Their footsteps echoed hollowly on the shiny stone floor, where a few people wandered about waiting for trains to arrive or depart, and several pigeons landed hopefully nearby. A policeman eyed them suspiciously, then walked away, and Garth said: 'If we get arrested, I shall blame you *entirely*, I want you to know that,' and Arwenna answered:

'I've never been arrested. I wonder what it feels like?' He grabbed her arm firmly, then took hold of her hand and held it as if he would never let her go.

'Come on,' he said, 'let's go back. I'm a respectable citizen and if you dare break any windows I shall deny I know you.'

She laughed, and kissed him, and he looked startled. 'What was that for?' he demanded.

'Because the policeman's looking, so you won't be able to deny it,' she said. He stopped walking, took her in his arms, and kissed her soundly, to the interested speculation of two women cleaners walking wearily past towards the platforms.

'What was that for?' she asked, and knew quite suddenly that she loved him with all her heart, and wondered why she hadn't realised before what was happening to her.

'Nothing. Just to shut you up,' he answered.

They walked out. Arwenna was silent now, and when Garth flagged down a passing taxi she made no protest. She

had just discovered something very disturbing and frightening, and it had shaken her so much that she didn't know
how she would ever look at him again without giving herself away. She sat back in the taxi and thought, oh dear, I
wish it hadn't happened. I wish I hadn't woken up—but it
would have happened later if not then, she knew. It hurt. I
didn't know it would be like this, she thought. I didn't know
it would be like a pain inside, an ache—

'You're very quiet,' he commented, and she saw that they
were back at the car park, and had left the taxi and were
walking towards the lift.

'Yes,' she answered. 'I'm sorry, I should never have
dragged you out so early,' and as he opened the lift doors
she burst into tears, and was horrified, but couldn't stop
herself.

Garth led her into the apartment, closed the door, and put
his arm round her. 'What on earth's the matter?' he asked,
sounding quite shaken.

Sobbing helplessly, she couldn't even begin to attempt an
answer, and what did she say, anyway? How could she tell
a man who had admitted that he wanted an affair with her,
simply to get her out of his system, that she had gone and
done something utterly stupid like falling head over heels in
love with him? She didn't. Or she was asking for trouble.
There had been enough trouble already, when she hadn't
even liked him. And as far as Garth was concerned she
would be just another woman in a long line stretching back,
and forward, to infinity.

He sat her down firmly on the settee and sat beside her,
and began to rub her hands as if they were cold, as they
might have been, for all she knew. 'Please stop,' he said.
'Please—Arwenna, stop crying.' He sounded very fraught,
not at all the man in command, and she hiccuped, and
stopped crying, startled at that strange phenomenon.
Garth—fraught?

'Thank God,' he muttered. 'Look, was it something I
said?'

She shook her head and sniffed, and he produced a neatly ironed handkerchief and said: 'Blow your nose,' so she did so.

'Can I get you a drink?' he asked. 'A cup of tea?'

'N-o—' Her voice was faint, almost a squeak. He sighed, and sat back as if she had exhausted him.

'Can you tell me what made you cry?'

She shook her head. Garth stood up and looked down at her for a moment. She had her head down and could only see his shoes, and she kept her eyes fixed firmly on them. The next moment he was kneeling before her, lifting her chin, so that she had to look at him. She swallowed hard.

'All right,' he said gently, 'I won't ask again. Would you like to go and lie down? It's not eight yet.'

'No, I'm all right now.' She gave a tremulous smile. She had to start now. *Now,* before he could guess anything, before he could see. He must never know, or she would be lost. 'I'll make breakfast, and then, if you'll give me some work, I'll get started.'

'If you think that's best, fine.' He was obviously going to agree with anything she said. Men were supposed, traditionally, to be frightened by a woman's tears, but she hadn't thought it would have had this effect on him.

She dabbed at her cheeks, tucked the handkerchief away in her pocket, and stood up. Garth stood watching her as if she might break into pieces if he moved too suddenly. She took a deep breath. When she walked out she glanced back. He was lighting a cheroot, and he looked as though he had just been hit very hard.

ARWENNA WORKED all morning. Garth had gone out about nine, saying that he would be back for lunch, and did she want him to fetch something to eat, or make lunch himself, or would she?

She said she would make something, and what would he like, and he assured her that absolutely anything would do, and was she sure she was all right? After being assured that she was, he left. She worked hard until noon, then stopped to prepare food. She was meeting Zack at four, and was visiting Aunt Daisy before that. Apart from telling her that he would call in and see Aunt Daisy during the morning, Garth had not told her where he was going.

During the morning's work it had been easy to not think about her feelings for Garth. Preparing the meal in the kitchen it was no longer possible to keep the thoughts from crowding in. She longed to see him again—and she dreaded it, both at the same time; a difficult mixture. The intercom telephone rang in the kitchen as she was making a cheese sauce to go with the marrow she had prepared. It was Fred, the day-time doorman, to tell her that a friend of Mr Vanner's was wanting to come up.

'He's not here at the moment,' she told him. 'Who is it?'

'A Mr Spence—he's a frequent visitor, madam,' Fred answered. 'Says it's important.'

'Mr Vanner will be back soon. Please send him up, will you?'

'Right you are, madam.'

She hung up. She had no way of contacting Garth. He hadn't left a number. She took off her apron as the door buzzed and went to let the unknown visitor in. A tall attractive man stood there, sober-suited, fair-haired, blue-eyed. He smiled, looking faintly puzzled. 'Good morning, I'm sorry to call in like this, but I do need to see Garth quite soon. Will it be convenient for me to wait? My name's Jason Spence, and I'm an old friend of his.'

'Yes, do come in, Mr Spence. I'm Arwenna Holmes. I'm just preparing lunch at the moment. I'm sorry, but I don't know where Garth is, but he should be in soon.'

'Can I help?' He followed her through to the kitchen before she could say yes or no, and seated himself at the table. Arwenna looked at him in some amusement as she put her apron back on again.

'Not unless you want to peel potatoes?' she grinned, looking at the immaculate grey suit.

'Fair enough.' He stood up and took off his jacket and laid it neatly over the back of the chair. 'Got a spare apron?'

'Good heavens, I was joking!' she exclaimed.

He looked at her, as amused as she was. 'I'm not.'

'You've got yourself a job.' She found a tea towel and he draped it round his waist with the air of a master chef donning an apron.

Arwenna stirred the cheese into the blended sauce and left it to be heated later, checked the steak simmering gently in a wine sauce. It smelt delicious, as did the mushrooms.

She prepared the marrow as he peeled three large potatoes, then said: 'If you'd like to stay to lunch, you'd better do a couple more. They're in the rack over there.'

'That's extremely kind of you.' He looked pleased.

'It's no trouble. You say you're an old friend of Garth's. Do you live in London?'

'No, Colchester. I came up last night, intended to phone, and got tied up. So, as I was passing, I called in instead. He has been known to be in on a Saturday morning.'

But not after silly women like me burst into tears, she thought. 'He won't be long now.'

'Are you an—er—old friend of Garth's?' he enquired with some delicacy. He wasn't making a bad job of peeling the potatoes into the sink with the waste disposal unit either.

'Not really. I'm working for him. And my aunt's had an operation at the clinic of his friend Bill Chisholm. Do you know him?'

'Oh, Bill! Of course! I introduced them seven—oh—eight years ago.'

That was a conversational opener if ever there was one. Arwenna told Jason about the previous evening's visit there, and they discovered almost instantaneously that they got on very well with each other. Jason was extremely funny, a witty raconteur, and one topic led to another, and they were deep in conversation over two glasses of sherry in the kitchen, supervising the cooking at the same time, and Ar-

wenna's laughter pealed out just after Jason finished telling
her about a disastrous holiday he had once had in Austria,
when Garth walked in.

They looked round, startled, Jason leaning well back,
sprawling in the chair, long legs under the table, jacketless,
tea towel-clad, laughing helplessly—seeing Garth at the
same moment that Arwenna did.

'Garth!' Jason jumped to his feet, whipping off the tea
towel, and the two men shook hands. Garth said:

'I see you two have introduced yourselves,' with a slightly
raised eyebrow towards the bottle of best sherry on the table.

'Arwenna's been entertaining me in between letting me do
all the work, yes,' said Jason, and gave her a wink. It was
difficult to tell Garth's mood. 'And she's invited me to
lunch.'

'Good.'

'It's nearly ready. If you men want to talk privately, when
would you like it serving?' She prodded the potatoes with a
fork. Another five minutes would do it.

'Look, Garth, it'll only take a few minutes,' Jason gave
her an apologetic look. 'Will you excuse us for five minutes? No more, I promise.'

'Of course. Five minutes,' she nodded. They went out,
and she grinned to herself. That meant ten. She set out mats
and cutlery, put plates to warm, and poured herself some
sherry.

Everything was ready when she heard them coming back,
laughing and talking like the old friends they clearly were.
Lunch was splendid. Arwenna was pleased that Jason was
there. It smoothed over what might have been a difficult
situation, and Jason was excellent company, taking charge
of the conversation, as it were. Although Garth was obviously pleased to see him, he seemed fairly thoughtful—at
least to Arwenna's sensitive awareness of him.

After they had eaten she excused herself, ostensibly to get
ready for the afternoon, in reality to give them an oppor-

tunity to talk. Garth had been to see Aunt Daisy, and had returned with some fruit and soft drinks for her. She decided she would go alone, and when she went into the lounge, changed into her favourite blue dress—washed and ironed by the competent Mrs Holt—she told them so. They were sprawled out on the settee, talking quietly. Both men stood up when she went in, and she was aware of Jason's admiring all-encompassing glance.

Garth looked at his watch. 'We'll all go, what say you, Jason? Aunt Daisy's quite a character.'

'Love to.' Jason emptied his glass, and put it down.

'What time are you meeting Zack?' asked Garth.

'Four o'clock outside Foyle's.'

'Zack?' enquired Jason, with an ever so polite smile.

'An old friend,' Arwenna explained, as Garth seemed disinclined to do so.

'Ah. Right, Garth. My day's free—now we've got that little matter sorted out, we'll go off somewhere when we've dropped Arwenna.'

She went to gather up her bag, and the basket of fruit, and Jason rushed to help her. Then they set off to visit the clinic.

ZACK WAS sitting outside Foyle's as the car drew up at the curb. Arwenna turned to Jason. 'It was nice meeting you,' she said. 'Goodbye.'

'And you. Thanks for a delicious lunch. I may see you later. *Au revoir,* Arwenna.' She slid out of the car, and Garth leaned over. 'How long will you be out?' he enquired.

'I don't know.' She looked towards Zack, who was crossing the pavement towards them, as the traffic honked behind them, annoyed at Garth stopping. 'About eight?'

'See you then. Take care.' He was gone, the powerful car accelerating swiftly to be swallowed up in the traffic. Zack kissed her.

'Hi, beautiful. Let's have a coffee first, then a wander round, okay?'

'I am in your hands entirely,' she answered.

'Mmm!' he groaned. 'I wish you were, honey.' He took her arm possessively. 'Still with that bloated capitalist, I see.'

'I'm afraid so.' She looked at him as they walked along arm in arm. 'Not jealous, are you?'

'What do you think?' he laughed. 'Insanely jealous, maddened—foaming at the mouth jealous.'

'You're an idiot!'

'I know—I must be. Come on, this place does a nice coffee. Then we'll go and feed the pigeons in Trafalgar Square, then we'll make our way to Hyde Park and stroll among the lovers and perhaps I'll persuade you—'

'No,' she said, laughing. There were never any tensions with Zack. Not like Garth. Easy-going, humourous, he was the ideal companion for Arwenna in her present state. It was so ridiculous to have fallen in love with a man like Garth. She wished she could put him out of her mind, and just enjoy her time with Zack. And that, after a few minutes of his conversation, in wit and humour and warm affection, was precisely what she managed to do.

It was nearer nine than eight when at last, feeling rather tired, she said farewell to Zack. He was going on to a party, and tried to persuade her to go, but she had had a long day, which had caught up on her. He insisted, despite her protestations, on walking with her to the corner of the street where she was staying. 'See you again some time soon, honey,' he said, looking deep into her eyes. 'Be good. Don't do anything I wouldn't do.'

She laughed, and stroked his rough beard. 'I'll try and remember that.'

Zack was holding her hands then. 'Don't fall for him,' he said, and she didn't need to ask whom he meant. 'He'll break your heart. He's the kind who uses women.'

'I know,' she answered softly. But she didn't tell him his advice had come too late. That was her secret—and always would be. 'I'll phone you, Zack, before I go back home. We'll keep in touch as well.'

'Okay, honey. 'Night. Take care!'

'I will.' She watched him lope away, whistling, then turned and began to walk slowly towards the main entrance. Zack was wrong about one thing. The danger from Garth lay not in his attitude to women—but in his dominant personality. She could compete with other women, but she couldn't have her life taken over, and he could easily. Arwenna was too independent-spirited to ever allow that to happen. She loved him. She couldn't help that, but she could help the way she reacted to him, now and in the brief future they had. She ran up the steps, and the evening porter was on duty, reading a paper. He got up when he saw her and went over to the lift.

'Mr Vanner's at home, madam,' he told her.

'Thanks, George.' The lift whisked her up, and she pressed the bell on the door.

Garth opened it, and she could tell by the faint blue haze of cigar smoke, even before she saw Jason, that he wasn't alone. Jason rose to his feet as she walked in. The table was littered with papers, both men were jacketless, and with ties loosened, and two glasses and a bottle of whisky on the table told of a busy evening.

'Hello,' she greeted him.

'I said we'd meet again,' he answered, and grinned. 'Did you have a nice afternoon out?'

'Very pleasant, thanks.' She regarded the table. 'I can see you're busy, so I won't disturb you.'

'We've finished,' Garth answered. 'Haven't we?'

'Yes.' Jason began to gather up the papers. 'Thank God. I've had enough for one day. Come and sit down and talk to me.'

'Want a drink, Arwenna?' Garth asked.

'I'd like a coffee more than anything. May I?'

'Of course.' There was something wrong with Garth. She didn't know what it was, a certain reserve, no more than that.

'Would you both like one?'

'I would,' answered Jason. 'Let me help you.'

He followed her to the kitchen, leaving Garth in the main lounge putting papers away. 'We've not eaten,' he said. 'Have you?'

'No.' She was filling the kettle while he banged about opening cupboard doors. 'Have you been working all this time?'

'Since we left you? Yes.' He laughed. 'You don't know Garth very well, do you?'

'Hardly at all,' she answered dryly. 'If you're hungry I'm sure I could whip something up.'

'If it's as delicious as that lunch, I'd say yes, but let's see what old Garth suggests, shall we? I'm sure you're not here to slave over a hot stove as well as doing all that mound of translating for him. You're quite a girl, aren't you?'

She glanced at him as he passed her three beakers, and his eyes were gently admiring. 'Why, thank you, sir,' she smiled, and gave a little curtsey, and he laughed.

'I'll go and ask him,' he said, and went out. Arwenna made coffee, put it on a tray with milk and sugar, and carried it in. They were talking as she went in and looked round, and Garth came forward to take the tray from her and put it on the now cleared table.

'We're all hungry,' he said, 'so why don't we go out and eat?'

'Not me. I'm too tired,' she answered. 'I'll have a piece of toast and an early night, I think—'

'Nonsense,' Jason cut in. 'It's only nine. You're in London, and the night is young, and so are you. I wouldn't hear of it, and neither would Garth. I've got a much better idea. How are you on a flutter at the tables?'

'Gambling?' she laughed. 'I don't know. I've never done any.' The two men exchanged glances.

'Then that seems to be settled,' said Jason smoothly. 'I'm a member of a very nice club that does excellent food, and has a casino better than any Monte Carlo has to offer. Let's drink our coffee and go.'

Arwenna sat down weakly. 'No,' she began. 'It sounds lovely, but I don't think—'

Jason sat beside her. 'All you have to do is go and change into your prettiest outfit—though you look perfect anyway—we'll go and have a bite, a quick flutter, and then home to bed. What more could a girl want?'

'And you might have beginner's luck,' said Garth.

She looked at them both. Why not? 'All right,' she agreed. 'Thank you.'

'Good.' Jason finished his coffee in one and stood up, rubbing his chin. 'Can I borrow your razor, Garth?'

'Help yourself. You know where everything is.'

Jason went out. Arwenna picked up her beaker and drank her coffee. Now that they were alone, she didn't feel easy. She had been having many thoughts over the past hours, even minutes, and they were rapidly crystallising into something less tenuous. Everything that was happening, and had happened, only served to make her realise that she could not go on much longer staying with, and working for, Garth. She had to get away soon, before it was too late.

He was planning on taking her to France after Aunt Daisy was home. She knew, in the things that had already happened, as though they were clues to a situation, that if she went she would somehow never be free. France was a country for lovers. Here she was strong enough, but there, miles away from home, all would be so different. How would she resist the inevitable? She looked up at Garth, and he was watching her silently, face expressionless. She looked away again, down at the tray on the table, and a shiver ran down her spine.

She knew one thing, it wasn't going to be easy. But with Garth, nothing was.

Not yet. Not yet. There would be the time when it was right to speak. But it wasn't yet. 'And what are you thinking nów?' he asked softly.

'Nothing important,' she answered. 'Nothing that can't wait.' She looked up at him again, eyes shining with her new-found inner strength, and saw him catch his breath. It was almost—for a moment—as if he knew. He couldn't, of course, but she would have to be careful. There were many things to be considered, very many things, before she made the break. 'I'll go and get ready,' she said, and stood up and walked away from him. It seemed somehow symbolic of what was to come.

CHAPTER ELEVEN

THEY TOOK a taxi to the casino, the three of them, Arwenna and Garth and Jason. Arwenna had put on her new pink suit, her highest heeled sandals, and carried a warm white stole. She had opened the envelope and taken out of it ten pounds and put that in her purse. She would gamble some of that, no more. She had no idea then how high the stakes were...

The place was full when they went in, and as they crossed the crowded lounge to the restaurant she saw the three of them in a wide wall mirror—she between the two men, tall, yet overshadowed by them both. Garth and Jason were well over six feet, Garth slightly the taller of the two, and the picture they made was impressive, even in this place of wealth, and golden, elegant men and women. The mirror image was to remain in her mind for a long time afterwards, and she was aware that others looked at them, and remained looking, and some smiled in recognition, and were greeted in return. She felt like a princess, and smiled inwardly at this small conceit, but it was pleasant to feel so, even if only for a while.

They were escorted into a discreetly lit small dining room, and Jason ordered champagne, and Arwenna studied an ornate menu while a waiter hovered by, pencil and pad poised. She ordered smoked salmon, and scampi with salad. The champagne arrived, and by the time her smoked salmon came she had had several glasses and was feeling decidedly happy and relaxed. No longer tired either, amazingly, but wide awake. Both men were good company—no tension

with Garth now. He too seemed totally relaxed. She loved
him so much that just to be with him was both bliss and
pain. She knew what she was going to have to do, but that
was in the future, and now was now, so she lived for the
moment, glowing with the inner warmth she felt, and more
than one pair of male eyes lingered on her—a fact not unnoticed by either man.

She was practically floating by the end of the meal, when
they entered yet another darker room filled with tables, and
silent intent people. It was a whole new world to Arwenna,
whose only knowledge of casinos had been via television and
films. This was real. The smoke drifted and hung wreathed
about the lights over the tables. Roulette, blackjack,
chemin-de-fer—all was fascinating. She looked at the serious faces round the tables, piles of chips at their side, heard
the voices of the croupiers at the roulette table as they stood
by one, quiet and watchful. *'Merci, mesdames et mes-
sieurs, faites vos jeux...'*

Jason moved away. When he returned, he held a stack of
plastic coins, and handed Arwenna several. 'Go on,' he said
softly, 'have a go.'

'But I—' she began, and was shushed by an elderly dowager by her side.

He whispered: 'Watch this game. See where they place the
chips. Watch.'

'All right,' she mouthed. She observed, saw the chips
placed in various parts of the numbered green baize,
watched the ball click-clicking round the moving wheel, then
the croupier's long-handled rake raking in, then giving to
others. Simple, it looked, but she still hadn't a clue how the
winnings were worked out.

She leaned over and placed three of the chips on number
three, for no reason except that she might as well start
somewhere.

She didn't realise that she had won until Garth put his
hand on her arm. 'Beginner's luck,' he whispered in her ear,

and Arwenna, rather dazed, gathered up a pile of chips and stared at them.

'Mine?' she gasped.

Jason took her away from the table, away from the annoyed dowager. 'You've just won three hundred pounds, my dear girl,' he told her.

'What!' She looked at him. '*How* much?'

'Three hundred,' he said. 'Told you. How are you on pontoon?'

'The card game? Do they play it here?'

'Something like it. It's called blackjack. Come on.' He led her over to a horseshoe-shaped table and sat her down, remaining behind her. Garth had disappeared. Dazed, Arwenna took a card, following Jason's whispered instructions, and some half hour later had won nearly a thousand pounds.

She couldn't believe it. Totally bewildered, she sat at a quiet corner table and looked at the chips before her. Garth stood there, silent. It was Jason to whom she spoke. It was almost as though he were not with them. Jason handed her a glass of champagne. 'Drink that,' he ordered.

'I need it—thanks. This money's yours,' she added, 'not mine. I can't believe my luck, but I don't want to play any more.'

'Very sensible, but may I ask why?'

She shrugged. 'I don't know. It's not for fear of losing, not that, because it's like pretend money as far as I'm concerned—it's not *real,* you know. I've just decided, I'm not really a gambler. I've enjoyed coming here very much, and I wouldn't have missed it for anything, but it's over now.' She handed him the pile of multicoloured discs. 'Thanks.'

'You little idiot! *You* won it, it's yours. Pay me back what I started you with if you must, but what you won is yours.' He looked at his watch. 'What say we have another bottle of champagne and then go?'

Garth nodded. 'You'll stay the night, of course?'

'I was hoping you'd ask. Yes, I will.' He took the chips and left, and a moment later a waiter appeared with a bottle of champagne in a bucket.

'Did you gamble?' asked Arwenna.

'I lost a few pounds at roulette, that's all. I rarely gamble. Jason's keener than I am.' He sipped the champagne thoughtfully. 'But you're not, I take it?'

'No, it's been fun, but quite enough to last me for a lifetime. The money I won—it's not mine. I shan't let Jason give it to me.'

'It's yours. He staked you, that's all. If you'd have lost do you think he'd have demanded his money back?'

'No, but—'

'Well then, it's yours. Take it.' Garth looked away as if the subject was closed. Arwenna stared hard at him, trying to understand the way his mind worked. That was impossible. Perhaps he didn't even know himself. He had veered from charm to almost silence within the space of a few hours, and she wondered why. Perhaps she would never know. There she was wrong. She was soon to find out, far sooner than she could imagine. It was after three in the morning when they went into the lift and up to the flat. Arwenna was tipsy, she knew she was, but there was nothing she could do about it. She stumbled slightly going down the steps into the lounge, and both Garth and Jason took an arm and half carried her to the settee. 'Whee!' she sighed, and hiccuped. 'Oh, do excuse me!' she giggled helplessly, and Jason said to no one in particular:

'I think I'll make some nice strong coffee,' and strode away. Arwenna dropped her bag beside her. It contained nine hundred pounds in twenty-pound notes. She had never even seen that much before, let alone possessed it, but Jason had been adamant. It was hers, the matter was closed. She couldn't think as clearly as she would have liked, but it seemed as if in some way the money was going to help her with something. She didn't have a headache, or any unpleasant sensation connected with drinking. She felt delightfully happy, as if some weighty problem had been resolved, and all was well with the world. It was quite sufficient for her. In the morning, if it ever came, she would try and work out why.

Garth had left her, and Arwenna kicked off her sandals and lay back comfortably on the soft cushions of the settee, closing her eyes. Memories of the evening danced in her head. Their arrival, seeing them in the mirror, the meal, the people, playing roulette, and afterwards cards, and drinking more champagne . . . all wonderfully hazy but colourful.

'Okay, take a sip.' Jason offered her a cup, and she took it.

'What is it?'

'Coffee.'

'Oh.' She sipped and pulled a face. 'Ugh, it's strong!'

'Mmm, I know. You're slightly sloshed.'

'So I am.' She laughed. 'And I'm very happy.'

'Lucky girl—to be happy *and* rich. Very nice.'

'But I don't feel as if it's mine—I didn't mean that—'

'Please, no more,' he ordered. 'I won too, you know. Not as much as you—but enough. My dear Arwenna, I was delighted to see you doing so well. I've had a good evening too, and that's yours to do as you wish. Buy some clothes with it—you're going to France next week, aren't you? Well then, buy an outfit to knock 'em dead with.'

'No, I'm not,' she said, and was aware, as she spoke that Garth had reappeared.

'Not going to knock 'em dead?' asked Jason, amused. 'Okay, put it in the bank.'

'No, I didn't mean that.' She put her cup down. 'I mean I'm not going to France.' The words fell into a still, small silence, and she saw Jason glance up towards Garth. And then—something changed. She could feel it, sense the growing sudden tension in the room, and her heartbeats quickened. She had said what was in her mind, almost without thinking about it, her tongue loosened by champagne, and it had been the correct thing to say at the time. Only now, too late, she knew she shouldn't have.

Slowly, very slowly, she looked up at Garth. So did Jason, who stood, as if at a signal from the other man, said: 'Excuse me,' and walked away from them. Then he'd gone taking his coffee with him, and she knew he wouldn't be back.

'That's news to me,' said Garth. 'May I ask why?'

'No, you may not,' she answered. 'I'm going to bed when I've drunk this,' and she picked up her cup. The next moment it had been taken from her, and she was being pulled to her feet. Startled, she looked into Garth's face, and saw an anger greater than anything she had ever seen before. She wriggled to free herself, but he held her in a steel-like grip and repeated:

'Why?'

'Let me go!'

'When you've told me.'

Her head was clearing with shock and she looked calmly at him. 'I don't want to go with you,' she said. 'That's why.'

'That is not a good enough reason,' he said softly. 'We have an agreement, remember?'

'I've been thinking about our "agreement",' she answered. 'And about a lot of other things—and about you. And I've come to my senses.' She reached out and prised his fingers from her arm, then from the other one. 'I don't want to go anywhere with you. And before you remind me of my aunt, and about James' father, and all the other little bits of blackmail you've tried, I'll tell *you* something. I'm going to pay back every penny of what it's cost for Aunt Daisy to have the operation, and for having those two women running the café. I was going to anyway, I'd already decided that today, but what I won tonight will help. And as for James' father, I've realised—belatedly—that I'm not responsible for other people's lives. I'll see him when I get home, and tell him what you did, and it's up to him to sort something out—not me. You've tried to take over my life, and you nearly succeeded, but that's over now. I'll return the money you gave me, and—'

'You've said enough,' he cut in. 'You'd better get to bed. We'll talk in the morning.' His voice was hard and angry.

'I haven't finished,' she shot back. 'Just because you don't like what I say—'

'No, I don't. But I'm in no mood to argue with a drunken woman.'

'I'm not drunk!'

'I don't know what the hell you are, then.'

She stood in front of him, wishing she were a man. She was trembling with reaction, and anger, and she hated the hard, scornful look on his face, as though she were being stupid. 'Damn you,' she whispered. 'Who the hell do you think *you* are?'

'I know who I am.'

'You're ruthless!'

'Yes, I am. So are you in your own way—'

He got no further. Arwenna struck out at him and he caught her hand and pulled her up to him—the coffee cup was knocked, went flying over her skirt, staining it badly.

'Oh!' she gasped, and looked at it. Then, turning, she ran away from him and into the bedroom. She closed the door and stripped off her skirt and took it into the bathroom to sponge it, then her door crashed open and Garth came in, white-faced.

'Get out!' she snapped. He followed her into the bathroom. She wore a waist slip beneath the skirt, and that too had been caught. She turned to him as she filled the bowl with cold water. 'Will you go?' she demanded.

'No. We'll finish this now—one way or the other.'

'You said I was drunk before—'

'You're not. You're as sober as I am.'

She pushed past him, into the bedroom, and put on her dressing gown. Icily she stared at him. 'I'm going to take off my slip,' she said. 'You've ruined that as well. I hope you're satisfied!'

'If you hadn't landed out at me it wouldn't have happened.'

She ignored that and slipped the underskirt off, carried that into the bathroom and began soaking the affected parts with cold water, gently and carefully, though with an effort to control her temper. When she was satisfied, she rolled both up in her towel, then laid them over the side of the bath.

'There's nothing more to say,' she told him. 'So it's useless you waiting—and don't try any of your strong-arm tactics on me. That won't persuade me to listen to you. I've had enough from you, all I'm going to take—'

'And where will you stay until your aunt is well enough to leave the clinic? Here?' he asked.

'No! I'll go—Steve and Zack will put me up. Don't worry, I'll manage.'

'I'm sure you will,' he answered icily. 'That should be nice for you, sleeping in one large room with—how many—four young men? You'll enjoy that won't you?'

'You can sneer as much as you like. I'll be *safer* there than I am here,' she snapped. 'At least they've never made a pass at me!'

'Don't be so naïve. Probably because they've never had the chance!'

She tried to push past him, to go into the bedroom, incensed, trying not to listen, but he caught her and held her, struggling in his arms. 'You stay here,' he said, voice low and cold.

'No, damn you, I won't!' Her eyes were wide and brilliant, lit with the anger that consumed her. 'In fact, I'll go now. Do you hear that? *Now!*'

Garth shook her hard, as if caught by something beyond his reasoning, and then, with a groan, took her to him, and kissed her.

Sobbing, frightened at his violence, Arwenna struggled to free herself, but it was impossible. She hated him, she hated herself—she hated his kiss—only then suddenly, moments later, she didn't. It was a savage, punishing kiss, intended as such by a man nearly beyond reason, and she fought and struggled to escape his mouth at first, then, as she went lightheaded with the combined effects of alcohol and anger, she found herself, to her horror, responding with a fierceness to match her previous resistance.

It was no use. Her own confused emotions were too much for her to cope with. The kiss changed, deepened, became more intense, and she sensed his growing excitement and responded with her own, helplessly.

'Dear God,' he whispered, after an age, 'you drive me insane,' and he buried his face in her thick tumble of hair, holding her as if he would never let her go.

'You're hurting me,' she said, voice shaking. 'Please—'

'I want to hurt you. Oh God, I want to—' His hands were upon her, and she trembled at his touch, her senses responding in a way she understood only too well, now, to his feverish lovemaking. He was a man almost beyond control, and she whimpered with pain as he suddenly pushed her away and staggered towards the bed, and sat down as if he could no longer stand. Anguished, she saw him go, then followed him, and struck out at his shoulder, sobbing with sudden anger at the rejection.

'Go—get *out!*' she shouted, voice torn, and Garth reached up, put his hands up to shield his face as if he could no longer defend himself from her attack, and Arwenna, knowing it, pushed his hands away and struck him. 'I hate you!'

She stumbled with the force of her own anger, fell against him, and the next moment they were in a tangled heap on the bed, and she was pummelling his chest with her fists, and crying.

He had no strength left, or so it seemed for a few moments, as he neither resisted nor defended himself—then, as though with a supreme effort, he found strength and caught her flailing arms, and said, brokenly: 'I can't fight you.'

'Then go—get out of my life!' she sobbed, the tears coursing down her face, her body against his, legs quivering with the effort to get balance again, but she couldn't, and, weakened by her own efforts at resistance, at struggling against such an overwhelming force as he, she lay back at last, panting and exhausted. Garth leaned over her, looking down at her, and his eyes were very dark, and his face shadowed, with deep lines of pain etched there, a man who had reached the end of his tether.

He groaned and said her name as if it hurt him, then again, then he leaned down his head and rested it against her breast, and closed his eyes. Arwenna could feel that he was trembling. She felt the tremors course through her own body, and she lifted up her arms and held them round him, to still the anguish that communicated itself to her.

'Oh, Garth,' she whispered. 'It's no use—don't you see—we'll destroy ourselves—' She held him closely to her, torn with love and despair for this man she would trust with her life, whom she loved more than life itself, but who would never love her, because he didn't know what love was, and because of that knowledge she had to go, to get out of his life and be safe. She was sure that she brought out the worst in him, as well, and that was the terrible thing. She had seen him with others, with his friends, and he was different, charming, well liked. Ruthless, yes, in business certainly—and with her—openly with her. There's something wrong with us both, she thought, as she felt him relaxing against her, gradually losing the tension and overwhelming anger that had filled him. Some chemistry that's triggered off whenever we are alone. Something dreadful and beyond the understanding of us both.

Oh, my darling, she thought. If only you knew my feelings for you! Lying there, closely, with him, was sweet torment. To touch, to hold him, to know his kiss and the caress of his hands, was more than she could bear. His body was hard and muscular, relaxed now in the calm after the storm, and perhaps now that the fury had abated she could say what she had to, and he would listen.

'Whatever happens, whatever you decide,' she whispered, 'I can't stay. I know you want me, I know you said we ought to get each other out of our systems, and in a way you're probably right. But it's not my way. I've known you for only a week, and my life is altered. Don't you see? I must be free.'

'I know,' he said, so softly that she barely heard the words. 'I know—' and he groaned and moved slightly away from her, lifting his hand to lay it on her cheek, then closed his eyes. His face was shadowed in the soft light that came from the bathroom; she hadn't switched on the bedroom lamp. She saw his mouth move, as though he tried to speak, but no words came, then he put down his head, and his body was shaking, as though he was weeping.

It was more than she could bear. She cried out something, softly, and cradled his head against her breast, soothing him as a mother soothes a child, then she kissed his cheek, murmuring words she didn't understand herself, seeking only to release him from the intolerable prison of his pain.

Gradually he became still, and the minutes passed with no words spoken, and at last Arwenna knew that he was asleep. She leaned over very carefully and pulled up the coverlet from the floor, his side, and covered them both. Then she too fell asleep, in his arms.

It was already light when she awoke. Garth was fast asleep, and his arms were round her as if he would never let her go, and her lips were touching his hair so that she tasted the faint sweetness of it. They had slept for how long—perhaps four hours. She dared not move to look at the clock, for fear of disturbing him. It was the first time she had slept with him, and undoubtedly the last. Soon she was going to leave him. If he stayed on in Raneley she would see him again, that was unavoidable; it was not a big place, but they would never be alone, she would make sure of that. And

once Aunt Daisy was fully recovered, Arwenna might go
away again, if life proved impossible—if she still loved him.

He stirred in his sleep, then, as if realising where he was,
made a sound in his throat, a questioning sound.

'It's all right,' she said. 'We fell asleep.'

He sat up and rubbed his hair. 'Here? I've been *here?*'

'Yes.' She began to get off the bed, but his hand clamped
over her wrist.

'You let me stay?' he asked huskily.

She shivered. It was cool, even with the dressing gown on.
'Your reputation is safe,' she murmured. 'I shan't tell anyone. And if you leave now, Jason won't know.'

Slowly, inexorably, Garth drew her towards him. Then he
kissed her. This time she didn't struggle. Her senses were still
blurred from sleep; his arms were warm and very strong—
and gentle. She put her hand to his heart, and it was quick-
ening, beating strongly and faster than normal. The heady
longing turned to fire, and it was no longer cool. She was
burning, burning. The skin of his face was rough with
stubble, but she scarcely noticed, for she was lost in the
heady sweetness of his lips as they searched hers.

All was lost, timeless, beyond logic or reason. She knew
nothing any more save the bliss of being with him that carried her away from the world she knew into another place,
another time...

ARWENNA LOOKED back once as she went out of the door,
and made a small kiss with her mouth. Goodbye, she
thought, goodbye. She could not stay. She could not face
him. Even though she loved him, nothing had been resolved between them.

She gathered up her clothes and crept out, leaving Garth
sleeping inside her bed. She unlocked the door with her key,
put the key on the table where he would find it, and went
towards the lift. It was eight o'clock on Sunday morning,
and when she was outside she was going to telephone Steve
and ask him if he would collect her.

She took the lift to the basement and walked out into the street, looking for a telephone box. There had been no time or desire to pack. She had what she stood up in, and her toothbrush, and handbag. The streets were quiet, no one about, and the telephone rang for a while before Steve himself answered it, sounding half asleep, and not a little annoyed.

'Steve? It's Arwenna.'

'Arwenna?' He was instantly alert. 'What is it? This sounds like a pay phone. Where are you?'

'Can you come and meet me?' she begged. 'I've left Garth's flat—I need somewhere to stay.'

'I'm on my way. Where's the phone booth?'

'Just round the corner from the flats. I'm sorry to call you, but I've nowhere to go—'

'Stay *right* there. Are you okay?'

'Yes, I'm all right.'

'Thank God! I don't want to know why you need me—but you do, and that's enough. Hang up, love, and let me get started.'

'All right. I'll be here. 'Bye.'

She hung up and remained in the booth. Fifteen minutes later a bright orange Mini screeched to a halt outside the kiosk, and half an hour after that she was sitting in the small kitchen of the flat drinking hot tea and eating burnt toast, and recovering slowly.

They spoke in whispers. Snores issued from the living room, which was also a bedroom for four, and three sleeping men didn't even know they had a female visitor.

Steve had closed the door, sat her down by the window and put the kettle on. 'You'd better tell me what happened,' he said.

She shook her head. 'Not yet. I'm not sure myself.' Which was a lie, but if she told him the truth he might go round to Garth's apartment and start tearing the place apart. She didn't want any trouble like that. She had already had enough to last a few lifetimes, in less than a week.

'I just decided I couldn't stay any longer. We—we don't get on,' she sighed. 'There's a complete clash of personalities. I just ran out—cowardly, I know, but it seemed the only way. I'm sorry to drag you out of bed, but I had nowhere else to—'

'Listen—hey, love it's *me*, Steve, remember? Considering I'd quite happily climb the highest mountain, crawl over broken glass, etcetera, etcetera—do you think I mind coming out at eight on a Sunday morning to save you? You've got to be kidding!'

She laughed, near to tears, and buried her head against his chest as he put his arms round her and hugged her. 'Oh, I don't deserve you,' she said.

'Well, you've got me—for as long as you want me. You've not fallen for him, have you?' He drew away and looked suspiciously at her.

'I'm afraid I have.'

'Hell's bells! I can hardly go and duff him up now, can I?' She shook her head, biting her lip. 'Does he know where you are?'

'No. When I left, he was still asleep.'

'Is he likely to phone—see if you're here?'

'I don't know.'

'If he does, do I say yes or no?'

'Tell him. It's better—he might worry. Yes, it's better.'

'Okay. Now, I don't know exactly where you're going to sleep tonight, but we've got a day to fix something up. When does your aunt come out of the clinic?'

'I'll find out tomorrow. I didn't think about the finer points of everything— Oh, Steve, I'm so tired!' She had had very little sleep for ages, and it was telling at last.

He nodded. 'You look it. Look, get into my bed and I'll crawl on to the settee for a while, then when they wake me up, I'll—ahem—warn them you're here.'

'You're an angel!' she smiled mistily.

'I know,' he grinned. 'I might as well go down and collect the Sunday papers and do a crossword or something. Come on, bed.'

Five minutes later Arwenna was fast asleep in his bed.

WHEN SHE woke up the room was empty, and fairly tidy, and she was alone.

She sat up and looked round her, puzzled. A large piece of paper was pinned on the settee, and she went over, yawning, to read it. 'Dear A,' it said, 'We've all adjourned to the pub to let you get your beauty sleep. If you want to come down it's the Oddfellows Arms at the end of the road on left. We've fixed up a bed for tonight. I had to restrain Zack from ravishing you as you slept. Back at two, Steve.'

She looked at her watch. One-thirty. They must have woken and crept out. She felt better, but not much. She washed in the kitchen and then set out to do the stack of unwashed dishes piled precariously on the draining board. When they were done she found a carpet sweeper and duster and began to work in the living room, dusting an incredibly untidy mantelpiece, when the door opened and she turned to see Garth walking in.

She froze, panicked, and sent a small ashtray flying into the hearth. For a moment it seemed as if her heart stopped beating. He looked across the room at her, then walked towards her.

'All right,' he said. 'I don't know what you want, but you can have it.' His words didn't make sense. Arwenna stood there motionless, duster still clutched in one hand, and gazed at him.

'Why—are you here?' she asked at last.

'Why do you think?' He looked haggard and almost ill, but he managed a faint smile. 'It's where I knew you'd be.'

'You must know why I left,' she said faintly. 'After—what happened—it's impossible—'

'I know. That's what I told myself when I discovered you'd gone. I know what we do to each other, and you're quite right—only it hit me so hard that it was like a physical ache inside me. I didn't mean it to happen like this, Arwenna, but, God help me, life suddenly had no meaning any more. I love you. I don't think I can live without you. If you don't come back, I'll have a damned good try—but it won't be worth much.' He took hold of her hands, and she felt the fine tremor in his. 'I couldn't even drive my car here, I had to get Jason to bring me. He's outside. I know all you accused me of—and you were right. I was taking over—because I was frightened of being taken over. I've never said this to anyone before—but I need you. For God's sake don't send me away.' His voice broke, became husky. 'Say something, even if it's only Go to hell!'

She shook her head. 'I don't want to say that. Don't you know why *I* left? Can't you guess?'

'I can guess. You told me last night why.'

'No, not only that. I found out—on Euston Station to be precise, at about seven in the morning, when you kissed me because that policeman was watching—that I'd done something very stupid. I discovered that I'd fallen rather badly for you.' She looked slowly at the hands that held hers, then back to his face. His beloved, wonderful, gentle face. 'But I never dreamed I'd hear you say you loved me.'

'We've only known each other a week. It's madness, I know that. I don't do mad, stupid things. I'm hard and realistic, and I know that love's an illusion—I know all this, Arwenna, with the practical side of me, and yet,' he lifted one hand to touch her cheek, to smooth the soft skin, 'and yet, when I see you, my heart lifts, when I touch you, like this, it's so special and wonderful, that I know there's no illusion. I love you for what you are, for what you have become, in a short time, a special person to me, someone I want to love and cherish for as long as I live.'

He took her in his arms then, enfolded her tightly, and held her to him. 'It's no good us fighting it any more. And I was fighting it—and you—because I tried to deny that I could ever need anyone. I've lost that fight—I knew I'd lost it when I found you gone.'

Arwenna smiled, but it was one of delicious anticipation. 'Oh, Garth, I wanted you so much, and I tried to deny that too. I've never wanted any man before.'

'Will you go to France with me—as my wife?' he asked. 'Will you marry me and come with me wherever I go—and wherever you want to go, and stay with me for ever and ever?'

'You know I will.'

He gave a deep sigh. 'There'll be no more quarrels. I love you too much to ever hurt you. We're both strong personalities, and we may not always agree, but we'll work it out together, one way or another.' He kissed her very gently. 'Where are your two friends?'

'At the pub. I was just tidying up—'

'So I see,' he said gravely. 'We'd better wait for them, hadn't we? They both love you—and I know why now. Do you think they'll be heartbroken?'

She shook her head, smiling. 'I don't think so, somehow. They're special friends—always will be.'

'Then I'll have to look after you, or else I can see—'

As Garth said the words, the door opened, and Steve and Zack came in. They were carrying several cans of beer.

'Oh,' said Steve.

'Oh, no!' sighed Zack. They looked from Arwenna to Garth, and back again.

Garth gently released her. 'I'm sorry,' he said, 'but I'm afraid you've just lost your new flatmate.'

Steve looked at Zack, who gave a resigned shrug. 'We're going to be married,' said Garth.

Zack crossed over to Arwenna. 'Do you love him?' he asked.

She nodded. 'Yes.'

'Aw, hell!' He glared at Garth, then stuck his hand out. Solemnly they shook hands. 'Look after her, or I'll kill you,' Zack said pleasantly.

'I know—and I will. That's a promise. I don't suppose it's any use asking you to the wedding?'

Zack shrugged. 'You could try. Where's the reception? I've never been to the Ritz, actually.'

'Why not? We'll let you know the time and date. Thanks for looking after her.' He took Arwenna's hand, and she gently disengaged herself and went to kiss both Steve and Zack.

'Goodbye. Thanks for everything. I'll be in touch.' Her eyes were shining. Then she and Garth walked out, and down to the car where Jason waited.

CHAPTER TWELVE

BUT THERE was more. When they were both in his apartment, and Jason had vanished discreetly—sensing perhaps that he was no longer needed, Garth told her the final truth.

They sat comfortably side by side on the settee near the window; it was Sunday afternoon, sunny outside, a perfect day. 'You know, Jason didn't come here by chance,' he said. 'He told me after you'd gone out. He'd come to see you.'

'Me? But he didn't even know—'

'Ah, but he did. He'd heard via the grapevine about the little incident with Marcia, and also had a word with Lucy, whom he knows—her lover is an old chum of his—and Lucy had found you a fascinating person, and told him that she suspected not only that you might take Marcia's place, but that she could see me falling head over heels.'

Arwenna began to laugh, softly, eyes shining. 'Dear Lucy,' she murmured.

'Quite. All this intrigued Jason sufficiently to "drop in" by chance—and get to know you.' He hugged her. 'And he agreed. He thinks you're quite special.'

'I like him too.'

'As long as that's all,' he growled, and kissed her.

'Of course,' she agreed. 'How could I ever look at another man? I've got you. Oh, Garth, I do love you, truly.'

He stroked her hand thoughtfully. 'There's more,' he said softly.

'More? About Jason—why?'

'No, about me.'

She was intrigued. There was something in his voice . . .

'Go on,' she said, her heart thudding.

'Four months ago, when I went back to Raneley for the first time in fifteen years—I was in the estate agent's car, and it had stopped at the lights—you crossed the road in front of us. I saw you, and something odd happened to me. I can't explain what it was because nothing like it had ever happened before—but I had to know who you were. I asked the agent, very casually, and he told me.'

'Old Mr Brown? I've known him for years.' She smiled.

'So he said. As he drove to Raneley Hall he told me all about you—and I knew then that I was going to get to know you, one way or another. He also told me that you were engaged to James Rhodes. It was enough. My dearest love, you didn't have a chance after that day—although you didn't know it.'

'You angled it so that you could get to know the Colonel, didn't you?'

'Mmm.'

'You crafty devil!'

'You could say that.' Garth laughed and pulled her to him. 'How does it feel, knowing you'll never get away from me again?'

She turned her face towards his, put her hands up to his face, and touched his cheeks gently. 'Let me show you,' she said, and kissed him.

THE AUTHOR

Mary Wibberley lives in Manchester, England, with her husband, son, daughter and a large assortment of animals. She has published more than thirty Harlequin romances, and her simple philosophy is revealed in her writing. "Life isn't all worry. It's fun as well." She likes her characters to have a sense of humor and finds that they sometimes turn out to be quite independent, developing personalities of their own. Mary confesses that she will never tire of the enjoyment of writing and wondering what will happen next.